HEART
OF
NIGHT
AND
FIRE

BOOKS BY NISHA J. TULI

HEART

OF

NIGHT

AND

FIRE

NISHA J. TULI

SECOND SKY

Published by Second Sky in 2023

An imprint of Storyfire Ltd.
Carmelite House
50 Victoria Embankment
London EC4Y 0DZ
United Kingdom

www.secondskybooks.com

ISBN: 978-1-83790-487-7
eBook ISBN: 978-1-83790-486-0

For every brown girl who wanted to be the chosen one too.

AUTHOR'S NOTE

Welcome to *Heart of Night and Fire*! Inside these pages, you'll find a fantasy romance series with all the tropes and themes you love—enemies to lovers, slow burn, family secrets, ride-or-die friendships—and so much more, all inspired by Indian and other South Asian lore and culture.

While you're reading, it's important to note that it wasn't my goal to be historically or even mythologically accurate to the letter. When I say inspired, I do mean *inspired* in that I used mythology as a jumping-off point and then added my own vision and twists to suit the plot—much like you'll find in fantasy novels written from a Eurocentric point of view.

I have also borrowed the dress, customs, food, and culture from across time periods and regions of India and other parts of South Asia, combining them to create a glittering world that bloomed in my imagination.

As an author of the Indian diaspora, I have been influenced by both the place I grew up in and the place my ancestors came from, and what you'll find here is a combination of all the histories and stories that have influenced my life.

I hope you'll enjoy the magic, adventure, and romance of Zarya's story.

Happy reading!

Nisha

ONE

Zarya always hunted the demons at twilight. They were at their weakest when the sun was sinking over the horizon, in that nebulous shift between night and day. For years, they had been spreading their taint along the southern coast of Rahajhan, ravaging everything in their path.

The naga spent their days cowering in the murky depths of the swamps where she now found herself crouched. She knew how to draw them out as the last of the sun's power faded away.

Starlight. For reasons she'd never understood, her magic called the naga from their lairs, dragging them to the surface.

Zarya lifted a hand towards the scattering of pale stars and pulled down glowing tendrils of light, twisting them between her fingers where they twirled like smoke caught in a breeze.

From her position low on the ground, she unfurled the ball of tangled ribbons across the swamp's oily surface. They sparkled in the waning light. A river of brilliance against the gloom. In her free hand, she gripped the hilt of her long, curved talwar and waited.

It never took long. The naga were greedy, monstrous things.

The surface of the water lay as still as glass. Except for a soft breeze rustling the blackened trees, the swamp was silent. The birds, the insects, and the animals that once called this forest home had all fled this oppressive bleakness long ago.

Zarya's stomach churned with anticipation as she remained focused on the water. Even the slightest error could mean her undoing. She shuddered at the idea of being towed to the bottom of the swamp, choking out her last stuttered breaths where no one could save her.

A moment later, a gurgle bubbled up from the surface, morphing into a squeal that tore through the silence. In a cascade of mud, an eyeless head burst from the pool. Translucent white skin stretched over the skull of a serpent-like monster, its jaws spreading wide. Rows of needle-sharp teeth snapped before it lunged, but Zarya was ready.

Swinging her talwar in a smooth arc, she sliced cleanly through the naga's neck in a practiced maneuver. Its head landed with a meaty squelch at her feet while its thick body slithered back into the sludge. She let out a deep breath as a tingling rush of adrenaline cooled in her blood.

After pulling out the khanjar tucked in her boot, she set to work, draining the naga's venom into a small glass jar. The inky liquid dripped in slowly as she twisted the knife deeper into its already greying gums.

"Zarya! What are you doing?" came a familiar voice through the trees. She frowned, her shoulders hunching at the interruption as Aarav's tall, slender form emerged through the dark leaves. Ignoring him, she finished with her work, stashed her khanjar back in her boot, and pocketed the vial of venom.

"Nothing."

She snatched up her talwar and stalked towards him, knocking him with her shoulder as she passed.

"What is the point of this exercise, hmm?" he asked as he trailed behind her like a buzzing mosquito she'd like to squish with a firm, well-placed slap. "There's no one left to buy that stuff."

He was right, but that wasn't the *point* at all.

She used to sell the venom in the nearby fishing village of Lahar—the locals said it was useful in their traps to keep certain predators away. But now the village, too, had been consumed by the swamp, forcing everyone to flee north, where the blight had yet to take hold.

Hunting the naga gave her something to do, though. Something to tame the restlessness that scraped her bones like a scourge. Peddling venom in Lahar had been the only time she'd ever been allowed a reprieve from her prison. But it hadn't been enough. It would never have been *enough*.

Zarya passed the line of rune-marked trees that held the swamp at bay and protected her home. The crush of dark branches and blackened leaves gave way to the lush and abundant flora that had defined all the forest only a few years ago.

She emerged to find Row waiting for her with his thick arms crossed. Clad in a black kurta that hugged his broad frame, his dark hair hung to the middle of his back, braids woven throughout.

Row wasn't Zarya's father, but he was the only guardian she'd ever known.

No, he definitely wasn't a parent. He was her fucking warden.

He'd kept her here nearly every day of her life, his magic preventing her escape. Even after everyone else had evacuated this ruined coastline, their wretched little trio remained here for some inexplicable reason he refused to share.

She felt like a spitting cobra caged inside a basket, longing to escape.

"Where have you been?" he asked, glowering as she approached.

"I caught her hunting naga," Aarav said, coming up behind her like a perpetual pain in her ass.

Zarya looked over her shoulder, throwing him a dirty look. "Gods, Aarav, do you ever get tired of being an utter dipshit?"

She turned back to Row. "Yes, I was hunting. Are you also going to scold me like a child?"

At nearly a head taller than Zarya, Row loomed over her like a disapproving mountain. Only a mountain would probably be more sympathetic. "You know it's dangerous."

Zarya threw up a hand. "Oh, everything is dangerous, according to you."

"If anyone saw you use your magic—"

"*Who's* going to see me, Row? There's no one out here."

His mouth flattened with displeasure. They'd had this conversation a hundred, no, a thousand times before.

Not waiting for his response, she turned to walk away.

"Come back. It's time for your training," Row called after her.

She stopped in her tracks and sucked in a long breath that did nothing to calm the rage that frothed in her chest like a bubbling cauldron of acid.

There were days she fantasized about killing them both in their sleep. Not that Row treated her poorly. Not exactly. He'd tried, in his own graceless way, to mimic a sort of paternal presence in her life, but his endless secrecy chafed like sand lodged in her boots. She was approaching her twenty-first year and was no longer a child. She didn't need this brand of *protection* anymore.

But if she did kill them, she'd be even more alone than she was now. She also worried Row's magic wouldn't release upon his death, and then she'd be trapped here forever. But she wanted freedom. She wanted answers. Mostly, she wanted to experience something other than this tiny strip of coastline that made up her entire world.

She spun around to face her oppressors with her jaw clenched. "Fine. Let's fucking train, then."

Row's nostrils flared as Zarya charged for Aarav without further warning just as he swiftly drew the weapon hanging from his hip. With her talwar still gripped in her hand, she swung it down overhead. He blocked it at the last moment, their blades clashing, the harsh sound shattering through the silent swamp. She'd caught him by surprise, forcing Aarav to stumble from the momentum of his swing. She allowed him only half a second to recover before she swung again.

"Get your shoulder up," Row ordered as she spun around and thrust at Aarav. She wasn't *trying* to kill him, but if an *accident* were to happen, then it certainly would be no skin off her nose.

"Your right side is open!" Row yelled at Aarav, who grunted as he arced his blade down over hers.

Aarav's face pinched together in concentration as he fended her off. They were mostly matched in ability, usually trading victories, but Aarav was battling more than just the skill Row had honed every day of her life. Aarav was also battling the endless fury of her frustration and the resentment that wove through her spirit, oozing into every cell. No amount of preparation could combat her brand of pure, unfiltered rage.

After another swing and another block, steel met, flashing in the descending light.

Zarya feinted and then lunged in the opposite direction, catching Aarav off guard as she kicked out a foot and swept his legs out from under him. He landed on his back with a groan, and she dropped on top, pinning him to the earth with a knee dug into his sternum.

She slapped the blade from his grip as he snatched his hand away with a cry. Pulling the short khanjar from her boot, she lifted it high overhead before sweeping down in a wide arc.

Then she stopped, the sharp tip hovering an inch over Aarav's face, right between his widened eyes.

She had no qualms about fighting dirty when it suited her aims.

"Enough!" Row barked, his arms folded tightly across his chest. "You've made your point. Let him up."

Zarya snarled and released Aarav. He rose to his knees, coughing and sputtering.

Aarav flung an accusing finger at her. "She wants to kill me."

She scoffed. "Don't be so dramatic."

"Stop arguing. I'm sick of listening to this," Row said with a scowl.

Aarav struggled to his feet, glared at Zarya, and stalked into the forest, his shoulders hunched with indignation.

"Must you do that to him?" Row asked, turning on Zarya.

"Do what? You want me to train, so I'm training." She flicked her long black braid over a shoulder. "You know what you could do? Let me out of here. Find someone in Dharati to challenge me."

"We've been over this a thousand times," Row said, before turning and heading towards the whitewashed cottage they all shared. Whenever Zarya veered them in the direction of this topic, Row donned his best impression of a ghost and disappeared.

"Yes, and you still haven't given me a reason for keeping me trapped here. I turn twenty-one in a few weeks. You can't keep treating me like a child!" She yelled the words at his back just as the door to the cottage slammed, leaving her standing alone outside. "Oh, are we done here, Row?!"

She huffed. Peering into the trees, she wondered where Aarav had gone, ever envious of his freedom to come and go as he pleased. As Row's apprentice, he wasn't bound by the same magic that choked off *her* air.

She followed the path where Aarav had disappeared but knew the further she ventured from the house, the harder Row's magic would fight against her. By now, she knew the precise distance she could walk before the weight of his power would grow too heavy, eventually knocking her out before she'd wake up on her back, staring at the sky.

Usually, to find Row standing over her with a judgmental scowl on his scarred face.

With a resigned sigh, she headed into the house, where she found Row preparing supper in their small kitchen. After he put a pot of rice to cook on the burner, he began slicing onions with the same dexterity he brought to all his actions. He was an experienced warrior, and despite his size, he flowed through life with the grace of a dancer.

Zarya went to help, retrieving a bowl of chicken already marinating in a mixture of turmeric, chilies, and dried coriander. She skewered the pieces onto thin metal rods and placed them on the grill.

They worked in silence side by side, their movements practiced and efficient, though the unspoken tension that hung between them was thick enough to cut and serve along with their supper.

While the food cooked, Zarya laid out the plates, glasses, and cutlery. The door to the cottage slammed open, and Aarav stormed in, still sullen and scowling. He parked his wiry frame at the small wooden table without saying a word, his knee bouncing under it.

Row set out the food, and they ate in silence, as they so often did.

Arguments between Zarya and Aarav were as common as the sunrise, and they all dealt with them with the efficiency of people who had no idea how to communicate with one another.

But Zarya's heart softened at Row's expression, his black eyes darting between her and Aarav. He wanted them all to get along and find whatever might pass for happiness. But resentment gnawed at her edges, leaving them worn and frayed and easily pulled apart.

Rage and loneliness were her only loyal friends.

The only constants she could remember.

She wasn't really hungry, so she picked at her food. Row and Aarav nibbled at theirs, too. It seemed all their appetites were suffering.

After finishing his meal, Aarav stormed to his room and slammed the door without another word. Zarya sighed. At least she wouldn't have to deal with him anymore today.

Once the dishes were cleared, she poured herself a generous portion of pear wine, grabbed a book, and headed into the garden.

A stone path, lined with colorful zinnias and lilies, led her to a wooden pergola, where she settled onto one of the cushioned benches. Dozens of floating lights illuminated the garden, casting everything in a warm coppery glow.

Zarya sipped her wine, its flavor crisp and tart, enjoying the way it softened her organs.

The cottage sat on the shores of the Dakhani Sea, where the water gleamed deep blue against the starry sky. Around her, frangipani, hibiscus, and jasmine grew in bursts of color that mingled with foliage so green it glimmered like the rarest emeralds.

She stared at the water, listening to the soothing roar of the ocean.

It wasn't an unpleasant prison, but a firefly trapped in even the most ornate jar would still die without air.

Around her neck was a thin gold chain that anchored a clear turquoise pendant she rolled between her fingers. The size of a thumbnail, its faceted edges were cut to form a teardrop. Row claimed it had once belonged to her mother, and it was the only thing she had from either of her parents. Zarya didn't even have memories of them to comfort her.

She blew out a long, slow breath and let the book fall open in her lap to a page she'd read countless times. She loved nothing more than losing herself in her beloved romance novels, hoping that someday she might find anything resembling that kind of yearning and passion and her eventual happily ever after. Of course, for that to happen, she'd need to venture more than thirty paces from this cursed spot.

A few minutes later, she heard the shuffle of footsteps and, from the corner of her eye, watched Row sit down next to her. She closed her book but kept her gaze focused ahead, scanning the horizon, wishing she could see the worlds and people that lay beyond.

"I'm not trying to torture you," came Row's rumbling voice, his tone laced with uncharacteristic sympathy. Zarya had never been entirely sure whether he simply didn't experience the heavy emotions that burdened most people or if he just had difficulty expressing them. He must really be feeling guilty to be articulating this rare show of compassion.

He placed a large hand on her shoulder, and she glowered at it but didn't shake him off.

"Just forget it, Row. I don't want to talk about it."

"There is nothing out there for you, Zarya. You aren't missing anything."

She fixed him with an incredulous glare. "You can't possibly think I'd believe that."

He sighed and ran a hand down his face, creases furrowing his brow. "I need to stop bringing you so many books."

Zarya snorted. "Right, you don't want me getting any more *ideas*. Why not imprison my imagination, too? I suppose it makes no difference to you."

Row exhaled with the weight of a thousand buried secrets. "One day, you will understand."

"You say that over and over, and yet nothing changes. When is 'one day'? What really happened to my family? Why won't you tell me anything?"

"You know I took you in after your parents died." He gritted his teeth, already losing his patience with this conversation. So much for those five seconds of sympathy.

"That's the story you keep telling." Zarya turned away, throwing back the rest of her wine. "But you are conspicuously light on details. Who were they? What happened to them? Why am I here?"

With his hands braced on his knees, Row paused, possibly debating what to say next.

"I realize this is hard for you. But I made a promise, and I vowed to keep it, no matter what."

With that, he stood and walked back into the house, leaving Zarya alone.

"If that's what helps you sleep at night," she said into the wind as she scrubbed away the tear that slipped down her cheek.

TWO

The next morning, Zarya awoke with the sun and dressed in a black salwar kameez, embroidered with silver stars that caught the light as she moved. She spun in the mirror, admiring herself from several angles.

Row trekked to the city several times a month and always returned bearing an armload of gifts. Romance novels and luxurious handmade clothing were Zarya's favorites. He wielded them as a peace offering, as though material possessions would make up for this half-life. She supposed this was his way of communicating the emotions he seemed to have so much trouble expressing.

Regardless, it was at least a distraction from the monotony of her days, and, for a brief time, they'd ease into a weak sort of truce with one another.

She swept the top half of her glossy black curls from her forehead, securing them with a silver clip before she adjusted the tiny star-shaped stud that pierced the left side of her nose.

Satisfied, she quietly made her way down the hall. After passing the closed doors of Row's and Aarav's bedrooms, she emerged into the living room, dominated by a large stone fireplace. This far south, they used it only a handful of times a year on the stormiest nights. Row had installed it years ago in a rare bout of nostalgia for the cooler climes of his northern homeland, and Zarya loved to listen to the crackle and pop of the wood with a warm mug of chai in her hands.

On the opposite side of the room, the kitchen countertop lined the farthest wall, where a bank of windows faced the rolling sea. In between was a small wooden table surrounded by four chairs—not that they'd ever had a visitor to occupy the extra one—and an array of plush seating. The wooden floors were covered with intricately woven rugs that provided some much-needed color.

With everyone still asleep, Zarya started on breakfast, heading for the icebox and pulling out a plate of stacked aloo paratha. After setting a tava to warm on the cooktop, she dropped in a generous dollop of ghee before frying the potato-stuffed flatbread until it was golden brown on both sides.

While they cooked, she boiled a pot of chai on the stove, tossing in an extra cinnamon stick, just the way she liked it. Bracing her hip against the counter, she stared out the window, watching the sun rise over the churning waves of the sea.

Eventually, a bleary-eyed Aarav wandered out of his room, rubbing the top of his head, causing his short black hair to spike in wild disarray.

"Good morning," she said in a singsong voice, knowing it drove him crazy when she was perky any time before eight in the morning.

Only acknowledging her with a grunt, he poured himself a cup of chai before downing the entire thing in one long gulp. Then he grabbed a flatbread from the table and tore into it, leaning his back against the counter. On his narrow frame, he wore a cream kurta that fell to his knees and a loose dhoti made of light beige cotton.

"Where's Row?" he asked through a mouthful of potato.

"Good morning to you, too, Zarya. Thank you for breakfast. I appreciate all you do for me," she replied in mock falsetto. Aarav squinted and ripped off another piece of paratha, baring his teeth.

"Maybe he's still sleeping," he said, ignoring her comment. He then pushed himself off the counter and tromped towards Row's bedroom as Zarya frowned after him. It was unusual for Row to stay in bed this late.

"Are we heading to Dharati today or what, lazybones?" Aarav flung open the door and paused.

Zarya came up behind him, stretching on her tiptoes to peer over his shoulder. "What is it?"

"He's not here," he said, looking back at her.

"Then he must be in the garden."

Zarya rushed outside, scanning the plants and trees for signs of her guardian.

"Did he already leave for the city?" she asked as Aarav came up behind her.

He shook his head. "I was supposed to go with him this morning."

Zarya pursed her lips, biting down on the retort perched at the tip of her tongue. How very nice that Aarav was invited to Dharati today, and they would leave her here alone. *Again.*

Aarav strode back into the house. The morning air was already heavy and humid, pulsing with heat. She caught a tendril of a cooling breeze skimming off the turquoise water and closed her eyes with a deep breath. Maybe she'd go for a swim later.

Aarav returned to the garden a moment later. "His sword is still here."

A worried line formed between Zarya's brows. Row rarely went anywhere without his sword.

Aarav had his own weapons clutched in his hands now. He buckled on his talwar before heading towards the stables.

"Where are you going?" Zarya asked, trailing behind.

"To look for him. Something is wrong."

They came to a stop when they saw that Row's horse, Ojas, was also still there. While Row *could* use magic to travel quickly, something felt off, uneasiness settling over them as thick as the air after a monsoon.

"I don't want to stay here alone," Zarya said, her eyes fixed on Ojas as worry tickled the back of her neck.

"You stay here alone all the time."

She ground her teeth. "Yes, but this is different."

Aarav hoisted himself onto his horse and peered down at her. "You can't come with me. You know that."

"Break the tether," she said, clenching her fists in the fabric of her kurta. "Release me from this. I'll come with you. I can help."

Aarav pinned her with a hostile glare.

Both Row and Aarav were Aazheri—a sect of nearly immortal mages who wielded five different branches of elemental magic: earth, air, water, fire, and spirit.

Zarya understood little about how it all worked, but what she *did* know was that Row possessed a deep well of power, while Aarav's magic was a shallow puddle in comparison. That meant he was incapable of severing Row's enchantment, and she wanted the words to sting.

Aarav had spent their lives holding his gifts over her, and she felt no remorse about reminding him that while he might have magic that was stronger than hers, he still wasn't very powerful amongst his kind.

She imagined it was part of the reason he was such a complete ass.

He didn't respond, instead throwing another dark glance her way before kicking his horse into a trot and heading into the blighted forest.

"When are you coming back?" Zarya shouted, but Aarav disappeared into the shade of the trees without another word.

She watched him go, wishing yet again that she wasn't bound to this tiny strip of land. Gods, how she hated this. With a cry of frustration, she stormed back to the house, throwing herself on the living room's plush divan with her arms folded, while she stewed in the mire of her indignation.

She spent the day pacing, listening for sounds of Row's or Aarav's return. But as night fell, an uncomfortable restlessness began to set in. If Row really had met his end, what did it mean for Zarya? Would she be trapped here forever?

The walls of the cottage grew oppressive, closing in on her in a way that felt all too familiar. Sometimes the suffocating weight of her confinement sat so heavy on her chest she struggled to draw more than the shallowest of breaths.

Deciding she needed more air, she grabbed a blanket and a bottle of plum wine and headed outside.

White crystalline sand lined the shore where she laid the blanket before sitting down with her legs crossed. She uncorked the wine and drank it straight from the bottle, staring out at the sea.

The sun was setting over the horizon now, the sky a smeared wash of oranges and pinks. Before long, stars twinkled overhead.

Zarya looked over her shoulder, peering into the dark, listening intently for sounds of her guardian's return. Thankfully, Row's barrier of magic prevented the swamp's creatures from wandering too close—there were far worse things than just the naga lurking out there. She was safe enough right now, even if she was desperately alone.

To settle her nerves, Zarya drew on the stars, lifting a hand to the sky. Ribbons of light bloomed between her fingers like iron shavings gathering around a magnetic force. She didn't understand how it happened, only that as a small child, she'd discovered this strange talent mostly by chance. But other than its ability to call the naga, it was a useless, if pretty, trick.

Row had spent many years working with her, trying to coax out something more, but this insipid gift comprised the extent of her magic. Every time she tried, Row sighed with what seemed like equal parts relief and frustration when nothing else manifested.

But that didn't stop him from insisting no one could ever know about it, either.

It was just one more mystery to which she had no answer, and no matter how much she demanded them, Row remained as tight-lipped as a spy caught behind enemy lines.

Zarya stared at the light twisting between her fingers, lost in the tenderness of their soft glow. Then she stretched her hand, allowing them to float away before they misted into the night sky.

With another heavy sigh, Zarya drained the wine bottle, her head spinning slightly now. Deciding she couldn't face the confinement of her bedroom tonight, she lay down in the sand, pressing her cheek to the blanket, imagining a day, somewhere in her muddled future, when maybe her life would finally begin.

THREE

Eventually, Zarya fell into an unsettled sleep and dreamed of a forest swirling in mist and shadow. The trees were tall, with expansive trunks and leafy branches reaching into a brilliant violet sky, streaked with thick rivers of twinkling stars.

But it didn't feel exactly like a dream. It was too real to be only in her head. The grass tickled her cheek where she lay, and the soft breeze caressed her hair and rustled the leaves. Confused, she slowly stood up, walked towards a small clearing ahead, and stopped, scanning her surroundings.

She was sure she'd never been here before, but there was something familiar about it. Like a scent from a memory you'd nearly forgotten.

The stars overhead beckoned—she'd never seen so many of them in one place before—and she reached up, drawing on their brightness as their light twirled between her fingers. She studied the effect, more substantial and dense than her normal magic.

Surely, this had to be a dream, but it felt like something more. *This* felt like magic.

A small breath of surprise escaped her lips when she realized she wasn't alone. At the edge of the clearing stood a hooded figure, surrounded by mist and shadow. Though her mind ordered her to be on her guard, something about the stranger told her she was safe.

The figure was tall and broad, suggesting a male body. He lifted his head, just enough so she could make out the flash of dark eyes and the angle of a defined cheekbone. A hint of an inky hairline and the corner of a full mouth. She could tell from the crescents reflected in his eyes that he was watching her. Intently, it seemed.

Unable to look away, she stared back, the silence fractured only by the soft buzz of dragonflies and the twittering of mynas in the trees. Energy filled the air and spread across her skin like waves lapping at the shore. The hairs on her neck stood up as a shiver rolled down her spine.

But she wasn't afraid.

An abrupt moment later, Zarya winced as sunlight burned through her eyelids, scorching her retinas.

She groaned as she rolled over, both from the dull throb in her temple and the stab of pain that shot through her hip from sleeping on the packed sand. The empty bottle of wine lay next to her—a reminder of why her stomach was currently doing its best impression of an acrobat spinning over a pit.

It took her a moment to remember why she was lying outside as she blinked over and over, shielding her eyes from the sun. Where had she gone in her dream? Who had stood with her in that clearing? Why had it felt so familiar?

It was then she remembered Row and Aarav. Were they back? Why hadn't they woken her up?

With her head spinning, she staggered to her feet and then paused, leaning forward with her hands braced on her knees.

"Fuck," she muttered as she clasped a hand to her mouth and held her breath, fighting down a wave of cresting nausea.

Once it had passed, she pressed herself up and stumbled into the cottage.

"Row! Aarav! Are you here?" she called as she crossed the living room. No reply came as she flung open Aarav's and then Row's bedroom doors, finding both spaces empty.

Where were they?

Supporting herself against a doorframe, she clutched her hand to her stomach and waited for another wave of nausea to pass. Inhaling through her nose and out through her mouth, she willed her gut to settle.

Then she headed back outside, trotting in the direction Aarav had left yesterday, hoping she might intercept him and Row already on their way home. She wound her way down the narrow path, overgrown with bushes, their black leaves tickling her legs with a soft rustle. But there was still no sign of them.

She continued along her path, approaching the spot where she knew Row's magic would start to weigh her down. That telltale pressure that squeezed her limbs, alerting her she was nearing the edge of her cage.

But nothing happened.

A soft breeze tangled her hair as she stopped and looked around, wondering if she was still dreaming or perhaps the victim of an elaborate prank.

Row didn't really have a sense of humor, though.

But this was where his magic *should* be weighing on her with the crushing force that stuck in the back of her throat.

She took another careful step, as if tiptoeing barefoot over broken glass, but still nothing happened.

And then another.

Still nothing.

Up ahead was the point where she usually blacked out.

She approached it with a sense of wary caution, expecting Row's magic to leash her down at any moment.

Nothing.

She stopped, her feet planted apart and her hands out, once again analyzing her surroundings. Was this the right spot? Of course, it was. She knew this place, every branch and leaf and bush like she knew her own heartbeat.

She continued walking, placing one foot in front of the other, hardly daring to believe this might be real.

The magic was gone.

More confident now, she sped up until she was running, her feet churning up dirt as she pounded through the brush. She let out a hoot, racing as fast as her legs would carry her, dodging the slender trees that stood in her path.

Her chest began to burn, and she came to an abrupt stop. She had never ventured this deep into the swamp.

That's when her muddled thoughts focused into razor-sharp clarity.

This was her chance.

Moving too quickly to second-guess herself, Zarya ran back to the house and burst through the door. Her chest heaving with effort and a rush of hope, she checked the bedrooms again.

Empty.

Pressure built inside her head, her tongue burning with the tastes of panic and endless possibilities. With her hangover now miraculously forgotten, she dashed to her room. Her hands shook as she packed a bag, trying to think of practical clothing options conducive to running away.

Running away.

That's what she was doing. Right?

An anxious lump formed in her throat.

Zarya changed out of the damp salwar kameez she'd slept in and into a pair of plum-colored leggings and a sleeveless cream kurta embroidered with purple flowers. She braided her hair and slipped into a pair of short leather boots, already imagining all the places she'd travel. The mountains she'd climb. The oceans she'd swim. The strangers she'd meet.

She reached for the weapons Row had spent a lifetime teaching her to wield with the proficiency of a soldier: her talwar, various daggers, and her bow and arrow. He'd made her train for hours every day, polishing her into a weapon of his own making. She'd never understood his motivations, other than he seemed to think everyone should want to learn the art of war. But it had at least been something to pass the time, and so she'd played along, reasoning that if she *did* ever get out of here, it would be a useful skill in her arsenal.

She gazed longingly at her sagging bookshelves, the worn spines evidence of how much these stories had been loved. But carting along the heavy volumes would be foolish and definitely impractical.

Besides, it was long past time to write her own story and stop living inside the pages of a borrowed reality.

But she decided one couldn't hurt, so she stuffed her favorite—a steamy rakshasa romance with a happy ending that she'd read at least a hundred times—into a pocket, then slung her pack over her shoulder.

With blood pounding in her veins, Zarya retrieved Row's saddlebags from where they sat in the corner of the living room and packed as much food as they would hold. Then she headed outside towards their small stable.

Row's horse, Ojas, regarded her warily but allowed her to strap on his saddle and load on the bags. She was about to mount him when she stopped and ran back into the house. Her heart was beating so hard she could feel it in the backs of her teeth.

She found Row's sword leaning against his bed. It was a different style than the talwar she used; its steel blade was straight, its hilt unadorned, save for a few shining runes embedded into the leather wrapping. She picked it up, clutching the scabbard in one trembling hand.

She wasn't sure why she wanted it, other than it felt like something she'd need.

Then she crossed the room to where a desk sat against the wall. Zarya tugged open the top drawer and found several bags of gold coins. Choosing a full one, she tested its weight in her hand and then hesitated, suddenly unsure of herself.

This was stupid. The enchantment would stop her, as it always did. She'd imagined it. She had been standing in the wrong spot. She'd drunk too much wine last night.

With those thoughts nagging on a loop and the sword and bag of gold clasped in her hands, Zarya forced herself back outside. She wouldn't play the coward. Not when she was *finally* being handed an opportunity like this on a golden fucking platter.

She'd regret it forever if she passed up this chance.

Zarya fastened the sword to the saddle, stashed a few coins in her pocket, and stuffed the rest deep into a bag. She touched her head to the horse's saddle, whispering a silent prayer to the gods, wondering if they'd ever notice her.

Then she took a deep breath and lifted herself onto the animal. From her perched height, she peered through the trees, dizzy with anticipation, sure Row and Aarav would approach at any second, catching her in the middle of her crime.

But her surroundings remained quiet. She was alone. She was doing this.

Taking the reins, she nudged Ojas into a slow walk. It had been years since she'd ridden anywhere. There had been no need since Lahar had succumbed to the blight. She wasn't a skilled rider, but she knew enough not to fall off and break her neck.

Ojas obeyed her gentle nudges as they once again approached the spot she knew so well. She closed her eyes, praying to any gods who were listening, to the gods who had abandoned her, that she hadn't been hallucinating.

As they ambled forward, Zarya still felt nothing. Only light-
ness. Only a tangible scream of elation sparking against her
skin. No press of magic to hold her back as Ojas stepped
through the trees. They kept moving deeper while Zarya's lungs
constricted, her breath coming in snipped gasps, her hands
sweating on the reins. Her heartbeat wild.

They passed the point where she normally blacked out, and
again nothing happened. This was impossible.

Now it was time to contend with the biggest decision of her
life.

She swallowed the searing knot of conflict in her throat and
hesitated. She had little sense of what waited beyond the
boundaries of her prison, and Row would never forgive her for
running away.

But freedom beckoned.

Zarya tasted it in the air, sweeter than the ripest fruit. More
tempting than the rarest treasure.

And right now, nothing else mattered.

This was the only thing she had ever wanted.

This wasn't the moment for indecision.

This chance might never come again.

And seriously, fuck Row.

Wherever he was, he was a powerful Aazheri who could
take care of himself. He would be fine. And Aarav? Zarya was
content to never lay eyes on his ugly face ever again.

With a last glance back, Zarya studied the home that had
been her entire existence for nearly twenty-one years. It stood
serenely on the shore, its tidy whitewashed walls belying the
truth of what it had contained. *Who* it had contained. A pretty
prison sitting by the sea.

Zarya closed her eyes, hoping it would be her last glimpse of
this place, too.

Not allowing herself to waver any longer, she pressed
forward, flicking the reins and shouting, "Run, Ojas, run!"

The horse sped forward, and Zarya lifted her face to the sun, the wind whipping at her hair.

And in that moment, she didn't just run—Zarya finally flew.

FOUR

The initial exhilaration of Zarya's freedom soon gave way to sobering reality. She was unprotected for the first time in her life, exposed and vulnerable. For all her bravado, her earlier confidence offered only a thin shield against the outside world, as ephemeral as smoke.

She shifted in the saddle, her body unused to riding for extended periods. It ached, sore spots forming where her skin rubbed against the leather. The sun beat down, forming beads of sweat on her brow. She wiped it away with the back of her hand before she reached for her canteen and took a deep drink.

As she picked through the trees, Zarya headed north, keeping the ocean at her back. The queendom of Daragaab was the largest territory in Rahajhan, occupying the southeastern corner of the continent where her home lay. It sat bordered by the Dakhani Sea to the south and the Nila Hara Sea on the east. Zarya's destination was the capital city of Dharati, which lay northeast of the seaside cottage, about a day and a half's ride away.

Numerous villages and farms once dotted the southern portion of the region, but these, too, had been abandoned as the blight had spread. No one knew where the blight had come from or what it meant, only that it was growing day by day. She'd often listened to Row talk about the challenges it presented and how no one understood its source, nor, more importantly, how to push it back.

The ground beneath Ojas's hooves was boggy, his weight leaving deep depressions in the soft earth, where murky puddles and mud oozed in every direction.

While Zarya maintained an uncomfortable truce with the swamp back home, out here, alone, a faint nausea settled in her stomach, the tiny hairs on the back of her neck standing at attention.

As she continued, her surroundings grew more intimidating. Worried she'd taken a wrong turn, her confidence wavered. She'd been riding for hours and had no sense of how far she'd come or how far she had yet to go. She'd spent the day watching and listening for signs of Row or Aarav, and she'd paid little attention to the route she'd traveled.

Right now, floating lights would be casting their coppery glow over the vibrant greenery of her garden as the sun set over the azure ocean. The comfort of her snug bed and her room full of books and treasures called. Here in the swamp, the ground crooked a finger, bleak and uninviting, as she allowed thoughts of returning to the cottage to seep into the hairline cracks of her conviction.

She peered over her shoulder, watching the trees sway in the dimness. She wasn't sure she'd even be able to find her way back anymore.

She pressed her lips together and shook her head. *No.* She was never going back. The anger. The hurt. The frustration. The loneliness of her captive existence. This was only a bout of nerves—the swamp always made her edgy, and the desire for freedom outweighed her need for security right now. The last thing she wanted was to be dragged back to her prison with this brief taste of liberty curdling on her tongue.

In the fading daylight, she focused her senses, alert to the things that inhabited the swamp. The worst she'd ever encountered were the vetalas—humanoid demons that feasted on human flesh and possessed unnatural strength. They hadn't seen one around the cottage in years—Row said they preferred to gather in areas of denser population—but that didn't mean she was safe out here in her solitude.

Weary and sore, Zarya's heart leaped when the outline of a house appeared in the falling light, and she urged Ojas towards it. As she approached, she saw it was one of several cottages ringing a tiny village. The homes sat dark and empty, their walls and roofs mimicking the black and dreary canvas of the forest.

Chills dimpled Zarya's flesh as she dismounted and eased open the door of the closest house. It stood mostly empty, only a few scattered belongings—a teapot, a stained pillow, a broken chair—littering the floor.

She tied Ojas up next to a patch of blackened grass on which he promptly began feasting. She watched him, hoping it wasn't toxic, but there was nothing else, so she didn't stop him. In her haste to leave this morning, she'd failed to consider the horse's needs.

Drawing out Row's sword from her saddle, she held it aloft and went to search the other homes, relieved to find them all empty.

When she'd completed her surveillance, she circled to the first house and laid out her cloak to cushion the hard floor. She then sat against the wall and pulled out the roti and channa masala she had packed that morning. After stretching out her sore neck, she tore off a piece of flatbread and scooped up a mouthful of curried chickpeas.

But just as she brought the food to her mouth, her stomach twisted, like a fist closing around her intestines, stealing her appetite. She dropped the food back in its container, deciding to forgo supper tonight.

She pulled up her knees and rested her head against the wall, thinking of Row and Aarav. If they'd already returned to the cottage, they would have come home to a cold stove and no dinner. Not that they expected her to wait on them—Row helped when he was around, and Aarav feigned usefulness—but the household tasks naturally fell to her. She hated it. The monotony. The tediousness. The absolute lack of adventure.

Glowering out the window, she watched the last of the day's light fade. It had been a prison, or no better than one. For a crime she had never committed. They had kept her in a cage for almost twenty-one years, refusing to tell her why. She had no idea where she'd come from. No friends, no family, no true companionship. No one with whom to share her thoughts and dreams. She'd never experienced the magic and wonder of the world. She'd never even been properly kissed.

Sure, there had been that one boy in Lahar with whom she'd had a few hurried fumbles, hiding behind the boats in his father's shed. But he'd fucked her without passion, and it had been over before she knew it. It wasn't anything like the stories she'd read. Either those had been exaggerated with the freedom of literary license, or he'd been just as clueless as she was. In her optimism, she chose to believe it was the second reason and that she was just waiting to meet the right person who would make her knees go weak with a single look.

Whatever the case, Zarya had read enough of those stories to know she desperately wanted to be kissed in a way that mattered. And then fall recklessly, passionately in love. She would never settle for anything less.

With that thought in mind, she pulled out her novel and flipped through the pages, turning to the parts she'd underlined. Namely, the naughty bits she was sure Row had no idea existed when he'd chosen these books for her.

But tonight, not even the promise of stolen kisses under moonlight could settle the anxiety thrumming in her veins. Tonight, the swamp seemed heavier and more oppressive than usual, the air distended with its unnatural silence. She kept Row's sword on the ground next to her within easy reach. Just in case.

Despite every worry and misgiving she had right now, she was sure leaving had been the right choice.

If Row found her, she'd kill herself before she'd let him drag her back to the cottage. She would fight like a demon to get away. Admittedly, it was hard to completely silence the lifetime of warnings he'd burdened her with, but she would take her chances with whatever waited out here—*anything* was better than her cage.

With a kernel of resentment popping in her heart, Zarya spread out the edge of her cloak and tried to force her mind towards more comforting thoughts.

Perhaps today marked the beginning of something auspicious. A life defined by friendship and love rather than secrets and loneliness. Maybe she'd find a family. Maybe a friend. Or maybe she'd meet a handsome warrior. Stories of brave heroes falling in love were her favorite kind.

As night waned on, she tried to sleep, but every crack of a branch or rustle of leaves had her jumping with nervousness. Her chin dipped against her chest for what felt like a thousand times before the first rays of sun became visible through the window. She was exhausted, but she had to keep moving lest Row or Aarav catch up to her. Now that daylight crept upon the forest, she felt more confident about venturing back into the trees.

Her stomach growled in protest, and Zarya reached for her abandoned dinner. But the queasiness from yesterday persisted, the sight of the food making her stomach flip. Instead, she settled for a gulp of tepid water from her canteen and hoped this nausea would pass soon.

Another noise stirred her attention, her focus snapping to the doorway of the house.

Slowly, she reached for Row's sword and eased up to stand with one hand braced on the wall. Footsteps squelched in the mud, the sound drawing closer to her hiding place. Zarya swore under her breath, realizing Ojas's presence would tell the intruder that someone was nearby. There were only two small windows, neither large enough to accommodate an escape. She was trapped in here.

She crept closer to the door, trying to peer around the corner. A figure appeared, filling the doorway.

She reacted instantly, slamming into the intruder with a shoulder to their chest, attempting to knock them aside before she took off running.

"Zarya?" choked out a familiar voice.

She stopped in her tracks, spinning around.

"Fuck! Aarav! What are you doing? Why are you sneaking up on me?"

"What am *I* doing?" He rubbed his chest, his body hunched and his eyes blazing. They both lifted their blades, pointing them at one another. "What are *you* doing out here? And why do you have Ojas? For a minute, I thought you were Row."

They faced off for several tension-filled heartbeats, neither willing to concede. But there was no point in them fighting out here right now. Still breathing heavily, Zarya lowered her sword, and then Aarav eventually did the same.

"So, you didn't find him?" she asked.

"No," Aarav said, running a hand through his hair. "There's no sign of him anywhere." He narrowed his eyes. "How did you get out here? How did you get past Row's magic?"

She thought about lying. Telling him she'd managed it on her own, but she knew he'd never believe that.

"I didn't," Zarya said finally, her eyes shifting away. "It was... gone."

"Gone?" Aarav's eyebrows drew together. "What do you mean, gone?"

"Just that. I simply walked out."

They shared a look deep with implications, the full weight of that knowledge sinking in.

Aarav straightened and then sheathed his sword. "You shouldn't have done that."

Zarya rolled her eyes at the chastisement in his tone. "Why not?"

"You *know* why."

His hands hung loosely at his sides, his feet spread as if he were expecting her to bolt. She considered it but was worried about getting lost in the swamp after yesterday. Besides, she needed Ojas, and Aarav would surely stop her before she could untether him.

"We're going to go back home to wait for him," Aarav said, grabbing her arm.

She yanked it from his grasp. "I'm not going anywhere with you." She was *never* returning to the cottage. She brushed past him and went to untie Ojas.

"Stop this, Zarya. You had your fun. We're going back *now*."

"No," she said, refusing to look at him as she soothed the horse and adjusted the saddle.

"Zarya, be reasonable. What is Row going to say if he finds you out here? You know this isn't safe."

"Why isn't it safe, Aarav? Why am I the only one who never gets to leave that fucking place?" She gestured in the direction she'd come.

His mouth pressed together, and for the briefest second, she wondered if she caught a flash of contrition in his eyes, but it was quickly replaced with a harder edge.

"We can't stay out here any longer. Come on."

He turned then and headed towards his own horse, grabbing the reins and leading it down the path Zarya had followed yesterday. She didn't move, looking in the other direction, feeling everything slipping away. For the briefest moment, she had tasted it—the freedom she'd longed for every day of her life, and now it was crumbling between her fingers like ash.

"Zarya," Aarav called over his shoulder, his tone sharp. "I can't be responsible for how Row will react if he finds you out here."

The words were heavy with repercussions, and Zarya nodded, tears stinging her eyes.

She grabbed Ojas's reins and silently followed, her head down and her eyes on her feet as she felt herself slowly pulling apart. This had been a stupid idea, anyway. Of course, she wasn't destined for freedom. What had she really thought? There was something more for her?

The cottage was her life, and she'd grow old and die there, lonely and bitter, and that was it.

They walked for a short while, leading their horses across the boggy ground as Zarya's mood grew darker and darker. She'd sworn last night that she'd never return to the cottage. What *if* she just jumped up on Ojas and ran? She could hide in the swamp. What was the worst that could happen? Could she outrun Aarav? He'd know she was headed for Dharati, and eventually, he'd find her.

The soft murmur of voices caught her attention. Both Aarav and Zarya came to a halt at the sound, their gazes meeting in wary apprehension. Zarya released Ojas's reins and quietly shuffled to the edge of the path to peer through a set of low, dense bushes.

On the other side, two men were dismounting from their own horses. One with shoulder-length silver hair, the front pieces tied back with a small strip of leather, and about half a dozen braids woven throughout. The other had bright emerald eyes and short black hair that fell in waves around his ears.

They were talking in low voices, and Zarya couldn't make out their conversation. It was rare to see strangers in the swamp, and she couldn't tear herself away.

The black-haired man sat down on a log, stretching his long legs out in front of him before crossing them at the ankles, while the other peered into the muddy pool before them, scratching his chin.

Not just men, she realized with a jolt.

That burnished brown skin, those bright eyes, those slightly elongated canines—she'd read enough stories to recognize them for what they were. Rakshasas. A nearly immortal species of elemental being known for drinking blood. Many lived in Dara-gaab, the seat of earth magic in Rahajhan, and most were of noble birth. Zarya tried not to gawk at this fairy tale come to life before her very eyes.

Aarav came up behind her and whispered in her ear. "Let's go. You can't be seen."

Zarya threw him a dark look and turned back to the rakshasas, watching their graceful movements, wishing desperately she could speak with them.

They were still talking to one another when something heaved in her stomach, and a moment later, two naga burst from the swamp. They were massive, like tree trunks—longer and thicker than the one she'd killed two days ago.

Zarya gasped as she watched one of them wrap itself around the dark-haired rakshasa's torso, pinning his arms so he couldn't reach the sword that hung from his side. His silver-haired companion was now occupied by the second naga, which was currently taunting him, darting its mashed face in and out, snapping its mouthful of razor-sharp teeth.

The dark-haired rakshasa was being dragged off the log and towards the water, his legs kicking and his body bucking as he tried to free himself. Zarya parted the bushes, preparing to dive through, when Aarav grabbed her and pulled her back.

"Where are you going?"

"To help them. He's going to die!"

"No, Zarya, they can't see you. We're leaving. They can take care of themselves."

Zarya made a face of disgust. "You're pathetic, Aarav."

She shoved Aarav with all her strength and plunged through the trees with Row's sword in her hand. With her feet planted apart, she lifted the sword high before slicing through the first demon's neck, shearing off its head in one neat slice, freeing the dark-haired rakshasa from its hold. She'd killed enough of these things to know exactly where to strike.

At the same moment, the second naga turned its attention towards her and lunged, clamping its mouth onto her leg. White and pulsing, the gelatinous mass of its body slithered on the ground, pulling her off her feet and flat onto her back. She cried out as the sword tumbled from her grasp, the naga's sharp teeth digging into her calf and shin. She screamed as it dragged her towards the murky water.

Clawing at the boggy ground, she tried to find something to grasp, but the soft mud came away in her hands, her fingers trailing deep gouges in the earth. Row's sword glinted where she'd dropped it, too far out of her reach.

Another scream tore from her throat as the naga's fangs ground against bone, burning as blood mixed with mud. The smell of rotting flesh wafted from its maw, its hot, fetid breath making her gag.

She twisted towards the snake, using her free leg to kick its face as hard as she could, hoping to dislodge its grasp.

Then something fast and small whizzed by Zarya's head, followed by a sickening squelch just before the pressure eased on her leg. She gawked at the arrow now sticking straight out of the naga's forehead right before it flopped over, dead.

FIVE

Her heart beating wildly, Zarya collapsed to the ground, panting. She blinked a few times, trying to clear the black spots twirling in her vision.

"*What* were you thinking?" asked a curt voice. The silver-haired rakshasa was crouched next to her, setting down a large wooden bow and throwing an angry glance her way.

Zarya frowned at him and then at her leg, surprised at the amount of blood. Long gouges punctured her skin, leaving her pants in tatters and her boot lost forever.

"I was trying to help you," she snapped, irritated at his tone. In fact, she'd almost died trying to help them, and she didn't appreciate the attitude.

The man offered her a skeptical look, his eyebrow arched in disdain, as he dropped the bag slung over his shoulder and then rummaged through its contents. He pulled out a small box and opened it.

"This will neutralize the naga's venom. You'll need to hold still." He held up a vial of colorless liquid and looked at her with clear, grey eyes. "And it will hurt." His tone suggested he wasn't about to apologize for that, though.

Zarya nodded, her heart still thumping erratically in her chest.

"Squeeze my hand," said his darker-haired companion, who had recovered from his own confrontation with the naga. With his knee planted in the mud, he clasped Zarya's hand with both of his.

"Hold on," said the first rakshasa as he poured the clear liquid over Zarya's wounds. The sting hurt almost as much as the naga's teeth. She sucked in a breath, willing herself to stillness as the pain flared hot and then slowly subsided. The silver-haired man continued scowling, saying nothing as he worked with practiced efficiency, cleaning her wound.

"You don't want an infection," he said. His tone again suggested he didn't care either way.

"Vikram, put this on." He held out a roll of white gauze. Vikram took it and began wrapping it gently around her calf. He wore a dark green, high-collared jacket with gold buttons and detailing at the cuffs. The other man wore a similar uniform in dark grey. Both wore black pants and tall black leather boots, along with an array of weapons strapped to their bodies.

"I am Commander Vikram Ravana, and this is one of my officers, Lieutenant Yasen Varghese." Vikram gestured to his companion. "We are soldiers in Rani Vasvi's army."

"I'm Zarya," she said as Vikram helped her sit up. Aarav hovered behind Vikram, a deep scowl marring his face. "And that idiot is Aarav."

"Where did you come from?" Yasen asked, his eyes narrowing. "And why are you out here? It's dangerous to go beyond the city walls."

Now that his role as nursemaid had finished, Yasen studied her with an intensity that caused her neck to flush. She didn't like the way he was glaring at her, as though she were a fly that had landed in his soup.

She shared a look with Aarav before answering.

"Our... father disappeared a few days ago, and we were looking for him. We live on the southern shore."

She decided on a loose version of the truth, still conscious of Row's warnings.

"You live out here?" Vikram asked, his tone sharp.

She nodded, wary of revealing too much to these strangers.

"Hmm." He scanned the trees. "You shouldn't be out here. I'm taking you into custody on behalf of Rani Vasvi. Come with us."

"We haven't done anything wrong," Zarya protested. "I rescued you!"

Yasen made a derisive snort. "Yes, *you* rescued *us*."

"We need to get back home," Aarav said, his voice pitching into a whine.

"Thank you for your help," Vikram said, looking between Zarya and Aarav. "But you will both come with us." Though the words were polite, the edge in his voice implied he wasn't taking no for an answer.

Vikram helped her to stand up, her injured leg throbbing. Row's sword still lay on the ground, and Zarya reached for it, but Yasen scooped it up before she could grab it. He gave her a dark look that suggested he wasn't about to trust her with this or any other weapon. She returned his glare, wondering what the fuck his problem was.

"Zarya," Aarav said, his fists clenched.

"Oh, just listen to them, Aarav. What choice do we have?"

She was pretending to be irritated, but the truth was she could barely keep her smile contained. After Aarav had tried to drag her back to the cottage, she was thrilled these two were taking them to Dharati, even if it did feel like they were being arrested. She was sure they hadn't technically done anything wrong, though. Perhaps *there* she could escape, ditch Aarav, and set out on her own.

Aarav grunted and stomped towards the bushes, but Yasen intercepted him.

"Where do you think you're going?"

"To get our horses."

"Stay here," Yasen ordered, before he pushed through the bush and called over. "There's only one horse."

They waited for Yasen to lead it around, but it wasn't Ojas. He must have run off during the attack. Zarya cursed her luck. Now she had no clothes, no food, and no money. And her only weapon had just been confiscated by the queen's soldiers.

How would she escape Aarav now?

"You can ride with me," Vikram offered, helping her limp to where the rakshasas' horses stood nearby and hoisting her up onto a white gelding. A moment later, he settled in behind, pulling up on the reins.

She shivered at being so close to another person, enjoying the way his body felt all warm and hard against hers. And this was not just any person, but a handsome rakshasa. The very same beings she'd fantasized about countless times, thanks to her books.

Though she'd read enough stories to know that you didn't throw yourself at the feet of the first man you met. Zarya was smarter than that.

Perhaps she should have been more cautious, but she couldn't muster the worry Row had tried to drill into her every day of her life.

She resisted the urge to reach out and pinch both Vikram and Yasen, just to make sure they were real. Finally seeing faces that didn't belong to Row or Aarav was worth the trouble of almost getting her leg bitten off.

Vikram seemed friendly enough, though Yasen was decidedly more off-putting. If they meant them harm, surely they wouldn't have tended her injury. *Right?*

They'd go to the city, explain their situation, and then Zarya could find her own path. Free of Row's shackles, maybe she could finally uncover why she'd been locked away her whole life.

They set off, hope stirring in Zarya's chest as she headed towards her new and uncertain destiny.

* * *

They picked through the swamp, side by side, mud squelching under hooves, while that same eerie silence hung in the air like a bubble on the cusp of bursting. Even the wind seemed to hold its breath as flashes of movement slid in and out of Zarya's vision. Trying to catch sight of the source, she'd whip her head around, only to find nothing but blackened trees and decay wherever she looked.

Their slender trunks grew together like claws reaching skyward, a canopy forming overhead. Coal-black vines looped through the boughs, hanging so low that they had to duck to avoid being caught in their snares.

As they plodded on, the swamp began to give way to a healthier forest, as withered bark and dull leaves transformed into fresh greens and rich browns. The boggy ground eventually firmed into hard-packed earth, easing their travel.

"How far does the swamp go, exactly?" Zarya asked.

Yasen's forehead pleated before he shifted in his saddle and flicked his reins in an impatient gesture, apparently not deigning to answer her question.

"*Where* did you say you lived?" Vikram asked from behind, a guarded thread in his tone.

"The southern shore," she replied, wondering if she should have ever revealed that information as she took in Yasen's deepening frown.

Sure, Row's constant reminders of her safety had been schooled into her for as long as she could remember, but they had also never made any sense. Why was the world okay for everyone else and not for her? Row was just an overprotective guardian, and he had to understand that she was no longer a child. There was no harm in these two knowing where they had come from.

As the swamp receded entirely, the forest seemed to be compensating for its dreary neighbor as flowers burst in every direction, their petals thick and glossy with every color under the sun. The wind rustled vibrant green leaves, and a peacock strutted through the bushes, its arced tail resplendent in hues of emerald and turquoise.

Zarya gasped with delight, pointing towards it right before her stomach clenched again and her shoulders rounded. She clutched at her midsection just as the sounds of rough snarls rippled from deep in the trees.

"Yasen, we need to move. Kimpurusha in the forest," Vikram called as his arm tightened around her waist.

"Hold on!" Yasen barked, addressing both her and Aarav, who rode on Yasen's other side. "And get low." He snapped his horse's reins, and it shot forward as they arrowed through the brush, leaves crunching as shadows closed in around them. The growling grew louder, and the queasiness in her stomach spread, her insides roiling.

Yasen spurred his horse forward, and Vikram followed close as Zarya clung to the horse's mane, one of Vikram's arms still banded around her. It seemed to take forever to reach the edge of the forest as darkness pressed in, filling Zarya's lungs, clogging them with sludge.

Finally, they broke through the tree line, and the landscape spread onto a rolling, grassy plain. The sun was visible just above the horizon of the Nila Hara Sea to the east, casting the sky and water in brilliant hues of pink and orange.

With nothing barring their way, they opened up their horses and streaked across the sun-beaten grass. Shadows chased them, their howling growing louder, their snarls hungry and desperate. Zarya swayed in the saddle, her nausea dragging her through churning darkness, causing her vision to smear at the edges. Vikram again tightened his arm around her, keeping her upright, his shallow breaths in her ear as the horses thundered across the plain.

As they rounded the crest of a hill, a city came into view up ahead. Its high golden walls stretched out for miles, everything lit so brightly that a dome of golden haze bled into the descending darkness. Even with bile burning a sour line in her throat, it was the most magnificent thing she had ever seen.

But she would have to admire it later because something swiped at her injured leg. With a cry, she kicked her bare foot, meeting only air. Vikram veered his horse to the left, trying to evade a second hit.

Stealing a glance over her shoulder, Zarya caught sight of a pack of lion-like creatures chasing them across the plain. They were white and translucent like the naga, but where the serpents had been fleshy and corporeal, the lions shimmered in and out of focus like apparitions. She'd never seen this manner of demon before.

A flash of copper split the darkness as long white teeth snapped and lunged for the horses, who sped faster and faster. She caught another flash of light from the corner of her eye, dirt, and grass leaping in the air, forcing the white shadows to retreat. The horses ran harder still, but whatever had slowed the kimpurusha had been temporary, and the demons gained on them again, giving chase like they had wings on their paws.

Ahead, a pair of enormous iron gates stood open at the city's entrance. At least forty feet tall, they looked strong enough to withstand an army of thousands. But with horror, Zarya realized that the gates were currently shuddering closed.

Whispering a prayer, she bowed her head, clinging to the saddle. Vikram bent over her, gripping the reins with his free hand. Sweat ran down her back and down her temples as her stomach heaved and churned.

"Almost there," Vikram said, his voice faint on the wind. Zarya looked up. The iron gates were almost fully closed now. They had only seconds before they would slam shut, leaving the four of them out here alone with these monsters. Her stomach twisted again, and she fought down another wave of nausea that threatened to upend her stomach.

Yasen shouted a command, spurring his mount harder. Another flash of copper light sent the demons scurrying back. Zarya looked over her shoulder as Vikram threw out his arm, sending two more blasts of light behind him. The earth shuddered as chunks of soil and grass slammed into the lions, throwing them off course.

It slowed the kimpurusha for a moment, but they shook off the attack and took up the chase again. Vikram flicked his reins, shouting out another command. His voice rang out over the thundering of hooves and the rushing wind.

Less than a hundred feet stood between them and the gate as it groaned on massive hinges, only a small sliver of light winking through a narrow gap that was currently shrinking far too quickly for her liking.

Eighty feet.

Forty Feet.

Ten feet.

Zarya held her breath as they pounded closer and closer, certain the gate's immense weight would crush them.

With only the slightest opening left, she felt a swoosh of air as they stampeded through, Yasen and Aarav right on their heels.

The gates slammed shut with a resounding quake as Zarya threw herself off the horse, staggered several steps, and then heaved out the contents of her stomach against Dharati's magnificent golden wall.

SIX

Zarya wiped her face with the bloody, dirt-stained hem of her kurta. Vikram's brow furrowed with concern, while Yasen's upper lip curled in disgust.

"What?" she asked, standing up straight and tossing her braid over her shoulder, trying to pretend she wasn't covered in vomit and missing a shoe. Her stomach had settled again, but she couldn't figure out why she'd felt so ill a moment earlier. Perhaps she was coming down with something.

She took a step, and her injured leg crumpled beneath her, sending her collapsing to the stones. Vikram leaped to her rescue, and as he helped her stand, he wrinkled his nose, though she could tell he was trying to hide it.

"Sorry. I don't smell my best right now."

His answering smile was kind, his striking green eyes crinkling at the corners.

"It's quite all right. Do you need help walking?"

She nodded and slung her arm over Vikram's shoulders.

Yasen exchanged a few words with the guards at the gate, their expressions grim as they surveyed the wall that was the only thing protecting them from what festered beyond it. It seemed solid enough, but Zarya hoped it was stronger than it appeared. It would take more than stone and mortar to keep the demons out forever.

Vikram also gave the guards a stiff nod before escorting a hobbling Zarya into the streets of the city. Yasen led their mounts while a sullen Aarav shuffled along, glaring at everyone with suspicion as though someone might peel away from the crowd and kidnap them all.

What was he so scared of?

Zarya took in the vast scope of her surroundings, the air in her lungs turning to mist. Dharati wasn't just a city—it was a cacophony: layer upon layer of color, people, carts, and animals roving through the crowded streets.

Zarya took a deep breath, barely able to comprehend so many people together all at once. After spending so much of her life alone, it was overwhelming. The sheer audacity of so much existing in one place. Lahar had been *nothing* like this. There had been a few hundred people at most living on the shore, and this blew all of her expectations to dust.

She watched a man and woman arguing in the middle of the maelstrom, their hands flying while they spoke with heated words. But after a moment, they stopped yelling and smiled, embracing each other with such tenderness that Zarya's heart ached.

This was it. The life she'd been chasing. The chance to experience something more.

As they proceeded down cobbled streets and through a packed bazaar, vendors shouted at passersby, gesturing to towers of fragrant spices, rows of shiny baubles, and stacked bolts of embellished fabric. Animals and fruits and vegetables and an array of things that Zarya couldn't name lined every walkway in gravity-defying piles.

It was everything she'd dreamed of and so much more.

Everything she'd been denied. Everything Row had claimed she hadn't been missing.

Vikram and Yasen led them through winding streets, past taverns, and coffee houses, where outdoor chairs and tables played host to animated conversations as people gathered at the end of the day.

They turned down a wide boulevard dominated by the sprawling facade of a glittering palace. Situated along the shore of the Nila Hara Sea, it gleamed like it had been dipped in broken glass.

Slender minarets and curving gold domes reached into the sky, and the luminous marble walls looked as if they'd been poured from heavy cream. Lattices wrought in marble and pale wood, sparkling with gemstones, covered rounded windows and gently pointed arches, and every surface was intricately carved with flowers, people, animals, and leafy vines.

"Jai Mahal," Zarya breathed. She had seen drawings and read descriptions, but nothing could have prepared her for the actual thing. Jai Mahal defied her most vivid daydreams.

Vikram steered her towards the palace's grand courtyard.

"Wait? We're going inside?"

She stopped, tugging him back as she pulled her arm from his shoulders, finding she was able to put weight on her leg again without too much strain.

Vikram gave her a quizzical look. "We are taking you to see the queen. This is where she lives."

Before them stood a set of towering doors painted a dazzling shade of sky blue, decorated with ornate white scrollwork.

"Why not just let us go? We won't cause any trouble."

Vikram raised a brow, clearly unmoved by her words.

"We found you wandering alone in the swamps, and you claim to live out there. Her Majesty will need to know about that."

"But why?" Zarya asked, descending into panic.

"Hiding something?" Yasen asked her with a dry smile.

"No," Zarya said curtly, trying to reel in her distress and smoothing down the front of her kurta. "Of course not. I just don't understand why you'd want to waste the queen's time with the two of us."

"I assure you, it's fine," Vikram said, his tone indicating he wasn't interested in hearing any more of her arguments. She nodded slowly, nervousness making her stomach flip, threatening a repeat performance. Vikram took her by the elbow, and she limped towards an immense tree standing in the center of the courtyard.

The Jai Tree. It stood at least a hundred feet across and several hundred feet tall, like a beacon watching over Dharati. The bark of its wide trunk was so pale it was almost white, and its arching branches reached towards the brightening stars overhead. Flowers bloomed in a riot of colors, carpeting the branches and forming a rainbow canopy that enveloped the palace and the surrounding streets. Zarya stretched her neck, inhaling the intoxicating perfume of thousands of blossoms on the breeze.

The sight was so staggering that she almost forgot to be concerned she was being escorted to the queen by two of her soldiers. All while covered in vomit and missing a boot. It didn't make for the most royal of first impressions.

"Welcome to the seat of Rani Vasvi," Vikram said as they entered through the Jai Tree's towering doors, these ones carved from dark green wood. The space inside glowed with ethereal light, the roof soaring overhead and curving into a pointed arch. The walls, the floor, and the ceiling were all carpeted in a layer of viridescent moss that muffled their footsteps as they approached the far wall of the cavernous space.

Zarya marked dozens more rakshasas milling around the circular room, all dressed in layers of rich fabric and dripping with even richer gold and jewels.

Vikram caught the eye of a man who could have been his double, sporting a neatly trimmed beard. His bright green eyes glittered as he watched their tiny procession make its way to the dais. Vikram rolled his shoulders before his brows pinched together.

Before them stood a high wall covered in shifting leaves, branches, and flowers that made it seem alive. As Zarya stared at it, the features of a face emerged. A pair of soulful amber eyes opened and blinked as a woman appeared amidst the greenery. Or rather, it was the shape of a woman sitting on a throne, her long hair a cascade of blooms and her dress fashioned from over-lapping leaves.

Zarya made out the high cheekbones and curving lines of the queen's nose formed by a tangle of twisting roots and branches. She was enormous, at least four stories tall, but there was kindness in her gaze. She looked down on the four of them with a curious glint in her somber eyes.

Zarya stood in awe for several seconds, unable to believe such a being could exist. She was going to tear a strip off Row when she saw him again. She thought of the last words he'd said to her the other night. *Nothing out here for her*, indeed. How dare he act like the outside world wasn't full of wonders like this and she'd been missing all of it?

A young woman sat at the queen's left, her back straight and her head tipped their way in curiosity. She was stunning, with luxurious black hair, deep brown skin, and the same amber eyes as the queen. Zarya exchanged a smile with her, wondering how glorious and magnificent, how free and big her life must be, living in this opulent palace that sat at the heart of everything.

To the queen's right stood another creature, bent and gnarled, his face deeply lined with skin like bark, as though he'd been forged from the trees themselves. He wore long robes and a turban in the earthy hues of the forest. He peered at Zarya with inky black eyes before turning to Vikram.

"What is this, Commander?" he asked.

"This is Zarya and her brother, Aarav. They assisted us during a naga attack in the swamp." He stood straighter, his shoulders arching back. "Steward, the southern swamp has progressed past the River Naveen. There was no sign of the missing garrison, and the map Professor Dhawan sent us with is already out of date. He'll need to be notified. The blight is moving more quickly than ever. We almost didn't make it back before the gates closed."

His tone was clipped, his mouth tight, and Zarya sensed he hated admitting this.

The creature huffed and stamped the staff clutched in his right hand. "Foolish. You fly too close. Take too many chances. I suppose this was your influence, Lieutenant?" He turned to Yasen, who shrugged.

"We had plenty of time. It's not our fault senseless girls intrude where they shouldn't." His gaze flicked to Zarya, who made an indignant sound.

"And where do you two come from?" The gnarled creature now turned his attention to Zarya and Aarav, who both recounted the same manipulated version of the story they'd given the rakshasas earlier. Mostly, that they were searching for their missing father.

The steward tilted his head, contemplating them. He shuffled forward, using the staff as leverage, before stopping a few feet away and taking a long sniff. Conscious that she was coated in sweat and vomit, Zarya grabbed her elbows and hunched her shoulders.

Regardless, her scent didn't appear to offend him. In fact, a light of satisfaction flared in his dark eyes as his mouth turned up into a crooked smile. He dipped his head. "Please remain in the palace as guests of Rani Vasvi. At least for tonight."

"No," Aarav said. "Thank you, but we must return home."

Zarya opened her mouth to object, not about to go

anywhere with Aarav, when the creature raised an authoritative hand in dismissal.

"Nonsense. It has been decided. You cannot leave the city once the gates are closed for the night, and the queen is nothing if she cannot care for her subjects." He gestured to a group of servants dressed all in white, hovering off to the side. "Show them to their quarters."

Turning to Vikram, he said, "Commander, keep an eye on our guests."

He then gave Zarya a pointed look. "And mind you stay out of trouble, young lady."

She nodded as she was led away by Vikram and Yasen.

They followed the trio of servants through the palace's gleaming white hallways, where vines, flowers, and branches flowed over every surface.

"Who was that man?" she asked Vikram, her voice echoing in the quiet hallways.

"Tarin," replied Vikram. "He is the queen's steward since she cannot speak for herself. She rules through him."

"Why did he sniff us?"

"He's astomi—they have poor eyesight and thus perceive things most clearly through smell."

"I'm surprised he didn't throw me out of the city immediately, then." She gestured to her filthy clothes as Vikram laughed.

"I'm sure he's smelled worse." He winked, and her neck flushed as wings fluttered inside her stomach. Gods, he was handsome.

"And who was the woman sitting next to the queen?" she asked.

"The Princess Amrita. Rani Vasvi's heir, who will one day take over the throne of Daragaab." A strained look passed over his face that Zarya couldn't interpret.

The servants paused at a door and showed them inside.

Zarya noted that each servant was tattooed with a single line of interlocking stars around their neck. The stars marked them as vanshaj, or the "descendants," those relegated to performing society's most menial tasks. She'd read about them in books and knew they had apparently once been tied to a dangerous and ancient power. The enchanted ink was applied around their throats at birth to strangle their magic, preventing them from ever accessing it.

But as she watched the man and two women drawing aside curtains, fluffing pillows, and tending to various tasks about the room, it was hard to see how they could pose any sort of threat to anyone. Their eyes remained downcast, and their postures curved as if they were trying not to take up too much space.

She touched her stomach with a sense of unease, but Vikram and Yasen appeared used to their presence, their eyes passing over the three servants.

Zarya, on the other hand, watched them with a hot wave of fury, understanding a thing or two about what it was like to be caged against your will. Even if it was inside a palace filled with luxury and jewels.

After going about the room, the vanshaj seemed satisfied with their tasks and pressed their hands together before quietly leaving.

Zarya stared after them for a moment, then turned to take in her surroundings, the vanshaj still weighing in the back of her thoughts.

They stood inside a large room with a small turquoise pool in the center, surrounded by low divans laden with cushions upholstered in cream and gold.

The bedrooms branched off the central room. Aarav went left while Zarya opted for the one on the right, a wide, airy space where scalloped arches surrounded a huge canopied bed draped with heavy fabric. The large windows, some covered in delicate latticework, overlooked the sea. The waves crashed outside, churning up the scent of salt and reminding Zarya of her quiet corner of shoreline back at home.

"I trust you'll find this suitable," Vikram said, plopping himself down on one of the low white divans sitting against the wall.

"This is too much," she said, dropping down next to him and examining the bandages on her leg. It was feeling much better, and she unwrapped the white strips, shocked to discover the cuts had almost healed, leaving only a few crusted scars.

"Enchanted bandages," Vikram said, noting her surprise. He grabbed a bowl of cashews from the table next to him and popped a few into his mouth. "Courtesy of the palace healers, and particularly useful when you're out getting chewed on by swamp demons."

"Incredible." Zarya unwrapped the rest of the bandages, marveling at her nearly unblemished skin. Row had some skill with healing, but he said only a mage gifted with the magic of Niramaya—a powerful branch of healing magic—was truly adept at it.

"Please make yourself comfortable," Vikram said, standing and smoothing down his jacket. "I'll have some food sent in. You must be hungry and exhausted. Yasen and I will pay you a visit in the morning. Would you like a tour of Dharati? Based on your reaction today, I think it's your first time visiting?"

"Oh, I'd like that very much," she said. "Thank you."

Vikram smiled while Yasen continued to glare, his mouth pursing like he'd bitten into a lemon. "Make sure you take a bath," he said, his nose wrinkling.

She rolled her eyes as he turned stiffly on his heel to leave.

After the door closed behind them, Zarya went to explore the enormous marble bathroom. A round tub sat in the center, and a large archway beyond opened towards the lapping sea.

Water had already been drawn, steam curling off the surface and smelling of roses and jasmine. She undressed and sank into the tub, closing her eyes, realizing how tense and sore her body had become over the past two days. She washed her hair and luxuriated in the water for a while longer, before stepping out and wrapping herself in a thick robe.

In the sitting area, she found plates of food had arrived. Morsels of spiced meat, lentils, and chickpeas floated in copper bowls filled with creamy sauces. Mounds of soft flat naan brushed with butter and garlic and flaky samosas filled with spiced peas and potatoes accompanied bowls of fragrant saffron rice, glass jars of tangy raita, and spicy mango pickle. It was more than she could possibly eat on her own.

A decanter of pale, sparkling liquid caught her eye, and she poured herself a glass. The bubbles danced on her tongue, fruity and crisp, while the food warmed her rumbling stomach that, thankfully, had settled from her earlier nausea.

There was no sign of Aarav, and as she stared at the closed door of his bedroom, she wondered where Row was right now. Had he returned to the seaside? Was he desperately looking for her, wondering how she had escaped?

She hoped he was worried and distraught over her absence. He would deserve every ounce of heartache.

Zarya prayed she could evade Aarav and hide from both of her captors. She needed to get away from Daragaab and venture further into one of Rahajhan's other regions. Disappear to a place where Row would never find her.

She didn't know nearly enough about her surroundings. Row had kept her conveniently ignorant of the lands that lay beyond her prison, and she'd need to be resourceful if she didn't want to lose her way completely. Perhaps during her tour with Vikram, she could begin to fill in the gaps of her education.

A wave of fatigue caught up with her. The past two days had been stuffed with more adventure and excitement than she had experienced in a lifetime. Tonight, she would sleep in the palace's opulent bedroom, and tomorrow, she would figure out what came next.

Whatever happened, she was finally free, and she intended to stay that way.

SEVEN

Waves crashed against the shore, rousing Zarya from a deep and dreamless sleep. She slid out of bed and padded over to the doors that led out to a balcony overlooking the ocean. With her face tipped to the sun, she inhaled a deep breath of fresh sea air and stretched her arms overhead, sighing at the ache in her muscles.

It was still nearly impossible to believe she'd just spent a night sleeping inside Jai Mahal. She'd gone from the loneliest corner of the world to the bustling luxury of a palace. If she had anyone in her life to tell, this would have made for a very good story.

Zarya returned to her room to change, where she found a salwar kameez made of shimmery, bright pink silk.

In the sitting room, she found breakfast laid out on one of the low tables. Vikram and Yasen sat talking with plates balanced in their laps. Aarav's door remained firmly shut, and she tossed an irate scowl his way, even if he couldn't see it.

Both rakshasas looked up when she entered, Vikram giving her a crooked smile that sent a flurry of butterflies bursting in her stomach.

"That color really suits you," he said, his gaze skirting her from head to toe as her cheeks flushed.

On the table was a large pot of chai. Zarya gratefully poured herself a cup and leaned back with it cradled in her hands.

"So, you promised me a tour of the city?" she said, looking expectantly between the two rakshasas.

"I'll take you," Vikram replied. "Yasen is on duty at Ambar Fort this morning."

"What's Ambar Fort?"

"It's where most of the queen's army trains and lives. We can stop there. Yasen loves it when I bring visitors." Vikram grinned and slapped his friend on the back. Yasen glared at him and then at Zarya.

"Speaking of which, I should get going." Yasen stood, his shoulders stiff. "Enjoy the city." He tossed Vikram a pointed look before marching out of the room.

"He must be fun at parties," Zarya said, biting into a crispy piece of fried dosa and gesturing to the door.

Vikram snorted. "Don't mind him. He's harmless. Shall we?"

Zarya nodded eagerly and wiped her hands on a napkin before jumping up from her seat.

When Vikram held an elbow out, she hesitated, chewing the inside of her lip.

"Is something wrong?" he asked, his green eyes brimming with concern.

While she was enjoying his attention, it was also over-whelming to finally be noticed. Being in the presence of anyone who wasn't Row or Aarav was going to take some getting used to. She shook her head at her foolishness, wondering when this feeling would pass—this breathless sensation of surfacing from a lifetime lived an inch below water. But Vikram would think she was being ridiculous if she told him the truth.

Given all of Row's warnings, maybe she should have been

less trusting and more careful about the strangers she'd met, but she had a good feeling about him. Besides, the need for freedom warred with her sense of self-preservation, and caution was just another cage keeping her in.

And so, Zarya's smile grew bright as she accepted his arm before he escorted her out of the palace.

Outside, the streets were as busy as the night before, and they wandered through the masses as Vikram pointed out landmarks and introduced her to so many wonders that she couldn't seem to open her eyes wide enough to take it all in. No matter what happened, no matter how angry Row was when he returned, she'd never regret taking this chance.

A tiny voice in her head reminded her not to get too comfortable here. She had to get out of Dharati in case Row did return because he wouldn't allow her rebellion to go unchallenged. She needed to find a way to earn some money so she wouldn't be destitute when she left, but right now, she was also content to enjoy the tour and Vikram's very enthusiastic company.

They passed the iron city gates they'd come through yesterday. They stood open again, revealing the forest and plains beyond. Zarya shuddered at the memory of the demons that had chased them to the city walls, while Vikram's eyes darkened as he scanned the area.

"Yesterday, when the kimpurusha chased us, you did something with your hand. It held them back?" she asked.

The concern on his face cleared as he looked back at her. "It was just a bit of magic thrown at them. The demons recoil from it, but it isn't enough to harm them. Not as effectively as an arrow through the skull, anyway." Vikram pointed a finger at his forehead and made a popping sound, and Zarya laughed. "The city walls are enchanted by the queen to keep them out, so we ensure everyone comes inside before night falls. But the magic can only do so much, and a special force known as the Khada patrols the perimeter after the sun sets, fighting off anything that gets too close. It's a dangerous job, but it's the only way to keep everyone safe."

"What exactly are they? The creatures? I've encountered naga near my home, but I've never seen ones like that before."

"No one really knows. Demons of myth and legend who haven't been seen in these lands for centuries. Things that should have remained in storybooks, rather than arriving at night to knock down our doors."

Vikram's forehead creased as he stared at the gates again, clearly unsatisfied with that answer. She remembered Row expressing similar frustrations about the swamp that was consuming their surroundings.

"As the blight has spread, they've moved nearer to the city. The queen is forced to use more and more of her power to keep them out. Once, they remained confined to the southern shore where it first started all those years ago, but we've found the nastier ones like to be close to people. That's probably why you only saw a few where you lived."

He paused, clearly wanting to ask more questions about *why* she had been living there, but she distracted him by asking, "Do you have other magic?"

He nodded. "Some. The queen and her heir are both yakshis, a species closely aligned with rakshasas. Yakshis are the original keepers of earth magic, but as we've comingled and bred together over the centuries, our powers have mixed, granting rakshasas many of the same abilities. Albeit at a lesser strength than yakshis, of whom there are only a few purebloods left.

"My father is strong for our kind, and I inherited only some of it, much to his eternal disappointment." A muscle in his jaw flexed. "Our earth magic means an affinity for growing plants and flowers. For the strongest, it can mean the ability to shift the ground itself. A rare few can shapeshift into animals as well, an ability that comes from the rakshasa side of our lineage."

"That's incredible." Zarya thought of her own limited power, wishing she could accomplish anything close to that.

Vikram threw her a wry smile that felt forced. This was clearly a touchy subject for him, and while she wanted to ask more, even she knew not to pressure people into talking about unpleasant things when she barely knew them.

"If you're interested in magic, you might like this." He pointed across the plaza to a white marble arch suspended over a pair of silver columns wrapped in swathes of red and purple fabric.

"What's that?"

"The Maya Quarter," Vikram said. "Home to the best and worst magic tricks, cures, maladies, and hexes." He waggled his eyebrows. "For humans and devakin with little magical ability, it is tempting to grab what they don't have. But be wary of what traps you may fall into. Some are powerful, and some are extremely dangerous. Of course, much of it is pure nonsense and works based only on illusion, with no connection to reality and the true source of magic."

He grinned at her, his posture at ease once again.

"Devakin?" Zarya asked.

"Those of both human and magical parentage. It generally results in a child of limited or no magical ability."

Zarya bit the corner of her lip. Was *that* what she was? Surely Row would have known about that, though?

They entered the quarter, the street lined with shops and carts. Vendors sold various teas and tinctures, bottles of potions, and incense in every shape, size, and scent. As they walked, Zarya kept her arm through Vikram's, their bodies brushing against each other in a way she certainly didn't mind.

She wondered why the queen's steward, Tarin, had

assigned Vikram as her overseer. Surely an army commander had better things to do than act as her tour guide?

But she wasn't complaining. What luck he should be the first person she'd meet.

To their left, they spotted a wagon covered in hundreds of mirrors of various sizes and styles. A woman sat on a stool next to it. Fiery red hair reached almost to her knees, contrasting with her mahogany skin.

"Would the lady like a window to her future?" the woman asked slyly, shoving a tarnished silver mirror into Zarya's hand. "Go on, take a peek."

Zarya looked at Vikram, who nodded. She shrugged and stared into the mirror's slightly warped surface, blinking at the reflection of her own hazel eyes. A moment later, her face swirled away, morphing into a forest with lush black trees and a violet, star-streaked sky.

Her mouth parted in surprise. It was the same place she'd seen in her sleep the night Row had gone missing—she was sure of it. Instinctively, she searched for the same figure who'd stood there earlier, but this time, it was empty. That same calming peace settled over her shoulders as she stared into the mirror.

She couldn't shake the feeling that this was a place she belonged. Like it had been waiting for her to arrive. She felt herself drawn into it, pulled forward. Her balance tipped, and she jolted back to the busy street as the mirror tumbled from her fingers, shattering into pieces on the ground at her feet.

EIGHT

"Oh," Zarya said, coming back to herself as her surroundings sharpened into focus.

"What is it?" Vikram asked. "Are you okay? Did you see something?" He placed a gentle hand on her arm.

"I don't think... no. I didn't see anything. Just a distorted reflection. Just a bit clumsy, I suppose." She wasn't sure why she wanted to keep this to herself, but it felt like something she wasn't supposed to share.

She forced an awkward laugh and turned to the woman, who was staring at the broken mirror with her lips pressed into a disapproving line.

"That will be three coppers," she said, throwing a sharp glance at Zarya.

"I'm so sorry. I don't have anything to give you for it."

The woman shifted as though she were about to stand, and Zarya braced herself for a verbal lashing.

"I've got it," Vikram said, stepping between them and pulling a few coins from his pocket. The woman's ire instantly melted away as she accepted them in her cupped hands with a tip of her head.

Zarya wanted to argue with Vikram about paying for her mistake, but she had nothing to offer, and he was already leading her away.

"Thank you," she said. "I'm so sorry. That was so careless."

He waved her off. "It's no problem."

"But I—"

"Really. It's fine."

She nodded but wasn't happy about the situation that had just transpired. It drove home the need to find a way to support herself and get out of here. She might be free of Row, but she was also helpless and, right now, relying on the mercy and charity of strangers.

As they moved down the street, Zarya cast a final look at the cart of mirrors, wondering what to make of what she'd seen. What was in the forest? Why did it call to her, and was it dangerous? What if this was what Row had been afraid of all along? She wasn't sure why the strange mirror had shaken her so much, but it was hard not to connect the introduction of these new visions with her escape from the cottage.

Row's admonishments that she wasn't safe anywhere outside signaled a warning that she was trying to ignore. She didn't want to go back, and she'd fight to keep her freedom. But she also wasn't a fool and had no intentions of dying just when her life had finally started. She would just need to remain cautious, that was all.

She forced herself to put the encounter out of her head and enjoy her surroundings. After all, she'd been craving this for so many years.

Once they'd explored several more streets, Vikram guided her out the other side of the Maya Quarter, where they emerged near a squat, red-brick building that stretched over several city blocks. Inside a fenced courtyard out front, dozens of people were sparring, firing arrows, and aiming knives at distant targets.

Zarya caught sight of Yasen across the yard, dressed in a fitted indigo kurta with the sleeves rolled up to expose a pair of thickly veined forearms. He was shouting orders to various sparring pairs, either correcting their form or adjusting a grip on a weapon.

"What's this?" Zarya asked.

"This is Ambar Fort," Vikram said with a sweep of his hand.

"Tarin called you 'commander' yesterday. Are you in charge?"

Vikram smiled. "I am. Though Yasen and my other lieutenants do most of the hard work. I'm really just for show."

He winked, and Zarya smiled, sure she didn't believe a word of that.

She noted a line of armed people at the entrance of the courtyard. A woman at the front stepped forward, shaking hands with one of the soldiers.

"We invite the locals to challenge us," Vikram said, nodding to where the woman had paired up against a male soldier. "It gives the citizens a thrill to see if they can best one of the queen's guards. Some of the most skilled are even invited to join the Khada quarterly trials. It's an honor to be chosen."

Yasen had come to join them, his shoulders looser than they had been at breakfast. A light sheen of sweat covered his brow, which he wiped away with the back of his wrist.

"Daragaab's former commander believed a populace that could defend itself was stronger," Yasen added. "This is his legacy. It's a stroke of foresight that's benefited the queendom more than once."

Vikram threw an annoyed glance at Yasen, who didn't appear to notice, his attention still on the woman who'd just entered the yard. She carried a wooden staff, and she approached the soldier, who was easily twice her size.

"This is amazing," Zarya said. "Can I try?"

Yasen's look was as dry as desert sand as he eyed her up and down.

"Don't look at me like that. I know how to use a sword. My... father taught me." She stumbled on the unfamiliar term, and Yasen raised a dark grey eyebrow, obviously skeptical about her claim.

"Fine, but you have to fight me, then," he said.

"Oh, you're on."

With a smirk, Yasen tossed her a talwar and chose one of his own.

"Don't cut yourself with that," he taunted. "The blade is sharp."

Zarya glowered but said nothing, focusing on Yasen, who was prowling around her, his stance relaxed. She thrust the talwar, and he effortlessly dodged it, swinging around and bringing his blade down as she just barely managed to deflect him.

With a grunt, she spun and feinted before lunging towards him from the other side. That caught Yasen off guard, and he stepped back, nearly tripping in his haste. She brought down her blade, and he blocked it, but only at the very last second.

Vikram let out a whoop of support on her behalf, just as Yasen recovered and then leaped. But she was ready, blocking his thrust with a ringing clash of blades. They parried back and forth, talwars flashing in the sunlight.

She might have been imagining it, but Zarya thought she saw a begrudging shadow of respect dawn on Yasen's face. She silently thanked Row for his unrelenting focus on her training all these years—the one concession she was prepared to give him.

The truth was, Zarya loved the feel of a weapon in her hand. It had given her some measure of control in a life where she'd had almost none. But even that had proven ultimately unsatisfying, with Aarav and Row as her only opposition.

Yasen was a trained soldier, and eventually, his skill and size overtook Zarya as he drove her back, knocking her down and pointing the sword at her heart.

The ghost of a smile appeared on his face before he tilted his head. "Well done, Swamp Girl."

She narrowed her eyes. While Zarya didn't care for the new nickname, she supposed this was high praise from the taciturn soldier.

He reached out a hand and pulled her up. She was dusting off her pants when a hushed murmur muted the din of the courtyard.

Every eye had swung to the fort's entrance as four figures emerged from the brick building. They radiated a commanding energy that spread through the crowd, compelling everyone to stand at attention.

In the middle strode the two most striking women Zarya had ever seen. One was tall and willowy with a sheet of silvery white hair and bright silver eyes that contrasted vividly with her copper-brown skin. She wore tight leather pants and a short jacket, all in creamy white, but her most remarkable feature was a pair of snowy white wings.

Next to her was a woman so pale she was almost blue. She sported a wild mane of hair that flowed from sea green at the roots to turquoise at the ends. Her angled, hooded eyes were the color of the ocean, and she wore a dress in hues of green and blue that, like her hair, danced around her as if she were perpetually floating on an invisible current.

On the flanks of the women walked two men. One with wavy black hair and light brown skin, wearing a black velvet jacket trimmed in red, black pants, and leather boots. On the opposite end was a man with a deep brown complexion and eyes that gleamed like golden lanterns. A yellow cloth was wrapped across his muscular body and slung over one chiseled shoulder.

"The Chiranjivi," Vikram whispered in Zarya's ear. "Emissaries from the kingdoms of Rahajhan and the most powerful magical beings in the continent. They've been here trying to solve the problem of the blight."

The Chiranjivi stopped in the center of the courtyard as the crowd cleared, giving them space for whatever was about to happen. Zarya pushed forward, hoping to get a better look.

"Are we ready for a demonstration?" the blue-haired woman asked, raising her hands to a chorus of cheers.

"That's Suvanna," Yasen said, coming up next to Zarya. "She's a merdeva from Matsya and, as you'll see, a powerful wielder of water magic."

Zarya shivered as the air pulsed with anticipation, noting that Vikram was now conversing with the man in the black coat.

"And that's Kindle," Yasen added, indicating the man Vikram was speaking with. "An agni from Bhaavana—kingdom of fire magic."

Zarya stretched on her tiptoes to get a better look as Suvanna spun around and flung a hand behind her, water springing from her fingers. It arrowed straight to where Kindle and Vikram stood, but the agni didn't miss a beat. He sidestepped to his right before fire burst from his palms, melting into the wave as it dissolved the water into a fine mist that floated into the atmosphere.

A wild chorus of cheers and clapping accompanied Suvanna as she spun around and shot out another blast, this one aimed at the white-winged woman who swung out an arm as a wave of something Zarya couldn't see slammed into the water, driving it upward. She realized it must have been a force of air as every eye in the courtyard followed the water's trajectory.

"That's Apsara," Yasen whispered next. "Air and ice are her specialties."

The winged woman changed hands, and Zarya felt the ripple of another invisible force before every drop of water crystallized into ice, forming a canopy of hovering crystals that hovered above the crowd amid squeals of delight.

Realizing those shards were about to come spearing down over their heads, everyone ducked, covering themselves until the dark-skinned man with the golden eyes stepped forward and raised his arms. A glowing yellow shield spread around him, forming an umbrella that sheltered the entire courtyard. The icy shards sparkled with gold through the haze of the translucent barrier as they gently melted away to nothing.

"And that was Koura," Yasen said with a wry grin. "He's into the whole protection thing."

Zarya joined the cheering crowd as the four Chiranjivi lined up and offered a bow. Row could perform magic, but she'd never seen him do anything like *this*.

Vikram smiled as he shook each of their hands before ordering everyone to return to their training. They slowly moved to do his bidding, their eyes still focused on the Chiranjivi, who now strode through the yard towards the gates.

They all nodded at Yasen, who tipped his head in acknowledgment. As they passed, Kindle did a double take when he saw Zarya, his eyebrows pulling together as confusion flickered across his expression. Why was he looking at her like that?

A moment later, the Chiranjivi swept out of the courtyard, followed by a wake of silence before the tension broke and training resumed.

"What was that about? Why did Kindle look at you like that?" Yasen turned to her with his grey eyes blazing. Gone was the affable manner they'd shared only a few moments ago, and in its place was the surly guard she'd met yesterday.

"I don't know." Zarya stared after Kindle's retreating back and was even more surprised when he cast another fraught look over his shoulder. "I've never seen him before."

Yasen narrowed his eyes, and Zarya got the sense she'd just

done something wrong, though she couldn't imagine what. She sucked in a tense breath as he took a slow step towards her.

Zarya had to look up to meet him in the eye, and she did her best not to cower under his penetrating stare. "Are you keeping something from us, Swamp Girl?"

"Do *not* call me that," she said through clenched teeth.

He smirked, but there was not a trace of amusement in it. "How are you going to stop me?"

"Shall we get some lunch?" Vikram clapped his hands right between their faces in a clear attempt to distract them from whatever this was. They turned to look at him, their stances locked for a fight. "Yasen! Join us."

Zarya took the opportunity to take a step back, distancing herself from Yasen's line of questioning. Yes, she was hiding things, and the less anyone knew about where she'd come from, the better.

"Yes, please," she said, keeping her eyes on Yasen, watching for any sudden movements. She didn't trust him for a moment. The silver-haired rakshasa glowered at her and then nodded slowly.

"Excellent," Vikram said, steering Zarya away by the elbow, a note of relief in his voice. "I know just the place."

NINE

Yasen spent lunch with his arms crossed, glaring at everyone who passed, and Zarya was immediately sorry Vikram had invited him. They sat outside a tavern next to the palace, overlooking the water, their table shaded by the flowering boughs of the Jai Tree. The scent of blossoms permeated the air, mixing with the scent of the nearby ocean.

Zarya couldn't get enough of the city. The feeling of being lost in the masses, just one normal person going about their life with a home and a family and people who loved them to return to at the end of the day. That's all she wanted. It's all she'd ever wanted.

Their server brought out bottles of wine, along with platters of chili chicken, chapatis, and savory fried vegetable pakoras with tangy tamarind chutney. She also brought a stone carafe and two stone cups from which Vikram poured a stream of thick red liquid before handing one to Yasen.

"Is it true, then?" Zarya asked, leaning forward, sure of what she'd witnessed but dying to confirm it. Had her books been accurate about rakshasa lore? She sat back abruptly, her face heating. "I'm sorry. That was rude."

"It's okay. Yes, rakshasas drink blood. Is that strange to you?" Vikram asked, with a curious tilt of his head.

"I've never met one of your... kind. Only read about you." She winced, realizing how pathetic that sounded.

"How very strange. There are many of us in Daragaab. You are very mysterious, Zarya. Have you never ventured beyond the southern shore before yesterday?"

She noticed Yasen stiffen as if he were now paying attention to their conversation, waiting to hear her answer, when he'd been pointedly ignoring both her and Vikram until now.

"Oh, of course," she said, waving a hand. "It's just been a long time. I was much younger. I must have met rakshasas then. I just forgot." Her laugh sounded forced even to her, and Yasen glared her way, but Vikram just offered another one of his patient smiles. She couldn't tell if he found her charming or absolutely brainless.

"Can I ask..." Her unfinished question hung in the air.

"What?" Vikram asked, while Yasen continued watching their exchange, one arm across his broad chest, the other holding his stone cup in mid-air.

"What sort of blood is it?"

"This is human," Vikram said, taking a sip and laughing as Zarya cringed. "Don't worry. Willing donors are paid handsomely for their gift." He winked. "Of course, devakin blood is much sweeter. Aazheri blood is the most succulent, but they aren't particularly willing snacks most of the time."

He took another sip and then smiled broadly, exposing his sharp and elongated canines.

"What are the teeth for if you drink it from a cup?"

Yasen sputtered, choking on his drink as he slammed a fist to the middle of his chest.

"Sorry, that was rude. I'm sorry. I don't have a lot of experience with conversation. I'm not good at this." She flapped her hands and covered her face.

"The teeth," Vikram said, apparently not minding her curiosity, "are for biting, yes. Many hundreds of years ago, our ancestors subsisted on hunting animals and humans. But as we mated with yakshis and other species over the centuries, our tastes slowly changed. We are far more civilized now. While we still crave blood and need it in small doses, we also enjoy the same foods you do.

"Animal blood isn't particularly satisfying but will do in a pinch. There is a thriving market of blood procurement for rakshasa tastes."

"Oh," Zarya said, her cheeks turning hot as she considered her next question, wondering if her books had been faithful on this next—and very important—point. "Do you also use the teeth for... other things?" The question came out as a breathless whisper.

Yasen barked out a laugh and leaned forward with a wicked gleam in his eyes. "Oh, tell me she's asking what I think she's asking."

Vikram rolled his eyes at his friend. "These days, most rakshasas save their biting for the bedroom," he said, twitching his dark eyebrows.

Zarya felt herself go red straight to the roots of her hair, so she grabbed a chapati, stuffing a piece in her mouth to cover her embarrassment. While she longed to know more about how exactly the biting worked beyond the pages of her books, she was also much too reluctant to ask. Sure, she'd imagined it, but what was the reality like?

To say she was curious was an understatement. Maybe she could find a shop and stock up on some new reading material. This was something she absolutely needed to know more about, and it was best to always do one's research. Row had always stressed the importance of preparation, though she was pretty sure this wasn't what he'd had in mind.

They tucked into their food as Vikram talked about the city, and Zarya listened in wonder, her touch-starved senses intoxicated by Vikram's careful attention. He kept grazing her arm and brushing her hand as he reached across the table. A bit more bread, a top-up of her wine.

Her thoughts wandering again to what Vikram had said about rakshasas and their teeth, Zarya caught a flash of his, and a surge, long held dormant, shot to the space just below her navel. She was an adult with all the needs and urges of a woman, and she'd had so little freedom to explore them other than with herself.

What would it be like to have Vikram's arms around her with his bare skin pressed to hers? To have his weight on top of her body and his hand between her legs? She sipped her wine, fully immersed in her daydream now, as she imagined the feel of those teeth grazing her skin...

"Zarya!" someone shouted, dragging her from her reverie.

She closed her eyes in pained resignation, knowing that irritating voice all too well. How did he always manage to find her? Aarav stormed up to the table, murder in his expression.

"I have been looking everywhere for you! You thought you could sneak away?" Aarav glared at Yasen and Vikram, pointing a finger like the jackass he was. "With *them*?"

"Relax, Aarav. We went for a walk." She pushed herself up from the table.

"This is enough. We're going home. *Now.*"

He grabbed her arm, but she wrenched it from his grasp.

"How many times do I have to say it? I'm not going anywhere with you."

"This is quite the family squabble, isn't it?" Yasen quipped, and Zarya whirled, planning to unleash her rage on him when, without warning, the ground began to rumble.

Frantic cries filled the air as diners leaped up from the tables that were now bouncing against the trembling earth. The buildings shook and debris rained down. People scattered

in every direction, running for cover down the wide boule-
vards that led away from the palace, parents clutching
screaming children in their arms. The palace's slender
minarets swayed like blades of grass in the wind, and the Jai
Tree shuddered, its petals falling to the ground as the earth
rumbled harder.

Zarya clutched the table, unsure of where to go.

A thunderous crack split the air, followed by more screams,
their pitch growing frantic. Zarya turned to the sound and saw
the earth itself had broken in two. A large fissure was spreading
down the road. It raced along the paved street, growing wider
and longer, people toppling off the edges and into the chasm,
their final screams swallowed by the darkness below.

Zarya watched a woman tumble off the side just as someone
grabbed her, pulling her back with a great heave before they
landed in a tangled heap on the ground. She breathed a sigh of
relief, but it evaporated almost instantly as she realized she was
now standing directly in the path of the lengthening rift.

It continued to widen as the tables and chairs lining the
boulevard toppled sideways and disappeared into the
expanding hole. Zarya backed up as the fissure gathered speed.
She turned and ran, the ground shaking so hard she struggled to
keep her footing.

The crack gained on Zarya as clouds of black fog belched
out of the opening, wrapping around her and blinding her to her
surroundings. She gagged at the stench; it filled her mouth and
nostrils, and her stomach roiled in protest. She stumbled and
tripped, her knees slamming into the ground, sending sharp
bolts of pain through her hips. Hacking and coughing, her eyes
watering, she tried to regain her footing.

And then the earth gave way beneath her, and there was
nothing but emptiness as she began to fall.

A scream tore from her mouth as Zarya reached out for
anything to grab on to as she plummeted, her stomach lifting

into her throat. But she found only air, the black fog muffling every sound and sight.

A moment later, she came to an abrupt, jarring stop, screaming at the jerk of her shoulder popping out of its socket. A hand gripped her wrist and began hauling her up.

She braced her feet against the side of the chasm, trying to find a hold, until another hand grabbed the back of her tunic and heaved her over the edge, where she collapsed to the ground with her face pressed to the stones. Her breath came in tight sips as she rolled to her side, coughing the black fog clear of her lungs. She swallowed hard and squeezed her eyes shut, willing her stomach to settle.

"You're okay; you're safe," Vikram soothed. She opened her eyes to find him kneeling over her. Covered in dirt, with blood smearing his cheek, he rubbed her back as she hacked and sputtered.

Nearby, she saw Yasen haul Aarav from the edge of the chasm before they both crumpled in the dirt by the edge. She'd have to talk to Yasen about rescuing that idiot later.

It took a moment for Zarya to realize the earth had stopped shaking. She sat up, stunned at the sight before her. The entire street was gone—the wide chasm now stretched at least half a mile from the palace and ran alongside its northern courtyard wall, leaving only a gaping rift of nothing.

Vikram was up on his feet and shouting orders to the palace guards to secure the area along the fissure. "Alert the fort!" he shouted as soldiers leaped into action, following his orders. "Get General Amjal and the Khada out here!"

Zarya clutched her arm as a sharp pain radiated from her shoulder. She winced, attempting to stand up so she could help, but collapsed to her hip at another stab of pain.

As she surveyed the aftermath, she noticed one of the Chiranjivi—the muscular, golden-eyed man—was moving between the injured, placing his large hands on broken limbs and bloody cuts. Even from here, she could see how careful and gentle his touch was. Flashes of soft golden light flared beneath his fingers that closed wounds and healed bones, leaving only the faintest traces of faded bruises and scars.

This must be the healing magic of Niramaya that Row had told her about. A group of healers followed Koura, carrying bandages, tubs of water, and vials of medicine.

With her hand still clasped to her aching shoulder, Zarya turned to the sounds of shouted commands coming from the courtyard.

The bottom bricks of the high courtyard wall were sliding towards the chasm, and chunks of the earth were falling away under the weight of the stone.

With her snow-white wings fluttering, Apsara stood on the far side with her legs staggered, her arms stretched towards the wall as if she were holding the bricks in place. Dust swirled in the air as sweat beaded on her brow. After seeing the demonstration at the fort earlier, Zarya was sure the woman was using air to hold the stones in place.

"I don't know if it will hold. The bricks are sliding," she said through gritted teeth, her voice carrying over the chasm.

Suvanna then added her own layer of magic, reaching out her arms as she formed a thick barrier of water. It shimmered and roiled like a massive raindrop suspended in time.

"Freeze it," she shouted to Apsara.

Apsara flicked her wrist, and the water turned to solid ice. She buffeted the block with another blast of air, attempting to force the stones back into place.

Onlookers held their breath as if they were peering over a canyon with their toes already dangling off the edge.

But it wasn't enough.

Cracks formed in the ice, thin lines webbing out from the center of the sheet as it was pushed to failure. A moment later, the ice shattered, exploding into countless shards. Zarya covered her head as tiny fragments of ice scraped her cheeks and peppered her clothes.

When she looked up again, the glistening marble wall was beginning to slide.

It paused for a heartbeat as if taking a bow at center stage, a final moment to honor its role as guardian of the sacred Jai Tree. Then it released with an echoing boom as shattered stones toppled one over the other, thundering into the abyss below.

TEN

Wails of anguish punctuated the crushing silence that followed.

Zarya clutched her shoulder, the pain spreading through her entire left side. The black fog had dissipated from the rift, but the nauseating churn in her gut remained. It was the same queasiness she'd suffered when the kimpurusha had chased them. Something otherworldly and wrong, all jagged claws and snapping teeth.

Apsara and Suvanna peered into the chasm. The entire courtyard wall had sunk into its depths, tearing off a chunk of the palace as well. Stones continued to topple over one another, clinging to the rough edges of the break before shearing away with a clatter. A tangle of thick tree roots jutted from the exposed face of the chasm, and Zarya thanked the gods that the Jai Tree appeared unharmed, its rainbow canopy still casting a benevolent blanket over Dharati and its battered citizens.

A mercy. Zarya dared not comprehend how anyone could save Rani Vasvi if she was ever in danger. The queen was trapped here, her form one with the wood of the tree. She would be utterly helpless should her home be threatened.

Zarya then caught sight of Princess Amrita being consoled

by Apsara and Vikram, her round face streaked with tears. Eventually, someone led her away and back into the palace with her shoulders shaking.

Zarya surveyed the damage. Puddles of water from the shattered ice littered the surrounding streets, mingling with the falling dust and ash.

Aarav groaned nearby, still lying on the ground, his face pressed to the mud. Zarya threw him a dark glare, kind of wishing he'd fallen into the chasm. Maybe not kind of. He looked up and frowned in her direction as if hearing her thoughts.

"You're hurt," Vikram said, approaching Zarya, who was still clutching her throbbing arm. "Come. Koura will fix you up."

He pointed towards the muscled Chiranjivi warrior. The man was still moving quickly between the injured lying prostrate on the street, his manner calm and eyes soft. Prayers and gratitude were murmured in his wake.

Fire ripped through Zarya with every step she took. Vikram walked alongside her, a hand on the small of her back. She tried not to groan as they approached the healer, whose hands now rested on the forehead of a woman with a long gash, blood coating the side of her face. That warm yellow glow emanated from Koura's hands as the wound sealed, leaving behind only a faint, crusted scar.

Koura's bright gaze then swept to where Zarya stood clutching her shoulder. Up close, he was even more enormous. He towered over her with his broad frame.

"What seems to be the problem?" His voice was as rich as honey-soaked cakes.

"My shoulder," she said with a wince, and he smiled before reaching out to wrap a hand around her bicep. The touch sent an arrow of pain through the side of her body. Koura frowned as she flinched, the corners of his eyes soft.

"I can fix it, but this will hurt a bit."

Her vision blurred with pain, tears leaking from her eyes, Zarya nodded. "Just do it, please."

Koura placed his other hand on the back of her shoulder and then focused his attention. Warmth and light seeped from his hands as a spear of agony preceded the rub of bone against bone, the joint popping as it slipped back into its socket. Then Koura's power flared once again as the vestiges of her pain drained to nothing but a dull ache.

"Better?"

"Much." Zarya rotated her shoulder. "Thank you."

He gave her a quick nod and then moved on to assist the next person needing his attention.

"What happened?" she asked, turning to Vikram. "What was that?"

Worry flashed across his handsome features as he stared into the chasm, just as Apsara approached from the other side.

"*That* is a good question," she said, eyeing Zarya up and then looking back at the chasm. "Whatever is plaguing Daragaab is growing stronger. We'll need to shore up the Khada now that it's breached the perimeter. The queen will also need to tap into her reserves of magic. If anything gets through the city walls, we're all in danger." She studied the gaping split in the earth, running her thumb over her bottom lip.

A moment later, Aarav came up beside Zarya. "*Now* we're going home," he said in her ear. "I'm not asking you again."

Apsara looked over at them. "You're the people they found yesterday in the swamps."

Zarya nodded, and the woman's eyes shifted.

"I recognize you," she said to Aarav. "You're Row's apprentice? What do you mean, go home?"

"Who exactly are *you*?" Suvanna demanded of Zarya, hands planted on her narrow hips, her eyes devoid of any warmth.

"Meet Suvanna," Apsara said. "She's not one for formalities."

Suvanna flicked her searing gaze to Apsara and back to Zarya.

"She's no one," Aarav said, again grabbing Zarya by the arm.

"Stop!" She wrenched herself from his grip.

"Someone explain this. Now. You live with Row, too?" Apsara asked.

Zarya nodded with reluctance but didn't see how to hide the truth anymore. "You know Row?" she asked tentatively.

"Yes, we all do. Row is one of the Chiranjivi," Apsara said.

What? Row had been keeping even more secrets from Zarya than she'd realized.

"Enough," Aarav interrupted with a hiss. "Do not tell her anything more. We are leaving."

"Why do you live with him?" Suvanna asked, her cold eyes boring into Zarya. "He has no children."

She hesitated. Row had kept her a secret for so many years, and now everything he had protected was unraveling. Could she trust these people with the truth if Row hadn't? But Suvanna looked like she would scoop Zarya's brain out with a spoon if made to wait much longer for a satisfactory answer.

Zarya sighed. "I'm not his daughter. My parents died when I was a baby, and he raised me."

Zarya's fury rose once again with the admission. The seaside cottage. Her prison. Her endless loneliness and the constant secrets. A torrent of words burst forth as she lost control of her emotions. She needed *someone* to hear the truth.

"He kept me trapped in that cursed house for almost twenty-one years," she said, desperation urging her on. "A few nights ago, Row went missing. And when *he* set out to search for him"—she pointed at Aarav—"I escaped." Aarav glared at Zarya, his hands twitching at his sides. "And I am *not* going back there. You'll have to kill me first."

"With pleasure." Aarav stepped towards her with a snarl.

"Enough!" Vikram unsheathed his sword and pointed it at Aarav, the tip hovering an inch from his throat. "She's asked you to stop."

But Zarya had already started moving. She grabbed Aarav's arm, using it to yank him forward. He stumbled as she gripped the back of his kurta, kneeing him in his crotch and aiming the side of her hand at his neck. Aarav dropped like a stone to the ground, clutching his injured cock and gasping for breath. His eyes watered where he lay on the ground, groaning.

Zarya leaned over him, shaking with rage. With a hand clenched in his hair, she pulled his head back and leaned in close. "I told you, I am not going anywhere with you. Fucking touch me again, and I will not hesitate to kill you. I've fantasized about it enough, and it would bring me endless satisfaction. Are we understood?"

Aarav looked up at her, naked loathing in his eyes, but he said nothing.

"I'll take your silence for a yes." She let go of his hair, and Aarav's head fell to the ground.

She dusted her hands, satisfied he'd finally gotten the message.

When she looked up, four sets of eyes watched her. Vikram's were wide, while the corners of Yasen's were wrinkled in amusement. Suvanna crossed her arms, scrutinizing Zarya with something akin to respect, and Apsara let out a breath of exasperation.

"So, Row is missing," Suvanna said, brushing past their confrontation, her stormy blue eyes growing darker. "For how long?"

Zarya glanced at Aarav, who was struggling to get back up. "Three days."

Apsara and Suvanna exchanged a look.

"And you have no idea where he is?" Apsara asked.

Zarya shook her head. "His magic—whatever prevented me from leaving the house—was gone." She worried her bottom lip as they all pondered the implications of that information.

"And he's kept you against your will all this time?" Vikram asked, his tone sharp. "That is monstrous."

Zarya nodded, that familiar cluster of emotions—rage, confusion, sadness—squeezing in her chest.

"So, you were the one he was always buying dresses for," Apsara said with a snort. "And we were all placing bets that he had a secret lover."

Everyone else burst out laughing, and Zarya turned red, lifting her chin.

"There was no reason I had to *look* like a prisoner."

"Indeed," Apsara said, mirth dancing in her eyes. "But why? And why did none of us know of your existence?"

"I wish I knew. And now I fear I may never find out."

"And you know nothing?" Apsara addressed Aarav. "You've checked his haveli?"

Eyes narrowing, Aarav nodded. "Of course I did. I was there earlier. I didn't find any evidence that he'd been there since our last visit to the city."

"Typical Row," Suvanna said as she folded her arms. "Stubborn as a goat. More secrets than a labyrinth."

The two women analyzed Zarya, causing her insides to squirm with discomfort. Her plan to run away had been reckless, but she also didn't see how she'd had any other choice in the matter. Her senses prickled with uneasiness, thinking about how livid Row would be when he found her. She had no doubt that no matter where she tried to hide, eventually, he would.

"Now that's out of the way, perhaps we should focus on more pressing matters?" Vikram interrupted, gesturing to the surrounding damage. "What caused this? And how do we protect the queen? Without her magic, the city will surely fall."

Zarya's shoulders relaxed, grateful for the change of subject and shift in focus away from her dubious upbringing.

"It is the darkness," Suvanna said, her fists planted on her hips. "I've said this. Only dark magic could work this way. It's why it continues to resist all our efforts." Her blue-green hair seemed to float on the waves of her agitation.

"There is no dark magic left," Koura said, coming up behind them, wiping his hands with a cloth before taking it to the sweat on his brow. "You know that, Suvanna. Do not call forth with your heresy things long since buried."

She shrugged as if to say she didn't believe that, nor was she bothered by his accusation.

"Koura is right," Apsara added. "It isn't possible."

"What do you mean by darkness?" Zarya asked, the question slipping out. She'd never heard of such a thing. Likely due to how frustratingly tight-lipped Row had always been. While he was content to bring her all the fantasies she could consume, he'd kept her in the dark about anything too grounded in reality.

Apsara's response was another suspicious look, but whatever she saw in Zarya's face convinced her to continue.

"The darkness is magic that was eradicated from Rahajhan centuries ago. The northern kingdom of Andhera was once the most powerful in the continent, thanks to dark magic. Surely, Row told you the stories of the Aazheri brothers who ruled there. The Ashvin twins. Their mother claimed they were born together, and so they ruled as one."

"He didn't," Zarya admitted, feeling foolish as everyone else nodded, clearly familiar with the tale. "What did they do?"

Apsara sighed. "As the Ashvin's magic grew, so did their ambition to rule all of Rahajhan. During the Hanera Wars, they used their power to unleash the foulest of demons, enslaving citizens across the continent. Darkness spread, finding its way into every corner. Many have been told these stories since they were children, mostly to frighten them into shunning the vanshaj." Apsara's mouth flattened at that.

"Driven by ego, the two Aazheri had traversed all of Rahajhan, fathering hundreds of children, leaving thousands of their heirs living here in the present. Though the vanshaj are born with magical abilities, they were punished for the acts of the Ashvin twins. As retribution for their sins, their descendants have been confined to lives of servitude.

"But most forget how the Ashvins were finally stopped. A young ruler from the water queendom of Matsya set out to defeat them. She petitioned the rulers of every region to band together and fight as one. Each heeded her call, and together they formed a link so powerful they were sure of their victory.

"But the Ashvins' power had grown, too, and the alliance wasn't enough. Even linked, the seven kings and queens of Rahajhan weren't strong enough to destroy the brothers. Instead, they sealed them up and locked the darkness away forever."

"Since then, dark magic has been inaccessible to those who dare to try," Apsara continued. "Very strong Aazheri can often feel their power brush against it. Row has told me it feels like a wall blocking the limits of his abilities, but it remains impenetrable. It has been a thousand years since anyone has touched it."

"Exactly as I said," added Koura. "The blight is not dark magic—it is something else we don't understand yet. It could be Aazheri magic or just a clever use of the elements."

"And *I* say someone has unlocked the darkness," said Suvanna. "They have discovered a way through the wall. The blight is a manifestation of this power, and it has been gathering strength, biding its time. And today"—she pointed to the ruined street—"today it demonstrated just what else it is capable of. *This* is only the beginning."

She pinned each of them with a defiant look, daring anyone to disagree with her.

ELEVEN

Later that evening, Zarya was cleaning up in the palace bedroom when a knock came at her door. She opened it to find Aarav and immediately backed up several steps, wary of his presence and his intentions.

"What do you want?"

He lifted his palms in a gesture of surrender and rolled his eyes.

"Relax, will you?"

Zarya's nostrils flared in irritation. *Relax? How dare he?*

"I think we should both move to Row's haveli. It's right across the street, and it makes more sense than staying here. It's where Row and I normally live when we're in Dharati."

"Why haven't you mentioned this? Is this a trick? Some scheme to get me back to the cottage?"

"It's not. I'll take you there now." He raised a finger. "*But* I will be keeping a close eye on you, and you will stay within my sight."

She didn't care for the sound of that but agreed that staying here in the palace and relying on the queen's good graces didn't make sense for the long term. Besides, maybe she could find some clues about Row in the house. Things he kept here so she would never see them.

"Fine, then. Let's go," she said. "But you will not be 'keeping a close eye on me.'"

"We'll see about that," was his only reply. She vowed to find some way to shake him off.

After thanking those in the palace for their hospitality, they made their way across the boulevard towards the haveli with nothing but the clothes on their back. Constructed from buttery yellow and cream marble, it sat overlooking the Nila Hara. Inside were gleaming marble floors and wide windows that looked out upon a jewel-blue sky and the clear rolling water.

As Zarya explored its rooms and halls, the ornate furniture and opulent décor, it was hard not to feel a certain bitterness about how grand these surroundings were in comparison to the simple cottage where she'd spent her entire life.

Why had Row tried to keep her from all of this? While he wasn't her father, she'd always got the sense he cared for her in his own awkward—if distant—way. He had never been deliberately cruel, but the longer she was free from that place, the more she was questioning everything.

She was pleasantly surprised to find a pile of packages by the front door stuffed with jewelry, books, and clothing, clearly intended for her. Row must have stashed these here, intending to bring them home to the cottage. Despite everything, something squeezed in her heart as she imagined the way Row had collected these treasures, knowing they would bring joy to her grey world.

While her goal had been to leave the city as soon as possible, she also had few resources at her disposal—most worryingly, a lack of money. Maybe there was some around here, though she would feel a little bad about stealing from Row again. Especially since she'd lost all the coin she'd taken from the cottage the first time.

Lugging the packages up the stairs, she chose one of the bedrooms, requisitioning one as her own until she could figure out her next move.

* * *

The following morning, Zarya stood on the balcony, listening to the city spring to life. She could sit here for hours just watching the vendors setting up their carts and the restaurants catering to patrons while people went about their day. Grey clouds gathered overhead, signaling rain.

"I still think we should head back to the cottage," came a voice that tore through her pleasant thoughts. "Row is going to kill me when he finds you here," Aarav said, coming closer. "And you, too, for that matter."

"Do you think I care?" Zarya whipped around to face him as they now stood toe-to-toe. "I meant what I said—I will die before I become his prisoner again."

"Was it really that dreadful? We took good care of you, didn't we?"

Zarya balled her fists, wishing she could punch him. Could she? What would he do?

Reining in her temper, she instead threw up her hands and stormed away, entering the hall and turning towards Row's suite. She heard Aarav following her, and she stopped, whirling on him.

"Do *not* follow me."

Aarav hesitated, clearly on the brink of arguing with her some more.

"Please," she said, her tone softening. "I need some space."

"Fine. But stay in the house."

Eyes cast heavenward, Zarya huffed out a breath and stomped away, her grey skirts swishing along the polished marble floors.

Thunder now roared overhead, and the first drops of rain pattered against the windowpanes. As she entered the living area of Row's suite, Zarya caught another glimpse of the rolling sea through a set of arched windows. Dharati was truly a magnificent city.

Apart from the fact she had no idea where to go, part of her reluctance to leave was focused on the desire to find out what Row had been keeping from her and why. He'd hid the fact he was one of the Chiranjivi from her, and there had to be a reason. What else had he been concealing from her all these years? If she left, then she wouldn't be able to question him when he finally returned, and she couldn't spend the rest of her life wondering.

His study seemed like the perfect place to start searching for answers.

Inside the room, a low table was surrounded by sofas covered in deep red fabric strewn with gold and black pillows. On the table were haphazard stacks of books and papers with no apparent method of organization.

She sat down on the sofa and started flipping through the books at random. The cottage had always been kept so neat and tidy, but this room was an absolute mess in comparison. Again, she wondered if she really knew anything about the man who had raised her and had been her only true sense of foundation.

She found texts on history and magic, as well as maps of Daragaab, but nothing that hinted at the answers Zarya sought.

A book of stories caught her eye, and she flipped it open, landing on a tale Row had told her many times as a child. She had always loved hearing about the Bayangoma—blind birds that bestowed great knowledge on the worthy. All they asked in return was for a few drops of blood, willingly given. As a girl who had grown up under a cloud of secrets, she had dreamed of voyaging to their grove someday and uncovering the knowledge they might bestow.

If Row wouldn't reveal her secrets, then perhaps she'd have to resort to more drastic measures.

Of course, none of that answered the question of where she'd find the birds or how she'd ever get there. She let out a sigh, puffing a lock of hair from her forehead, and sank back into the seat, frustrated by everything.

"Find anything useful?" Vikram asked, startling her out of her reverie as he entered the room with Yasen on his heels.

Zarya closed the book and looked up. "What do you mean?"

"I presumed after you told us about Row keeping you prisoner, you would be searching for some clues as to why that was. That can't have been easy."

She offered a wry smile as the rakshasas settled onto the sofa across from her. "You're right. But no, I haven't found anything." She glanced at the door. "I'm surprised Aarav let you in here."

"We didn't give him much choice," Vikram said with a quick smile before he leaned back and closed his eyes. "I can't believe you spent twenty years locked up with that asshole." Vikram opened one eye and peered at her. "I can kill him if you want."

She snorted. "Don't think I haven't thought about it many times."

Yasen picked up a book from the side table and began flipping through the pages. "We could make it hurt, too," he said, still looking at the book and smiling to himself. "A lot."

"You know it's bad if even Yasen is defending your honor," added Vikram.

In spite of herself, Zarya laughed. "My honor is very much intact when it comes to Aarav, I can assure you."

"Zarya," Yasen said, looking up with a puzzled expression. She was equally puzzled because she was pretty sure he had never said her name or addressed her directly before. "You're in this book."

"What are you talking about?"

"There is a picture of you. Right here."

Yasen held up an illustration, inked in black pen, of a woman wearing a dark sari covered in delicate white embroidery, a cascade of curls hanging over her shoulder. She sat on a chair, leaning over a thick book placed on a desk. The wall behind her was set with large rectangular stones and a scalloped window covered in intricate lattice. Papers and pens were scattered on the desk and floor, and a pen was tucked behind her ear.

But the woman in the image wasn't Zarya. It couldn't be. She'd never been in a room like that, and who would have drawn it?

Zarya walked over and took the book carefully from Yasen. It was true that the woman could have been her twin. With her finger tracing the image's outlines, she stopped on a tiny mole that sat in the crease beside her nose. "No, this isn't me—I don't have a mole here."

Then she noticed the teardrop pendant around the woman's neck, identical to the one Zarya had worn for as long as she could remember. Her breath snapped in two as she looked up at the two rakshasas.

"I think... I think it's my mother."

TWELVE

Zarya's legs trembled as she leaned against the sofa, her heart thundering in her chest. Tears stung her eyes with the enormity of Row's betrayal. Her mother. After a lifetime of wondering, finally, a clue. He'd kept this from her. Willingly left her in the dark when he had a picture of her hidden in this room all along.

Knowing this existed would have meant everything to her.

She stared at the page, overwhelmed by the complicated snarl of emotions tightening in her gut.

"I had no idea Row was such a bastard," Vikram said softly, as if he was worried she would shatter at the sound.

Zarya looked up. "I tried to accept there was a good reason. Tried to convince myself he was right, even if I didn't understand why. But what does this mean? Why does Row have a picture of my mother in a book? Why would he *keep* this from me? Who was she?"

Her voice was rising to a hysterical pitch as she flipped the pages, looking for more. But there were no other images of the woman, and the text was written in a language she didn't recognize.

"Can you read this?" She held it out to Vikram and Yasen

like an offering, hoping they could help, but they both shook their heads. Even Yasen seemed apologetic about it.

The world tilted at a dizzying angle. Zarya's head throbbed, tension building behind her eyes. She had come searching for answers, and finding evidence of her mother's existence made the shadowed corners of her heart ache with a longing so deep it felt like roots grinding through hard-caked earth.

For years, she'd always tried to keep the worst of her loneliness at bay. Tried to separate herself from the need to belong to something, but this discovery was blowing through all her hard-won defenses. Every emotion she hadn't allowed herself to feel came out in a rush.

"I'm not feeling well," she said, clutching the book to her chest.

Vikram came over and rested a gentle hand on her shoulder. "You are a little pale."

"I think I need to lie down."

"I'll walk you to your room," he said, taking her by the arm. "You look as if you might faint."

Zarya nodded, letting him guide her through the haveli's wide halls. When they arrived at her room, she settled on the bed, her movements mechanical and stilted, like she'd been hastily screwed together. Vikram held her shoulders and directed her to lay her head on the pillow.

She clutched the book tight to her chest, curling around it into a ball.

"Do you want me to stay?" Vikram asked, and she shook her head.

"I'd like to be alone. If that's okay."

"Of course. I'll check on you later," Vikram said, brushing a lock of hair from her forehead and tucking it behind her ear.

When he was gone, she let out a long sigh as one thought toppled over another. The weight of her past, or rather the complete absence of it, sat like a boulder in the middle of her chest. She had no past that she knew of, but she had a family *somewhere*.

Family had always existed as an intangible idea. She understood its shape and its texture, but it wasn't something she could ever claim. As much as Row and Aarav had been a *sort* of family all these years, their questionable relationship had always tainted any positive interactions they might have shared.

Even if her parents were gone, there must be aunts or uncles or cousins living somewhere in Rahajhan. *Grandparents.* Someone who would take her in and love her and give her the home she'd always dreamed of. For a heart-wrenching moment, Zarya pictured a different future for herself. A family. A life where she was wanted. Perhaps even cherished.

They might not even know she existed. Or what if they did? What if they'd been searching for her? What if Row really was the monster she'd supposed? What if she had been taken, not given, as he'd claimed? The only person who could offer any clarity was nowhere to be found.

She flipped the book open again and studied the image of her mother, searching for a clue. Something that might give her an answer.

A caption was printed beneath the image. *Aishayadiva Madan.* Was this her mother's name? Was she Zarya Madan? Was *Zarya* even her real name?

Someone must be able to read the unfamiliar language, but she was ever cautious about being too open with anyone in this new world of hers. This knowledge might be risky. What if Row had been telling the truth about needing to protect her?

Aishayadiva Madan wore a large ring on her left hand. A wedding ring? What about her father? Had they loved each other? As her eyes closed, Zarya envisioned a jubilant gathering of dark-haired Madans. A family event—a wedding. Maybe her own, full of food and laughter and dancing.

She lay back on the bed, allowing her swirling thoughts to

pulse and coalesce into a new pattern. She'd imagined so many scenarios for her life beyond the cottage, but which one of them might ever become real?

The rain drummed against the windows, white noise filling her ears. She opened her eyes at the sound of chirping crickets a second later. Or maybe it had been hours—it was hard to tell. She was back in the dream forest, lying on the ground.

There was the same river of stars in a deep violet sky and the same leafy dark trees. A rustle in the bushes called her attention, and she sat up, finding the same mysterious figure standing in the shadows. She could feel his gaze on her, pulling up gooseflesh across her skin.

"Who are you?" she asked, her voice a hushed whisper, conscious of upsetting the quiet stillness of this place.

He didn't answer, but he did move closer as a sliver of moonlight fell over his face—there she saw the flash of dark eyes. A straight nose and the hint of a mouth, along with a chiseled collarbone and a broad shoulder.

"Please. What is this place? Who are you?" she asked, pushing herself up to stand. "Why do I keep coming here?"

But the stranger remained frustratingly quiet, as still as the air that surrounded them. Was he a ghost? A projection? Was he real?

She moved closer, taking one step and then another, before she tripped forward like she'd stepped through a cloud, the ground melting away beneath her feet and her stomach heaving into her throat.

A moment later, her eyes popped open, and she was once again lying in her bed inside Row's haveli, confused and blinking up at the ceiling.

THIRTEEN

It took several moments to reorient herself to the present. What was that place? And maybe more importantly, who was that man?

She sat up and looked out the window, noticing the rain had let up, leaving the room humid and stifling. Deciding she needed some air, she went outside to the small courtyard at the side of the house with the book still clutched in her hand.

She dropped onto a bench situated under a pergola in the corner and opened it to the page with her mother's image. Lost in her thoughts, she jumped when someone called her name. The book bounced out of her lap and landed face down at her feet.

Apsara was staring down at her with her leather-clad arms folded across her chest. Her white wings gave a soft flutter as she took in Zarya's disheveled appearance. She raised a silvery grey eyebrow as she glanced at the book at Zarya's feet, her head tilting to read the cover.

"What are you reading?"

"Nothing. I like the pictures," Zarya said, retrieving the book and snapping it shut.

Apsara shrugged. "Will you come with me? There's something I'd like to verify."

"What?" Zarya asked, a shiver of unease running across the hairs on her neck.

Apsara didn't answer. Instead, she jerked her chin, turned on her heel, and walked away. Zarya supposed that was her cue to follow. Apsara led them into the streets of Dharati, where barriers of green silk cord now lined the edges of the chasm. The courtier they'd seen when they first arrived, who bore a resemblance to Vikram, stood at the opposite edge, surrounded by several other rakshasas who were fawning in his presence.

"Nawab Gopal Ravana," Apsara said, catching Zarya's gaze. "One of Daragaab's most powerful rakshasas and the highest-ranking noble outside the royal family. He functions as the ambassador between the rakshasas and yakshis."

Zarya paused to watch as Gopal stretched his arm over the chasm, focusing intently, before the earth shuddered in response. The two sides of the abyss groaned and then shifted inward, as if drawn together by a magnetic force.

"Ravana? As in Vikram Ravana?"

"His father." Apsara's mouth flattened in a line. "His earth magic is strong."

"Can he fix it?"

She shook her head. "No, that would either kill him or take months. There's only one rakshasa in Rahajhan with that sort of power, but the nawab can at least make it less of a hazard."

"But he has years. Rakshasas are immortal, right?"

Apsara nodded. "Nearly so, but I worry it's Daragaab's time that is limited."

"The blight."

"The blight," she replied. "But something else too, something irreversible. It's changing, shifting, becoming more unstable. And if it keeps spreading, how long will it be before the shadows encompass all of Rahajhan? The other realms can claim ignorance, but if we don't stop this, everyone will feel its taint before long."

With a grim expression, Apsara turned to Zarya. "But that's what I'm hoping you might be able to help with."

Again, Apsara walked off without explaining anything more. Zarya huffed but followed in her wake, catching up with her long strides.

"What about the queen?" Zarya asked. "Can't she help fix the rift?"

"The queen is busy guarding the wall. We can't have her expending her energy on trivialities we can learn to live with."

Zarya wasn't really sure how a giant crack in the middle of the city could be considered trivial, but she didn't press the matter.

"How about your magic?" Zarya asked next. "What I saw of your powers was incredible."

Apsara cast her a dubious look. "Yes. I'm vidyadhara, and my home is in Vayuu in the highest peaks of the Pathara Vala Mountains. My people are known for their abilities with snow and ice and wind."

"What's it like in Vayuu?"

"Cold," Apsara replied. "But it's home."

They had arrived at a small but tidy haveli deep in the city's heart. Apsara didn't bother knocking as she swung open the door and gestured Zarya inside. Kindle stood up from a table situated at the center of the room. He blinked at Zarya as if trying to clear a nest of cobwebs from his vision.

"Zarya." Kindle bowed to her. "It is a pleasure to finally meet you. Please have a seat." His eyes were kind and his manner gentle, and the tension in her shoulders loosened a fraction. She placed the book, still in her hand, on the table before sitting down.

Kindle was all elegance and polish in a black coat edged in scarlet velvet, along with black breeches and tall black leather boots. Midnight hair fell in curls just past his chin, and his light brown skin was as smooth as river-worn stone. Though his eyes seemed black, when they moved, flashes of red, orange, and yellow sparked in them like flames.

"Can I get you something to drink?"

"Apsara said you wanted me for something?" Zarya replied, tired of this evasiveness.

Kindle nodded and pursed his lips. "To the point, I see. Very well. Apsara, the vritrastone is in my top desk drawer, if you'd be so kind."

Apsara, clearly not a fan of being assigned errands, stalked off to the adjacent room, throwing Kindle a glare.

"Is this where you live?" Zarya asked, surveying the simple but charming space, curious about the Chiranjivi.

"Yes, the queen was generous enough to provide me with lodging away from the palace. I find it suffocating to witness all the bowing and scraping of the noble courtiers. It gives me a backache just watching them."

Zarya smiled, remembering the sycophantic crowd surrounding Gopal Ravana earlier, and thought she might like this soft-spoken man. A moment later, Apsara returned holding a shimmering grey rock.

"There is something I've been wondering," Kindle said. "Perhaps a clue as to why Row kept you a secret. We were—are —good friends," he said. "I was shocked to hear of your existence, though."

A wave of hurt lingered in his expression, but Zarya supposed a smart man didn't go around bragging about the young woman he had imprisoned in the forest. Zarya rubbed her chest, feeling that old wound that burned in her heart whenever she thought too long about Row.

Kindle gave her a sympathetic look, and the ache subsided to a smoldering ember. "I hope you don't mind. There is so much anger in you, especially for someone so young."

"What do you mean?"

"I am agni."

"I thought you had the power of fire."

"I do, but my abilities also allow me to sense and influence emotions in others. Bhaavana is the kingdom of love and passion, after all."

He offered her a kind smile, but Zarya curled her lip, not appreciating the idea of having her feelings manipulated by anyone.

"Don't be afraid," Kindle added. "Rumors of our power are exaggerated. I cannot make you feel anything you don't already feel. I can only influence those emotions one way or the other. In this case, I was taking the edge off your understandable rage."

"Don't do that again," she snapped. "I am entitled to my feelings as they are. Row is a monster."

Kindle gave her a sad smile. "I understand. If you ever change your mind, please come to me."

Zarya threw him a look that suggested that would never happen.

"But," continued Kindle, "I'm hoping while we await Row's return, we can put together some pieces of this puzzle. How old are you?"

"I'm twenty. I'll be twenty-one in a few weeks."

"You're sure?"

"You're doubting I know my own age?"

"We'll see." He held out the rock to her. "Take this."

Zarya sighed, hating being ordered around, but she held out her hand before he dropped the stone into her palm. About the size of a lemon, it was warm to the touch, its edges smooth and worn.

"Is it supposed to do something?" She tilted it, letting the light catch the shimmering flecks embedded into its surface.

"You don't sense anything?" Kindle asked, his eyebrows arched with expectation.

Zarya shook her head. "Nothing, except a little self-conscious that you're both staring at me like that. What is this?"

Kindle released a frustrated puff of air as he ran a hand through his dark hair. Apsara hovered behind Zarya with her arms folded like an irritating shadow.

"Will you sit down?" Zarya asked. "You're making me nervous, standing over me."

This entire encounter was beginning to grate on her nerves.

Without a word and without taking her eyes off Zarya, Apsara dragged a chair out slowly and sat down in the most exaggerated manner possible. She leaned back and spread out her arms as if to ask if Zarya was satisfied.

Zarya graced her with a dirty look and turned back to Kindle, who was now holding a second stone, this one pale and dull.

"Try this," he said, holding it out.

Zarya reached for the stone. They all stared at it, sitting in her palm. "Now what?"

"Do you notice anything?"

"What am I supposed to notice? It's a rock."

Kindle scratched his chin, and Apsara let out a huff of exasperation that had Zarya bristling. Apsara was the one who'd dragged Zarya here, not the other way around. What right did she have to be so annoyed? Zarya also didn't love the fact these two had clearly been discussing her, thus orchestrating this strange encounter.

"Well, it was worth a try," Kindle said, taking back the stone and stashing it in his pocket.

"What was? What did I do? Or not do?"

"I had wondered if perhaps you were Aazheri. This is vritrastone mined from the Pathara Vala Mountains. If you had magical ability, it would have responded to you."

Zarya blinked at those words slowly, as if emerging through layers of compacted sludge. *Aazheri.* No, if that were the case,

Row would have told her. *Right?* He'd always been confused by her magic. If she'd been Aazheri like him, surely, he would have known.

She considered telling Kindle and Apsara about her magic. Though her ability to capture starlight seemed harmless, Row had always been crystal clear about the need to keep it secret. But after all the risks she was already taking, she decided to heed his warnings on this point until she understood more about herself. He'd kept her entire existence from these people he called friends, and there had to be a reason for that.

"I've never been able to do magic," she said, finally.

The lie tripped off her tongue as she wondered if she was doing the right thing. Row had lied to her about so many things, what loyalty did she really owe him now? She was doing this for herself, though, not him.

"No, I suppose not," said Kindle. "Besides, you are too old. Magical abilities in Aazheri typically reveal themselves in teenagers, and if you haven't noticed anything yet... well, it was a plausible guess."

Sharp talons of grief raked against Zarya's heart. She understood her star magic was only a benign trick, but a part of her had always hoped it was something more yet to be revealed.

"If you notice anything unusual, see anything, experience any visions, or detect any shivers of magic, please come and tell me at once."

Visions. The forest with the violet sky. The strange man who said nothing. Was that magic? It certainly felt that way.

She lied again. "I will."

To himself, Kindle murmured, "I thought perhaps..."

"You thought what?"

"It's nothing," Kindle replied.

Zarya pursed her lips. "Can I go, then?"

Kindle dipped his head. "Thank you for humoring me."

With a curt nod, Zarya walked out and slammed the door behind her.

She wandered aimlessly through the bustling street, pondering everything that had just happened. With a start, she realized she'd forgotten the book with her mother's picture.

She turned back towards Kindle's haveli to retrieve it. Just as she was about to knock, she heard her name and stopped. Apsara's and Kindle's voices floated through the open window.

"Do you think she was telling the truth?" she heard Apsara ask.

"I'm not sure," Kindle replied. "Her reaction *was* strange when I mentioned it. But why would she lie?"

"Do you really think she could be Asha's?" Apsara asked. "We have no reason to believe there was a child."

"I appreciate that," Kindle said, a thread of whispered hope in his voice. "She looks so much like her, though. And why hide her? Row wouldn't have done so without good reason. Who is she?"

"What if she were Aazheri? Would we be able to use her?"

"Possibly," Kindle said, his voice grim. "Especially if she was Asha's."

Zarya frowned at those ominous words. Use her for what?

There were several beats of silence, then Apsara spoke, her voice soft. "I know he loved her, but I don't know that she ever returned those feelings. Where would she even have come from? It seems impossible. I know we're growing desperate, but she's just a girl. One who bears a passing resemblance to a woman you haven't seen in decades. A ghost from the past and a whisper of a future that is never going to be."

Gooseflesh erupted along Zarya's skin. Apsara's words felt almost like a prophecy or a vow.

"Besides, you understand how dangerous it would be if anyone found out she had a child no one knew about? Who is the father? It can't have been Kabir unless there's more at play here than we realize."

"These are all good questions," Kindle answered.

"Where do you think Row is?" Apsara asked.

"I don't know. I've sent out messages to my connections in some of the other realms to keep an eye out for him, but so far, there has been no sign."

More silence followed, and then Zarya heard the scrape of chairs along the floor. Apsara was preparing to leave, but Zarya needed her book, so she knocked, pretending she'd just returned.

Kindle opened the door. Apsara approached and studied Zarya for a moment before turning back to Kindle and shaking her head. Without another word, she stalked out of the house.

"I forgot my book." Zarya pointed to where it sat on the table.

Kindle retrieved it, searching her face as he handed it over.

"Thanks!" she said, overly bright, and then waved, cringing at her terrible acting. Before Kindle could ask if she'd been eavesdropping, Zarya hurried away, walking in the same direction Apsara had gone.

Apsara had said the name Asha—a short form of the name in the book. Had they known her mother? Did they imply Row had *loved* her? And why would her magic matter if she was Asha's?

She became a stirring roil of emotions as her resentment for Row became layered with something thicker and more dense. Something that smelled like more treachery than she had ever imagined.

What if Row was *never* who he had pretended to be?

Zarya thought again of the family she'd never known that might be out there waiting for her.

If Row ever came back, she wouldn't rest until he finally gave her the truth.

FOURTEEN

Slowly, Zarya began to settle into a routine, though it was clear she'd entered a city teetering on the razor-fine edge of balance. At night, she'd lie in bed listening to the sounds of the creatures that attempted to breach the city's defenses, worried about the welfare of those who fought valiantly to keep everyone safe. The wails of the demons against the cries of those defending the city formed a jarring, mournful melody.

She'd been spending hours at the fort with Yasen, watching the Khada train. The elite unit only allowed the most skilled within its ranks. Once a year, they held a series of trials for potential recruits. Receiving an invitation to participate from their leader, General Amjal, was regarded as the highest of honors in Daragaab.

Throughout the year, hopeful recruits were permitted to participate in some of their drills. Zarya had joined in several times, though Yasen had forbidden her from actually enlisting in the ones around the perimeter after the city gates closed at night.

She hadn't fought him too hard about it *yet*, mostly because being in close proximity to the demons reminded her too much of her life in captivity. But she couldn't deny her desire to see if she could succeed in the trials. She wore her fighting skills with pride. The next trials wouldn't be for many months, though, and by then, she hoped to be far away from here.

Today she faced off with Yasen in the blistering heat in the palace gardens, their blades flashing in the sunlight. Her sleeveless kurta and cropped white pants weren't doing much to keep her cool, nor was the hair she'd piled on top of her head in an effort to expose the back of her neck to a non-existent breeze.

"Who could read a foreign text for me?" Zarya asked.

"Why?" Yasen asked, swinging at Zarya.

"You remember the book with my mother's picture? I was wondering if someone could translate it." She had searched Row's room several more times, but nothing else useful had turned up.

Zarya kept her voice low, aware of Aarav lurking nearby.

"Possibly, but hundreds of old languages in Rahajhan have fallen into obscurity," Yasen said.

They fought, parrying back and forth as she tried to get in a hit. Finally, she managed to evade a swipe from his blade and then feinted before kicking a leg behind his knees, knocking him on his back. She raised her arms in triumph, thrilled to have finally gotten one over on him.

Never missing an opportunity to teach a lesson, Yasen leaped up, knocking her to the ground beneath him, the full weight of his body crushing her to the pavers.

"I've told you," he said, growling in her ear. "Don't start celebrating until your opponent is dead."

She laughed. "Yes, teacher."

Yasen lifted the corner of his mouth, pushing himself up and helping her stand.

She'd noticed during these past weeks that Yasen transformed upon entering the fighting yards at the fort. His usually furious demeanor shifted into something softer and far more benevolent as the soldiers clamored to learn from the army's most beloved teacher, his lessons firm but kind. It was a picture so at odds with the scowling rakshasa she was slowly getting to know.

A tentative friendship had blossomed the more time they spent together as Yasen's edges became less abrasive. On days off from teaching at the fort, he lived in the palace barracks, but he was too full of energy to actually take a day off and often roped Zarya into practicing with him in the gardens. She got the sense he struggled with attention from the other soldiers and needed to be around someone who wasn't there to be mentored or impressed by him. She did her part by insulting him every chance she got, and he reciprocated in kind.

A scowling Aarav watched them with his arms crossed, still intent on his self-appointed role as Zarya's bodyguard. It was driving her mad.

Aarav had also been spending a lot of his time at the fort, joining in the Khada's drills and constantly acting as her shadow. But he'd declined to join them today, choosing instead to hang on the sidelines, making everyone irritable. Zarya attempted to ignore him, but it was becoming increasingly tempting to stab him with a rusty nail with each passing day.

"It's sweltering out here," Aarav said, glowering at the sky as though it was the sun's fault.

"Then go inside," Zarya said. "No one wants you here."

"Someone needs to keep an eye on you."

"Aarav, I'll stay here with Yasen. I won't go anywhere."

Zarya launched an attack on Yasen, ignoring Aarav as his eyes darted between them. He grunted, then stomped into the palace's cool interior.

"Gods, he's a prick," Yasen said, staring after Aarav. "I don't know why you haven't killed him yet."

"At this point, it's only a matter of time." Zarya wiped her forehead with the back of her hand. A pitcher filled with ice, mint, and lemon sat on a nearby table. She dropped into a chair and poured a glass. "Gods, it's so hot out here today."

Yasen took a long drink from his glass. Despite the heat and activity, he hadn't broken much of a sweat. Zarya couldn't help but admire the pleasing lines of his profile and his finely honed body. Even with his bouts of surliness, he wasn't the worst company she could have found.

"Come with me." He put his glass on the table.

"Where are we going?"

"Can you ever just do what you're told?"

She crossed her arms and raised an eyebrow. "I have trust issues."

"Fine. Don't come." He turned and walked away.

When she realized he intended to abandon her there, she made a sound of protest and ran after him.

Yasen rolled his eyes as she came up alongside him. "So predictable," he drawled, causing Zarya to glare.

Yasen took them to a staircase that led down to a narrow beach. The Nila Hara sparkled before them, the frothing waves beckoning in the heat of the sun. Zarya immediately kicked off her shoes and rolled up her pants, heading into the surf with a satisfied sigh as the cool water swirled around her shins.

"Come on; it's perfect." She gestured to Yasen, but he shook his head, eyeing the water with mistrust.

"No, thank you. This is for your benefit. Rakshasas and the water don't mix."

She rolled her eyes. "That's really weird, but it's your loss."

Yasen chuckled as he leaned back on his elbows in the sand. "There's a scholar who lives in the northern forest. Professor Dhawan," he said as Zarya cupped water in her hands and dumped it over her head. "He might be able to read your book. He used to teach at the university in Gi'ana."

With a wistful sigh, Zarya said, "I'd love to go to university."

"It's mostly full of Aazheri. They study magic as well as

science, math, art, history." He gave Zarya a wry look. "You would fit in given the amount of time you spend reading."

"I would." She nodded, not taking the bait at the implied insult. Yasen smiled.

"Have you ever been there?" Zarya asked. "To Gi'ana?"

"Once. A long time ago. It was during the former queen's coronation. The city was a spectacle. They had acrobats dangling from roofs and massive rings of fire decorating the squares." He smirked. "I got myself into a lot of the good kind of trouble."

"That sounds incredible," Zarya said, swishing up water and sand with her feet, thinking about the worlds that lay beyond Daragaab. She still wanted to get out of Dharati, but she was warring with the desire to wait for Row's return so she could demand the answers she sought. Indecision was keeping her in place right now.

"Former queen?" she asked finally, picking up on Yasen's last comments. "Who rules in Gi'ana, then? The history books Row brought me were so hopelessly out of date."

"King Adarsh sits on the throne, but he will soon pass the crown to his eldest daughter."

"Why?"

"Power usually passes through the female line in Gi'ana. I'm not actually sure what the holdup has been about. Petty family squabbles and succession issues, I believe."

Yasen fell quiet, lost in thought.

Zarya went to sit next to him on the beach and nudged him with her shoulder, sensing there was something resting on his mind. "What is it?"

With his face tilted to the sun, he said, "There's been a lot of unrest in Gi'ana the last few years. Also in Andhera, which lies to Gi'ana's north."

"Who is Andhera's ruler, and what's causing the unrest?"

"Raja Abishek has been on the throne for centuries. He's

probably the most powerful Aazheri in Rahajhan. Andhera has always been deeply secretive, but stories of rebellion by the vanshaj can be suppressed for only so long. A resistance is rising, but the king has struck them down without mercy.

"I heard talk of him cleaning out an entire vanshaj quarter. Thousands of them were rounded up and forcibly marched into a mass grave where they were burned alive. Children, mothers, all perished in agony."

Zarya shuddered, the hairs on her arms standing on end. "Why? How could someone do that?"

"A message. A reminder of what their defiance costs. Smaller factions operate throughout the continent—most vanshaj have understandably had enough of their treatment— but the rebellion's roots lie in Andhera and Gi'ana. In Dara-gaab, the movement is currently small, but our stability is erod-ing. It's not only the blight that's offsetting the balance."

They again fell into silence, listening to the sea, lost in their separate thoughts. A moment later, swift footsteps sounded from the marble staircase. Zarya turned to find Aarav storming towards them.

"I've been looking everywhere for you. Who said you could leave the garden without me? And to come here alone with *him*?" He sneered at Yasen with the same derision one might reserve for a pile of steaming garbage. "These filthy rakshasas have only one thing on their minds."

Zarya was about to protest, but Yasen beat her to it, launching himself up and storming towards Aarav. "Watch your fucking mouth, Aazheri," Yasen snarled, grabbing Aarav by the shirt and slamming him against the wall. He dug his forearm into Aarav's neck, Yasen's strength and size easily overpowering him.

With his airflow cut off, Aarav sputtered, clutching at Yasen's arm. Zarya let him turn purple for a moment before reluctantly deciding she shouldn't let Yasen kill Aarav. Even if he completely deserved it.

"Yasen, stop." She placed a hand on his arm. "It's okay."

Yasen threw her a dark look, his grey eyes flashing. Then he dropped his arm before stepping back, growling at Aarav and baring his sharp teeth. Aarav flinched with fear, though it was obvious he was trying to put on a brave face.

Yasen snarled at Aarav one more time and then glared at Zarya before spinning on his heel and storming back up the stairs. She watched him leave, angry that the comfortable closeness they'd been enjoying had just evaporated thanks to Aarav.

"What is wrong with you?" Zarya whirled on him. "Did I not tell you to leave me alone?"

"I have a responsibility to ensure you are cared for."

"You mean watched." She resisted the urge to throttle him. "You don't care what happens to me. You just want to control me so you can report what a good little apprentice you are when Row comes back."

"I gave up everything to care for you the past twenty years! And this is the appreciation I get?"

Zarya scoffed. "You didn't care for me. You lorded over me. You took every opportunity to make me miserable. And why? Why do you hate me so much? I have nothing, Aarav. I've never had *anything*. What kind of pathetic man hates a girl with *nothing*?"

A sob escaped her throat at the thought of his cruelty and the way he'd made her doubt she could ever be deserving of anyone's love.

"You had Row," Aarav hissed. "He worshipped you. It was Zarya this, and Zarya that, Zarya will rise to greatness one day. And what was I? A worm? A lowly servant. A nursemaid to a spoiled little brat."

"What are you talking about? I did not have Row. What greatness? I was a prisoner! Have you lost your mind?"

Aarav seethed, his wiry frame trembling.

With her voice pitched low, she continued, "I hate you, Aarav. For as long as I live, I will hate you. You didn't have to help Row keep me locked in a cage. At the very least, you could have shown a *child* a little kindness. I will never forgive you for that."

Zarya offered him one last look, hurt blazing in her heart, before she also stomped up the steps.

At the top, she glimpsed Yasen disappearing into the palace, sure he'd been listening. The thought of him hearing that humiliating conversation stuck like tar in her chest, coating her heart in a thick layer of black fury.

After a final glance behind her, she released the pressure of her tears and ran from the palace.

FIFTEEN

The next afternoon, a knock sounded at the haveli's door. Sleep had been elusive, Zarya's mind a whir of conflicting emotions after her argument with Aarav. She had spent most of the night on the balcony watching the sea, recalling the harsh words she'd hurled at him. Though Aarav deserved every bit of her venom, guilt gnawed at Zarya's conscience.

She was thrilled to see Vikram at the door, his arrival a much-needed breath of fresh air. Between Row's disappearance, the encounter at Kindle's, the fight with Aarav, and Yasen's brooding, Vikram's easy smile was a welcome and very handsome distraction.

Elegant in a green kurta of soft brushed material, he wore dark brown pants and a pair of short leather boots. Zarya decided his hair was also curling in an especially adorable manner today. His emerald eyes sparkled with mischief as he held up a small basket.

"Care to join me for a ride in the northern forest? The palace kitchen prepared us lunch."

"Is it safe?" she asked. "What about the blight?"

Vikram smiled. "There are no demons living to the north of

the city, and it's daytime, so we'll be fine. Even if we did encounter one, they're at their weakest until the sun sets. We can handle them."

Still dressed in her nightgown, she nodded enthusiastically. "Okay. Give me a moment to get changed."

She ran upstairs, suddenly warm and flustered, and not because she'd just bolted up the stairs like her heels were on fire. Rifling through her clothes, she analyzed several options, conscious of Vikram waiting downstairs. She wanted to look nice for herself, of course, but it wouldn't hurt if he thought she did, too.

Finally, she chose a sleeveless purple kurta made of chiffon layered over bright pink silk. Silver beads were stitched along the hem, and the cut showed off her strong, lean arms, a result of all the extra training she'd put in with Yasen. After fussing with her hair for a moment, she left it down, black waves falling to the middle of her back.

Zarya found Vikram waiting in the living room. She hadn't heard Aarav return last night and assumed he'd been out drinking. At least he wasn't trailing her everywhere now. With any luck, he'd gotten so drunk he'd unwittingly stumbled into the chasm outside.

"All ready," Zarya said, putting Aarav firmly out of her mind and flashing Vikram a grin.

Heat flared in Vikram's gaze as he took her in from head to toe. "A picture of perfection."

Aware of her own heart speeding when he came to stand in front of her, she resisted the urge to lean into his scent of fresh grass and the salt of the sea. Vikram held out his hand, and Zarya took it, his fingers folding hers in his delicious warmth.

They arrived at the stables and mounted their horses before Vikram directed them out of the city and into the forests that lay to the north of Dharati.

After riding for a while, they approached a small clearing in the trees. The slim banyans created a leafy canopy that filtered in soft sunlight, while flowers grew in bursts of color, evidence of Daragaab's flourishing earth magic blossoming in every direction.

She remembered the days when the forests around her home had looked like this before the blight had taken over. Truly, this was so beautiful that Zarya wondered if she'd ever need to go anywhere else.

Of course, she still thought constantly about leaving Dharati—to escape Row and Aarav—but since the latter seemed to have abandoned his quest to drag her back to the seaside cottage, she was content to get to know her new surroundings better. And especially this handsome rakshasa. She watched him dismount, noting the bunch and shift of his muscle under his fitted kurta and the way the light caught his black hair.

Besides, after gathering too many scraps of information that didn't fit together, she wanted answers from Row. She was tired of trying to solve an invisible puzzle, and she'd take the risk of waiting for him to return so she could demand clarity. She simply couldn't leave here without understanding *why* he hadn't told her that he'd known more about her mother than he'd ever let on.

Vikram spread a blanket on the grass and began to unpack the basket. Zarya dismounted and joined him, kneeling down as he pulled out wrapped containers of golden pakoras with pear chutney, bright pink kaju katli, and slices of mango. And finally, a bottle filled with pale green liquid.

"Enchanted, thanks to Apsara, to keep it cold for hours," he said, pouring her a glass. She took a sip and sighed with contentment, picking up notes of lime, jasmine, and honey. They ate in comfortable silence for a few minutes as they listened to the insects and birds shaded within the trees.

Vikram stretched out and leaned on an elbow before reaching to run his finger along a scar on Zarya's forearm. The hairs on her arm shivered at the gentle touch. The scar had faded over the years, but the small ridge of raised skin remained as a reminder of her childhood.

"What happened?" He swept his finger back down her arm, his hand covering hers as heat stirred in her chest.

"A burn," she said quietly. "When I was seven, I was trying to cook dinner after Row and Aarav had left for a few days.

"Sometimes they would do that. Leave on an errand and be away longer than they expected. I was boiling water to make rice, and it tipped while I was adding the grains to the pot. I wasn't quite able to reach the top of the stove, and I bumped the handle. The boiling water came down on top of me.

"I started screaming, and it hurt so much I thought I was on fire. Of course, no one heard me. I managed to get it under some cold water, but then I fainted from the pain. I don't know how long I was unconscious. It was a day or two at least.

"Eventually, Row came home and found me sweating on the ground—infection had set in already. He used magic to treat me, but it never quite healed."

"Shit," Vikram swore under his breath.

"I'm sorry. I shouldn't have told you that. Row is revered, and a member of this sacred cabal that everyone respects, and I'm here telling everyone what a villain he is. He wasn't terrible. He tried. He was never cruel, but I just don't think he really understood how to care for a child."

Zarya covered her face with her hands, and Vikram sat up to pull them away.

"You are not responsible for the choices Row made. I don't know why he did this to you or if he thinks he had a good reason, but you are under no obligation to protect his reputation. If he comes back, he will have to answer for what he did. I will make sure of it."

Zarya let out a soft laugh. "Can you do that?"

He gave her a wry grin that made her chest twist. He handed her a pakora, and she munched on it thoughtfully.

"I didn't want much," she eventually said, staring into the distance. Vikram raised a dark eyebrow.

"Just someone to love and care for me. I haven't experienced very much of that in my life." She wondered how pathetic she seemed admitting that.

Vikram shifted closer so their thighs were touching. "That doesn't seem right. From the short time I've known you, I can see how beautiful and brave and kind and clever you are and that you deserve untold amounts of love."

Zarya's cheeks warmed, looking at the blanket as she chewed on her snack.

"I mean it." Vikram tucked a strand of hair behind her ear, letting his hand linger against her cheek. When she found the courage to look up, his green eyes were luminous with a soft sort of determination. Her heart was racing, and her breath quickened as his gaze remained on her.

She tipped forward almost involuntarily, willing him to do the same. She wanted to be kissed and held, and Vikram's arms looked so strong and inviting. She wanted to feel his body pressing against hers. Zarya was so tired of her perpetual loneliness. Of that space behind her heart left so cold and hollow like a crystal vase no one had ever thought to fill with flowers.

Vikram's hand trailed across her jaw, his thumb sweeping over her bottom lip as a fuse detonated deep inside the chambers of her heart. The past fell away, leaving only this moment.

She heard the hitch in his breath as he brought his face closer to hers. Zarya closed her eyes in a hum of anticipation. She could taste it—the bottled longing of so many years spent alone. So many nights wondering if there was anything for her beyond the walls of her contained existence. The sweetness of triumph made even richer by the denial of it for so long.

His lips touched hers, the barest flutter, so tender that her heart nearly fainted dead away in her chest. There was a firmer press and a soft moan as she gently parted her lips. She felt the sweep of his tongue and his hand cupping the back of her head before he tipped it back to take a deeper plunge.

At that precise moment, a sonorous crash thundered through the forest.

Zarya and Vikram snapped apart as an enormous boulder skidded towards them through the trees. He sprung up instantly and grabbed her arm, yanking her out of its path. The solid mass slid across the earth like an ice cube on a warm surface before it came to a halt directly where they had been sitting a moment earlier. Food and dishes had scattered everywhere, and the air had muted to stillness, like it was holding its breath.

But the intruder wasn't a boulder.

"It's... an egg?" Zarya asked, scrutinizing it at an angle before looking at Vikram. His forehead creased as they took in the strange object. Smooth as glass, its polished black surface was striated with veins of silver and gold. And something—a life force, a magnetism—pulsed in the atmosphere around it, like the beat of a swinging pendulum.

They looked skyward, searching for its source. A moment later, Zarya's stomach began to spin and churn, and that's when she was certain they were in danger.

Vikram emitted a strangled noise as he reached for her hand.

"We need to run," he said, the calmness in his voice belying the horror now unfolding above. Dozens of dark shapes were streaking across the sky, hurtling towards the earth.

And right towards them.

More eggs drove into the ground, blasting dirt and trees in every direction. Zarya and Vikram ran hand-in-hand, free arms thrown overhead to shield themselves from the onslaught.

"What are they?" Zarya shouted over the sounds of crashing trees and snapping branches.

"I don't know."

Vikram urged her to move faster as a flock of bright red birds filled the sky, their screeches high and piercing as they swooped above.

As she ran, Zarya looked up, trying to gauge the magnitude of this added threat. She watched as another egg oozed from the back end of a bird and slammed into the ground. Another bird flew past her vision, this one birthing yet another smooth oval, but that one didn't make it to the ground. Instead, it cracked open mid-air before releasing another clump of crimson feathers.

Good gods, what *were* they?

More and more eggs split in the air, birthing an entire seething flock of shrieking feathered demons. They had to find cover.

"This way!" Vikram veered through the trees. "There's a cave where we can take shelter."

The screeching grew louder as each new bird began its own assault, in a shower of eggs and feathers and claws. Vikram and Zarya ran, weaving in and out of the trees.

Zarya felt a sharp pain against her temple just before she tripped and fell to the ground, her head spinning, the roiling in her stomach twirling in tight nauseating waves. She needed to get up, but her arms wouldn't move. She was so dizzy that her eyes wouldn't focus.

She staggered back to her feet, stumbling sideways and feeling blindly before her. Her skin stung from the impact as she was pelted over and over with sharp bits of shell and debris.

An egg the size of a coconut slammed into her lower back, throwing her forward and bruising her hip before rolling off with a thud. She tried again to get up, and when she pushed the hair from her face, her hand came away sticky with blood. It oozed into her eyes as Zarya struggled to her hands and knees.

She fought down the urge to vomit, bile burning in her throat, the blood muddling her vision.

Hands then circled her waist as she was lifted up, cradled in strong arms. Vikram ran. The sky continued its torrent, objects hurling into the earth and sending up sprays of dirt as the sky darkened with ominous screeches and the flapping of wings.

The world twisted and whirled as everything in Zarya's vision went black.

When she awoke, they were entering a small cave. Vikram lowered her gently to the ground as eggs continued to rain from the sky.

With a moan, Zarya touched her head, her fingers coming away wet. Vikram's kurta was covered in blood, and she hoped none was his.

"Are you okay?" He lightly touched her head, and she gasped at the sharp sting of pain.

"Hold on." Vikram ripped off the bottom portion of his tunic and dabbed at the blood coating her face. Next, he ripped off the sleeve and wrapped it around her head as a makeshift bandage.

"You're going to have nothing left to wear if you keep this up," she groaned.

"You wish," he replied with a wry smirk.

She choked on a laugh and then groaned again as the movement made her head throb. "Don't be charming—I almost died."

Vikram grinned, but his smile dropped away as he looked outside.

The shower of eggs appeared to be tapering off. After several more minutes, the eggs finally stopped as the scarlet birds cleared away, disappearing into the clouds, their distant shrieks carrying on the wind.

"What *were* those?" Zarya asked, peering up at the sky.

Vikram shook his head, his brow furrowed with concern. "I don't know. Another demon returned from the storybooks."

"But it's daytime," she protested, and he regarded her with an expression that suggested he knew that and was extremely concerned about it.

"Can you walk?" Vikram placed a hand on Zarya's back as she staggered to her feet. "We need to get you back to the city to get this taken care of."

"I think so."

Zarya and Vikram slowly emerged from the cave to a picture of destruction spreading as far as they could see. Shattered and whole eggs littered the ground; their shells were chipped, the shiny, smooth surfaces blemished. The eggs ranged vastly in size, the smallest as compact as limes, the larger ones nearly as tall as a person, though none matched the size of the original egg that had landed on their picnic. Massive banyan and neem trees sagged, split through the middle, their roots torn from the earth.

Zarya's stomach had settled again, and she couldn't help but notice the way her body reacted whenever the demons were near. She was sure it had grown worse since leaving the cottage. Had that happened when she'd lived on the shore? Sure, she'd always felt a bit queasy in the swamp, but she'd always put that down to its sticky, cloying air and her need to always be on alert.

What Zarya *could* feel now was the eggs' life pulse, like a synchronized beat resonating through the forest.

"Do you hear that?" Zarya asked.

Vikram shook his head. "What?"

"There's a... feeling. Like the air is breathing. You don't notice that?"

"I don't," he said slowly, touching her head gently again, his brows drawn with concern. "We really need to get you to the healers. Come on."

Right. That's what it must be. Just a side effect of hitting her head. But she'd felt it when the first egg had fallen. Or at least she thought she had. She bit her lip as her heartbeat continued to thrum to the backs of her teeth.

Vikram looked around. "The horses ran off—do you think you can make it all the way back? I can leave you in the cave and bring help."

"No, don't leave me here. Not with these things. I'll walk." He nodded, holding out his hand. She grasped it, and they slowly picked their way through the forest.

"We should bring one of these back. Apsara or Kindle might want to examine one," Vikram said, bending down to inspect an egg, but Zarya tugged him away.

"No. Don't touch them. It's just a feeling, but I don't think you should."

He gave her a quizzical look but nodded in agreement. "We'll get you to the infirmary. We can send out soldiers to look for survivors. Let's hope these didn't land in the city, too."

The silence between them was tense as they walked. If the demons were acting during the day with this much impunity, it signaled things really were changing. How much worse would they get before the blight swallowed everything whole?

Finally, they crested a hill that brought them into view of Dharati, the city spreading out before them.

They stopped dead in their tracks.

"No," Vikram whispered before he broke into a run.

SIXTEEN

Zarya paused on the hilltop, surveying the scene. The north end of the city was now in ruins. Chunks had been scooped from the perimeter wall that now surrounded a row of jagged, broken outlines that once made up a series of houses and buildings. Smoke rose in grey plumes, and the screams of the wounded carried on the wind.

Vikram stopped at the bottom of the hill and looked up at her, the lines around his eyes tight.

"I'm fine. You go," she called down. He shook his head and waited for her to descend, taking her hand before they both picked up their pace.

The moment they passed through the city gates, soldiers descended on Vikram, seeking his orders on how to proceed. He began shouting out commands to search for the injured and to seal up the gates, along with demands for construction crews to begin work immediately on repairing the damaged portions of the wall.

"Someone alert the queen that her enchantment has been breached!" he shouted at a soldier who tipped his chin and ran off.

Zarya scanned the sky. For now, it was empty, but who knew when these monsters might return?

"Let's get you looked at," Vikram said, placing his hand on the small of her back and leading her towards the palace. Zarya caught sight of the eggs littering the ground, that same strange heartbeat still thudding in the back of her head.

"Don't let anyone touch them," she said to Vikram, grabbing him by the arm. He nodded and continued firing off instructions as they walked.

"I'll be fine," she finally said after he'd been stopped by yet another soldier in the throes of an emergency request. "You deal with this."

"You're sure?"

"Yes. Please. You have people who need you."

"Okay, I'll find you once things are under control here."

"Of course." She squeezed his hand once more, then made her way to the infirmary. Dozens of people already filled the cots, the injuries ranging from minor scrapes and bruises to broken limbs. Koura was moving amongst them, healing them with his warm yellow light.

"Oh my!" came a high voice that pulled Zarya's attention. "Let's get you looked at."

She found Princess Amrita standing in front of her, wearing a simple white kurta. Her black curls were piled on her head, and her cheeks were flushed with a sheen of sweat.

"This way," she said. "I'm Amrita."

She sat Zarya in a chair and began unwrapping the fabric tied around her head.

"I'm Zarya," she answered.

"I know. I remember when you arrived with Vik and Yasen. What happened to you?"

Zarya winced as Amrita pulled away the cloth. "I was out in the forest with Vikram when those birds attacked us."

A line formed between the princess's brows, and she looked into Zarya's eyes for a moment.

"Do you work in the infirmary a lot?" Zarya asked, and Amrita shook her head.

"Sometimes. I enjoy working with people, and it seemed like they could use a few extra hands," Amrita said with a smile before she stood up. "Let me get some supplies. I'll be right back."

The princess moved to a table covered in bandages and various jars and bottles. Just then, Vikram and Yasen walked in and approached Amrita, conversing with her for a few moments. Vikram glanced over at Zarya and spoke with another healer, who then walked over to clean and dress her wound.

As the healer worked, Vikram pulled up a chair next to her.

"How are you feeling?" he asked as Yasen joined them.

"I'm okay."

Vikram squeezed her hand. His skin was warm and welcoming, and her stomach melted into that same liquidy feeling she'd had when he'd kissed her so briefly. She wondered when they'd get a chance to pick up where they'd left off because she definitely wanted more.

"What happened out there?" she asked. "What *were* those things?"

Vikram ran a hand along the back of his neck. He was clearly under a lot of strain. "Kindle and Suvanna think they're called kala-hamsa. Another demon born of myth, like the naga and kimpurusha. These monsters should not exist here. Suvanna took a group of soldiers to examine the unhatched eggs, particularly the one that nearly crushed us. It's at least twice the size of any of the others. We wanted to make sure you were okay before we joined them."

"How many people were hurt?" Zarya asked, scanning the infirmary.

"Too many," he said. "A large section of the city is practically dust, and several people were killed. Many others injured."

"So much for it being safe on the north side," Zarya said to Vikram, her tone dry, though she didn't blame him for any of it. Of course, this was out of his control.

"You should be more careful where you go for *rides*," Yasen said. Fierce grey eyes bored into Vikram, heavy with meaning. Yasen then tugged on the hem of his green jacket, giving Zarya a perfunctory bow.

"I'm glad you aren't dead," he said before walking away.

"What's his problem?" she asked as Yasen's tall, broad form and his stiff shoulders receded into the crowded infirmary.

"You know how he gets," Vikram said. "He's just worried about all this."

Before she could respond, Apsara came storming in, stopping in front of Zarya and crossing her arms.

"You're okay?" she asked, her words clipped. "I need you to tell me what you remember. Leave out no detail."

"We were..." Zarya cleared her throat, cheeks warming at the memory of the short-lived kiss with Vikram. "Eating lunch," she said, with too much force. Apsara arched an eyebrow but said nothing. "And that giant egg came hurtling at us. We jumped up and ran for cover. Something must have hit me in the head because I was suddenly on the ground and covered in blood. I fainted and woke up in the cave where Vikram took us."

"And that's it?"

"I think so. What else should I remember?"

"You didn't notice anything unusual?"

Zarya bristled at Apsara's brusque manner. "You mean, other than hundreds of hard objects pelting us and screeching birds hatching in the sky? No, I'd say that's as unusual as it gets."

"And after you woke up?"

"I could hear them." She recalled the thrum of synced heartbeats again, like a clock ticking towards ruin.

"You heard them?" Apsara's expression turned to alarm.

"Apsara," Kindle called, striding into the room. "Something dreadful... Suvanna sent a messenger. She said they were examining the largest egg—" He paused and took a breath. "And it sucked in nine guards. One moment they were there, and the next moment they had melted into the surface and were gone."

They all stared at him. Something was alive in those eggs. Something hungry.

Vikram leaped up from his chair. "I need to go back out there."

"I'm heading out, too," Kindle replied. Apsara nodded, turning to follow them.

Zarya interjected, "I'm coming with you!"

Apsara turned her cool gaze on her. "No. You are staying here to rest and heal."

Without another word, she stalked off with Kindle and Vikram, the trio conversing in low voices.

She watched them go, but she had no intention of staying behind. Zarya waited for them to leave and then stood to follow as soon as they cleared the doorway.

* * *

A short while later, Zarya had changed into clean clothes and strapped Row's sword to her back. Yasen had returned it to her weeks ago, and in Row's continued absence, she'd claimed the strange weapon as her own. A few more knives and daggers were tucked into her boots and belt. The forest wouldn't catch her unprepared again.

As she left the haveli, she passed the ruined palace wall,

where a group of masons were building it back up. Gopal's magic had shifted the chasm enough that it was no longer a gaping hazard, and bridges had been erected across it, making transport more convenient. The edges had also been fortified so no one else risked ending up as its inadvertent victim.

Between the swamps, kala-hamsa, and the chasm, Daragaab was dangling on a fraying thread of security. Zarya had settled into a comfortable routine during her weeks here, but it seemed like something was trying very hard to kill them all.

Trapped on the seaside, Zarya had been living on the outskirts of reality, helpless and ignorant. She had no idea the world she'd emerged into was coming apart at the edges, but she'd found a tentative place here. She'd made friends. She was happier than she'd ever been. Now something threatened that existence before she'd even had a chance to enjoy it, and she couldn't let that happen.

She passed through the destruction that had fallen upon the city, noting the ruined buildings and pockmarked streets. Word had already spread about the danger of going near the scattered eggs, and people were keeping their distance as they scurried past. But as their glances darted to the side, it was obvious they also couldn't look away.

She reached the gate and entered the forest, determined to find the site of the original egg that had interrupted their picnic. She wanted to know what these things were. As she moved deeper into the forest, Zarya sensed their innate wrongness with increasing trepidation. Whatever they were, she was sure they didn't belong here. Their hearts continued beating as one, worming their way into her subconscious.

It felt like a signal, a warning.

But the message was conflicted.

Layered beneath her sense of alarm was another feeling that pulled her in as much as it pushed her away. The knock of a visitor late at night, begging to be let in and make themselves comfortable. Despite their sudden and violent entrance, their presence wasn't entirely threatening, either. Such was the inconsistent tangle of her thoughts when she found herself coming to a stop in front of an egg about the size of a melon.

Piqued with curiosity, Zarya kneeled in the grass and studied the egg, noting the striations that marked its surface. She wanted to touch it, though she couldn't explain why. She reached out before hesitating, thinking of the soldiers that had been sucked into the largest egg.

"Zarya, what are you doing?" She turned to find Yasen emerging through the trees. "Don't touch that. We just lost nine soldiers to one of those things."

"I know." Her hand hovered an inch over the egg. "But I think maybe I can touch it."

"What do you mean?"

"I can't explain it. I just know I can do this."

Yasen folded his arms, looking down his nose at her. "Don't be ridiculous. What if it eats you, too?"

"It won't," she said, not sure why she was so certain but convinced, nonetheless.

"What happened to your so-called trust issues?"

"I trust this feeling, okay? Leave me alone if you're just going to be an ass."

Perhaps sensing he wouldn't talk her out of it, he crouched down and sighed loudly. "Fine, but I'm going to hold on to you in case it tries to bite your face off."

Zarya nodded.

With her hand hovering above the egg's surface, she noted the way its energy spiraled with its own center of gravity, like a planet moving in the heavens. Zarya had spent her entire life held captive by secrets and understood the sound of their call, so she pressed her hand against the egg.

The surface was warmer than she expected, and for a moment, nothing happened. But then a sensation like being swept on a tide engulfed her, her limbs and body turning amorphous at first and then becoming solid.

When she opened her eyes, she wasn't entirely surprised to find herself standing in the dream forest at the edge of a small clearing, the violet, star-strewn sky shining brilliantly overhead. This place obviously meant something. But why did she keep coming back here? She spun around, searching for a clue.

Lush black trees were silhouetted against the endless, velvety sky. The hairs on the back of her neck stood suddenly at attention. She twisted abruptly, her feet tangling, sending her toppling over. She landed on her ass with a grunt, her teeth clacking together.

Across the clearing now stood the most beautiful man Zarya had ever seen. She was sure it was the same one she'd seen before, only this time he stood cloaked in moonlight instead of shadows.

Straight black hair fell to his shoulders. Tall and broad, his muscled chest and arms strained against his black kurta. A straight nose was centered between high cheekbones and full lips. And his eyes—as dark as the forest but shifting with flecks of gold in the light.

The man said nothing but looked straight at her, his head tilted. His brown skin glowed with the telltale luminescence Zarya recognized as unmistakably rakshasa.

She was too mesmerized to be embarrassed by her fall, and she couldn't pull her eyes away as he approached her, something dangerous in the way he moved, graceful and fluid, more animal than human. Pale scars marked his hands, another over an eyebrow and one visible above his collar.

As he stood over her, Zarya looked up into the hard planes of his face. The ferocious blaze in his expression. Beautiful, but in a distinctly savage way. Nothing soft about him.

He held out a hand, and she looked at it before once again meeting his eyes and reaching out slowly.

A shock passed through Zarya as their fingers met, his skin hot as his large hand swallowed hers. There was the slightest flare of his nostrils before he stepped back, pulling her up.

"Are you hurt?" he asked, his deep, rough voice making something flutter in the lowest recesses of her stomach.

She shook her head. "Only my pride."

He responded with the barest curve of his mouth and the faintest flicker in his eyes. His calloused thumb swept over her knuckles, and Zarya's knees loosened to the consistency of jelly.

"Who are you?" Zarya asked, breathless. "What is this place? Why am I here?"

He blinked then, in a brief flash of uncertainty, before opening his mouth to speak. But before he could reply, she was suddenly yanked away.

Voices called her name and tugged her back, her hand slipping from his as she once again plummeted, coming apart and then back together, landing with a thud on the grass.

Now it was Yasen and Apsara hovering over her like two grumpy clouds coming to rain on her parade.

"What did you do?" Zarya demanded, sitting up. "Why did you pull me away?" Jumping up, she brushed the grass from her leggings.

"Excuse me? You were in a trance, and I was worried about you dying," Yasen snapped. "We were helping you. How about some gratitude?"

"I was fine!" Zarya couldn't explain why she was so angry. She rubbed her chest at the strange hollow in the center. Upon breaking the connection to her vision, an overwhelming sense of loss scored marks along her insides, leaving a jagged, stinging ache.

"Stop," Apsara said, raising a hand for silence. "I told you to stay in the infirmary and rest."

"And I didn't listen," Zarya countered, then turned to Yasen. "What do you mean, I was in a trance?"

"Exactly what I said," Yasen replied, his tone icy. "You were touching that thing, and your eyes glazed over, and you went all stiff. When I tried to pull you away, your hand was stuck. Apsara heard me and came to help, but we couldn't tear you free. I thought it was going to suck you right in. And then your hand released, and you started yelling at me."

Yasen shuddered, likely remembering the soldiers they'd already lost. Zarya felt guilty for snapping at him. Some of them had probably been his friends.

"Sorry. I was startled. Thank you for your help."

Yasen appeared only slightly mollified by her apology, his jaw still hard.

"What did you see?" Apsara asked.

"Nothing. Just darkness. An empty blackness, like the lights had been dimmed," she lied. She had no intention of revealing the truth until she understood more about Apsara and the other Chiranjivi, especially if these visions were somehow connected to her magic. There was a reason Row had kept her existence a secret, and there was *definitely* a reason she was having these episodes now. This all had to be connected. "And then you were pulling on me and calling my name."

"That's it?" Apsara regarded Zarya, tilting her head. "I suppose it's encouraging you survived."

Apsara clearly suspected the lie, but Zarya didn't care. The forest and the beautiful rakshasa were her secrets to keep for now. She owed nothing to this woman.

"Well, you're out here now," Apsara continued. "Come on. We should tell Kindle about this."

Zarya nodded, and they picked their way through the ruined forest to the clearing. She could still feel the eggs pulsing against her skin, wondering why she seemed to be the only one to sense it.

As they approached the site of their earlier picnic, she saw the scattered food and dishes still lying in the grass. Remnants of an afternoon that had taken an unexpected turn in more ways than one.

Her heart skipped as she remembered Vikram's feather-light kiss. She touched her mouth, still feeling the ghost of his soft lips. Across the clearing, Vikram caught her eye, his gaze darkening as though he'd been having similar thoughts.

Apsara went over to where Kindle and Suvanna were conferring. Zarya could tell Apsara was relaying what had just happened to her with the smaller egg, and she gestured for Zarya to come over.

Nervous, she approached, hoping they wouldn't force the truth from her.

"Tell me what happened when you touched it. Don't leave out any detail," Kindle said, his brow furrowed. As she gave him the same report, Kindle scratched his chin in contemplation.

"You, there," Suvanna said, pointing to a young soldier loitering nearby. "Come here. We're doing a test. Would you say the one you touched was about that size?"

She pointed to one of the eggs, and Zarya shook her head. "Yes, but you're not testing anything on him! That's barbaric. What if he disappears? What if he dies?"

"He's a soldier in the queen's employ. This is his duty," Suvanna snapped, and gestured to the man to touch the egg.

"What? No, someone stop this!"

"My lady," the soldier said to Zarya, "she is right. I appreciate your concern for my welfare, but I am happy to offer my services." He issued a quick bow and bent towards the orb at his feet.

"What? No! Kindle? Apsara? Do something!"

They regarded Zarya silently, Kindle with an apology in his eyes and Apsara with a combined look of irritation and resignation. Zarya searched the clearing for Vikram or Yasen, sure they'd object to one of their soldiers being used this way, but they had moved deeper into the trees and out of sight.

The soldier had ignored her and had already placed a hand on the orb as Zarya glared at Suvanna in disgust. For a few moments, nothing happened, and she breathed a sigh of relief just as the soldier made a startled noise. His hand had begun sinking into the egg's surface, slowly pulling him in.

"Get him out!" Zarya cried, bending down and circling her arms around his waist. She tugged with all her strength, but the egg dragged him in further.

"What's going on?" She heard Vikram's voice before he appeared beside her and moved in to help. The guard was screaming now—in pain or in terror, she wasn't sure. Probably both.

As the guard wailed, the egg made a wet, crunching sound, devouring flesh and bone. Bile rose in Zarya's mouth as the guard sunk to the middle of his forearm. The egg was anchored to the ground, resisting every attempt to dislodge the man from its vise.

"Someone, do something!" she screamed. He was almost to his elbow now, but the guard had stopped screaming, shock setting in. His face was white and covered with a thin sheet of sweat. Vikram and Zarya tugged and heaved, but it made no difference.

Zarya saw Suvanna approach from the corner of her eye, the merdeva pulling out the sword anchored to her back.

"Stand aside." She raised the sword over her head, and Zarya realized what Suvanna intended.

"No! Gods, stop!" she screamed.

"He's going to die otherwise! Move out of the way!" Suvanna curled a lip, her eyes glowing vividly blue.

Zarya looked into the soldier's terrified face, her eyes filling with tears, understanding Suvanna was right. She nodded and leaned away from the soldier, putting a hand on his shoulder.

"Look at me." He turned to her, his eyes rolling in his head. "Keep looking at me." She willed him to be brave. She willed *herself* to be brave. Zarya gripped his free hand, holding it against her heart.

She locked eyes with him, trying to ignore the nauseating flash of steel, the whoosh, the sickening crack. The guard fainted as blood gushed from his severed appendage, and Zarya clung to his limp, free hand. Then they all watched in grim fascination as the egg devoured the remaining stump with a squelch. A collective shudder ran through the clearing as Zarya collapsed to her knees, trying not to retch.

"Healers!" Suvanna shouted. "Help him!"

Vikram strode towards Suvanna, his jaw hard enough to crack stones. "Who do you think you are? My soldiers aren't yours to dispose of at will. I will have you arrested for this!"

Suvanna put a hand on her hip, the other gripping the bloody sword dangling at her side. "I did what was needed. Your queen wants us to stop the blight using any means necessary. Try to arrest me, Commander. See how far that gets you."

Suvanna and Vikram stood inches apart, noses almost touching. Suvanna was several inches shorter, but she managed to fill the difference.

"Arrest or no arrest, if you *ever* try something like that again, I will have the queen throw you out of Daragaab. Permanently," Vikram said, his teeth bared.

Suvanna stepped back, her lips pursed into a thin line. She said nothing else before she turned away and stalked into the forest.

"How could you do that? That man was innocent!" Zarya shouted at Suvanna's back. A healer had swooped in and was busy bandaging the comatose soldier's arm.

Suvanna stopped and turned to glare at her. "I *don't* need to explain myself to you, little girl. Just because the others trust you doesn't mean that I do."

Zarya recoiled as if struck, with no idea how to respond.

"Ensure the entire affected area is barricaded to prevent anyone wandering too close to these things," Suvanna said to no one in particular before she disappeared into the trees.

SEVENTEEN

"Why can't I come?" Zarya asked Yasen as she followed him through the streets of Dharati the following day.

"Because," was all he said as he walked, his long legs eating up the distance. With Row's sword strapped to her back, Zarya had to scramble to keep up. This thing was heavy, but it had become like her security blanket, coming with her everywhere.

"But you know I can fight! I want to help."

After the attack on the city, the Khada had chosen to hold an emergency round of the admission trials with the goal of rapidly shoring up their elite force. Today would be the first of several testing rounds, and hopefuls from all over the queendom were eager to throw in their lot. Zarya included.

"I've been training just like everyone else has."

Yasen stopped so suddenly she practically crashed right into him before he spun around to face her.

"It's dangerous," he said, his brows drawn together. "You don't know what's out there." He gestured in the direction of the high stone wall that served as their main line of defense. But its effectiveness had been thrown into question when the kala-hamsa had breached it yesterday.

"I lived out there!" Zarya said as Yasen continued walking. "I know that better than anyone."

Yasen stopped again, whirling on her. "Yes. And don't you think that's a little suspicious? What are you hiding, Swamp Girl? You've been keeping secrets ever since you arrived. How am I supposed to trust you?"

"I'm not hiding anything," she snapped. "Row used his magic to protect us."

Yasen gave her one more skeptical look, then continued his march through Dharati, ignoring her pleading. That didn't stop her from trailing after him. She had absolutely no intention of sitting this out.

"Why are they being so picky, anyway?" Zarya asked Yasen. "Shouldn't they want all the help they can get?"

Yasen looked at her with an eyebrow raised. "Because the Khada are a bunch of snobs."

At Ambar Fort, the fighting yards were buzzing with activity. Dozens of sweat-soaked bodies were practicing their sword techniques, sparring in friendly duels. The different stations for the trials were already set up. Targets for archery, an open ring for fighting with weapons and hand-to-hand combat, and off to the far side rose a giant contraption that seemed to function as a sort of obstacle course, with balance beams, swinging ropes, and ladders that fell on the worrisome side of stable.

There were also a handful of Aazheri and rakshasas practicing magic, ribbons of bright light in various colors emanating from their fingers. She watched them for a moment, thinking of her meeting with Kindle and Apsara, still wondering if what they'd concluded about her magic was the entire truth.

Yasen surveyed the press of bodies before his eyes settled on Zarya once more. "You still want to join them?"

She swallowed a nervous knot in her throat and nodded. "Of course I do. I want to help."

Yasen tipped his head as though to suggest they'd see about that, then resumed his progression through the crowd.

He was stopped constantly by eager young recruits begging for advice or requesting an analysis of their form. Yasen pretended to be put out by it, but he also didn't hesitate to help everyone who asked. She pressed her lips together, suppressing a smile as he retained his usual scowl, but it was obvious a part of him enjoyed this.

His trail of admirers followed him through the training yards like ducklings. Zarya felt a twinge of jealousy at seeing how encouraging he was with everyone else when he kept telling *her* to go home.

Eventually, they reached the far end, where a long table had been set up for those wishing to join the Khada's ranks. A stern-looking man wearing the Khada's red-and-gold uniform stood guard over piles of parchment, where each potential recruit had to sign their name. Yasen made small talk with each hopeful warrior who stopped by to add themselves to the register.

Zarya caught sight of Aarav, who was bent over the table, scratching against the parchment. They hadn't spoken since their argument on the beach and she didn't imagine they would do so any time soon.

As if feeling her eyes on him, he looked up and frowned, his brown eyes darkening. He dropped the pen and straightened. For a moment, she thought he might come over to say something, but he looked past her and walked away.

She watched his narrow frame disappear through the crowd and sighed.

"Ready, Swamp Girl?" Yasen asked, pulling her attention away from Aarav.

"Stop calling me that."

"If you're really planning to do this, get yourself in line," he said, ignoring her comment. He pointed to where dozens of people were queuing up, one next to each other. "If you die, don't blame me."

She rolled her eyes. "I'll keep that in mind."

The day would include a series of trials that tested agility, combat with various weapons, archery, and for those who had magic, spell casting. Zarya squeezed her fist at her side, knowing she had to keep her powers hidden, though she wasn't sure what good her insipid magic would do, anyway. It might be useful for calling the demons, but no one here would thank her for *that*.

Nervous energy permeated the air. Never before had the Khada done this outside of the usual schedule. Beneath the excitement rippling through the crowd was an undercurrent of fear that this drastic step was necessary at all.

A low murmur dropped over the yard as a line of Khada emerged from Ambar Fort, wearing their distinctive red-and-gold uniforms. At the center marched Vikram, resplendent in his own green commander's sherwani. Next to him walked another rakshasa in the blue and gold of the Khada's general.

The group came to a halt in front of Zarya and the other hopefuls.

She looked along the line, catching sight of Aarav about halfway down. He was focused intently on the Khada while he chewed the inside of his lip. Yasen stood off to the side with his arms folded, casually keeping an eye on the proceedings and, she was sure, complaining about her to whoever would listen.

Vikram raised a hand, calling for silence.

"Welcome, hopeful recruits!" he called out in a commanding voice that easily carried over their heads. "I am Commander Ravana, and I'm sure you all know General Amjal."

He paused for everyone to nod before continuing, but there was no need for introductions. Everyone standing in this yard knew exactly who these two rakshasas were. Zarya had already heard plenty of stories from Yasen about the general and his accomplishments with the Khada.

"Today will mark the first quarter of the trials. You are at the start of what will be a difficult journey. You must prove your worth and dedication if you wish to join the ranks of the Khada. Even in a situation this dire, it's important to remember that patrolling the wall is exceedingly dangerous, and we can only accept the very best."

Vikram scanned the assembled crowd, then continued in a more somber tone.

"Do not underestimate your duty here today. The Khada have been protecting this region of Daragaab for years, and we do not take on new recruits without careful consideration. We need warriors with strength, courage, and discipline."

He paused again briefly before clapping his hands together in conclusion.

"Let us begin! Each group will receive instructions on their first test, so listen carefully for your name! Good luck to each one of you!"

The crowd of hopefuls broke up in a clamor of voices and congregated around the Khada, who were busy organizing everyone into groups.

A shrill whistle announced the start of the first test.

Zarya waited as the Khada called out names in turn. Standing with her hands clasped behind her back, she tried to hide her nervousness. A young warrior was called forward, tipping a crisp salute before being directed to the archery range.

A few minutes later, a decorated Khada soldier stopped in front of Zarya and eyed her up and down.

"Zarya?"

She exhaled a tight breath and stepped forward. "Yes."

"I'm Lieutenant Batra. Lieutenant Varghese tells me I should go hard on you to discourage you from this endeavor."

Zarya narrowed her eyes, glaring at Yasen, who was still

leaning against the wall with his posture loose like he didn't have a care in the world. When he found her staring, he gave her a smug grin. She looked back at Lieutenant Batra.

"Yasen should mind his own fucking business," she said, and the soldier laughed.

"I admit, I *was* inclined to ignore him." He winked, and Zarya smiled. "We're up next. What's your weapon of choice?"

She gestured to Row's sword on her back. "The blades."

Lieutenant Batra's eyes crinkled at the corners. "Perfect. Then let's go."

She followed him to the middle of a sparring ring, where they both drew their weapons. A crowd had gathered around them, other recruits looking for a distraction in between their own tests, as well as members of the Khada. She caught sight of Aarav and Yasen watching, too, and felt exposed and self-conscious.

For all her bravado, she suddenly wasn't as sure as she had been about holding up against one of Daragaab's most accomplished soldiers. She rarely won against Yasen, and Aarav had walloped her enough over the years to make it clear that she was far from infallible.

They circled one another, backdropped by the sounds of the others training, fighting, and falling. But she pushed down her nerves, knowing that fear was only a state of mind. Row had taught her that well enough.

She made the first move, darting towards the lieutenant and swinging her blade. He easily blocked it and countered with a light jab of his own. She dodged it, raising her blade to deflect his next attack. He blocked that one as well.

As they parried, their flashing blades met with the satisfying clash of steel. Grunting, she swung around, going in for another attack, knowing her reflexes were fast. Fighting was as much about thought as it was about intuition—another thing Row had taught her—and he'd trained her to look for tells that signaled what her opponent might do next.

She drew on that, trying to anticipate his moves and mostly guessing right. They traded blows as she met him strike for strike. Her body was starting to tire, though, and the lieutenant looked like he'd barely broken a sweat.

Just as Zarya was wondering how much longer she could hold on, he stopped and lowered his blade with a smile that made his eyes sparkle.

"Well done, recruit," he said, and she held her breath. Lieutenant Batra lifted his hand and signaled that she would be allowed to proceed to the next test. Several onlookers erupted into a supportive cheer, and she pressed a hand to her chest, her shoulders dropping in relief.

He held out his arm, and she grabbed his forearm in a show of solidarity. "Tell Yasen I tried."

She laughed, and he let go, offering her a bow before moving on to the next recruit, leaving Zarya in shock over her accomplishment. She couldn't quite believe that she had actually prevailed against an experienced Khada warrior. She hadn't beaten him, but she'd held her own, and that was something to be proud of. Yasen could get bent. She had as much right to be here as anyone.

Over the next three days, Zarya faced challenge after challenge and managed to complete every task, usually dragging herself to the finish line. Each night she went to bed with aching muscles, only to wake up to them screaming even louder. She wasn't sure if her body would ever recover.

Slowly, the numbers in the fighting yards dwindled as those cut from the trials took their place along the walls, nursing their battered bodies and egos. About a third of the original recruits were left, and Zarya still couldn't believe she was one of them. Again, she silently acknowledged the fervor with which Row had taught her to protect herself. She didn't think he'd had *this* in mind, but he also wasn't here to complain about it.

Aarav stood across the circle where she waited with the others, about to embark on his final test. Zarya supposed it wasn't surprising he'd also gotten so far, given he'd been Row's student, too.

She tried to make eye contact, but he looked away just as General Amjal summoned him. He jogged over to the obstacle course, his joints clearly stiff from the rigors of the past few days.

Zarya rolled her neck, thinking of how strenuous the obstacle course had been. And she'd just barely finished it, at that. She'd been fresher then and wasn't sure she'd manage it now after the punishing regimen they'd all been put through during the last few days.

Aarav pressed his hands in front of his heart and bowed to General Amjal before he turned and shimmied up the side of the contraption.

Zarya watched with her breath held as he tumbled over logs, scaled walls, ran through rings of fire, and swung from one platform to another. He was quick and determined, and despite herself, Zarya found that she wanted him to succeed, even if she was still angry with him. Besides, if he failed here, he'd probably find some way to make it her fault, and she didn't need that.

Every eye in the ring followed him as he grabbed a swinging handle and launched himself over a pool of murky water. But one of the ropes securing the wooden crossbar snapped, causing Aarav to lose his grip. For a moment, he seemed to hover in the air as his arms and legs windmilled like a puppet cut from its strings. The entire yard fell into a horrified silence that was shattered a moment later when Aarav popped up, gasping for breath. He dragged himself out, his dripping clothes forming a puddle where he stood.

"Recruit has fallen!" shouted one of the Khada's lieutenants, but he didn't move to signal whether Aarav had actually failed the task. Zarya watched several Khada eyeing one another, apparently unsure what to do.

Vikram was now conferring with General Amjal, their heads bent together. Aarav's shoulders rounded as he watched the pair intently, his hands opening and closing at his sides.

She saw Vikram and the general shake their heads before General Amjal gestured to Aarav that he had been eliminated from the task. He was met with a mixed chorus of boos and cheers as Zarya watched the air whoosh out of Aarav like someone had kicked him in the stomach.

"Wait!" Zarya cried. "That's not fair. It broke. He couldn't control it." She didn't know why she was defending him after the horrible things he'd said the other day, but this didn't feel right.

"I'm sorry," Vikram said. "Things go wrong out on the wall, too. A failure is a failure, regardless of how it happens."

She could see the apology in his expression, but it was clear his hands were tied.

"Recruits!" General Amjal said. "Congratulations on making it this far. Those of you still standing will join the Khada on the wall in one week for your final test. Keep up your training and get some rest in the meantime."

There was a chorus of cheers from the remaining hopefuls, but Zarya's own victory was soured as she watched Aarav, whose face was an expressionless mask. She couldn't tell if it was the water or if those were tears running down his cheeks.

She was about to go and console him, but he pinned her with such a dark look she stopped, knowing anything she said to him right now would only make things worse.

With a heavy heart, Zarya watched Aarav walk away, disappearing through the crowds of Dharati until she could no longer see him in the distance.

EIGHTEEN

"Let's do something fun tonight," Vikram said at breakfast a few days later. He sat with Zarya on the haveli's balcony off the back garden, overlooking the water, with Yasen and Aarav sitting across from them. "Things have been far too serious lately, and I'm guessing you've never been to a peri anada."

"A what?" Zarya asked, sitting up in interest.

"Drinks, dancing, fun. You'll love it," Vikram promised with a playful smile.

Yasen sipped his chai and rolled his eyes. "Oh, this will end well."

"Don't be such a scorpion in the sand," Vikram said to his friend.

"Yes," Aarav said, brightening, as Zarya glanced at him with suspicion. He'd been even more moody than usual since his disappointment at the Khada trials. "That is a brilliant suggestion."

"Who invited you?" Zarya asked, but hurt flashed in his eyes, and her irritation turned to guilt. Despite his foul mood, Aarav *had* been giving her a wider berth since their argument on the beach, and she was wary of antagonizing him in case he decided to pick up the hobby of becoming her bodyguard again. "Fine. That does sound like fun."

"Perfect. We'll pick you up later. Yasen and I will be at Ambar Fort today, so try not to get into too much trouble without us."

"Please," Yasen said, eyes raised to the ceiling, his hands pressed together in mock prayer.

* * *

Later that day, Zarya returned to the haveli after visiting the soldier who'd lost his arm in Suvanna's macabre research with the eggs in the forest. Raj was twenty-four and had spent five years as one of Rani Vasvi's guards. For now, the healers were managing the pain, and soon, Koura would begin the long and painful process of regrowing his arm. Raj would recover completely in time.

Nevertheless, a sting of contrition gnawed in her stomach. Zarya suspected her weak vein of magic was the reason she'd been able to touch the egg without harm. If she'd been honest with Suvanna and the others, perhaps the merdeva would never have risked Raj's life in such a reckless manner. It would have been completely her fault if he'd died.

To assuage her guilt, she had gone every morning to visit him. He was cheerful to a point that bordered on maniacal, and she marveled that anyone could be so positive after such an experience. Nevertheless, she was relieved there didn't appear to be any lasting psychological damage. The Chiranjivi were a mostly cold and merciless lot. Row must have fit right in.

She knew it didn't make up for the fact that she'd lied to everyone, but she felt sure that keeping her magic hidden was tantamount to her safety. She'd always scoffed at how dramatic Row had been, but surely there had been some reason for all of his worrying? And there was still Apsara's suggestion that they could "use her" to consider. Whatever that meant.

Zarya spent the rest of the afternoon getting herself ready for the peri anada. She wore a lehenga made of raw black silk covered with intricate black beads fastened with silver thread. The choli fit snugly across her chest, leaving her midriff bare from just under her breasts to a line low on her hips where the sweeping floor-length skirt hung.

It was nice to finally have a place to wear the pretty clothes Row had chosen for her, rather than stare longingly at them hanging in her closet back at the cottage, or worse, trying them on only to be forced to wander the beach alone and without a soul to admire them.

Vikram and Yasen arrived shortly after Zarya had finished dressing, divested of their usual uniforms. Vikram wore an embroidered gold kurta that went to mid-thigh, worn over slim black pants, and Yasen wore a kurta of dark blue that contrasted beautifully with his silver locks.

Vikram took her in, looking at her with an intensity that made her stomach drop in response. Though she had limited experience in such matters, she was sure she wasn't imagining his interest in her beyond friendship. At least she really hoped she wasn't imagining it. He'd basically kissed her during their picnic, and who knew what might have happened if they hadn't found themselves in the middle of a demon onslaught? He also hadn't mentioned it since, but she was trying not to let that bother her.

Aarav came out on the balcony wearing the same rumpled brown kurta and beige dhoti he did every day. He'd thrown a cream vest over the garb, and Zarya supposed that was his attempt to dress up for the occasion. She'd never seen him wear anything else in all the years they'd lived together, and all three of them surveyed him with a bemused look.

"What?" Aarav asked, looking down at himself with his hands spread. "Is something wrong?"

Yasen closed his eyes and pinched the bridge of his nose as if begging for patience, muttering something Zarya couldn't make out under his breath.

"Where are we going?" Zarya asked, turning away from Aarav, not about to let him derail her excitement.

Vikram held out a crooked elbow towards her. "It's a surprise." There was that unmistakable burn in his gaze again, his eyes sweeping her over as nervous anticipation bloomed in her stomach. Zarya hoped this was going to be a night to remember. The kind of night someone might write about in one of her books.

They left the haveli and headed towards an area of the city Zarya hadn't explored yet. As they entered the bustling fray of the Rata Quarter, it was evident Zarya and her companions weren't the only ones with revelry on their minds tonight. They skirted past teeming taverns, music and chatter spilling out their open windows.

All around them, exuberant Dharatis shared drinks, food, conversation, and much more. Zarya noticed a man and woman having a very private moment on the edges of an extensive seating area, the woman straddling the man's lap and his hands gripped around her waist. The woman rolled her hips as their mouths clashed in a frantic kiss, seemingly oblivious that they weren't alone.

Zarya exhaled a breath, wondering if Vikram had noticed the couple as well. Their eyes met, and something told her he had and was maybe—hopefully—having similar thoughts to hers.

They stopped in front of a building made of smooth white marble carved with intricate designs. Music thundered from inside, so loud that even the ground outside vibrated with the beat. Lights flashed in the open windows that ran almost the height of the wall, letting in the evening breeze and revealing a large room packed with dancing people.

Zarya grinned, in love with absolutely everything tonight. A broad-chested devakin stood at the door. A small winged tattoo at the corner of his left eye marked him as half vidyadhara.

Zarya had learned that devakin bore their half-magical lineage as a point of pride, and the practice of declaring one's heritage with a face marking had become fashionable across the continent. Wings delineated one as vidyadhara, while a flame was used for agni, a water drop for merdevas, a leaf for rakshasas, and a circle for healers. Zarya again wondered if her latent magic meant she was devakin, except that her star power didn't align with any of the known branches of magic. She was an anomaly in every way, it seemed.

Vikram exchanged a few words with the vidyadhara devakin, gesturing to Zarya, Yasen, and Aarav before the man nodded and pulled aside the green velvet curtain that hung over the entrance. The devakin flashed them all a puckish grin as they entered.

Through the curtain, an indoor luminescent forest revealed itself. Reminiscent of Rani Vasvi's throne room, the floor was covered in a thick carpet of springy moss. Trees lined the walls, their branches and leaves creating a high canopy overhead. Low branches and vines brushed the ground, and everything was covered in flowers of every size, shape, and color imaginable.

Copper lights hung suspended overhead, where tiny winged creatures flitted through the air, darting in and out of the greenery. "Peri," Vikram said into Zarya's ear, his hand pressing into the small of her bared back. She shivered at the brush of his warm breath on her skin, watching the human-like forms swooping and diving in the air.

The peri anada hummed with an array of humans, devakin, rakshasas, and an assortment of other species for which Zarya had no name. The most noticeable and striking were the dozens of stunning beings pouring drinks, serving tables, and standing around looking decadent enough to eat... amongst other things.

"Fairies. Half human, half peri," Vikram said, his voice dropping with a hint of suggestion. "Here to make *all* your wildest fantasies come true."

She glanced up at him, both shocked and definitely intrigued by the idea.

The fairies' skin glistened in gold and silver and blue and pink and purple, their brilliant jewel-toned hair falling in long, thick curls. Their enormous sparkling eyes encompassed a rainbow of hues, and they wore clothes that could barely be called that—thin gossamer scraps covering only the bits that needed covering, exposing lean thighs, taut bellies, and miles of lush skin.

Zarya and the others were ushered to a table in the corner, where they sat and absorbed the surrounding activity. A long bar lined the back wall where several male fairies, all bare-chested and chiseled with muscle, were pouring complex drinks in hues of orange and yellow and gold and green. They tipped them into intricate glasses that looked almost too delicate to touch.

A curvy female fairy made her way over to them. Her skin sparkled purple, and her hair was a cascade of pure white streaked with a shocking shade of violet. Her amethyst eyes were surrounded by thick black liner and the longest lashes Zarya had ever seen. She oozed flirtatiousness. Her barely-there dress was made of a thin, lustrous material that scarcely covered her perfectly rounded ass and magnificently propped up her ample breasts. Zarya couldn't take her eyes off her.

"Drinks?" she asked, one hand resting on her cocked hip, the other balancing a crystal tray at her shoulder. Yasen ordered a round for the table, and the fairy sauntered away, her hips swinging in a way that had more than one set of eyes devouring the sight of her departure.

Zarya turned her attention to the dance floor where two green-skinned male fairies were dancing together—if one could call it that. They were gyrating around each other, their hips pressed together with not an inch of space between them. They flipped around, back-to-back and then front-to-front. Zarya felt her cheeks flushing further, noting the way it was affecting them both, thanks to the tiny scraps of tight clothing barely covering their hips.

The shimmering purple fairy returned, this time with her tray laden with crystal glasses garnished with fruits, flowers, and sparkling stir sticks.

Zarya grabbed a pale green glass adorned with candied pineapple and a thick swirl of coconut. She took a tentative sip and almost choked as the alcohol seared her throat.

Yasen laughed and slapped her on the back. "Peri concoctions are known for packing a punch."

He took a deep draft of his drink that gleamed ruby red in the flashing lights, a cluster of raspberries sitting at the bottom of the glass. Zarya took another sip, this time prepared for it. Once she got past the initial prickle, she could taste the tropical notes of coconut and pineapple layered with something more earthy and subtle. It was delicious.

"Care to dance?" came a deep voice from behind Zarya.

One of the male fairies she'd been watching earlier was holding out a pale green hand. She twisted in her chair and saw his companion at the next table, bowing to another young woman, also in invitation.

Zarya exchanged glances with the woman—who seemed just as scandalized and curious as she was—and they grinned in mutual solidarity.

"Sure, why not?" she said, turning back to the fairy waiting for her. She picked up her glass and tossed the contents back, grimacing as it burned down her throat.

"A little liquid courage—good idea, Zarya," Yasen said with a wicked gleam in his eyes.

She glared at him but then stood and looked up at the fairy. He was so tall that Zarya had to tilt her head up to look into his bright green eyes, framed by a fringe of emerald hair.

He pulled her into the press of bodies, wrapping his hands around her waist and tugging her against his gold-dusted chest as he moved his hips. Despite his suggestive movements, she sensed a distance, a reserved boredom in his eyes, like this was all a chore he wasn't particularly fond of.

"What's your name?" she asked, placing her hands on his firm biceps so she could stretch onto her tiptoes to speak in his ear.

"My name?" he asked, his thick eyebrows furrowing. She nodded, and he hesitated, glancing around the room. "I'm not supposed to talk about myself."

"But I asked."

He couldn't seem to meet her eyes as his slipped away, once again searching the corners of the room.

"I'm sorry. I didn't mean to pressure you," Zarya said. "Forget I asked."

"It's Amandeep," he said quickly, in a low voice.

"I'm Zarya. It's nice to meet you."

He blinked and smiled, something in his demeanor shifting. "Are you having fun tonight, Zarya?"

She grinned and nodded as Amandeep began moving again, his movements less seductive and more friendly. His manner became warmer, and she wrapped her arms around his neck, letting him take the lead. The alcohol was taking effect, and she laughed with abandon. She couldn't remember a time when she'd ever felt this unburdened.

Before long, the song ended. Amandeep backed up, his hands dropping from her waist.

"I need to move on to the next patron," he said. He took

Zarya's hand and touched his lips to it, peering up at her through endless eyelashes. "It was a pleasure, Zarya."

"Thank you, Amandeep. For me as well."

After a tip of his head, he walked away, and she looked out across the dance floor to where Aarav was being similarly entertained by a female fairy, his eyes as wide as saucers and his mouth hanging open. It made her wonder what kinds of entertainment he got up to when he spent time in the city without her.

The crush of bodies surged around Zarya, and she let herself sink into the music, swaying with the beat. A warm hand landed gently on her back, and she looked up to find Vikram standing behind her.

"May I join you?"

She nodded as he passed her one of the glasses he was holding—this one a pale purple with floating pansies.

She sipped while they rocked with the music and the thrumming beat. Zarya lost count of how many songs they spent on the dance floor but was thoroughly breathless when she placed a hand against her stomach.

"I think I need a break."

Vikram took her hand and guided them through the throng of people back to their table.

Yasen and Aarav were gone, and Zarya spotted them sitting at an enclosed booth with three men wearing the distinctive red uniforms of the Khada. Hands moving about in animation, Aarav was talking excitedly about something. Yasen leaned back, his arm slung over the bench, looking bored.

Zarya narrowed her eyes at Aarav, who looked more energetic than she had ever seen him. He looked almost... happy. After his sullenness lately, she wondered what was perking him up.

"Are you having fun?" Vikram asked, pulling her from her thoughts of Aarav as he leaned in close, his warm hand enveloping hers. She nodded. She was having the most fun she'd ever had in her entire life.

"This is exactly what we all needed." She waved a hand at her face. "Although I am so hot, I'm melting."

Vikram gestured with his chin. "Let's go outside to cool off —there's a garden you'll like."

They left through a set of glass doors at the back of the building, and the evening breeze was a welcome change from the heat of bodies and the smells of sex and dancing inside.

"Oh, this feels so good," she said, lifting her hair to allow a breath of cool air to touch the back of her neck.

The garden continued in the same theme of an enchanted forest, where leafy branches strung with lights hung over sparkling fountains and small bonfires, and the scent of jasmine, roses, and lilacs perfumed the air.

Vikram and Zarya found a secluded corner with a woven carpet laid on the grass next to a burbling pond swimming with hundreds of rainbow-hued fish. They sat side by side against a pile of cushions, laughter floating on the air from around the garden.

Vikram took Zarya's hand, his thumb tracing circles on her skin, the touch sending tiny sparks of awareness up her arm. She leaned against him, loving the way his body felt pressed against hers. With his other hand, he ran his thumb along her jaw.

"We were interrupted the other day."

She nodded, but her heart was pounding so hard she couldn't form any words. Zarya flicked her eyes skyward as if to check for falling eggs, and Vikram laughed.

"Our luck can't be that bad."

"Let's hope not," she finally whispered.

He was staring intently now, his eyes dark with lust and need in a way that made her insides tip and spin. As their surroundings receded, Zarya felt only his eyes on her and the responding shiver of her skin.

But he was being so careful, and she couldn't wait any longer, so she summoned a thread of courage and leaned forward.

"Kiss me," she said, her voice raw and filled with emotion. Her words seemed to snap something loose because Vikram's arms were around her in an instant, as his mouth finally crashed into hers with all the desperation she had craved for so long.

He kissed her urgently, their hands roaming over each other's arms and hips and curves. He shifted so he could lower Zarya to the ground before rolling on top of her, one elbow planted beside her head and a hand gripping her waist.

With her long skirt bunched around her thighs, she wrapped her legs around his hips as he planted a line of hungry kisses down the side of her neck and across her collarbone, dipping to a spot just above the swell of her breast.

He rolled his hips, and she moaned at the unmistakable hardness of his cock, pressing to the wet ache at her center. She met his thrust, craving more pressure, as he traced his tongue along the top edge of her low-cut choli.

His hands didn't stop moving, his fingers tracing circles along her ribs, tickling along the edge of her top. She whimpered at the spread of his breath, hot against her skin.

She wanted more—she wanted all of him touching all of her body. This was nothing like it had been with the fishing boy in Lahar. This was alive and electric. Vikram knew how to touch her, how to move his body to pull these soft moans from her mouth.

He kissed her harder, his tongue tangling with hers, and she groaned. This was more decadent than Zarya had ever imagined. It was no wonder an entire canon of poetry existed dedicated to this act. She *knew* it had to be better than her limited and uninspired experiences of the past.

He teased along the waist of her skirt, and she wondered how much further they would go. She was dimly aware that they were outside and might have an audience, but she was having a hard time caring. It was clear this place catered to and encouraged this kind of behavior within its walls.

"Vikram," a frosty voice said, and they both stilled. Gods, not again.

Zarya looked over to find Yasen watching with his eyebrows drawn together and his shoulders tense. A muscle in his jaw ticked as he stared at his friend.

Vikram scrambled off Zarya. She sat up, adjusting her skirt and pulling up the strap that had slid down her shoulder, feeling foolish and exposed. What had been so electric and thrilling a moment earlier had just turned cheap and tarnished. And she didn't understand why.

Vikram opened his mouth to say something to Yasen, but nothing came out.

Making a sound of disgust, Yasen gave him another piercing glare before he stormed off.

She exchanged a glance with Vikram. "What just happened?"

Once again, Vikram seemed at a loss for words, so Zarya didn't wait for a response. She pushed herself up and pursued Yasen, catching up to him as he entered the club, the music and lights folding over them.

"Yasen!" She grabbed him by the hand and forced him to turn towards her. "I'm sorry, I didn't know that you—" She broke off, not really sure what the problem was. "There's no reason to be jealous—I thought you and I were just friends. I'm sorry."

Yasen shook off her hand and took a step closer, leaning down to speak directly into her ear. "I'm not *jealous*," he said, his voice chipped from the heart of an iceberg. Yasen stepped back, glared again at Vikram, who had come to stand behind her and stalked out of the club.

"Why is he so angry?" she asked.

Something inscrutable crossed Vikram's expression as he watched Yasen's silver head melt into the crowd.

"We got into an argument while you were dancing earlier, and he's still mad at me. He'll be fine."

She was sure she caught a flash of hurt in Vikram's eyes as he attempted to brush the incident off. He turned to her and smiled. "How about another drink?"

"Okay," Zarya said, letting him lead her towards the bar.

Despite a nagging thought that she had missed something important, she wasn't ready for the evening to be over yet. Whatever had upset Yasen could wait until tomorrow. They ordered another round of drinks and spent the rest of the night in a glorious haze of music and kissing.

NINETEEN

With her head pounding, Zarya awoke to find Vikram fast asleep beside her, his cheek pressed to the pillow and his hair falling over his eyes. They were in the same bedroom where she'd spent her first night in Jai Mahal, sunlight streaming through the windows.

She blinked rapidly, wondering what she had done last night, but relaxed when she realized they were both fully clothed. A drunken fumble was *not* the evening Zarya had planned now or ever again. Next time she had sex, she wanted what she'd read about in books. She wanted fireworks and sweet nothings whispered in her ear. She wanted the stars and the moon and someone who knew what the fuck they were doing.

That kiss last night had suggested Vikram definitely knew what he was doing, and she wanted to remember every moment when it happened.

Vikram's eyes peeled open as she shifted on the bed. Clasping her hand to her forehead did nothing to ease the pounding she could feel in the backs of her eyeballs.

"Do you feel as terrible as I do?" he asked, squinting as though his retinas were melting.

"Worse," she replied, mashing her face into the pillow and groaning.

Then she lifted her head and looked at Vikram.

"We didn't—you know..." She gestured to the space on the bed between them, wanting to be absolutely sure.

He gave her a wry look. "I assure you, that would not be something you'd ever forget."

Then he rolled over on his back and closed his eyes, pinching the bridge of his nose. Zarya picked up a pillow and swatted him in the face. He grabbed it, laughing.

"No, I was a perfect gentleman. And you passed out as soon as you crashed on the bed. Very charming."

It was her turn to laugh, but it was cut off with a groan as her head gave another sharp throb.

"How about some water?" Vikram asked as he eased himself up and shuffled into the bathroom. He returned with two full glasses and handed one over. Zarya took a large gulp and then wrinkled her nose at the smells of food wafting from the sitting room, sure she couldn't keep down anything in this nauseated state.

Nevertheless, Vikram coaxed her into the main area where breakfast had been set out. What she needed was the biggest cup of chai she'd ever had in her life. A small glass jar with tiny white pills sat next to the teapot, and she picked them up, examining the bottle.

"What are they?"

"Pain medication," Vikram said. "Magically enhanced to work quickly and effectively."

Zarya shook the bottle and popped off the lid. "I guess someone knew we were out last night?"

She tipped two pills into her palm and passed the bottle to Vikram before swallowing them with a big slurp of water. She sighed in relief as they took effect almost immediately, just as he'd promised.

Now that her stomach had settled, the waiting food looked much more appealing. She placed a paratha on her plate and topped it with a generous spoonful of raita, suddenly ravenous.

As they ate in exhausted silence, Zarya caught a movement in the garden outside. She pushed herself up to investigate, swinging open one of the glass doors.

Yasen lay on a bench, his kurta unbuttoned at the neck and his long limbs askew. He was snoring loudly, his mouth gaping wide.

She stifled a giggle as she stepped out onto the stone patio. Clearly, Yasen had detoured after he'd stormed off last night.

A moment later, she choked out a sharp laugh at the sight of Aarav in nothing but his underwear, lying face down in a flower bed. The noise jolted both Yasen and Aarav awake. Yasen lifted his head to blink at her, and Aarav let out a long and agonized groan.

Holding up her skirt, Zarya stepped over the stone garden border and reached down to help Aarav up, dirt and flower petals sticking to his skin. He braced his hands on his knees, panting while he leaned forward as if willing himself not to vomit.

"What happened to you two?" she asked, pressing her mouth together to suppress a smile. The last thing Aarav needed right now was her laughing at him.

"He is absolutely terrible at Rani's Cradle," Yasen said in a disgusted voice and flopped an arm in Aarav's direction. "It takes a special sort of talent to be that horrendous at anything."

Aarav groaned again as he dropped to his knees and began crawling towards the door, leaving a trail of garden detritus behind him like peri dropping a trail in the forest so they didn't lose their way.

Vikram now stood in the doorway, leaning against the frame

with a grin. Yasen swung his legs off the bench and leaned forward, burying his head in his hands.

"I ran into this idiot after I left the club," Yasen said, again gesturing to Aarav, who was now lying face down on the stones, his quest for the door currently abandoned.

"They kicked me out of the Khada trials, and it wasn't my fault," Aarav said, his voice feeble but indignant. "I wanted another chance."

"The Khada we were speaking with told him if he could win a hand, they'd let him try," Yasen continued. Vikram arched an eyebrow, and Zarya guessed he wasn't too pleased the Khada were allowing disqualified recruits to gamble their way back to the trials. "So, we spent the entire night between gaming dens while he lost every match and every coin in his pocket."

Zarya covered her mouth, trying hard not to laugh.

"And then he lost his actual pockets when he bet away his clothing. Why anyone thought his rumpled vest was a fair deal is beyond me." He curled his lip.

"So, did they agree?" Zarya asked.

"Eventually," Yasen said. "He had nothing left to bet, but they appreciated the effort."

Yasen looked up from where Aarav was lying at her feet. "They said he could redo the obstacle course this afternoon. They would clear it with General Amjal if I could clear it with Vik."

"This afternoon?" Zarya asked, eyeing Aarav dubiously. It would be a wonder if he could stand up by this afternoon, let alone complete the Khada's trial. The healer's magical pills might help, but he was clearly a mess.

Aarav took a shuddering breath and curled his hand into a weak fist. "I can do it," he said with a feeble sort of confidence that Zarya hoped he could translate into action.

Zarya exchanged a smirk with Yasen, whose eyes crossed as he stood up, pausing to swallow hard.

"Come have breakfast. You'll feel better after some tea, and Koura sent some magic pills."

Yasen slung his jacket over his shoulder with one finger and stepped over Aarav, who had resumed his wayward journey for the door.

Once they were inside, Zarya passed food and tea to Yasen while Aarav eventually made his way to the sofa, lying on it with his head back and legs splayed out. His head kept drooping, since he was having trouble keeping his eyes open.

The silence that settled over them was awkward, the tension from last night's argument still hanging between them. Yasen chewed his food, pointedly ignoring Vikram, who kept looking at his friend with a frown.

"I have to be at the fort in a half hour," Yasen said as he stood and grabbed the bottle of pain pills, shook two out, and swallowed them. "It's up to you if you want to let him try out this afternoon." He flicked his gaze to Vikram for a brief second before studying the still-prostrate form of Aarav. "If he's in any state to do so."

He then turned to Zarya and gave her a quick bow. "Thank you for breakfast. I apologize for the undignified state in which you found me."

Yasen left the room without another word, his back straight and his shoulders stiff.

Zarya paused before putting her teacup down, jumping up, and running into the hallway.

"Yasen," she called.

He turned around, his posture still rigid.

"The scholar in the forest that you told me about? Will you take me to see him later? I want to show him the book with my mother's picture."

Yasen's eyes softened, his shoulders relaxing slightly. "Professor Dhawan? Yes, of course—I'll pick you up after dinner."

Once again, he turned and walked down the hallway.

"Where did you go?" Vikram asked when she returned to the suite.

"Yasen promised to show me something," she said, not wanting to reveal anything more right now. Vikram gave her a doubtful glance but didn't press the matter any further.

She was consumed with a growing awareness that nothing she understood about herself was true. But she was ever wary that she still didn't know whom she could trust. The fewer who knew her truths, the better.

* * *

After dinner, Zarya dressed in a simple kurta with leggings and short leather boots. She paced the haveli's front hallway, waiting on Yasen, a leather bag containing the book slung over a shoulder. Finally, Yasen knocked at the door.

"Sorry, I got held up. The swamp was behaving erratically today."

Zarya stopped pacing. "What do you mean?"

"It's becoming volatile and unpredictable. Before, it was just a slow creep, but now it's jumping. Pockets of rot are appearing in detached areas. And the demons are becoming stronger and bolder. A pack of vetalas killed three Khada soldiers this afternoon."

The lines around Yasen's mouth grew tight, and she walked over to place a hand on his arm. "I'm sorry. Were they your friends?"

He shrugged, though she sensed he was trying to make the gesture appear more casual than it was. "I trained them. But that's the life of a soldier. Friendships are always temporary when death is your constant mistress."

Zarya didn't like that answer at all. Despite his general abrasiveness, she was worried about him. She sensed there were secrets and truths he was holding tight. Things that were painful for him to examine too closely, something she understood all too well.

"Be careful when you're out there," she said. "I wish you didn't have to go."

"Now you see why I didn't want you joining them?" he asked as he held open the door and they left the haveli, entering the bustling streets of Dharati before taking a shortcut through the palace to get to the stables.

"I want to help," she said again, and he let out a resigned sigh.

As usual, dozens of vanshaj scurried about the palace, laden with bedsheets and towels, trays full of food, pitchers of wine and water, along with whatever item someone had demanded from the other side of the sprawling compound.

Zarya watched Yasen eyeing a woman as she passed, her head bent low and her eyes on her feet. She saw the way his fist tightened and remembered how impassioned he'd been when he'd spoken of the uprisings in the northern part of the continent. While she'd first assumed he was unaffected by their presence, it was now obvious it bothered him as much as it did her.

"This is what I signed up for when I joined the queen's ranks," he said as they continued, picking up on their earlier conversation. "Kind of."

"What do you mean 'kind of'?"

"I always knew I'd join the army. But I dreamed of traveling throughout Rahajhan, fighting battles for Daragaab across the continent. Or maybe as a mercenary with no one and nothing to answer to. I've always wanted to see more than just this place."

They found the palace stables and selected a pair of horses.

"You don't like it here?"

"After a hundred years of conquest, Daragaab's borders have been secure for decades. Rani Vasvi is impervious to magic, and our military is renowned, so our enemies are few. For a soldier, it can become tedious.

"I've considered going to Gi'ana or even Andhera to join their ranks. The nexus of three regions, plus the Saaya in between, ensures things are never really settled.

"What's the Saaya?"

"It's unceded territory both regions have been fighting over for centuries."

"Why?"

"Just a few hundred untapped diamond mines."

Zarya whistled at that. "I guess I can see why no one wants to let go."

The corner of Yasen's mouth ticked up. "But I can't abandon Vikram," he added.

"He doesn't want to leave?"

Yasen shook his head. "His father would never allow it. The Ravanas are essentially royalty, and Vikram has duties he must fulfill."

Something in Yasen's voice told Zarya *this* was at the heart of their argument, but she didn't want to pry. While he was being amicable, she didn't want to risk getting on his bad side again, so she let the matter drop for now. It was none of her business.

"At least the blight has kept things interesting."

She gave him an incredulous stare.

"What? I realize it's unfortunate those soldiers were eaten today, but at least it was a little excitement."

"Honestly," she said, muttering under her breath as Yasen laughed.

"If you can't keep a sense of humor, then you risk losing yourself to despair."

Zarya gave him a side-eyed glance and said in a dry tone, "Oh, sure. 'Funny' is the first thing I'd write on a list of qualities describing Lieutenant Yasen Varghese."

His answer was a snort, and she couldn't help but mimic his smile. He didn't do it often enough.

They rode through the city, exiting through the northern gate. Since the kala-hamsa attack, travel outside the walls before nightfall was still permitted out of necessity for those residing in the northern forests and smaller towns throughout the kingdom. The army had already been discussing if they'd eventually need to evacuate the entire region into Dharati. Of course, this presented the challenge of where all those extra people were to go. The city was already overflowing with swamp refugees who had been forced to flee their homes in the south.

After riding for a short while, Yasen and Zarya arrived at a cozy little house tucked into a copse of bushes. Warm light shone through the windows and a gentle curl of smoke reached into the sky from the squat chimney.

They hopped down from their mounts, tying them to a nearby tree.

A short man wearing dark blue robes stood before a large garden adjacent to the cottage. He didn't seem to notice their approach as he dug into a small pouch hanging from his belt, pulling out a handful of yellow powder. He proceeded to scatter it in a neat line, forming a square around a patch of withered roots. He then stared intently at the ground. A moment later, the lines of yellow powder ignited, flames erupting in a perfect square. Bright green shoots burst open, revealing a bouquet of glossy orange, red, and yellow flowers.

"Oh!" Zarya said, causing the man to look over. He stared, speechless, for a moment, his skin turning ashen as his eyes went wide.

"Aishayadiva," he said, his voice barely above a whisper. "In all the living world, I never thought—" His hand went to his throat, gazing at her with equal parts terror and amazement.

Zarya and Yasen exchanged an uncertain glance.

"Professor Dhawan. Please meet Zarya," Yasen said. "She came to Dharati for the first time a few weeks ago. Before that, she lived on the southern shore with Row."

She gave Yasen a sharp look, wondering why he was telling him this, but Yasen shrugged. Professor Dhawan started at the sound of Yasen's voice, his face regaining some of its color before he peered again at Zarya.

"With Row? That is most curious."

Not in the mood for another discussion about Row, Zarya gestured to the garden. "What did you do there? With the powder?"

Dhawan smiled and gave a jiggle to the bag hanging from his belt. "Aga phula. Native to Bhaavana, but I've always had a soft spot for them."

He plucked one of the blooms, tipped it upside down, and gave it a shake, releasing a puff of yellow dust. "They only bloom like this in the presence of fire, and their pollen is particularly useful for creating controlled lines of flame. It helps farmers clear away dead brush for their crops."

Still watching Zarya with a mix of wonder and trepidation, he shuffled towards the cottage. "I was about to have supper, and since you've already interrupted me, you might as well come in."

He swung open the low wooden door and ducked inside. Yasen had to bend practically in half to enter, but the cottage's ceiling was tall enough to accommodate him, though just barely.

"Sit," Dhawan said, pointing to the rough wooden table at the center of the room. His tone brooked no arguments, so both Yasen and Zarya slid into a seat without comment.

In the corner was a small, unmade bed. In another was a worktable covered in an assortment of books, vials, and beakers filled with colored liquids, along with a collection of measuring scales.

"Have you eaten?" Dhawan asked, heading for a small kitchen in the opposite corner. Without waiting for an answer, he began spooning a thick yellow stew with lentils, peas, and potatoes into large wooden bowls. He plunked them down in front of Zarya and Yasen.

"Eat." He picked up his spoon and took a slurpy gulp. Yasen eyed his bowl but didn't move to pick up his spoon. Not wanting to be rude, Zarya took a small bite and made a sound of appreciation. Dhawan looked up from his bowl and narrowed his eyes with suspicion.

"What brought you to Daragaab, Professor?" Zarya asked, trying to make conversation since Yasen was doing his very best impression of a rock. "Yasen said you're from Gi'ana?"

"After many years of serving the royal family, I came here to retire," Dhawan answered. "I like the solitude of the forests. However, I've also been aiding the Chiranjivi in suppressing the blight, so it seems I was never truly meant for peace."

"Are you Aazheri?"

Dhawan barked out a laugh, settling back in his seat.

"Well, I'm certainly not a rakshasa with this face and this body." He patted his rounded belly and gestured to Yasen. Zarya choked on a laugh, and Yasen couldn't seem to decide if he should be offended.

"What's so funny?" Dhawan asked, but his eyes gleamed with mischief. "Yes, I am Aazheri." Dhawan took another loud gulp of his stew before licking his lips, humming in satisfaction.

"Eat," he said again, eyeing her. Zarya swallowed another tentative bite while Yasen continued to ignore his bowl.

"Do you know Row?" she asked.

He nodded. "I know Row, of course. You've met the others in his little band?"

Zarya nodded, and Dhawan grinned, leaning forward with his forearms braced against the table. "What do you think of the charming Suvanna?"

She let out an involuntary shudder.

"Merdeva." Dhawan snickered. "Beautiful but wicked crea-tures. Useless magic—water. Bah." He waved a hand as if batting away a fly, and Zarya couldn't imagine what might happen if he ever said that within earshot of the cold and hard warrior. She'd probably turn him into a barnacle.

"How long have you known Row?" she asked, wondering if she might be able to learn something useful from Dhawan.

"Forever. He's as old as dust. They all are. Not as old as me, mind you."

He barked out a laugh again and began digging into his stew, chuckling to himself as if he'd just told an extremely clever joke.

She had a thousand questions for Dhawan. About Row and about the fact he'd just called her Aishayadiva. The same name she'd read in the book under her mother's picture. Zarya was now certain beyond a doubt that woman was her mother.

They ate for a few minutes. At least, Dhawan ate while Yasen and Zarya exchanged increasingly awkward glances in the thickening silence.

"Now, what brings you into the forest?" the professor finally asked. "It wasn't to ask about Row. You could have asked pretty boy, here."

Zarya snorted as Yasen sat up straighter, definitely offended now. She might develop a fondness for this cantankerous man. Anyone who could put Yasen in his place deserved some respect.

"I was wondering if you could read a book for me? It's in a language I don't know."

"Strange question for a girl from the swamps to be asking."

Zarya swallowed, conceding his point, but she ignored the question, instead saying, "Yasen said you also used to be a professor."

He regarded her intently, his bushy dark eyebrows knitting together. Zarya was sure he could sense she was hiding something, but he let the matter slide.

"Let me have a look, then," he said, holding out his hand.

Zarya opened her bag and pulled out the book. He held it out in front of him, tipping it this way and that, scrutinizing the cover.

"A professor I used to be, but there are thousands of languages and dialects across this continent," he said, flipping it open and thumbing through the pages. "This appears to be written in Tangsa, an old language that fell out of favor centuries ago. It was once widely used in Andhera and Gi'ana before the Hanera Wars."

"So you can read it?" Zarya asked eagerly.

The Aazheri shook his head. "Alas, not even I am fluent in them all."

Her heart sank. Of course, it had been foolish to hope. She'd have to find another way to learn what Row had been hiding.

"How long did you say you lived with Row?" Dhawan glanced at Zarya, the question casual if a little probing. Since Yasen had already told him where she'd come from, she reasoned there was little point in lying about it now.

"My whole life."

"Here? In Daragaab?"

"Yes. Why do you ask?"

The professor lifted his shoulders. "Idle curiosity, my dear. It's peculiar he kept you hidden. Do you know why?"

She shook her head.

"Did you never wonder?"

Her anger swelled, hot tears threatening to fall. She wiped them away roughly. "Of *course*, I wondered." It had occupied her every waking thought.

He patted her hand, his expression now soft and his eyes kind.

"I'm sure he had his reasons, hmm? Don't give in to rage. You're much too young for that."

She blinked hard, willing her tears not to fall.

"We should go—we're sorry to have bothered you," she said, suddenly needing to be out of this stifling room.

Dhawan's eyes held an apology as he leaned away. "Come back and visit me."

Zarya stuffed her book in her bag and nodded. "Sure."

"You." He pointed a finger at Yasen. "Look out for her."

Yasen glanced over at Zarya, his expression unreadable, before looking back at Dhawan and placing a fist on his heart. "With my life."

After Dhawan had closed the door behind them, Zarya gaped at Yasen.

"What?" Yasen scowled. "Don't look at me like that. And don't get any notions that I like you. I *tolerate* you."

Yasen mounted his horse, looking down his nose at her. She smirked and hopped onto her own, and they turned towards Dharati.

Zarya said nothing as they rode, lost in her thoughts.

"Are you okay, Zee?"

"I'm not sure." She paused and looked up at the sky. "Yasen, do you think someone can assume one thing their entire life only to discover everything they understood was a lie? Do you think it's possible to change the course of your life?"

Yasen's face was earnest, and he gave her a crooked grin. "Yes, I believe that. I think that is very possible."

"Also, did you just call me Zee? No more Swamp Girl?"

He lifted a shoulder. "I was trying it out."

She laughed then and flicked her reins with a smirk. "I knew you liked me."

As her horse leaped forward, she heard Yasen's soft chuckle.

TWENTY

The next night Zarya waited in the training yards with a line of other hopeful Khada recruits. Aarav stood further down with a determined set to his jaw. He had managed to peel himself off the furniture yesterday and complete the obstacle course to the satisfaction of General Amjal, earning himself a place back in the fold. Zarya decided that if Aarav could complete that thing as hungover as he'd been, then he *definitely* deserved this second chance.

They were all dressed in the light leather armor the Khada wore during their night patrols, giving them a layer of protection against the teeth and the claws of the demons they might encounter. Yasen had tried one more time to talk her out of doing this, but she was resolute in her desire to do her part to protect Dharati. The blight had been a presence in her life for as long as she could remember, and she had more reason than most to mistrust it.

To counter that, Yasen had suited up to join, too. She couldn't help but feel touched that he was worried about her, while also annoyed that he thought she couldn't handle herself. Why did he even care?

General Amjal was calling out instructions while Vikram looked on, his hand clasped around the hilt of his talwar. She hadn't seen him since he'd left her room yesterday morning, but she hadn't stopped thinking about the feel of his mouth and his hands on her skin.

His gaze fell on her for a flash before he looked away. She told herself he was just trying to maintain a professional distance—she was a soldier in his army's command—surely he had an image to maintain. That was fine. She'd carry the memory with her for now.

General Amjal finished relaying tonight's instructions and ordered them to their assigned sections of the wall. The sun had set a few hours ago, and they'd be relieving the shift currently on watch.

Zarya found herself in a battalion with Yasen, Vikram, and Aarav. She glared at Yasen, assuming he'd orchestrated this so he could keep an eye on her, but he just gave her one of his signature dismissive shrugs.

A series of fortified garrison doors allowed the Khada to easily pass from one side of the barrier to the other. As they approached their section of the wall, Zarya noted a raucous group of people standing on the roof of an adjacent building, looking out over the swamp. They were drinking and laughing and appeared to be having a very good time.

"Who are they?" Zarya asked Yasen.

Yasen curled an upper lip in distaste.

"They take bets each night on who might die," he said. "It's become big business. You'll find them all over the city."

"Well, that's a little rude," she said. "The Khada are risking their lives to protect *them*."

"Believe me, none of us like it. When we tried to enforce a ban, a few got it in their heads to go into the swamps and poach demons to sell on the black market, but the betting put a stop to that. It's the lesser of two evils."

Zarya threw a dark look at the revelers, who paid her no attention, then followed the line of her battalion to the other side of the wall.

There they found a long stretch of open plain that ended in a line of trees, already long with shadows. Above them, Zarya could hear the chatter and whoops of the onlookers.

"Spread out!" Vikram called as the Khada and the recruits positioned themselves at equidistant points in front of the wall. Zarya and Yasen moved to their positions and faced the forest.

The sky was midnight blue, a river of stars thick overhead. It was nothing like the dream forest that occupied her waking thoughts. That forest was a soft caress of silk. The one she stood before now was a monster sharpening its teeth.

"What do we do now?" Zarya asked.

"We wait," Yasen replied, giving her a sidelong glance. "Maybe if I'd told you this was really just a lot of standing around, you would have listened to me."

She tossed him a dirty look. "No, I wouldn't have."

He sighed as though she were the source of all his troubles. She ignored him, keeping her head up and scanning the trees for movement.

Hours later, Zarya was feeling the effects of being awake all night. Her feet were starting to ache, and they had seen nothing yet. Yasen must have been thinking along the same lines because he glanced down at her with a look of concern. "You all right?"

"Fine," she said, lifting her chin and forcing herself to stand a little straighter.

"Told you it was boring," he said.

"You said it was dangerous."

He lifted his shoulders as though the difference didn't matter, and she resisted the urge to make a snide remark. She shifted on her feet, wishing she were in her comfy bed back at the haveli and wondering if Yasen had been right after all. She had definitely been expecting a little more action than this. How much longer would they have to stay out here?

Even the carousing from the gamblers above had subdued to a hush, and she wondered if any of them were still awake. It would serve them right if they were all too exhausted to do anything tomorrow without the benefit of any entertainment to show for it.

Zarya was stretching a tense muscle in her neck when a rustle in the distant trees caught her attention, along with that unmistakable queasiness that signaled a demon's presence. She looked around, wondering if anyone else had noticed the sound. A few heads had swung towards the snap of a branch, and now she was sure she hadn't imagined it.

Pushing down a cresting wave of nausea, she pulled the sword from the sheath on her back, the zing of metal filling the quiet air. She looked to Yasen, who was also staring at the forest.

He grinned and drew his blade from his hip. "It's showtime."

Zarya scanned the horizon, watching intently for signs of movement.

Then she saw them—vetala.

Either her childhood memories had softened over time, or these things had become even more grotesque over the years. They were much taller than she remembered, their limbs too long and narrow to support their oversized heads. They walked with a stilted gait, their necks swaying from the weight, but they were also advancing at a surprising and alarming rate.

Some said they were reanimated corpses inhabited by vetala spirits, while others said they were born like this, mindless, aggressive, and violent. Whatever they were, their skin was an unnatural shade of bluish-black, like dead bodies that had been left unattended for too long, their mouths filled with jagged teeth, perfect for feasting on the flesh of their victims.

"What do we do?" Zarya asked as Yasen took a step forward.

The guard was advancing, and she stepped up, keeping herself in the line and trying to ignore the nausea currently swelling up her throat.

"We stick 'em full of holes," Yasen said, and tossed her a wry grin. "They're especially vulnerable right under the rib cage. Stab and then—" He jerked his sword up in a slicing motion. "Cutting their heads off is pretty effective, too."

Zarya nodded, licking her dry lips, nervousness settling into her limbs. She had faced plenty of the blight's demons, but there was a wildness in the air that set the hairs on her neck standing up. She remembered what Yasen had said about them growing bolder and more feral.

She could hear the vetalas now, beyond the rustling shuffle of their uneven gait. They made low guttural sounds like they were trying to send a message. If she listened closely, she thought she could make out a word or two, but when she tried to focus, they slipped away into garbled strings of nothing.

"Charge!" came Vikram's cry from further down the wall, and then, as one, the Khada and the recruits stirred into action. Zarya ran for the forest, heading towards a group of vetalas who lumbered past the tree line. Remembering Yasen's advice, she launched herself at the first one she reached and, with a roar and an almighty heave, gutted it through the torso before slashing upward as it collapsed at her feet.

But she was surrounded on all sides. The vetalas' mouths were open, making those strange sounds looping through her thoughts like she was dangling off the edge of a message. She shook her head to clear them away, steadied her stance, and raised her sword. She swung, heaved, and gutted until a pile of vetalas surrounded her in a grotesque wreath of dead limbs.

Yasen was nearby, dealing with his own group of demons, smears of black blood splashed across his cheek and hair.

Zarya's own armor was splattered with dark blood, the smell making her gag. Taking a deep breath and focusing her mind, she regrouped and jumped in to help cut down the remaining demons.

The vetalas weren't particularly difficult to kill, but what they lacked in brains, they made up for in numbers. There were *so many* of them. It seemed to take hours for the sky to lighten, signaling an end to the demons' strength. Now only a few vetalas were left staggering at the edge of the forest.

Zarya and Yasen stood back-to-back, breathing heavily as they watched for any stragglers. Zarya's earlier queasiness seemed to be abating now that the sun was rising.

Another vetala then materialized through the trees, but its appearance was slightly altered. Its limbs were more proportional to its body, and it didn't look quite so... dead. A flicker of premonition suggested this was a very bad sign.

Zarya gritted her teeth and lifted her sword just as it growled and then charged. It was definitely faster, too, and as she lunged for it, the vetala ducked, evading her blade with a troubling agility compared to its more awkward cousins.

Yasen came at it from behind, tackling it to the ground and rolling off right as Zarya snuffed it out with a precise stab between the shoulder blades.

She jerked the sword up through its body, feeling the snap and crunch of bones and cartilage. Back on his feet, Yasen made the final blow with a swift slice to its neck.

She was still breathing heavily when she registered the sounds of cheers and whoops coming from the gamblers, who were now alert once again. They had finally gotten the show they had all come for.

Covered in sweat and demon blood, she shot them a dark glare, furious that they were behaving like this was all some kind of game. Yasen was staring at them with a similar look on his face, and she wondered how many times he'd nearly died out here, only to have to listen to their carousing. It was an insult to everyone doing their best to protect Dharati.

But morning had arrived, and Zarya scanned the trees one more time, relieved to find the blighted forest was finally empty.

"Khada!" Vikram called out. "Fall back!"

There was a collective sigh of relief as the soldiers made their way to the wall. Some were limping, nursing injuries, and Zarya saw two men carrying a woman, her eyes closed and her arms hanging limply at her sides.

Zarya hoped she was just knocked out, but the gash across her chest was a grim sign.

They filed back into the city through the garrison door, while above, the gamblers were calling down to them, some with words of encouragement and some with suggestions of how they might improve their form next time. It took all her willpower not to shout at them to fuck off.

Suddenly, there was a scream, and the garrison door thudded shut. Everyone spun around at the sound of a second ear-piercing shriek from the other side, followed by a shudder of something hard and heavy, like a body, being thrown against it.

"What's going on?" Yasen shouted.

Several of the Khada were attempting to pry open the exit, but it was jammed.

"More vetalas!" Vikram shouted.

"They're stuck outside! The door won't open!" another soldier shouted. More vetala shrieks carried over the wall. They must have snuck up on the last of the Khada, somehow barring the door and preventing anyone from coming back out to help.

"Send word to the next battalion," Yasen shouted, pointing at one of the recruits. "Go. Run. Tell them to come through on the other side, now!"

The man was already sprinting away like his life depended on it.

"Who's still out there?" Yasen called to Vikram, and Zarya scanned the crowd, missing a familiar face.

"Aarav," she whispered. "Aarav!" she shouted louder, hoping she'd just overlooked him, but he didn't answer. Another hard bump against the door made the entire wall shudder.

"Aarav!" she shouted, spinning around, spotting the gamblers who were peering over the edge of the building. She was running before she knew what she was doing, taking the stairs two at a time until she reached the rooftop, bursting through the door.

Yasen was close on her heels as they shouldered their way through the tightly packed crowd. Zarya gasped as she leaned over the railing.

Aarav was surrounded by three vetalas—but they weren't the mindless beasts from their earlier fight. Those had all either fled or perished in the sunlight.

These were similar to the last one Zarya and Yasen had killed, the one that had seemed more whole and solid. And apparently, they were impervious to sunlight because they were currently dueling it out with Aarav and another member of the Khada.

A third soldier—Zarya recognized him as one of the recruits —lay dead on the ground, his skin already turning ashen.

"Aarav!" she shouted, but he couldn't hear her over the noise of the gamblers, and she didn't know what she would do to help, even if she could. She grabbed Yasen's arm and squeezed it, screaming when a vetala lunged for Aarav.

"Careful," Yasen said dryly. "One might think you cared if he lived or died."

She glared at him and turned back to watch Aarav fighting off the vetala, its sharp teeth bared as it snapped for his throat.

Aarav ducked and swung his sword to meet the demon's next impossibly fast move. He was battling with expert skill, but it wasn't enough. They were being overpowered.

The vetala's teeth flashed before it grabbed the soldier's sword, impervious to the sharp blade as it yanked it from her hand and tossed it to the ground before turning back with a monstrous grin.

From her vantage point, Zarya could see more members of the Khada scrambling to open the garrison door, but it was built to withstand an assault, and something was still blocking it, though Zarya couldn't see what it was.

A loud crack forced everyone into horrified silence. The soldier was stumbling backward, clutching her chest, blood pouring out of a gaping hole. The woman's heart now dripped from the vetala's long fingers. It rolled its neck and pounced before it began feasting as the sounds of tearing flesh and the woman's last sobs filled the air.

Zarya covered her mouth and looked away, but a movement caught her eye. While the demon was distracted, Aarav had maneuvered behind it and plunged his sword through the vetala's back before swiftly beheading it and then scooping up the dead soldier's dropped talwar. He did it all within the space of a second before the remaining two vetalas were on him again.

He became a whirl of motion as he fought with both blades flashing in the brightening sunlight. She'd never seen him move like that before. Was this what he'd been doing with all his hours in the city? Training and practicing? No wonder he'd wanted to join the Khada so much. He'd always been a decent fighter, but this was something else.

The crowd was out of control now, screaming their support. Vikram and the others had acquired a battering ram and were busy trying to break down the door.

Zarya scanned the far side of the wall, wondering why none of the other battalions had arrived yet. How far away were they? Had they been similarly ambushed?

Aarav ducked and speared his sword into the gut of a vetala, its black blood spilling out onto the ground. The other demon lunged for him, and Aarav hopped back, narrowly avoiding its claws. He spun around and drove his sword right through the creature's throat before bringing it crashing to his feet in a shapeless mound of limbs.

Aarav stood with his head down and his arms hanging at his sides as he stared at the slain demons, his body heaving with the effort of his breaths.

"Oh, thank the gods," Zarya said, pressing her forehead to the stone railing as she waited for the race of her pulse to settle. The crowd on the rooftop was roaring so loudly the entire building was vibrating as money exchanged hands and the winners gloated over the losers.

A great boom from below signaled the garrison door finally giving way right before Vikram and the rest of the Khada spilled through the opening. They surrounded Aarav, slapping him on the back and shaking his hand. He grinned, the weariness in his body seemingly chased away by their admiration.

"That was far too close for comfort," she said to Yasen, who was leaning with his elbows on the railing and his hands clasped next to her.

"At least it was an opportunity to prove himself."

She wanted to go down there and scream at Aarav for scaring her like that. As much as they didn't get along and she joked about killing him, she didn't *really* want him to die.

Another figure emerged through the garrison door. It was General Amjal, and the Khada parted to make way as he strode towards Aarav. The general stopped, regarding Aarav for a moment.

His face split into a grin and he slapped him on the back. Aarav smiled back, beaten and weary, but Zarya didn't think she'd ever seen him stand so tall.

There was no doubt in her mind that Aarav had just been promoted to a full-fledged Khada. She exchanged a look with Yasen.

"Maybe you were right. This is too dangerous for both of us."

Yasen scoffed and shook his head. "You aren't going to be able to stop him anymore. He has that look in his eye. One of a man redeemed. Who has finally discovered his purpose, Zee. He won't stop until he's dead."

TWENTY-ONE

"Commander!" A soldier was making his way towards Vikram on the ground below, his face stern. Zarya and Yasen watched as they exchanged words, while Vikram's brows inched up with alarm.

It was then Zarya noticed the smell in the air as a gentle fall of grey flakes drifted down from the sky. Yasen wiped a speck off his shoulder, and his gaze met Vikram's.

"Fire," Yasen said, his pallor turning ashen before he spun on his heel and shoved his way back through the boisterous crowd.

She took off after Yasen, clamoring down the stairs, emerging to alarms blaring through the streets. A cloud of smoke hung over the palace, choking the air.

Zarya and Yasen dodged a mass of panicking crowds. Some were screaming and crying, and many were moving without any clear sense of purpose. Magic couldn't harm Rani Vasvi, but even she wasn't immune to fire, and they all understood what this might mean for their queen.

Zarya was exhausted from her already long night, but she pumped her arms and legs, rounding a corner right on Yasen's heels as they finally came into view of the palace. She almost lost her footing at the sight that greeted them.

The blue courtyard gates stood wide open, revealing the Jai Tree consumed by flames. The inferno was clawing its way up through the branches like a disease. It would take only minutes for every last flower, leaf, and twig to ignite.

Zarya and Yasen entered the courtyard, covering their mouths with their sleeves against the thickening smoke.

Vikram was already standing in the center, shouting orders to the palace guards, calling for water to be carried up from the sea. Clearly, they'd been drilled in the case of such a catastrophe because they were already forming a chain that wound through the palace, ready to shunt buckets of water between their outstretched hands.

"Someone find Suvanna!" Yasen yelled, and pointed at a palace guard. "Tell her to come immediately."

Good. That was good. Surely, with her magic, there was something she could do to help the queen. Zarya thought of Rani Vasvi trapped inside. That gentle being entwined with the wood that had now become her blazing coffin. Unable to move, unable to speak. Unable to save herself from one of the only things able to consume her.

The brigade was now moving at a full clip as buckets of water were dumped at the base of the trunk, but it was like a single drop falling into the sea. The blaze had grown too intense. They needed something more.

Kindle, Apsara, and Suvanna came pounding through the castle gates, stopping in the center of the courtyard, each momentarily paralyzed by the sight before them.

Apsara flung a blast of air at the highest branches, her magic whipping through them, pulling the flames like clothes blowing on the line. But her magic only fanned the flames, and the fire leaped higher, catching more branches.

Zarya heard Apsara swear under her breath as she changed

course. Next, she blasted out a sheet of ice that slammed into the trunk and formed a thick column, wrapping around the circumference.

For a moment, the wall of ice smothered the worst of the flames. Sweat beaded on Apsara's brow, her face tight with concentration as she fed more and more magic into the ice, trying to counter the radiating heat.

The roar of the blaze dimmed, and for a moment, it looked like it might work, but the ice grew shiny as drips started to run down the surface. The entire thing came crashing down, collapsing under its own weight, sloughing to the ground, while the fire continued burning on like nothing had touched it at all.

At the same time, Kindle was trying to take control with his magic, directing the heat away. His expression was masked with frustration as the blaze also resisted his efforts.

"I don't understand," he shouted. "This fire is completely out of control. What started this?"

No one answered him, either because they were too stunned to speak or, more likely because no one had any idea what had set this off.

Zarya's attention turned to Suvanna, who stood completely still in the center of the courtyard. She was an anchor amidst the chaos, and at first, Zarya wondered why she wasn't doing anything, but then she realized the merdeva was so deeply rooted in concentration she had slipped into a trance.

Her head was down, and her eyes were closed, her arms stretched out at her sides. A trickle of sweat ran down her pale temple as her blue-green hair sparked and swirled around her. She was stunning and fearsome, like a queen surrounded by destruction and chaos. Zarya couldn't take her eyes off her.

Apsara came to stand next to Zarya, her arms folded and the lines around her eyes tight with worry as she watched Suvanna.

"What is she doing?" Zarya asked her.

"There isn't a large enough source of water in the courtyard. She's trying to draw more into the air from the Nila Hara, but without being directly adjacent to it, she needs to concentrate. It's very complicated magic."

Zarya looked up to the sky, where the water had begun to coalesce. One by one, tiny drops were soaring over the palace and joining together to form larger drops.

The suspended balls of water drifted slowly, drawing together in slow motion, bumping into one another and pooling together. It was like watching a lake being built from nothing.

Suvanna stood rooted to the spot, her hair a floating, swirling mass of blue and green. As her body trembled, the pool in the sky expanded. It ebbed and flowed, twisting and turning in the atmosphere as it grew.

While Suvanna worked her powerful magic, the brigade continued their dogged efforts, the fire crackling and flaring as it burned brighter and hotter. The entire tree was in flames now, the leaves and petals curling into black husks of ash. Soot rained from the sky, coating everything in a layer of death and decay.

Suvanna moved her lips, chanting a prayer or a spell or just a string of words to anchor herself. With her eyes still closed, she shook harder, sweat running down her forehead as her hair grew even wilder.

"Is she okay?" Zarya asked, worried by how much the merdeva was trembling. Apsara nodded, glancing up at the jittery pool of water dancing overhead. It seemed to breathe as if it were alive, pulsing with a heartbeat and breath.

"We'll need to get everyone out of here," Apsara said. "The water is going to come down. Move! Out of the courtyard!"

People slowly registered her shouts, though many remained fixated on the sight above them.

"Now! Everyone!"

They began evacuating, but it was clear they were reluctant to abandon their queen. Apsara kept yelling at everyone to move, her orders becoming louder and more demanding.

Suvanna had finally stopped trembling, her body now utterly still like she'd been worn into sea glass. A roar ran through the courtyard as the fire leaped higher. The pool of water had also calmed, its surface rippling gently. It seemed as large as the Nila Hara itself, hovering over their heads like a cloud.

And then Suvanna's eyes snapped open as silence fell and every head in the courtyard turned to stare. She was terrifying and mesmerizing—like a star drawing them all in.

"Run!" Apsara shouted, stirring everyone back into action. "Keep going! Everyone get out of here!"

Apsara grabbed Zarya's arm and tugged her towards the courtyard gates. Zarya, still unable to take her eyes off Suvanna, let herself be hauled away.

Where the atmosphere had been one of simple panic a moment ago, now it had turned into a tide of terror. Suvanna was slowly raising her arms with her head tipped skyward. Beads of water continued to jump from the ocean, feeding the hovering mass above.

There was a hush of paused breath.

A dimming of the senses, like everything had been coated in fog.

A calm before a storm.

And then Suvanna snapped her arms down, and the world exploded.

The pool in the sky burst apart, a thundering stream of water drenching the Jai Tree.

It cascaded through the branches and down the trunk, its waves spreading through the courtyard, knocking everyone still within its walls off their path. Zarya was hurled off her feet by a cresting wave. Its force dragged her along the stones, the hard surface biting into her thin leather armor, until she crashed into something hard and unyielding that sliced into her side.

Trying to keep her head above the water, Zarya sputtered and coughed as she was pressed into whatever blocked her path, stone digging into her ribs. Another wave crashed towards her, knocking her sideways, the stone tearing through leather and skin before the water tossed her into the chaos.

Zarya clawed at the surface, trying to keep afloat, only to see she was being dragged towards a low section of the partially repaired palace wall. Beyond it lay the chasm that had split the street apart a few weeks earlier.

Her heart thudded in her ears as she careened towards the opening, fighting against the wave, paddling towards a higher section of the wall. But she was too far away. She was being dragged too quickly.

Making a split-second decision, she sunk into the water, waiting for her feet to brush the bricks below. With every ounce of strength she could summon, she launched herself off the ground and streaked diagonally through the water, hoping she was on the right course. She uttered a silent prayer of thanks that all those hours she'd spent in the ocean at the cottage had made her a strong swimmer.

The distance felt endless. Her lungs burned, the effort of holding her breath turning her light-headed. Unable to hold it any longer, she swam up, emerging just past the point she'd been aiming for. The force of the water slammed her into the partially repaired wall.

The stones offered little in the way of handholds, but she gripped them with her fingertips, the waves intent on dragging her towards the chasm. A man swept past her, his arms flailing and his head bobbing as he wrestled against the current, but it was too strong.

She was too far away to reach for him, and she saw the moment he realized it was no use. That his end had come. Their eyes met, and all she could do was fight down a sob as he tumbled over the edge and disappeared from her view.

"No," she whispered before a scream caught her attention. A woman was barreling towards her, thrashing against the water, and it was obvious that she had no idea how to swim.

Zarya gripped the wall with one hand and lunged towards the woman. As she caught her wrist, Zarya noticed the linked black stars tattooed around her throat.

"Grab my hand!" Zarya yelled. The woman turned towards Zarya's voice, flailing harder, her movements jerky and frantic. She reached out, her nails scraping along Zarya's skin just before their fingers locked. They gripped each other as the water continued to pummel them.

Zarya felt the woman sliding out of her grasp, her grip on the wall weakening as she dug her fingertips into a line of mortar, trying to anchor herself.

"Hold on! Stop kicking!" she screamed, but the woman was delirious with fear, her hand sliding until they held on by just their fingertips.

"Hold on! You have to hold on! Stop kicking!"

"I can't!" The woman was sobbing. "I can't!"

"Don't let go! Don't let go." She gritted her teeth, trying to pull the woman in closer. But Zarya wasn't strong enough. The woman's fingers slipped out of her grasp, and the last thing Zarya saw was her face, frozen in terror, as she flipped over the edge of the chasm and disappeared into the abyss below.

Zarya clung to the wall, sobbing, as the tide finally ebbed. The water flowed out of the courtyard, gushing into the palace and out through the gate, pouring off the edge of the chasm that had just claimed the woman's life.

After what felt like a lifetime, the courtyard finally fell

silent, the deafening roar of water replaced by a heartbroken echo.

Zarya slid from the wall and collapsed to the ground in a shallow puddle.

Her tears mixed with the salt of the sea as her heart cracked in two.

TWENTY-TWO

Drip. Drip. Drip.

The sound filtered through the courtyard where Zarya lay on her stomach, shivering and soaked, water pooling around her. Her tears flowed as the cold spread through her limbs, everything numb and broken.

For all her talk about killing Aarav, she had never actually seen a person die before. The reality was a reminder of just how little she understood about the world she'd found herself in.

The woman had been right there, so close and yet unreachable.

Zarya opened and closed her hand. Her nails were torn from gripping the wall, and her hand stung where the woman's fingernails had left a row of bloody gouges. Zarya had held on as tightly as she could, but it hadn't been enough.

She could still see the woman's terror—the absolute certainty she was about to die written in every line of her face. It was a sight Zarya would never forget. She had looked about Zarya's age. So young, her life had barely begun. Zarya erupted into a fresh wave of tears.

"Zarya!" Someone called her name, but she couldn't

move, her body weighed down by what felt like a ceiling of iron. She closed her eyes, willing the voice to stop. Willing herself into quiet oblivion. She didn't want to talk to anyone right now.

But then a hand stroked her hair, and she slowly opened her eyes to find Yasen crouched in front of her, scanning her body from her head to her toes.

"Are you okay?" he asked, his voice uncharacteristically soft.

Zarya shook her head, unable to answer.

She didn't resist when Yasen's strong hands turned her over and scooped her up into his arms. It was nice to be held.

Zarya leaned her head against Yasen's shoulder. She could feel the thrum of his heartbeat, and she thanked the gods that nothing had happened to him. While they weren't exactly friends yet, he was definitely starting to grow on her.

Yasen carried her over to a stone bench and set her down carefully, leaning her against the wall.

"Are you hurt?"

"I'm fine," she said with a wince. Her head and back were aching, the cuts on her hands and fingertips throbbing lightly. But she was fine. She would be fine.

Yasen sat down and put an arm around her shoulders, pulling her close. At first, she resisted, unsure and confused, but then she realized he was trying to be comforting and she relaxed. He pulled her in, resting his chin on her forehead. She squeezed her eyes as a tear slid down her cheek before wrapping her arm around Yasen's waist. This, too, was nice.

The Jai Tree was now a charred black ruin, barely recognizable. The massive trunk was covered in soot, every groove and line plugged with thick, greasy ash. Branches pointed into the sky like skinny black arms, reaching for help that had come too late. The doors had collapsed into each other, and debris lay everywhere. It littered the courtyard in a carpet of ruin—

charred leaves and flowers, shattered buckets, and smashed stone.

"The queen," Zarya whispered as a weight pulled on her heart. She looked up at Yasen, who was staring at the tree. She wanted to know what he was thinking about.

"I need to help search for other survivors. Are you okay here for a minute?" he asked. Zarya gave him a small nod. "I'll be right back. I promise." His voice was edged with a concern that made her heart twist. He let go of her and strode across the courtyard to confer with his fellow soldiers.

In the center of the courtyard, Suvanna still kneeled on the ground, her head bowed and her hands spread on her thighs. Apsara sat next to her, running her hand up and down Suvanna's back, murmuring something into the merdeva's ear.

People lay everywhere. No, not people. Bodies.

Some washed away in the tide, some drowned, some battered to death by the awesome weight of the water. Children, men, and women. So many of them. Dozens and dozens. How many lives had been lost to save just one? Zarya thought again of the woman who'd died. She had been a servant with no freedom of her own. No one here would even care she was gone.

Zarya closed her eyes, her teeth chattering as her clothes dried and the temperature dropped. She opened them again briefly when a blanket was tossed next to her on the bench, but she ignored it. The cold reminded her of what had been lost. Reminded her that she was somehow still alive. She'd come so close to going into that chasm, too. Why had her life been spared when so many hadn't?

A moment later, she felt the blanket settle over her body, and she opened her eyes to find Kindle. Sodden but unharmed, he sat down next to her with a rip through the front of his coat and his black curls hanging limp over his forehead.

"Do you know if Vikram is okay?" Zarya asked, her throat raw from the smoke.

"He's fine. Helping with the survivors."

She let out a breath of relief, and the heaviness on her chest eased a fraction.

"Are you okay?" Kindle asked her.

Zarya didn't respond at first. It was taking all her effort to keep herself upright. In spurts, she told Kindle about the woman she had allowed to die.

"That wasn't your fault," he said, placing a hand on Zarya's knee. "You held on to her as long as you could. I'm sure it was terrifying to watch, but you are not to blame for that."

She didn't say anything for a moment, weighing Kindle's words.

"Zarya," Kindle continued. "I want you to know you can confide in me. In Row's absence, I feel a responsibility to ensure you're cared for. Row has always been a good friend."

Zarya turned to study him, reluctant to accept anyone's help. She still didn't know who any of these people really were. "I'm fine."

"Nevertheless, if you need anything, please ask."

"Thank you," she said eventually, sensing his concern was genuine.

"You didn't start the fire. You tried to save her. Most wouldn't have even done that," Kindle said.

"You aren't going to tell me I'm a fool for crying over the life of a vanshaj?"

The flecks of red and orange in Kindle's dark eyes flared for a second. "There's nothing less valuable about the life of a vanshaj. She deserved to be saved as much as anyone else."

A loud crack drew their attention towards the Jai Tree. One of its thick branches had splintered under its weight and was slowly bowing. Apsara and Suvanna jumped up from where they were still sitting in the middle of the courtyard. With her arms raised, Apsara used her magic to snap the branch from the tree before she eased it into a safer position.

Koura was circling the Jai Tree, gently laying his large hands on the bark and scrutinizing the surface, his jaw hard and his eyebrows bunched.

"What's going on?" Zarya asked Kindle, gesturing to Koura.

"No one has been able to get inside to check on Rani Vasvi," Kindle said, his voice low. "The door is blocked."

"Does it hurt her if the branches break?" Zarya asked, a horrified hand drifting to her throat. Kindle didn't respond. His lips were pressed together, and she supposed that was answer enough. She swallowed, thinking of how much pain the queen must be in right now.

"They need to get to her," she said, and Kindle nodded.

"They're trying. And not just for her sake. If she dies, there will be no enchantment protecting the city. Even if she does survive, I worry that she won't be able to hold it in this weakened state."

At that moment, half a dozen peri—the same tiny creatures they'd seen at the peri anada—streamed out from a hole at the base of the tree. Flittering around Koura's head, they bounced through the air, gesturing wildly. With the blanket wrapped tightly around her shoulders, Zarya strode towards Koura with Kindle on her heels.

"The queen is alive!" Koura declared, just as a group of soldiers entered the courtyard with axes slung over their shoulders. Koura began directing them, and the soldiers set to work. The thunk of metal hitting wood became the only sounds in the courtyard as everyone held their breath. A pained shudder ripped through the tree with each strike. Zarya imagined that if she strained hard enough, she could hear a distant scream.

Finally, the doorway shifted, and Koura shouted out a series of orders as people scurried left and right to obey. Before long, the door had been unblocked, and Koura ducked inside with his retinue of healers armed with supplies.

"Can they help her?" Zarya asked Kindle.

"I hope so. The queen's imperviousness to magic includes the healing power of Niramaya, but they will do what they can."

Zarya caught sight of Vikram and Yasen handing out blankets and checking on injuries. Guards were collecting the dead, lining them up in rows to be identified by their loved ones. Zarya's throat constricted as she thought of the woman's family who would have no body to bury. Nothing to hug one last time.

Someone thrust a steaming mug of chai into Zarya's hands, and she looked up gratefully to find Vikram.

"I'm so relieved you're okay," she said, accepting the cup and taking a sip of the hot tea.

He studied her face and asked, "What's wrong?"

She shook her head. "I'll tell you later."

Reluctantly, he nodded and turned towards the burned tree with his brows furrowing, his pale face contrasting with the dark circles under his eyes.

"I'm sure she'll be okay." She placed a hand on his arm. "I know she means a lot to you. Koura will do everything he can."

Vikram nodded, his expression grim.

The queen's steward, Tarin, had entered the courtyard with the Princess Amrita clinging to his arm, her face crumpled with worry. Zarya heard him demanding to be let inside to see the queen, his gravelly voice rolling over the courtyard stones.

Apsara blocked the entrance with her arms crossed and her expression inviting little argument. "Once Koura has examined her condition, you may go inside to see her," she said.

Tarin grunted, smacking his cane on the ground, clearly displeased with her answer. He told her he would stand here and wait. Apsara shrugged as if it made no difference to her.

"Is the princess okay?" Zarya asked. She wasn't entirely

sure what Amrita's relationship with the queen was, but it was obvious Rani Vasvi meant something to her. "I should go and speak with her. She was so kind when she helped me in the infirmary."

Vikram looked over to Amrita and then back to Zarya, rubbing his forehead.

"No. I'll go and check on her," he said. "You stay here."

Then, without another word, he turned and walked away.

Zarya found a place to sit and await news. As she sipped on her tea, her chilled blood finally started to thaw.

While the day waned, courtiers, servants, and guards milled about the courtyard, some mopping up the water while others aided the injured. Survivors left for the infirmary while others returned to their rooms and homes. Many stayed, wondering about the fate of their queen and the city she protected.

Hours passed as Vikram paced back and forth, unable to settle. Yasen approached Vikram, putting a hand on his shoulder and whispering something only Vikram could hear. Zarya was happy to see them talking again after their argument the other night.

Vikram nodded at Yasen, gripping his arm in thanks.

After several more hours, Koura finally emerged from the Jai Tree, glowing with a sheen of sweat. Everyone waited with their breaths held.

"She is alive," he said, his deep voice resonating across the courtyard. Murmurs of relief rippled through the crowd, their collective tension softening. "The damage is severe. She may not survive, but for now, she is stable."

Zarya studied the stricken faces around her. Though she had only spoken with the silent queen once, it was obvious she was loved by her people.

Vikram looked broken, his expression haggard and his hair sticking up from where he'd run his hands through it.

"You should get some rest," Zarya said, placing a hand on

Vikram's back. After being up half the night with the Khada, they were all running on pure adrenaline.

"I'll take him to his room," Yasen said. "You should lie down, too. I've arranged for you to stay in the palace tonight. You look exhausted. And kind of terrible."

He grinned at her, and she rolled her eyes. Yasen winked as he led Vikram away, and she found herself smiling at his infuriating but kind of loveable irreverence.

With the blanket still pulled tight around her, Zarya walked back to her usual room, where a warm bath awaited her. A wave of sorrow for the vanshaj rose in her chest, knowing it was the silent and subservient people who worked around the clock, ensuring everyone's comfort, who had been responsible for this.

Zarya stripped off her Khada armor, still damp all these hours later. She wiped her hands on the blanket, transferring a layer of black soot and yellowish dust before dropping it on the pile of clothing.

She stepped into the hot bath and sighed as it chased away the chill that permeated her bones. When she was done, she stepped out, still shivering, and dressed in a soft nightgown before covering it with a thick robe.

A swell of exhaustion overtook her, and she climbed onto the soft bed, her eyelids weighed down like anchors. She didn't think she'd ever been this tired before in her life. She blinked heavily, her body melting into the soft mattress.

When she opened her eyes a moment later, Zarya lay in the black and violet forest, her cheek pressing into the soft grass. Tension instantly dissolved from her tight shoulders as she inhaled the fresh scents drifting on the night air.

Footsteps crunched in the grass, and Zarya didn't need to look up to know who walked amongst the trees. His presence tugged at the corners of a secret place deep inside her spirit.

She watched his feet as he came to a stop and lay down in

the grass next to her, his gaze skyward and his hands clasped over his stomach.

They lay in silence for several minutes, and Zarya couldn't remember ever feeling so at peace. Something about this place made all the events of the day feel like a distant memory.

"What magic created this forest?" he finally asked, breaking the silence.

"I don't know," Zarya said. "I thought maybe you knew."

He turned to look at her. His eyes weren't cold, but they were acute, as if considering everything.

"Who are you?" Zarya asked.

"I'm Rabin." His eyes widened briefly, as if he were surprised he'd offered up that fact.

"I'm Zarya," she replied, feeling no need to hide it from him.

"Zarya," he repeated, and she liked the way her name sounded in his mouth, like a stroke of lightning casting the world in brilliance.

"Why does this forest feel so"—she paused, searching for the right word—"good?"

Rabin raised his dark eyebrows. "And yet, something is bothering you."

It was her turn to be surprised at his perceptiveness. She let out a long breath.

"I let a woman die today." She clenched the soft grass, the blades tickling her fingers.

"What happened?"

"There was a fire and a flood, and I was trying to hold on to her, but I wasn't strong enough. She fell, and I lost her."

"That doesn't sound like it was your fault."

"The worst part is she was vanshaj, and no one is going to care. Dozens died to save one, and they will all be forgotten."

"It sounds like you were very brave," he said, his voice like a tumble of weather-worn stones, the words fused with such certainty that some of the pressure in her chest released.

"Thank you," she said as she let out another long breath.

They lay quietly for a few minutes, the rustling leaves and whirring insects creating a gently tuned symphony. She studied his profile as he stared up at the sky. He was so achingly beautiful.

"How do we leave this place?" she asked after a few minutes.

"Do you want to leave?" He turned to look at her again.

"No. I don't." Their eyes locked, and Zarya marveled at the muted slivers of gold in his gaze, warmth blooming in her stomach.

"I'm not sure how. This is all a mystery to me," he said as though resigned to some inevitable fate.

His hand now rested in the grass, inches from Zarya's. Slowly, she stretched out her arm and curled one finger around his pinky. He blinked, pausing for a heartbeat, his stare never wavering as he folded his large hand around hers.

Zarya sighed in relief as her tired eyelids finally fluttered closed.

The last thing she remembered was the warmth of Rabin's hand, safe and calm, before she spun away into the welcoming arms of sleep.

TWENTY-THREE

The queen continued to live under Koura's constant care and attention, but she teetered precariously on the edge of life as Daragaab held its breath. Without the power of Niramaya, Koura and his helpers were pushed to the limits of their skill with little success. Only Tarin's particular vein of astomi earth magic seemed capable of rendering any sort of improvement on the beloved queen.

No one knew what had caused the fire that had rendered her nearly helpless. For now, the queen's magic was holding on, keeping the enchantment that guarded the city in place, but it felt like they were all straddling an ever-widening crack.

Zarya's shifts with the Khada had been anything but boring, the demons attacking with vigor, as if they could sense the queen's power was failing. On her nights off, she'd listen to the screeches in the distance, waiting for the alarm that signaled a breach.

She hadn't thought about leaving Dharati in a while—she'd been too distracted by the people she'd met and the life she'd been finally living, savoring every drop like they were the last ones scraped from a dry well. With the city lingering between stability and ruin, she knew she couldn't run. She was only one person, but every pair of hands was one more chance against the blight.

It had been almost a week since the fire, and Zarya lay on the divan in the haveli's living room, staring out a window that overlooked the sea. Lost in her thoughts, she also couldn't get her last encounter in the dream forest with Rabin out of her head.

Who was he? While she'd learned his name, she knew nothing else about him. Why did they keep meeting there? Did he truly not understand it, either, or was he lying to her? Something in her gut told her he was being honest, but even with her limited experience, she knew not to trust the words of a strange man who kept appearing in her dreams. No matter how beautiful he was or how he caused that liquid flutter in the pit of her stomach.

She could still feel the warmth of his skin against hers, his rough fingers caressing her hand, and yet, she wondered if he was real or some phantom conjured from the hallows of her overactive imagination.

What if she'd created him out of her sense of loneliness? What if the entire thing was simply a product of her eroding sanity? Sure, she'd escaped Row's prison, but that didn't mean she didn't have a lifetime of trauma to overcome. And she'd always been very good at spinning fantasies in her head.

She still hadn't had the time or space to fully process the effects of a life lived chained to a proverbial yoke, but it would be foolish to think that the concealed shadows of her past wouldn't come out to haunt her someday.

Eventually, she'd have to face down those demons, but right now, she needed answers. About where Row had gone and what he'd been hiding. Focusing on this goal settled the voices in her head that told her she was a broken woman held together by fraying threads who would somehow need to be put back together.

She rubbed her chest. Ever since the fire, it had felt like a band was squeezing her ribs, making it increasingly harder to catch her breath. A tight cluster sat behind her heart, wrenching tighter and tighter. Her temple pulsed, and her legs and arms ached as if she'd just endured a strenuous bout of training. She blamed her nights on the wall, but the soreness seemed more persistent than usual.

Maybe she'd inhaled more smoke than she realized, or maybe she just needed more sleep. She considered asking the palace healers, but they were still run off their feet, healing those who'd sustained far worse injuries, and she didn't want to add to their burden.

She grunted at a stab of pain as her ribs contracted again.

Pushing herself up from the divan, she decided she'd head over to the infirmary at least. If they were experiencing a rare lull in their duties, she'd ask someone to examine her.

Wandering across the road, she skirted past the rift, again thinking of the woman who had fallen. The masons were back at work now, rebuilding the wall as quickly as possible to prevent more fatalities. Though Zarya reasoned, a lot of the damage had already been done.

The palace was quiet as she entered. Since the fire, the entire city had dimmed to a hush, as if everyone was afraid of upsetting its tenuous balance.

A chorus of raised voices drew Zarya's attention. She recognized Kindle's soft timbre, his rolling r's, and that tempered cadence, distinguishable from the others. Then she heard Suvanna's sharp tone, and she drifted closer, curious to hear what they were arguing about. Because it was obvious, they were angry about something.

She tiptoed to the edge of the doorway and inched forward until she could see all the members of the Chiranjivi standing at the far end of a small library. They were facing one another, backdropped by a large window. Even Koura had taken a break from the queen's bedside. Zarya also noticed Professor Dhawan seated in a plush armchair, his dark eyes surveying everyone, concern pleating his brow.

"We must *do something*," Suvanna said with a hiss, smacking her chest with her palm. "This place is devouring us. More and more people keep dying. A queen is almost dead. Hundreds of lives have been lost. This can't go on any longer. It is the darkness. You can't deny this anymore."

"It is not the darkness," Koura said through clenched teeth, like he'd said it a thousand times already. *The darkness.* Those words sent a chill racing down Zarya's spine. "This is powerful magic, but the darkness cannot be awakened. It has been a thousand years, Suvanna. It was banished. *Forever*." Koura gestured to Dhawan. "Tell her."

"He is right," the professor said. "If there were anything to touch, then I would feel it. The wall is still firmly in place."

"Then what is it?" Suvanna asked. "Tell me. You know what those demons did the other night to the Khada. They survived the sun. They *barred* the door. They *knew* what they were doing. These *things* are not mindless savages anymore." Suvanna faced Koura with her arms folded, not at all intimidated by him, despite the fact she barely came up to his chest.

Koura ran a hand down his face and breathed a weary sigh. He glanced at Kindle, who sat on the window ledge with his elbows braced on his thighs and his hands clasped.

"I don't know," Koura admitted.

"We are trying, Suvanna," Kindle added. "We have left no stone unturned. We have tried everything. Read every book in Rahajhan. Tried every spell. Nothing seems to *touch* that damned blight and whatever lives in it."

"We have *not*." Suvanna stamped her foot and pointed to the ground, glaring at each of them in turn. "If you would all just admit what is in front of you, there would be other options."

Apsara was leaning next to the window, her arms folded with one leg propped against the wall. She dropped her stance and approached Suvanna, laying a gentle hand on her arm. "No. You are giving in to your fear, my friend," she said. "This is not our way."

Suvanna shook off Apsara's touch with a snarl, and Zarya saw the hurt that flashed across Apsara's expression.

"If it is the darkness," Dhawan said, picking up their conversation, "then stopping the blight will be the least of our troubles. A world where dark magic flourished was nothing but devastation and ruin.

"The books tell only half the story of those black days. It would mean the end of everything we love. Everything that matters to us. When the Ashvins' demon armies marched across the land, nothing was spared. Entire nations were razed to the ground and left in piles of smoke and ashes. Suvanna, this is not a thing to hope for."

Suvanna huffed an angry breath. "I'm not *hoping* for it." Her voice rose as she spread her arms wide. "I am hoping you fools will see sense before it is too late. Before this becomes too powerful for all of us to take on, even together."

"Who?" Apsara asked then. Her smooth white hair shimmered in the light that filtered through the window where she'd once again taken up her post. "Suvanna, if you really believe this, then who? Who awoke the darkness after all these years? Who would have the means? No one alive in Rahajhan is that powerful."

Zarya noted how everyone else's eyes tried not to meet as if avoiding something none of them wanted to say out loud.

But Suvanna held no such compunctions.

"Don't pretend you don't know it is Row's *king*."

Suvanna spat the word "king" from her mouth like a bitter curse as Zarya caught her breath.

Who was Row's king?

Suvanna continued, flinging a pointed finger at the window that faced north. "It is Raja Abishek. It is Andhera's cursed Aazheri and their eternally tainted magic. They did this before, and, given enough time and freedom, they will do it again. The sixth anchor existed once. Don't fool yourselves into thinking it has been lost to time."

Zarya watched the fury building in Kindle as his jaw hardened and his stance stiffened before he approached, stopping inches in front of Suvanna. Zarya was sure they were about to come to blows. Who knew what kind of damage these five could do if they allowed their power to run loose?

"How dare you?" Kindle said, his voice low and dangerous. "How dare you accuse a man of something like this when he isn't here to defend himself? Row is one of us."

Suvanna scoffed and tipped her head. "And where is he? Isn't it convenient things seem to be getting worse just as he disappears? What is he doing, Kindle? Why did he up and leave in the middle of everything?"

Apsara and Koura both fidgeted where they stood, each of them rolling their shoulders and tugging on their clothing as they still avoided one another's gazes. Clearly, similar sentiments had crossed their minds.

"You are refusing to see the truth," Suvanna said, her bright blue eyes flashing. "I am tired of being helpless. Every day that we do nothing, the people of Daragaab are in more danger. The swamps grow, magic is consuming us, the demons are getting more powerful, and people are suffering. The queen is in no condition to hold it back much longer. How soon until this spreads into all our homes? This won't be only Daragaab's failure. *Everyone* is going to *die* if we don't do something."

Kindle's jaw hardened again. "You mean like drowning dozens of innocent people?" he asked, giving her a pointed look. His eyes sparked, his anger clearly on the brink of erupting.

Suvanna took a slow step towards him, her fists balled at her sides.

"It was them or the queen. I will not apologize for doing what needed to be done. Her survival is far more important than a few insignificant lives." She stared at Kindle, daring him to defy her. For a few seconds, they glared at one another until something guttered out in Kindle's expression before his shoulders sagged.

He stepped back, shaking his head.

"The girl," Kindle said. "Row must have been keeping her secret for a reason."

"I'm afraid the girl is a false hope," Dhawan interrupted. "She is already twenty-one."

"You see?" Suvanna said to Kindle, slicing her hand through the air. "The girl is nothing."

Zarya started at Dhawan's comment and realized he was right. It was her birthday today, and she'd completely forgotten, too consumed with the strange turn her life had taken and everything that had been happening. But how had *he* known that?

She felt a surge of the same disappointment her feeble magic always invoked. To be called *nothing* tore away at something tender and raw in her soul.

The Chiranjivi had obviously been talking about her. But why? Kindle and Apsara had already confirmed she wasn't Aazheri. Did they know something else?

"There must be a way," Apsara said, her voice soft but full of certainty. "We are missing something. We are five of the most powerful beings in Rahajhan. There *is* a way to stop this without giving in to something we cannot return from. We just have to search harder."

Suvanna made a spitting motion, her chin jerking. "You are all fools. We are wasting time, always talking and waiting. Never *doing* anything." Her voice dropped to an ominous octave as the air around her seemed to shiver. "It *will* soon be too late."

She gave the group one last glare and stomped off in the direction where Zarya was eavesdropping. Zarya gasped and pressed herself against the wall.

Suvanna strode through the door, her steps full of purpose. Zarya breathed a sigh of relief as Suvanna passed her, but then the merdeva stopped. Zarya held her breath as Suvanna slowly looked over her shoulder, pinning Zarya with an angry glare.

She waited for an admonishment that never came. Instead, Suvanna scanned Zarya from head to toe, rage simmering behind her ocean-blue eyes. Then, without a word, she stalked off.

Zarya retreated in the opposite direction. As she hurried through the palace, she recalled Suvanna's ominous prediction. *We are all going to die here.*

She thought about what she'd just learned of Row. He hailed from the north. He was Andheran. Raja Abishek—the tyrannical ruler who had slaughtered all those vanshaj—was Row's king.

A new storm of questions now scattered her thoughts.

Was he still loyal to him? Was this why he'd always been so tight-lipped about his past? Was he ashamed or hiding something?

What was the sixth anchor Suvanna had mentioned? What was an anchor at all? Something told Zarya they hadn't been discussing nautical terms.

And finally, if Raja Abishek *was* the one unleashing dark magic on Daragaab, then what did that mean? Could they stop him? How powerful was he? There had been no mistaking the thread of fear that had run through that room when Suvanna had said his name. Even five of the most powerful beings in the continent were afraid of him. What kind of monster was he?

What if Suvanna was right?

What if the only way to stop the darkness was the darkness itself?

TWENTY-FOUR

Later that evening, Zarya once again lay on the divan in the living room, attempting to rest, her aches having grown steadily worse throughout the day. She pressed some ice to her forehead, but it did nothing to ease the tension thumping behind her eyes.

Even Aarav had been somewhat concerned, offering to bring her a cup of chai that now sat cold on the table next to her. Someone knocked at the front door, and she listened for him, hoping he would answer it.

Her chest constricted, and her aching joints flared. Closing her eyes, she tried to sleep, regretting that she hadn't made it to the infirmary earlier for some pills from the healers. Once she'd rested for a moment, maybe she'd go back over to the palace. Even better, maybe she could convince Aarav to run the errand for her.

But every time she closed her eyes, she was plagued by visions of the vanshaj woman flipping over the courtyard wall.

She also couldn't deny her increasing disappointment every morning she woke up and hadn't found herself in the forest with Rabin again. She wasn't sure if he was friend or foe, but she couldn't get him out of her head and desperately wished she had some way to control the visions or whatever those strange episodes were.

The conversation she'd overheard this morning was nagging her, too. It was true Daragaab seemed less secure with every passing day. Between almost falling into an endless void, being pummeled with falling eggs, and then nearly drowning, it felt as if something was trying very hard to get rid of her. For the thousandth time, she wondered if she *should* have stayed at the cottage. What if Row really had been right about it being dangerous out here? But surely he hadn't foreseen these strange events? This was all just a coincidence.

With a sigh, she flipped to the other side, attempting to find a comfortable position. She jolted at a clicking sound coming from the glass doors leading to the garden. Why was someone sneaking around outside?

Slowly she sat up before pretending to sort through the stack of books on the table. Row's sword, which she'd taken to carrying almost everywhere, sat propped against it. Zarya picked it up and made her way over to the doors, peering through the darkness.

Something hit the glass again, and she moved closer, carefully pushing down the door handle and stepping outside. The garden appeared to be deserted.

"Who's out here?"

"Zarya."

She whirled, sword up, ready to strike.

Vikram emerged through the bushes, hands raised in surrender. "It's just me."

"What are you doing? You scared me half to death!"

"You didn't look that scared." He glanced at her raised sword.

"It's an expression. *Why* are you hiding in there?"

"I knocked on the door, but no one answered, so I thought I'd check around here. I missed you."

Vikram grinned in a way she found maddeningly charming.

"This is a very strange way of showing it."

"Are you going to keep pointing that at me?" He placed a fingertip on the point of the sword. She scowled before lowering it to her side. Then she dropped onto a bench as another wave of pain seized her chest and head.

"Are you okay?" Vikram asked, sitting down and rubbing her back.

"Yes. I mean, no. I've got a headache," she said, not quite sure how to describe all the things she was experiencing. This didn't feel normal. This didn't feel like a typical set of aches and pains, and she was starting to worry something was truly wrong with her.

"Here," Vikram said, digging into his pocket. "Take some of these."

He shook two of the healer's pills into his hand, and she let out an exclamation of joy. "Gods, I could kiss you," she said, taking them and swallowing them dry. For a few moments, she sat with her eyes closed, grasping the edge of the bench and waiting for the pills to take effect.

"Does that mean I'm forgiven for startling you?" Vikram asked, and she tossed him a glare. "Don't be mad at me," he said, sliding closer, a playful grin on his face. "What I really want is to show you something."

Curiosity getting the better of her, she asked, "What?"

The pills had begun their magic, taking off the worst edge of her pain, though it still lingered in the background.

"C'mon," he said, standing up and grabbing her hand. "It's a surprise."

Despite the ache in her limbs, Vikram was enthusiastic enough that she let herself be tugged along.

He led her out of the garden and into the city. They wove through alleyways, avoiding the busiest streets, until they came to a small doorway set into the base of a tall, round tower.

She followed Vikram as he effortlessly bounded up a spiraling staircase. Her aching legs and tight chest protested, but Zarya trudged along behind, gripping the railing as she towed herself up.

Up and up they climbed, until they finally arrived at a circular observation deck. A wooden platform ran around the perimeter, offering a sprawling view of the city in every direction.

Zarya took in a deep breath as she beheld the millions of twinkling stars that shone overhead. Below them, hundreds of people traversed the streets, eating and drinking at outdoor tables, music playing, and conversations floating on the air. Families gathered on balconies, sitting down to dinner as they shared stories of their days. Even on the rooftops, lovers and friends embraced, heads tilted together, gazing at the brilliant sky.

It was the breathing, vibrant beauty of life.

Hope was a potent thing. Even when faced with innumerable dangers, the city found a way to celebrate. To bring light into the darkness. To smile in the face of adversity and find comfort in the shadows.

Maybe Suvanna was wrong. Darkness wasn't beaten with more darkness.

Darkness was destroyed by embracing the light, even when that seemed impossible.

"Look," Vikram said, coming to stand next to her and pointing to the sky, his hand gently resting on the small of her back. The sky was the deepest shade of midnight blue, sparkling with a vibrant sheet of stars. Far beyond the city, the rolling green hills of the forest beckoned. Facing this way, it was easier to ignore the threat of the blight marching from the south.

Lovely enough to make one *almost* forget what came knocking at night.

"It's my birthday," Zarya said, staring up at the sky.

"Is it?" Vikram smiled. "Well, happy birthday. I'm sorry, I wish I'd known. I would have planned something a little more special."

She shook her head. "No. Nothing could be more special than this. This is perfect."

And she meant it, feeling none of the sadness that usually accompanied another lonely passing year. For the first time ever, she had friends and people she cared about surrounding her. It was the only gift she had ever wanted.

A glittering line of silver streaked across the sky, and Zarya hopped in delight. A shooting star.

"Make a wish," Vikram said, whispering in her ear, and Zarya closed her eyes. She wished for everything she had right now. For this moment and the soft breeze on her face and the handsome rakshasa standing next to her. She wished for this version of a real life she'd craved every single day. She wished for it all to last forever.

"What did you wish for?" he asked after a moment before she opened her eyes to watch the star continue its journey across the sky.

"I can't tell you or it won't come true."

He smiled and leaned down to kiss her softly, his mouth warm and his lips like satin. She melted against him as he wrapped his strong arms around her.

She pulled back and looked into his eyes. "Thank you."

"For what?"

"For bringing me here. For reminding me I'm worth noticing."

The corners of his mouth turned down. "I'm sorry anyone has ever made you think you weren't worth that. You are worth all that and so much more."

Zarya leaned into Vikram again, resting her cheek against his chest, gazing out onto the city below. She sighed as his warmth eased some of the tightness in her sore muscles.

Then she looped her arms around his neck, pulling him in for another kiss. His arms circled her waist, pressing her in closer. Their lips met softly at first before the kiss grew more urgent. She let out a soft sigh as he nibbled her lip and then sucked on her tongue.

They pressed closer together as his hands slid lower. She wanted so many things right now. She had wished for this, too.

There was a lot for her to worry about.

A lot of questions Zarya had no answers for.

So many secrets clamoring for her attention.

But right now, none of it seemed to matter.

Being here on top of the world, being kissed, she could spread her arms and finally soar.

A moment later, Zarya collapsed as pain ripped through her chest, her scream shattering the stillness of the night.

TWENTY-FIVE

Agony flared hot and bright as Zarya's view of Vikram and the night tore away in a smear of color like an artist dragging her fingers through wet paint.

Torturous, twisting, shredding anguish clamped down on her muscles and bones, like her organs were swelling, ready to explode into atomic bursts of crimson tissue. A stab speared through her brain as blinding light and shattering darkness clashed and twisted, blurring her vision. Zarya screamed, wrapping her arms around her body, and crumpled to the ground, feeling nothing as her knees struck against the stone.

Someone called her name from a distance, the pitch drilling into her ears. She shut her eyes tight, trying to block it out. Her muscles seized, fighting off an invisible force that squeezed them. Squeezed her. Like bricks and stones piled one on top of another. Layer after bruising layer, crushing her flesh and blood and bone.

The midnight-blue sky and rolling green hills faded from memory, replaced by scarlet and black and grey, shifting, coalescing, and pulsating in foggy, dense clouds. It was a wash of nothingness. Her lungs constricted from a lack of oxygen.

She tried to breathe deeper, but it was like trying to inhale against a wall.

"Zarya!" She heard her name again as she clutched herself, lying on the floor of the observatory. She tried to clutch everything that hurt, but she only had two hands. *Everything* hurt. She was one giant mass of throbbing, pulsing pain.

"Help me," she moaned, or at least she tried to speak the words, but she couldn't tell if they were only in her head. Then she felt arms lifting her, and she tried to scream again, but her throat had swelled. The pressure of someone's touch against her skin was like a hissing brand, marking her forever.

Her consciousness blended in and out as there was a descent, winding down, down, down, as every step jolted her like a hammer strike.

A bite, a punch, a jab. She was being crushed. Whole cities, whole kingdoms, whole continents and civilizations coming down on top of her. The weight of the world grinding her bones to ash. She groaned, trying to curl into it, trying to crawl into a pocket of relief that wasn't there.

"I'm getting you help," she heard someone say, their voice cracking. "What's wrong? What's wrong? I'm getting help. I'm taking you to help." They repeated the words over and over again as they carried her. As they spiraled down the stairs, Zarya spiraled, too, down and down until darkness swept in and took her away.

* * *

Days passed, weeks, hours, seconds, minutes, years, centuries— it was impossible to know—somewhere between coherence and death. The only thing Zarya remembered was the pain. Like a living thing, it grew wings and claws and teeth and tore and shredded and bit. It hooked into her skin and her bones and each of the cells that were barely holding her together.

She perceived little, barely marking the people who came and went. Their voices and features blurred with the pain.

Koura hovered over her, his healing hands trying to offer her relief, but they made no difference. She was crushed and squeezed and twisted over and over again. He spent hours at her side, his sweat dripping onto her, his face a mask of frustration. And when Koura had done too much, when a river of red ran from his nose, he'd place something in her mouth, and she'd be taken away again.

Blink.

Kindle stood over her, magic moving on his lips. His hands rested gently on her body, but she felt the pain hammer at his power, unwilling to release her. It flung it away, scattering it like a pellet shot through a bubble. It resisted. It clung to her, pushing him away. Shielding her. Keeping the pain inside.

Blink.

Professor Dhawan sat at her bedside, a large book over his knees. He held a vial in his hand that he peered into, lines of concentration etched into his face. Zarya reached out, her throat burning. He looked at her, concern in his eyes, tears welling in the corners, and then he shook his head. She was lost.

Blink.

Vikram pressed a wet cloth on her face. It hurt where he touched her, but the coolness was a relief. She couldn't move. Couldn't tell him to stop. Didn't know if she wanted him to. Yasen stood behind him, his expression grim.

Blink.

She was wasting away. Her heart dripped blood, her insides poured out. Washing away like seashells on the tide. Swept by the surf, they would be lost to the deep forever. She fainted again.

Blink.

Zarya lay on her stomach in the dream forest, and for the first time in days or weeks or months, she reacted to something other than the pain. Today, the forest wasn't peaceful, though. Whatever magic normally comforted her held no power today.

Still, she let out a dry sob because she knew help was coming.

She didn't know why she was so sure of that, but she understood it in her crumbling bones.

The ground beneath her was both soft and hard. Roots dug into her ribs, where she lay as the breeze burned against her skin. She reached out to explore the texture of the moss beneath her, savoring something other than the pain. She was so thirsty. She was so tired. She felt like she'd been stretched and pulled like melted sugar until she'd dissolved into nothing.

She couldn't lift her head. All she could do was lie on the earth, focusing on her breath. *In and out. In and out.* When had breathing become so hard?

Where was he?

But then, through the shadow of pain, his presence tugged at her edges, now frayed and coming apart like threads off the loom, waiting for someone to weave them back together.

Like magic, Rabin appeared at her side. She felt him rather than saw him, but the sensation was unmistakable now. She would know his presence anywhere.

It wasn't *like* magic, though. It *was* magic.

He leaned down and placed a large, gentle hand on her forehead.

She cried out as something dipped into her chest, but then she felt it. The barest glimmer of relief. The pain dulled to a gentle roar. The waves, dark and huge and consuming, rolled through her body, washing the lost pieces of her back to shore. Maybe someday she would once again be whole.

She opened her eyes, blinking through tears, one slipping down across the bridge of her nose. He caught it and wiped it away. His touch was so warm, and she wondered how such an innocuous gesture could offer such relief?

"Who did this to you?" he asked, his rumbling voice low with wonder. "Why? Who *are* you, Zarya?"

His eyes flashed with hints of gold against a midnight canvas, and Zarya gazed into them, letting him anchor her. Letting him take care of her the way she sensed he was supposed to.

He gently turned her onto her back, and she studied the canopy of dark leaves that hung overhead, blowing in a slight breeze. The violet sky sparkled, and a pale golden moon hung so low it brushed the tops of the trees. Pinpoints of lights danced in the sky like they were signaling to her.

He placed his large hand in the center of her chest. It was so big it nearly covered her completely. Her heart reacted, beating wildly.

A dark wave crashed over her and then the pain began to leach away.

More tears leaked from her eyes as Rabin moved his hands, running them over her arms and legs. It was hard to believe someone who looked so fearsome could be so gentle.

The pain dulled, flowing away in eddies, like a thunderstorm easing to a spring shower. Her body, so tense and rigid, began to soften, bit by bit. Relief cascaded in shallow bursts, rolling over one another. A tempest blowing out. A squall gusting away.

With his head bowed, Rabin placed his hands on her stomach and went completely still. The forest held its breath, too, silence descending as every bird and insect and even the breeze paused, waiting.

Zarya felt it then—the vise leached away, pulling up through her body. First releasing her feet and then her shins and then her knees, rising up and up. It drew away through her fingertips, through her arms and her stomach and her chest and her shoulders and her neck until the pain gathered only in her head.

"Hang on," Rabin whispered. "I can't help you with this part, but it will be over soon."

Then the pain behind her eyes squeezed, and Zarya screamed. Her back arched off the grass as it echoed in every part of her, in every corner of her heart, moving through her, becoming her. She screamed and screamed until her voice cracked away, and then she continued screaming, her body robbed of sound.

Pressing against his hands, she thrashed and writhed and then Zarya exploded, coming apart in a thousand points of blackness like the night sky crashing down from the heavens.

It finally stopped.

Zarya stared up, her vision blurring. She sobbed, her tears flowing down her cheeks, touching her head, her arms, her stomach, searching for the pain. Only an ache remained. The soreness after intense physical activity. Muscles strained but free, no longer crushed by the weight of mountains. She floated on frothy tendrils of airy relief.

Rabin put a hand behind Zarya's back and helped her sit. Their eyes met, and she had the unmistakable sense of falling into something with no bottom. That this moment had just set her on a path that could never be undone.

"Thank you," she said, mourning the complete inadequacy of those feeble words. "I don't know how I can ever thank you enough. I thought I was dying."

He shook his head, his eyes boring into her, into that secret place only he seemed to be able to reach. "You don't need to thank me."

His hand lingered on her back, the touch warm and firm and inexplicably protective.

"Who are you?" Her raw voice barely carried above the din of the wind that had returned to rustle through the leaves.

"Who are *you*?" he countered.

"I'm nothing," she said, recalling Suvanna's callously tossed words.

With his other hand, he gripped her chin between a thumb and forefinger and drew her gaze towards him before he tipped her face up. They were so close she could feel his breath on her lips. She couldn't take her eyes off his mouth—the curve of his lips and how soft and inviting they looked.

"That isn't true," he said, and it sounded like a truth so absolute it could tear apart galaxies.

His gaze dropped to her mouth, too, just for a moment before he raised a dark eyebrow and said, "So, let's see."

"What?"

"Start with a flame. That's usually the easiest."

Zarya blinked, confused by his words.

He released his hold on her and then waited, intent but expectant.

"I don't unders—"

And then she noticed it.

Deep inside her heart was something new and tangible she couldn't name. A presence she'd never noticed before.

"Do you feel it?" he asked.

"What is it?" A part of her already knew, but she needed to hear the words.

"It's magic," he said, and at that precise moment, she understood that, despite everything, she had always known.

"Hold out your hand and search for a fire anchor," he told her. "It's different for everyone, but you'll know when you feel it."

An anchor, she thought, recalling the conversation she'd overheard between the Chiranjivi. So Zarya closed her eyes and focused on the new and sentient presence that sparked inside her.

Fire.

It called her name, flaring and flickering. Zarya opened her eyes, bewildered.

Rabin took her hand and flattened it so her palm faced up between them. "Focus on directing it here." He rubbed his thumb in the center, dragging it away almost reluctantly, sending a warm tendril of *something* directly into her stomach.

She did as he said. Fixated on her palm, she aimed the spark towards it, and a tiny flame ignited.

It hovered above her hand—a flickering sliver of destiny.

He nodded, the corner of his mouth lifting into an almost smile.

"That's better."

His hand flexed against her back, where it still rested. He leaned over and blew at the flame, his face close enough that she could smell freshly tilled earth and spring leaves. She longed to reach out and run the backs of her fingers along the dusting of stubble that covered his jaw.

The fire sputtered and died.

"Do it again, Zarya."

Her name resonated like a whirlwind blowing through a tunnel, and she didn't understand why she wanted him to say it over and over. She did what he asked again, the small flame winking into existence where it hovered over her palm.

He pushed himself up and studied her for a moment.

"Keep practicing," he said, before he turned and walked into the trees.

She watched his broad back until he disappeared.

Zarya turned back to her fire, watching the tiny light quiver in the palm of her hand as the entire universe reflected in the depths of the fire.

And for the first time in days, she smiled.

TWENTY-SIX

Sleep finally came. Freed from the pain, Zarya crumbled into exhaustion.

Koura came and went regularly, his magic filling her up and healing what had been stripped away. While Zarya had been lost, the queen's health had continued to decline, and thus Koura still spent most of his waking hours by Rani Vasvi's side but assured Zarya he'd find time to come.

As she dozed, medicine fogging her thoughts, Yasen, Vikram, and even Aarav sat by her side. They waited, they read —sometimes out loud to her—and sometimes they even sang. Zarya had a vague memory of Yasen plucking the strings of a small veena propped up on one knee, the sun turning his hair into starlight. Kindle sat with his head in his hands while Apsara watched her quietly, nibbling on her lip, questions written on her face.

Finally, Zarya woke in the familiar palace guest suite.

The lattice-covered windows filtered in a cool, gentle breeze, and the rushing sounds of the ocean soothed every tired muscle in her body.

Someone had cleaned her up, washed her hair, and put her

in a pair of soft pants and a sleeveless shirt. Scars ran down her arms, a ladder of thin lines forming a crisscross pattern. Self-inflicted fingernail scratches, she realized. They were already healing, but they must have been deep to still linger, even after Koura's care.

She shivered, grateful she couldn't remember that part at least.

Zarya lay with her hands folded over her stomach, savoring the quiet of the room and the wondrous clarity of her mind, finally at rest.

After sitting up, she poured herself a glass of water from the crystal jug next to her bed. It tasted of roses and pomegranates.

With unsteady legs, she placed her feet on the floor, testing her strength. She pushed herself up and hobbled slowly to the bedpost, reaching out to grip it for support. Already out of breath, she collapsed on the chest at the foot of the bed.

"Zarya!" Vikram exclaimed, entering the room. His midnight hair was sticking up in various directions, the way it got whenever he'd been running his hands through it. "You're up. She's up!" he called into the sitting room, and Yasen and Aarav appeared in the doorway.

"Get back into bed," Vikram said.

"Can we get you something to eat?" Yasen asked.

"Someone send for food. Soup!" Aarav called.

Vikram fussed over her, settling her back under the covers. Someone handed over another glass of water, and she gulped it down. A tray with a bowl of fragrant coconut broth and a steaming cup of chai was set in front of her.

Vikram sat on the edge of the bed, taking one hand as she sipped the broth with the other. "We were so worried about you. What happened?"

She shook her head. "I don't know." The warm soup soothed her throat, raw from screaming. "It was the worst pain I've ever experienced, and it just wouldn't stop. It was like something had me in a vise and just kept twisting and twisting. I never imagined I could feel so much."

Three sets of eyes scrutinized her with a combination of horror and concern.

"How long was it?" Zarya asked carefully, dreading the answer.

"Over a week," Vikram said. "First, you were in such pain. Oh gods, we were so scared. And then it just stopped, and you've been asleep ever since."

As she sipped her tea, her hands shook—partly from the strain on her body and partly from the fear of whatever had caused this. It was a miracle she wasn't dead. What if it happened again? Could Rabin help her? Why had he been the only one who was able to fix her? Was that why the forest called them?

"I need to lie down again," she said, feeling lightheaded.

Vikram propped a stack of pillows behind her, and she leaned into them. Then she noticed Aarav's black eye and the swollen cut on his cheek.

"How are things on the wall?"

The Khada generally refused aid from the queen's healers unless it was life-threatening, instead preferring to wear their minor injuries as badges of honor.

Aarav grinned. "I've killed more vetalas than any member of the Khada."

"Well, I'm glad you're not dead," she said, closing her eyes. "I think."

"I'm glad you aren't dead, too," came his reply. "I suppose."

Zarya smiled.

"Do you want someone to read to you?" Vikram asked.

"I'd prefer some quiet."

"Of course."

Yasen and Aarav said their goodbyes and then shuffled out of the room.

"Do you mind if I lie down next to you?" Vikram asked, sweeping a lock of hair off her forehead.

"I'd like that."

With her eyes closed, she listened to him kick off his boots and remove his jacket. The bed shifted as he crawled in next to her, and Zarya turned on her side as he wrapped an arm around her, scooting himself in close to cradle her body. Cocooned in the warmth of his embrace, she drifted off again.

When Zarya woke, Kindle stood at the foot of the bed, his hands bracing the footboard, lost in thought. He wore his usual black coat trimmed in red and a wide belt around his slim waist. His wavy black hair was swept back and out of his eyes. At her movement, he looked to her, and she caught those fiery flashes of orange and yellow in his irises.

At that moment, Vikram also stirred from sleep, where he'd dozed off next to her.

"You're looking better," Kindle said.

Zarya sat up, and Vikram rose from the bed and pulled on his boots.

"I need to be at the fort," he said, grabbing his coat. "And I'm already late."

Zarya nodded and smiled. "I'll see you later."

He pressed his hands together in Kindle's direction with a quick bow and then left the room. Kindle watched after him, something conflicted in his expression.

"Zarya, I offered to be here if you need someone to talk to, but in Row's absence, I feel it's my duty to ask that you be careful about who you get close to in the palace."

Zarya wondered where this was coming from. "I don't believe that's any of your business."

"No, I suppose it's not." He glanced back to the door. "Just... be cautious. You have been sheltered from the realities of life."

Zarya opened her mouth to argue, but she couldn't deny it.

It was true that despite how capable she liked to think she was, she didn't know much about life on the outside. Books could only account for so much. Still, she wasn't a complete fool.

Kindle sat down in the chair next to the bed so he was eye level with her.

"What happened? Tell me what you saw when you were bound."

"What do you mean, bound?"

He sighed. "Someone placed a binding on you. But it was not like anything I've ever seen before. It was beyond my ability to break." He hung his head in his hands. "I'm sorry. I can only assume this was Row's doing, but it's not something any of us recognized. We all tried. Dhawan, Apsara, Suvanna. Every time we had a hold of it, it would slip away. We couldn't hang on and even if we could, it was incredibly strong."

Zarya was surprised at the emotion in his voice, wondering why he cared so much.

"You don't need to be sorry. It wasn't your fault."

"How did you release it?"

She faltered. "I didn't," she replied, knowing she'd have to reveal something about her visions but feeling compelled to keep the details as vague as possible.

Details like the fact she knew Rabin's name but didn't know who he actually was. He might have rescued her, but she sensed he was dangerous. His warrior's disposition, the scars, the overwhelming intensity in his eyes—everything about him spoke of something dark and elusive. Mysterious and wild.

Her cheeks flushed as she remembered the way he'd looked at her and the way he'd said her name. She could still feel where he'd touched her, like a memory dipped in warm honey and wrapped in shadowed silk.

But he'd helped her. If he'd meant her harm, surely he wouldn't have done so?

"I was in a forest," she said. "It felt like a dream. There was a stranger."

"Who? Where?" Kindle sat up straighter.

"I don't know where it was. It was just a forest, and the person was hooded," she replied, massaging some of the details for her convenience. "I didn't see them. I don't know who it was."

Zarya flexed her hand, remembering the flare of fire she'd brought into existence. How it had danced before her eyes. A creation born of her very soul. She searched for that spark now, finding it twirling in her chest where it curled and purred.

"I don't understand. This makes no sense," Kindle said, furrowing his brow. "Was it a vision?"

Zarya shrugged, not meeting his eyes. "I'm not sure what it was. It felt more like a dream." That wasn't really the truth, either, but it was the only way to describe it.

He pursed his lips, clearly unsatisfied with that answer. "And now? Do you notice any difference?" he asked. He looked her up and down as if he could see a change tattooed on her skin.

"I'm just tired."

At Zarya's lie, Kindle's shoulders slumped.

"Are you sure? That binding was clearly meant to restrain magic that someone must have thought you possessed. Dhawan's theory was that it had been building up inside of you all these years and finally released, triggering this episode."

Inwardly, she cursed. Everyone was *so* close to discovering her truth, but she couldn't let it happen yet.

"I don't feel anything, Kindle. I'm sorry."

The deception withered on her tongue, but Row had been explicit: her magic must remain hidden. Had his attempts to coax more out of her for all those years really been a ruse? Had he actually wanted to conceal it so much that it had almost killed her? On an already lengthy list of grievances, this seemed one offense too many.

If Zarya ever saw Row again, she'd kill him on the spot.

Kindle made a sound of frustration. "Row, where are you?" he said softly, speaking into the distance. He slumped back in the chair and covered his hands with his eyes. "What haven't you told us?"

She wondered what would have happened if Rabin hadn't found her in the forest. How long would she have suffered, wasting away to nothing because of Row and his secrets?

"Why does any of this matter to you?" Zarya asked, growing suspicious of Kindle's continued interest in her magic. First the incident in the haveli and now this. "What do you want from me?"

There was a reason her magic meant something. Kindle had mentioned her when she'd eavesdropped on the Chiranjivi. They all wanted something, and she wasn't sure if she could trust them with her secret yet. Or secrets, rather. Zarya was starting to gather them like keys on a ring, each one unlocking another door to her present and maybe her future.

"Row and I have been friends for a very long time. Well, inasmuch as men like us can ever be friends," Kindle said, his tone dry.

Zarya thought she understood what he meant, given Row's imperiousness and aloof disposition, and almost laughed.

"But he never whispered a breath about a girl he had locked in a cottage by the sea. Who are you? Row does everything with a reason. And now he's been missing for months, and I fear the worst. But there is a reason he kept you there, and I'm sure it's important for us to find out what that is." He looked Zarya directly in the eyes, searching her face like she was a puzzle to solve. "I think *everything* may depend on it."

TWENTY-SEVEN

"I want to go for a walk," Zarya declared a week later as she dropped the book she hadn't actually been reading on the bed next to her. "I've had enough of this room."

Aarav looked up from where he was studying a hand of Rani's Cradle with a deck of cards on a table in the corner. Thanks to the constant stream of food and attention from the kitchens and Koura, her strength had noticeably improved. But she was going stir-crazy.

"I don't know." Aarav leaned back in his chair, his posture loose. "Koura said you needed to stay in bed."

Zarya narrowed her eyes, though there wasn't any heat in her annoyance. Aarav's disposition had shifted since she'd been ill, and he seemed to have altogether abandoned his role as her constant shadow. It appeared that nearly dying on the wall every night made him far more pleasant to be around. She couldn't help but notice the way he carried himself ever since that first night with the vetalas. It had clearly awoken something that had been sleeping inside of him. A new confidence and purpose.

Zarya had been banned from the wall herself until Koura deemed her one hundred percent fit to fight, and she couldn't wait to get back there. Reports had been streaming in that the demons had been battering the Khada with more ferocity than ever. Did they know that Rani Vasvi was weakened? Or were they just getting bolder? Either way, none of it spelled anything but trouble for Dharati.

"What Koura doesn't know won't hurt him, will it?" Zarya said, tossing her blanket off and climbing out of bed. After regular walks through the palace gardens, along with guided exercises, her legs were much steadier, and she was ready for more.

"Just a short one, I promise. Let's go to Rupi's—I'm dying for a gulab jamun. Or three." She pressed her hands together in mock prayer, imploring Aarav. The nearby bakery was one of the city's most popular, with a line out the door every day. "Oh, please, kind sir. Just there and back. I'll be ever so thankful."

"Fine," he said with a huff, probably realizing she wouldn't give up. Zarya smiled in triumph and clapped her hands together.

"Good. Now leave so I can get dressed." She made a shooing motion, and he threw her a half-hearted glare before leaving the room, her laughter following him out. Even if friendship was still an elusive idea between them, perhaps they could find an amicable middle ground.

Zarya turned to the closet and dug out a pair of black leggings and a green angrakha, a garment similar to her usual kurtas with a crossover neckline. She left Row's sword where it sat propped up in the corner, reasoning it wasn't warranted for a trip to the bakery, and she was still too weak to use it, anyway.

With the sun hanging high in the sky, Dharati was at the height of its midday bustle. There had been no further daytime attacks since the kala-hamsa had assaulted the city, but Zarya sensed a wary unease in the air. It was getting harder to ignore what was out there, and that wall would only protect them all for so long.

Along their route, they were stopped constantly. Or rather, Aarav was. Groups of men called out his name, shouting from rooftops, market stalls, and taverns as they walked by. They grinned and pointed, mimicking Aarav's moves on the wall. Sword chops, fist punches, and high kicks.

"The Tiger!" A man came up to shake Aarav's hand and clap him on the shoulder. Men followed behind, slapping him on the back and asking when his next shift on the wall would be as they growled and held up their hands, forming mock claws with their fingers.

Aarav lapped up every drop of their attention like a kitten with a saucer of milk. "I've got the next few nights off," Aarav said to a chorus of boos. "But word is that a new nest of vetalas have been stirring in the southeast corner of the swamps." The boos turned into oohs and whoops from the men as they mock-walloped each other.

Though she still wasn't a fan of these men gambling on the Khada's lives, Zarya watched with a smile, truly delighted Aarav had found something he could be proud of. She recalled Aarav's claim that Row had cared nothing for him and wondered if she wasn't the only person Row had wronged. Perhaps he had both of them to answer to, if and when he returned.

"Can we go now?" Zarya asked with her arms crossed, feigning impatience. "You became a local hero in my absence. How can I be in your presence? I am not worthy of this greatness. Aarav the Tiger. My, my, whatever will Row say?" She cocked her head. Aarav gave her a dry look and gestured for her to keep walking.

As expected, there was a line out the door at Rupi's—her

sweet fried balls of cheese soaked in rose syrup were the stuff of local legends. Zarya leaned against the building at the end of the line. With one foot propped against the wall, she closed her eyes and tipped her face to the sun.

As they waited for the line to move, more fans and well-wishers greeted Aarav. Refrains of "the Tiger" followed more growls and laughter. Keeping her eyes closed, Zarya smiled to herself again, happy that Aarav had found their admiration. Maybe he'd be less of a pain in her ass from now on.

"I've been looking for you!" came a female voice from some-where in front of Zarya.

She opened her eyes. Before her stood a plump rakshasa, who came barely to the height of her shoulder. With her other hand, she gripped Aarav's arm tightly, as if he might bolt.

"Have we met?" Zarya asked the woman, straightening up.

"No, no. But the boys have told us so much about you," she said.

Her black hair was shot through with streaks of silver, tied into an elegant twist on top of her head. Her smooth face made her appear ageless, and she was dressed in a low-cut blouse and an ornately decorated green sari in a style favored by the nobles.

"About how Row kept you prisoner!" She leaned in and lowered her voice to a stage whisper, pretending to be discreet, but everyone around them turned to stare.

"I'm sorry," Zarya said, trying to keep her tone polite. "But who are you?"

"I've been dying to invite you for dinner," said the myste-rious rakshasa, completely ignoring the question. "I said to myself, 'Diya, next time you're in the city, you're going to track down these newcomers and invite them to the manor.' And here you are! The boys are on leave from duty and are coming home for a few days. You'll come, too! We're celebrating the blessed union. It's going to be a splendid event."

Aarav and Zarya exchanged confused glances.

"By boys, do you mean Vikram and Yasen?" Zarya asked.

"Yes, who else would I mean? We'll make it a surprise! Vikram has been trying to keep you to himself, hasn't he? But I've got my spies." The woman wagged a finger and winked at Zarya. "And the party is tomorrow—we've been planning it for weeks. The whole family is just dying to meet you."

"Uh..." Zarya said, looking at Aarav for help. He just shrugged.

"I'll send the carriage for you tomorrow morning. It's beautiful in the countryside, and you're very pale. Everyone needs time away from the city. It's much too crowded here."

She pinched Zarya's cheek.

"Ow!" she cried.

"But don't tell the boys." Leaning in, she spoke again in a loud whisper, obviously meant to be heard by everyone. "I can't wait to see their faces."

Zarya rubbed her cheek but smiled. Clearly, this woman adored Vikram and Yasen.

"I'll see you tomorrow. And don't worry about bringing anything. We'll take good care of you." With a wave, she walked off with her generous hips swaying from side to side.

"Who was that?" Zarya asked Aarav, watching the woman leave.

"Vikram's mother?"

"Maybe? I guess we're going for a visit to the countryside?" she said.

"Apparently so. It would do you some good, though. She wasn't wrong—you really do look awful."

Zarya snarled as Aarav bolted for his life, disappearing into the bakery.

* * *

As promised, their ride pulled up in front of the haveli the next morning. It was hard not to gape at the green-and-gold carriage that waited for them, flanked by liveried footmen in white dhotis, royal blue vests, and bright red turbans, their backs ramrod straight.

On the other side of the carriage stood a contingent of six armed guards, all bearing weapons and wearing the queen's uniform.

"Who knew Vikram's family was *this* fancy?" Aarav asked as he slid into one of the plush green velvet seats. "I can't believe he sleeps in the army barracks when he's got money like this."

"I suppose a soldier is always a soldier," Zarya replied, taking the seat across from him. Aarav flipped through the various drawers and compartments that lined the interior of the carriage.

"Aha," he said, pulling out two glasses and a crystal decanter filled with wine from a small cupboard near their feet. The footman poked his head inside, scanned the small space, and apparently satisfied, closed the door, latching it in place.

A moment later, someone called out a command, and they lurched forward. Aarav and Zarya shared a grin. Despite the somewhat abrupt invite, this was already proving to be a thrilling adventure.

"Why are the queen's guards coming with us?" Zarya asked Aarav.

He shrugged. "I'd guess to protect us out in the forest."

"You'd think they'd have better things to do than watch over the two of us." Zarya sat back and folded her arms.

"I suppose," Aarav said. "Clearly, Vikram's family has pull with the queen."

As they exited Dharati, the carriage picked up speed, barreling through the countryside. A wall of trees lined them on each side, so thick it was impossible to see anything beyond the dense foliage. It was like moving through a living, verdant tunnel. After she grew tired of studying leaves, Zarya lay back and drifted off to the sway of their travel.

An hour later, she awoke as the carriage turned down a gravel road. They progressed through more leafy tunnels until a massive set of gates appeared before them. Golden bars twisted into intricate curls were anchored against a high stone wall where two guardsmen dressed in the same royal blue and red livery of the coach attendants waited. After the gates swung open on smooth hinges, they were waved through.

The carriage continued down another tree-lined tunnel before it opened onto an expanse of vivid greenery that sprawled far into the distance. Clusters of artfully arranged trees were interspersed with pristine fields of lush grass, shrubbery, low hedges, and huge plots of land bursting with a rainbow of flowers.

As the horses trotted down the stone path, the house came into view. Made of pale brown stone, edged in a delicate trim of white, it stretched across the flat horizon. A towering central building rose into a sweeping onion-shaped dome, surrounded by narrower buildings topped with smaller domes. Dozens of windows covered in intricate latticework curved into delicately pointed arches.

Zarya and Aarav poked their heads out of the carriage as they rolled towards the manor, studying the gardens furnished with white marble fountains, seating areas, firepits, and hammocks swinging between trees.

Flamingos stood in the crystal-clear pools, macaques swung from branches, and snow leopards lounged in the dense grass. Deer nibbled on flowers, peacocks strutted along the pathways, and even a baby lion splashed happily in a fountain. In the distance, an elephant raised its trunk into the air and let out a bellowing cry.

"Wow." Aarav's eyes were wide. "Why would Vikram and Yasen ever leave this place?"

Zarya wondered the same as the carriage pulled up in front of the house. An attendant swung the door open, proffering a stabilizing hand for Zarya. She took it and stepped from the carriage, trying to take everything in.

They continued down a short path where more animals frolicked amongst the plants and flowers. Tiny peri scurried about, some with skin like tree bark and others with smooth, leaf-green complexions.

Short, bearded men tromped about while plump, golden babies fluttered on feathered white wings. A group of tiny people—who looked like they were made of twigs—were having a tea party, while two purple-skinned peri clung together, fucking each other furiously under the shade of a large leaf. Zarya quickly looked away with a snort, covering her mouth. She widened her eyes at Aarav and they both snickered.

Green wooden doors, four times her height, stood partially open at the front of the manor. On the wide magnificent steps stood the familiar rakshasa who had accosted them at the bakery.

"I'm so happy you're here." She opened her arms wide, waving them up the stairs. "Come in, come in—you must be hungry. Lunch is all set up for you. Come and say hello to Amrita. She's been dying to see you."

They entered a cavernous space that boasted high, vaulted ceilings covered in colorful tiles that created swirls of flowers and leaves. Vikram had certainly been modest when describing his family and his upbringing.

A high-pitched squeal rang out, and they looked up to find Princess Amrita running down the stairs.

"You're here!" came her high, musical voice. "Oh, I've been waiting so long to chat with you again."

She ran up and hugged each of them, and Zarya felt

awkward about the instant display of affection, while Aarav grinned like a fool as she ruffled his hair.

"I know you're Aarav. I've heard all about your accomplishments at the wall. You must be very brave." Aarav's face turned a deep shade of red. "And Zarya! It's so good to see you're all better. I swear Yasen never stops talking about you!"

Zarya was sure the princess was mocking her, but there was nothing but sincerity in Amrita's gaze. The princess nodded, her curls bobbing as she clapped her hands, delighted about absolutely everything.

"And you've met Diya, of course." Amrita linked her arm with the woman who had invited them.

"Yes," Zarya said. "And I still didn't catch who you were, Diya?"

"I'm the nawab's wife."

She said it like Zarya should have known that all along.

"Right," Zarya replied as it occurred to her this arrangement seemed a bit strange. "And why is the princess of Dharati here at Vikram's family home?"

"Oh!" Amrita said. "Didn't Diya say? We're announcing the vowing tonight!"

"The vowing?" Zarya asked.

"Yes, between me and Vikram, silly. Surely, he told you. We've been promised for years!"

Amrita giggled again and hugged Zarya tight as thunder roared in her ears. Vowing? Promised? Vikram was *marrying* Amrita?

Aarav blanched and stared at Zarya, his mouth slightly open. She stiffened as Amrita gestured to the wide central staircase.

"I'll show you to your rooms," she said breathlessly as she led the way, oblivious to the reaction of her guests.

Promised. Vikram was promised. *To a princess.*

Aarav moved closer to Zarya and leaned in, speaking in a low voice. "Do you want me to kill him? 'Cause I will."

Zarya looked up at him, bewildered. Her mouth opened and then closed as Amrita took her hand and dragged her up the stairs.

Their rooms were situated across the hall from one another, with Zarya's sitting at the back of the manor overlooking a garden to rival the one out front. Emerald and gold silk lined the walls, against which sat a large four-poster bed made of pale wood, while a set of glass doors led to a wide, curving balcony.

Zarya stepped outside, hoping to relieve the building pressure in her chest. But the afternoon was sultry, and the air stood still as the sun beat down, making her want to jump out of her skin.

After retreating to the cooler interior, Amrita's high voice carried from across the hall, where she was showing Aarav his room. He caught her eye through the door, and it was everything Zarya could do not to burst into tears. She poured herself a glass of water from a pitcher on the table, taking big gulps that did nothing to settle the roil in her gut.

Gods, she was such a fool. He'd lied to her. Played games with her. Tricked her into believing he cared about her all this time. Of course, she'd turned at the first handsome man to give her a second look. Maybe she belonged back at the seaside cottage, after all. Who did she think she was, going out into the world? She had no experience and no idea what she was doing.

With a sick feeling in her stomach, she started to piece things together. Now she understood why Yasen had been so angry that night at the peri anada. Zarya gripped the bedpost, her blood pounding.

"Oh my," Amrita said, coming into the room. "You need something to eat. You're awfully pale." Zarya studied the princess, taking a proper look at her for the first time.

Amrita's brown skin was gleaming and rich. A tumble of

thick black curls framed an angelic round face and wide amber eyes. Her lips were pink and plump, and her ears swept up into delicate points. She was stunning.

"Come down to the dining room. Lunch is all set."

Again, Amrita pulled Zarya with her. They ended up in a small wood-paneled room with a large table at the center. Zarya and Aarav sat down as Amrita and Diya joined them, and a parade of vanshaj arrived with platters of food. Tureens of chicken and lamb, swimming in glistening brown and orange sauces. High stacks of naan drizzled with butter. Fresh salads of tomato, coriander, and onion seasoned with pepper and lemon. A huge silver platter piled with sliced coconut, pineapple, mango, and ruby beads of pomegranate.

Amrita kept up a constant stream of chatter about the house and the gardens and the party tonight. Zarya felt so stupid. So used. Was she destined to be lied to by every man in her life?

No, Zarya thought. She had done this to herself. Trusting the first charming rakshasa to show her a bit of attention. All the warning signs had been there, and she'd ignored them, confident she knew enough. But she hadn't.

"Huh?" Zarya looked up to find everyone around the table staring at her.

"Will you be my guest of honor at the party tonight?" Amrita had placed her hand on Zarya's and turned towards her. There was zero pretense or calculation on her face. "Vik and Yasen speak so highly of you; I feel like we're already friends."

Zarya nodded, miserable. Clearly, Vikram had not only lied to Zarya but also to his sweet and trusting fiancée.

"Of course." Zarya forced a smile. None of this was Amrita's fault.

"Oh, wonderful!" She clapped her hands together. "Then you'll sit with me, and you'll tell me all about the trouble those boys get up to when they aren't at the palace."

Aarav choked on his water, spitting it out and coughing until his face turned purple. Zarya gave him a sharp look.

"Sorry. Went down the wrong pipe," he croaked.

After a lunch that lasted three hundred years, Zarya extricated herself, locking herself in her room where she paced. The room was stifling, growing hot in the afternoon sun. Diya had said clothes had been provided, and Zarya dug into the closet for something cooler to wear. She found a light dress made of yellow silk that swept to the floor, leaving her back and shoulders exposed.

A knock sounded at the door, and Zarya opened it to find Aarav shuffling from foot to foot, his hands stuffed in his pockets.

"Uh, so, are you... okay, or what?"

He rubbed the back of his neck and looked down the hallway as if hoping someone would come to rescue him from this conversation.

"Don't trouble yourself, Aarav," she snapped, anger shortening her temper.

He opened his mouth, looking even more uncomfortable, before he wedged his foot right in and said, "I did say he was trouble from the beginning."

"You *did*?" Zarya clenched her jaw.

"Yes. Why do you think I wanted you to come back to the cottage? So things like this wouldn't happen." His voice rose, and she grew angrier.

"*This* is not my fault."

"I'm just saying—"

"How about you say nothing and get away from me? As usual, your presence is neither needed nor desired, Aarav."

Zarya slammed the door in his face as hard as she could. A moment later, she heard Aarav's door bang across the hall. She huffed and crossed her arms, pacing the length of the room again. She should leave. Go back to the city. Disappear into its masses. She didn't need any of this.

She wanted to yell. To pick up the expensive-looking vase on the dresser and smash it into a million pieces. Zarya ground her teeth, her pulse racing, and then shook her head.

No, she wasn't going to let Vikram squirm out of this and make it easy for him by disappearing. She would stay and he would face the consequences of his actions. This wasn't her fault, and Zarya would not be the one to run and hide.

TWENTY-EIGHT

With preparations for the evening's celebrations well underway, the manor house hummed with activity. Zarya heard the sounds of hurried footsteps and barked orders as the servants scurried about their duties.

She lay on the bed feeling sorry for herself as the smells from the kitchen wafted through the floor, causing her stomach to growl. She had barely eaten lunch, only pushing the food around on her plate, and was now ravenous for dinner.

A knock came at her door, and a young vanshaj woman stood on the other side holding a platter with samosas and a bottle of pale pink wine.

"Would my lady care for a snack?"

Zarya opened the door wider and invited her inside. "Yes. Thank you."

The woman's eyes were downcast as she entered. She wore a salwar kameez in royal blue, edged with silver, and a blue chiffon dupatta draped over her head. The ring of tattooed stars around her neck was so precise and black, Zarya felt like she could reach out and pluck one off.

Zarya couldn't take her eyes away as her hand drifted to her own throat, something tugging at her memory.

The woman looked up at Zarya's hand still lingering on her throat. She snatched it away, mortified to have been caught like that.

"I'm sorry," Zarya said, "I didn't mean—"

The woman held up both hands and pushed them in her direction as she shook her head. "It's nothing. Please enjoy your food."

"Thank you," Zarya said as the woman rushed away with her eyes down and her shoulders rounded. Zarya watched her leave, an uneasy ache blooming in her chest.

Her stomach grumbled again, and she reached for a stuffed pastry and poured herself a full glass of wine. Today wasn't a day for moderation.

While she savored the delicious food, she sat back, still stewing in her thoughts.

Vikram had hurt her, but he also hadn't made her any promises. Zarya didn't know what falling in love was like, but she was pretty sure what she felt for Vikram wasn't it just yet. Could it grow into something more? She wasn't sure. She had wanted to be kissed, and she'd *loved* being kissed by him, but had she been reading into something that wasn't there?

Regardless of what he did or didn't feel, he shouldn't have been kissing her at *all*. And when she saw him, she would make sure he would answer for that.

Now on her second glass of wine, she picked through the bedroom closet. Diya hadn't been exaggerating when she'd said they would provide everything. An array of colorful dresses hung in the wardrobe, each more elaborate and glittering than the last.

Zarya chose a golden silk lehenga covered in crystal beads and sequins with a choli that left her arms bare. The full skirt flared out to the ground in rivers of fabric and swathes of creamy lace, all of it accented in more beads.

She curled her hair and pinned it so it hung down her back before affixing a golden maang tikka along the center part with the small medallion resting on her forehead.

As she turned to study the mirror, Zarya had to admit she looked rather nice. She hoped the effect would produce a touch of remorse in Vikram, but more importantly, she hoped she'd meet someone even more handsome to dance with tonight. She wasn't above inciting a small dose of jealousy. That was, if Vikram even cared. Maybe she'd been nothing but a conquest. A notch on his bedpost.

After polishing off the rest of her wine, Zarya made her way to the main floor.

Vanshaj bustled about, laden with trays of food and drinks, giant vases of flowers, bolts of fabric, and even the occasional live bird contained in a gilded cage. Aarav waited at the bottom of the stairs, his posture stiff in a crisp sherwani. He shifted in his golden chappals, clearly uncomfortable in the tailored garments, but Zarya admired the knee-length jacket made of deep green velvet, along with the fitted beige pants.

"We clean up nicely," Zarya said, smiling at him.

"You're in a better mood."

Zarya shrugged. "I've had a few glasses of wine." She laughed at his expression. "Lighten up. What do you think I did all those nights you and Row left me alone?"

His eyes darkened, and she laid a hand on his arm.

"Aarav, I'm sorry. I shouldn't have snapped at you earlier. I was upset, and I took it out on you."

Aarav blinked a few times, and Zarya realized she'd never apologized to him after one of their arguments. A twist of guilt drilled into her gut. Maybe she needed to take more responsibility for the state of their relationship.

"It's okay. I meant it when I said I'd kill him for you. Just say the word," he replied, his tone light, but there was a coldness in it that released something in Zarya's heart at his violent but brotherly sentiment.

"I'll keep it in mind," she said with a half-smile. "Shall we?"

A young vanshaj man at the bottom of the stairs directed them towards the dining hall, where the night's festivities would soon begin. Inside, they found a long table running through the center, laden with flowers and golden plates rimmed in royal blue. At the front, a raised platform held four chairs that faced the other diners.

They were escorted to their seats, joining the dozens of other guests, many surreptitiously glancing at Zarya and Aarav with a range of expressions, from cool and indifferent to warm and curious.

Pale green cocktails with mint leaves floating in delicate crystal glasses were placed in front of them as more guests filed in. The drink reminded Zarya of the night they'd spent at the peri anada, where Vikram had kissed her with such passion. Her festive mood darkened a little at the memory, and she gestured for a refill.

Before long, the table was full of elegantly dressed courtiers, including several stunning fairies, who were dressed a little more conservatively than those she'd seen at the peri anada. But only just, Zarya mused, as she took in a female fairy with pale pink skin and hair, wearing a choli cut so low that her ample breasts were hovering on the edge of exposure. Next to her sat a handsome rakshasa with a pinched expression, who leaned over and brushed his lips to her throat, his tongue darting out like a frog. The fairy made a sound of pleasure, but her smile was noticeably tight. Zarya wrinkled her nose.

A hush descended on the diners as a greying man in a green sherwani stepped forward and cleared his throat. In a booming voice, he cried, "Make way for the nawab and his illustrious family!

"Rise for her Royal Highness Rajkumari Amrita Vasvi and his esteemed Nawabzada Vikram Ravana."

Zarya took a deep breath as the couple entered the room. Amrita was even more beautiful than earlier, wearing a dusty-rose sari embroidered with silver. Bubbling with excitement, she bounced as she clung to Vikram's arm. As handsome as usual, his black hair fell in waves around his ears, and his honed soldier's body was clad in a gold-accented royal blue sherwani with a red sash running across his body.

Behind them, Yasen walked in unannounced, his hand on his sword hilt as he scanned the crowd, scowling at everyone. He wore a sherwani similar to Vikram's but with fewer adornments. The blue was perfect against his silver hair.

The soon-to-be royal couple made their way down the room, pausing along the way to bow and shake hands with their guests. Yasen was the first to notice Zarya amongst the crowd. His eyes flicked between Zarya and Aarav before he froze. His face twisted with concentration, and she could practically hear him trying to warn Vikram with his mind.

Yasen caught her eye as she gave a small nod—yes, she knew, and she wasn't planning to make a scene. Yasen relaxed a breath.

Vikram noticed Aarav first, and his brow creased before he looked across the table to where Zarya stood, the blood draining from his face. With her hand planted on her hip, she raised an eyebrow at him, noticing his grip on Amrita tighten.

Amrita squealed as they approached. "Look who came! Diya found them in the city yesterday and sent the carriage for them. She told them to keep it a surprise. And aren't you surprised, Vikram? You've told me so much about them, and I knew you'd be so happy. Aren't you happy?"

Amrita turned her bright eyes to her fiancé, who gave her a strained smile and pecked her on the cheek. "Of course I'm happy. What a wonderful surprise, my beautiful rajkumari. Aarav, Zarya, how nice you could join us."

With his smile struggling to find his eyes, Vikram offered a stiff bow and settled Amrita into the chair next to Zarya. Everyone followed suit and Zarya found herself between Amrita and Yasen, with Vikram and Aarav across the table.

Vikram's complexion had shifted from ashen to a pale shade of green, as though he was precariously close to vomiting on the golden plates. At the front of the room, the next members of the Ravana family were being introduced.

"Please rise for the most elegant, beautiful, and charming Begum Jasmine Ravana, Begum Diya Ravana, and Begum Vamika Ravana accompanied by the most exalted, virile, glorious, and powerful Nawab Gopal Ravana."

"Wow, he's laying it on a little thick," Zarya muttered under her breath, and Yasen choked on a laugh.

Three female rakshasas entered, all clad in varying shades of blue. Diya walked next to a tall, slender rakshasa with dark mahogany hair, light brown eyes, and sharp, high cheekbones. They were accompanied by a curvy third rakshasa with inky black hair and dark blue eyes, a vacant expression on her face.

Behind them walked Vikram's father with the same tousled black locks and the same emerald eyes. But where Vikram's face was kind and open, the nawab looked like the kind of man who boiled baby monkeys for pleasure. The procession of four made their way to the elevated head table at the front of the room, settling in a line facing their guests. As the nawab took his place, vanshaj servants leaped into action, and platters of food started to stream in.

"Aren't you surprised? This is just so exciting." Amrita beamed at Vikram.

"Very," he said, practically choking on the word.

"I just knew you'd be thrilled. They're going to spend the next few days with us while you and Yas are on leave.

They've promised to tell me all about what you get up to in the city."

Amrita turned her shining eyes to Aarav. "I want to hear all your stories from the wall. My mother and Gopal say I'm not allowed to attend the betting parties, but it sounds so dangerous and just so thrilling."

Aarav grinned, more than happy to regale her with tales of his victories.

"Tell her how many times you've almost died." Zarya smirked, and Aarav glared at her, but it was half-hearted. They began chattering as Amrita launched a slew of questions in his direction.

"I'm sorry," Yasen said, his voice low and guarded. "I should have told you, but—"

"It's fine." Zarya cut in. "It's not your fault. He's your friend. You barely know me. You were being loyal."

"Zee, that's not how it was."

She waved him off, pretending it didn't bother her. "I'm fine, Yasen. You're not the one who needs to apologize."

He nodded, his lips in a tight line. "I'll kill him for you if you like."

Zarya snorted. Vikram was going to be lucky to survive the night at this rate.

"No, you won't, but I appreciate the sentiment."

At that moment, Amrita turned her attention to Zarya.

"Yasen says you know how to use a sword? And you've fought on the wall, too? Who taught you? Oh, I'd love to learn how to use a weapon."

"Why don't you learn, then? Yasen is a pretty good teacher."

Both Amrita and Zarya turned to stare at Yasen, who sat with his arms across his chest, glowering at everyone in the room before he slowly turned his head to find the two of them staring. If it was possible, his frown deepened further, and Amrita and Zarya both dissolved into a fit of giggles.

"No, I don't think there's much use in my learning how to use a sword," Amrita said, a tinge of sadness in her tone.

"Everyone needs to learn how to defend themselves. Yasen will teach you. Right, Yas?" Zarya smacked him on a firm bicep. He glared back, arms still crossed over his broad chest, saying nothing before he looked away.

"Fine, then. I'll teach you," Zarya said.

Amrita's eyes grew wide. "Would you?"

"Sure."

"I don't think that would be a good idea," Vikram interrupted, leaning forward with his teeth clenched.

"And I don't think anyone asked you," Zarya said with a cool stare before turning back to Amrita and sorting out plans with her for a lesson.

Once dinner started, Yasen sat back in his seat with his stony glare on everyone, while Vikram said little, drinking a lot and smiling when Amrita spoke to him, only replying in monosyllables. Zarya could sense Vikram trying to catch her eye, but she refused to give him the satisfaction.

Their little party was tense, and Zarya barely paid attention to the food while dinner dragged on forever. Finally, the parade of dishes stopped, and the mood around the table heightened.

As the plates were cleared, guests began to drift towards the attached ballroom, where upbeat music was already playing. Vikram and Amrita started off the dancing as Gopal and the three beautiful women lounged on a dais covered in thick pillows and bolsters. Zarya didn't miss the cold and assessing stare the nawab used to survey the room, as if assessing a threat from every side. Something about him made her skin crawl.

"Who are those three women?" Zarya asked Yasen.

"The Begums of Ravana. His wives."

"Rakshasas have harems?" she asked.

"Some. It's an old tradition, usually only for royalty. Gopal married Vamika, who failed to produce an heir for about a hundred years, and he couldn't let the Ravana line die out, so then he moved on to Diya, who only had a lowly daughter."

He paused at Zarya's scowl.

"Some things never change," he said by way of apology. "So, he moved on to Jasmine, who finally gave him two boys—she is Vikram's mother."

"I had assumed Diya was Vikram's mother. She seems so fond of you both."

Yasen's mouth tipped up at the corner. "Diya thinks she's everyone's mother." He said the words wryly, though there was a definite warmth in them.

At that moment, Gopal Ravana's gaze found both Zarya and Yasen, his expression darkening into menace.

"Well, he seems like a barrel of laughs," Zarya said dryly as she crossed her arms.

Yasen laughed darkly. "Oh, you have no idea." He said it softly, this time with something uncomfortable shadowing his voice.

Vikram and Amrita finished their dance and more couples moved out to join them. Zarya turned to Yasen, giving him a hopeful smile.

"Don't even think about it." He raised both his hands. "I don't dance."

"I wasn't," she said, her face falling.

"Don't pout. There are plenty of rakshasas who would be more than happy to indulge you." He pressed his hands together. "Enjoy yourself, my lady. *Try* to behave." At that, he grinned and walked away.

Sure enough, as soon as Yasen left her standing alone, a rakshasa male with cropped silver hair and crystal blue eyes that perfectly matched his form-fitting jacket asked her to dance.

Zarya glanced around the room, feeling Gopal Ravana's eyes on her again. She threw him a bland smile and then nodded to the handsome blue-eyed rakshasa.

"I'm Arjun," he said as he wrapped an arm around her waist, splaying a large, warm hand against her back.

"I'm Zarya," she replied, grinning like a fool. What did she need Vikram for, anyway?

"Has anyone told you that you are the most beautiful woman in the room tonight, Zarya?"

She barked out a laugh. "No, they haven't. Has anyone told you that you're a liar?"

"I speak nothing but the truth," he said, gracing her with a boyish smile. "How are you related to the intended pair?"

"A friend of Vikram's. Loosely speaking." Arjun gave her a bemused look. "You?"

He shrugged his broad shoulders. "A distant cousin. My mother sent me here hoping I might meet a nice girl to bring home and marry." Arjun gave her a smoldering look, and she couldn't suppress her answering grin.

"And did you meet a nice girl, Arjun?" she asked, batting her eyelashes. He grinned back, tightening his arm around her.

"We'll see, won't we?" He spun her around, and she laughed in delight.

Zarya spent the rest of the evening moving from partner to partner, coming back to dance with Arjun every few songs. He taught her the traditional dances of Daragaab, most of them fairly simple and intuitive once she got the hang of the basic steps.

Hours later, thoroughly flushed and a little tipsy from champagne, Arjun pulled Zarya into a recessed corner of the ballroom. With his hands pressed against the wall on either side of her head, he leaned down, bringing his mouth to her ear.

"I find you extremely enticing, Zarya."

His voice pitched low as he ran the tip of his nose along her throat, bringing one hand to her hip, tightening his hold. "I'd very much like to take you up to my room."

A gentle scrape of his elongated teeth brushed her sensitive skin, and she shivered at the idea of him biting her, acutely aware of the stories she'd read in her books. Arjun was so handsome and delicious, and the night had been so wondrous, and part of her, a *very* tempted part, wanted nothing more than to follow him and let him show her all the things she'd been missing.

But she'd made enough stupid mistakes for one day.

With a groan of frustration, Zarya pushed him back.

"I'm sorry. As much as I really, really want to—*really* want to—I don't think that would be a good idea. Thank you for the dancing. I had a wonderful night."

Arjun smiled. "Of course. I'll be here the next few days if you change your mind."

The corner of her mouth tipped up. "I'll remember that."

She placed a hand on his chest and slid it down slowly, caressing the taut muscles under her palm, and for a moment, her conviction wavered. Their gazes met, and he tipped his head in a hopeful question, clearly wishing she'd changed her mind.

She shook her head. *No.* Jumping straight to another man so quickly would be reckless. She would not make a fool of herself again.

With one more lingering look of regret, she pulled away. "Good night, Arjun."

He dipped his chin. "Good night, Zarya."

TWENTY-NINE

Tired and humming to the music in her head, Zarya strolled back to her room, still reeling from the strain of the last few weeks. A cool breeze greeted her when she entered her room. The balcony doors stood open, letting in the night air. Zarya stepped outside to cool off, still warm and flushed from dancing.

By moonlight, the gardens appeared even more alive. Floating lights bobbed in the air while jewel-toned peri glowed under the moon like fireflies. Delicate beams of illumination shimmered in the fountains and along the various stone pathways.

Zarya leaned on the railing, taking in the pulse of magic and mystery below. A soft knock sounded at the door, and she closed her eyes, already sure of who it would be.

"Can I come in?" Vikram had opened the door, half his body already in the room. At first, Zarya was tempted to tell him to leave, but she supposed this conversation was inevitable. She didn't answer, turning back to face the gardens to let him figure it out himself.

Clearly, he took her silence as a yes, because a moment

later, he stood next to her, also facing the night. Zarya trained her gaze forward.

"Zarya, I'm sorry—I've been a complete and utter asshole," Vikram said after a few moments of silence.

Her answering laugh was a wry snort. "Is that what you came to tell me? I already knew that."

"It's not what you think," he said in a rush.

She made a noise of disdain and straightened up from the railing. "What, you aren't engaged to the princess?"

"No. Yes. It's complicated." He turned towards her, running his hand through his hair.

She folded her arms, squeezing her elbows.

"So, explain it, then. Why did you lie to me?"

Vikram shook his head and let out a deep sigh. "We aren't engaged. At least not in the way you think. What we have isn't a romantic relationship. I'm to become her steward when Rani Vasvi passes on and Amrita takes her throne."

Zarya frowned. "What does that mean?"

"You've seen the queen. She cannot speak for herself. Cannot move from her position, so she relies on Tarin to be her voice. They can communicate through their minds, so he's able to share her wishes out loud."

"So, you're not getting married," Zarya said, something prickly loosening in her chest.

"Not technically, no." His shoulders dropped. "The position of steward is highly coveted, and my father fought for this honor for years. It's been his eternal frustration that yakshis have held the throne for so long.

"Daragaab has always belonged to them, given their original ties to its earth magic. The Jai Tree itself was planted after the Hanera Wars as both a symbol of their triumph over the Ashvins and a reminder of their power.

"But as the rakshasas' own abilities grew thanks to interspecies mating, they shut us out from the highest echelons of power, keeping us just within reach of ruling but not quite.

"It became paramount to their survival to procreate only with their own to keep their magic pure. But it was a lack of foresight on their part as the practice has reduced their numbers to the point where only a few pureblood yakshis now remain.

"Tarin was the first non-yakshi steward to ever take the position. Astomi also have strong ties to the earth, and I suppose were seen as a lesser threat than allowing a rakshasa to take the position. Astomis tend to live quiet, reclusive lives with little taste for the demands of court.

"Because of that, my father saw an opportunity to finally claim what he feels has been denied our people for so long."

Vikram chewed the inside of his lip and stared into the distance.

"When we are joined, Amrita will be queen of Daragaab and the effective ruler, but my role as her steward will give the rakshasas a position of power that is only slightly second to that. The queen is old, and she's closer to death, now more than ever. The time is coming much sooner than I expected."

He paused.

"Or hoped," he added quietly.

"You don't want this?" Zarya asked, picking up the despondency in his words.

"I've never wanted this. I'll be tied to the queen, never able to have a life of my own. I become hers in mind and soul."

Zarya swallowed a lump in her throat. "But then why was Yasen so angry when he caught us kissing at the peri anada? I thought it was because you were cheating on her."

Vikram's green eyes shone. "When I say I belong to her in every way, I mean that even my body is not my own. I am to remain celibate. Never to marry. Never to touch a woman in that way. I can never be the husband anyone deserves. While we aren't married in the traditional sense, this promise to each other amounts to the same thing."

"Oh," Zarya breathed. "I... see."

His shoulders slumped even further as he nodded. "When Rani Vasvi dies, I will spend the rest of my very long, nearly immortal life essentially married to a tree, expected to serve her and help solidify the role of rakshasas in Daragaab."

Vikram appeared on the edge of tears, and the hardness of her posture softened.

"Why did you lie to me, then? What happens if you break your celibacy?"

"Because you overwhelmed me, Zarya. That day in the swamp, when you jumped out to try to rescue us from the nagas, you were so sure of yourself. You'd spent a lifetime sheltered from the world, but nothing scared you. Without a moment's thought, you put yourself in danger for two complete strangers."

Vikram took a small step closer. "For many years, I have avoided getting close to anyone I might develop feelings for, knowing my future. I understood it, and I was resigned to it, but I hadn't counted on you blowing into my life. And it was selfish, but for a moment, I wanted happiness. I wanted to be with someone who made me feel something. Who might deign to choose me. Who I might at least get the chance to fall in love with."

There was so much passion in his voice that she found herself starting to sympathize with his situation.

"Who also didn't understand or know about your previous... commitments," Zarya added pointedly.

A blush of guilt colored his face. "I admit I took advantage of that fact," he said. "But I swear that wasn't why. It was you, Zarya."

She wanted to believe him. Wanted to believe that he'd been so enamored with her that he'd nearly abandoned his duty.

It would have been just like one of her books, but those always had happy endings, and she didn't see how this could possibly end in anything but heartache.

"I'm sorry—I lost myself. I pushed aside everything, focusing only on what I wanted. I thought if you knew the truth, you wouldn't want to get to know me. You didn't deserve that, and I'll regret it forever.

"As for what happens to me if I break my vow, I'd bring untold shame on myself and my family and possibly lose my position."

He reached for Zarya's arm, but he stopped and let his hand fall to his side.

"I have an older brother," Vikram continued, turning away again, his eyes once again focused in the distance. "This was supposed to be his destiny. Not mine. But he disappeared many years ago. We were never close, but I've never understood how he could walk away from his duty. How he could just leave me here to face this alone. One day I will see him again and—" He broke off, overcome with emotion, his eyes shining in the moonlight.

Anger, hurt, and confusion flashed in his expression. The anguish of loss and knifing family betrayal. Despite everything, Zarya found herself wanting to comfort him.

"What I do know is I don't measure up to my brother in any way my father deems worthy, even now. This arrangement is the only way I've ever been useful to him, so perhaps I should be grateful."

Vikram's expression softened. "Of course, none of this is your concern or your fault. I'm sorry. I didn't mean to cause you any hurt. You deserve to be with someone worthy of you. Someone who is free to love you openly."

They both fell silent again.

"What about Amrita? Does this hurt her?"

Vikram rubbed a hand down his face. "I'm not really sure, to be honest. We're friends and have been for a long time, but that's all. We don't share those kinds of feelings and we never have."

Zarya nodded. "Okay. Thank you for telling me."

"Thank you for hearing me out. It is more than I deserve."

"I haven't forgiven you yet."

He dipped his chin. "Of course. I understand. Please enjoy the estate. The gardens are a wonder to behold when you get a chance to explore them."

As he turned to leave, Zarya called out, "Wait." He stopped, looking back at her with one hand on the doorknob. "I'm sorry."

"For what?"

"That's an awful lot for you to bear."

"Thank you," he whispered and slipped quietly out of the room.

Zarya had been ready to collapse into bed, but she was once again buzzing with energy. She found a shawl and wrapped it around her shoulders before she headed outside, deciding to take Vikram's advice and explore the garden by starlight.

A symphony of sound greeted her as she emerged through a set of glass doors at the back of the house. Tiny peri chatted with one another in quiet voices while the insects and birds twittered, and an owl hooted in the night. It was all so peaceful. Zarya inhaled the scent of roses and jasmine and honey that drifted on the breeze.

As she wandered through the garden, many of the small creatures stopped to watch as she passed. Some waved, and some tipped their hats, and she smiled back with a wave of her own. Families were sitting down together with bowls in their hands, and some cradled the tiniest of babies wrapped in bundles.

An entire magical microcosm brimmed here, one so seemingly at odds with the cold and serious nawab who ruled this place. A man who would sell his youngest son into a life bonded to a sentient tree for the sake of his own ambition.

Zarya rounded a corner and spied a silver head of hair through the bushes. She recognized the back of Yasen, who currently had a male rakshasa pressed against a stone wall, their mouths locked and Yasen's hand shoved down the front of the man's pants.

"Oops," Zarya said, the sound slipping out before she slapped her hand over her mouth, hoping they hadn't heard her. She turned to scurry away, pretty sure Yasen would not be pleased by her interruption.

"Zarya." She stopped in her tracks and turned around with a sheepish grin.

"Sorry. I was just out for a walk, and I didn't mean to get in the way—"

Yasen had pushed himself away from his companion, who was broad and muscled, with long dark hair and striking violet eyes.

"It's fine," Yasen said. He whispered something to the other rakshasa. They shared a look, and the man grinned before he pressed his hands together in Zarya's direction before striding away.

"He didn't have to leave," she said. "I'm sorry."

Yasen shook his head and sauntered over to a fountain that sat in the center of the small courtyard where they stood. He picked up a glass with an inch of dark red liquid sitting on the edge and took a sip before he settled on a nearby stone bench.

"It's fine. I'll see him later. Come and sit," he said to her, gesturing to the empty spot with his chin.

"You sure?"

"Sit," he said, his tone offering no room for argument.

She obeyed his order and they both stared into the fountain. Silvery fish spooled around one another and occasionally leaped up in a spray of water before dipping below the surface.

"This place is really something. You grew up here?" she asked after a few moments of silence.

Yasen braced his elbows against his knees with his glass suspended between his hands and angled himself towards her.

"Zarya, I'm sorry about what happened. Vikram's been like a brother since we were children, but what he did... it's not like him to behave that way. And I should have told you—"

Zarya held up a hand for him to stop. "He apologized and told me everything. About Amrita, about their future."

Yasen's lips formed a thin line.

"It wasn't your fault. I don't blame you. I'm a big girl—I'll get over it. I really just feel sorry for him now."

Yasen gave her a sad smile.

"I understand why you were so mad that night at the peri anada now. I thought you were jealous." She tilted her head to him, her cheeks warming at the admission.

Yasen laughed, throwing back his head.

Zarya made an indignant sound. "Well, it's not *that* funny!"

"No," he said, shoulders shaking. "You are lovely—truly, but as you might have just noticed, you aren't really my type."

Zarya folded her arms and sat back. "Well, that's for the best because moody and brooding isn't really my type, either."

Yasen laughed out loud at that, and Zarya brightened at the sound, happy to see he was sometimes able to let go of the tight hold he kept on himself.

Also leaning back, he crossed an ankle over his knee and took a long drink.

"Thank you for offering to kill him, though," Zarya said eventually, nudging his arm with her elbow. "What with him being like a brother and all. I'm honored."

"Don't think this means I like you," he said, a grin splitting his handsome face.

She raised a hand as if she were taking a solemn oath. "I would never."

Their eyes met, and Zarya laughed as something warm shifted inside her.

"Does this mean we get to ogle handsome men together?" She tapped her chin with one finger. "I've discovered ogling handsome men is actually a specialty of mine."

"You name the time and place, Swamp Girl."

"We're back to Swamp Girl again?"

He winked. "Don't pretend you don't like it."

She thought about it for a moment. "The weird thing is, I kind of do."

He snorted. "Yeah, you're just as strange as I thought."

She gave him a playful shove. "Stop that. I just mean... I've never had anyone give me a nickname before because—"

She broke off, suddenly embarrassed.

"What?" he asked.

"Because I've never had a friend before."

She winced inwardly, realizing how clingy and pathetic that sounded. She waited for him to remind her they weren't really friends, but his expression softened.

"Well then. I'm honored to be your first," he said, and she could have exploded with happiness. Tears burned her eyes, and she smiled.

"Oh gods, you aren't going to cry now, are you?" he asked, and she shook her head, wiping the corner of her eye with the heel of her hand.

"No, of course not." She blinked rapidly, very obviously on the verge of crying.

He shook his head in annoyance, but she was sure that something had just changed between them. She sensed a lot of the emotions he wore were only for show. He clung to them so tightly, and Zarya wondered what had made him retreat into himself, erecting this shield of armor.

Her mouth stretched into a wide yawn that she covered with the back of her hand.

"Come on," Yasen said, standing up and holding out his hand. "You should get some sleep. You're still recovering."

Zarya looped her arm through his, and they returned to the house. Before going their separate ways, Zarya wrapped her arms around Yasen for a hug. He held himself stiffly for a moment. She thought he might back away, but then he softened and squeezed her tight.

"Night, Zee," he said.

"Night, Yasen."

Dead on her feet now, Zarya wobbled back towards her room through the quiet hallways.

A whisper floated out of the dark. "He loves you."

Zarya froze. She turned to find a figure sitting in the shadows of a small alcove. As Zarya approached, moonlight streaming through the window revealed Amrita, her eyes wet with tears.

"What?" Zarya asked.

"Vikram. I saw the way he watched you all night. The way he looked at you. I know he doesn't want this life with me."

The plush bed in Zarya's room called, and this was now officially the longest day of her life. While she'd mostly forgiven Vikram, she was going to tear a strip off him tomorrow and tell him to do something to assuage his princess, whether he wanted to become her steward or not.

With a sigh, Zarya dropped down next to Amrita. "I didn't know he wasn't supposed to be doing that. With me."

"I know that. And I certainly don't blame you. Or him. Not really. I wouldn't want to be in his shoes, either. I suspected something was going on when I saw you at the palace, but I assumed he'd told you about us." She paused. "I know they say it's forbidden, but I don't see what the big deal is. It's not like I can please him in that way."

Zarya sat up straight, shaking her head. "I'm not sure if

that's what I want. Sneaking around? Hiding it? It sounds miserable."

"It would make me happy to see him happy," Amrita pleaded. "I carry so much guilt that I've done this to him. That he has no life and no freedom because of me. If I thought being with you could offer him any kind of joy..."

"Amrita, you are very kind to worry about him," Zarya said, taking her hand. "But I can't let his cage become mine, too. I'm sorry."

A tear slid down Amrita's cheek, but she made no move to wipe it away.

"Go to bed, Amrita. Sometimes our destiny is not what we would have chosen. We can either seek to change it or learn to live with it. I don't know your paths, but that's up to you and Vikram to figure out. It can't have anything to do with me."

Amrita stared with her big amber eyes as Zarya stood.

"Good night."

Back in her room, Zarya kicked off her shoes, landed face down on the bed in her now rumpled lehenga, and instantly fell asleep.

THIRTY

The next morning, she found Yasen and Aarav seated across from one another in the small dining room. Aarav was studying a row of playing cards laid out on the table. After befriending several members of the Ravana guard, he'd spent the better part of his evenings losing and winning hands of Rani's Cradle.

Zarya sat down and watched Aarav shuffling the deck, noticing they depicted Rani Vasvi, Amrita, Tarin, the Chiranjivi, as well as some of the nobility, including Vikram, Gopal, and all three of his wives. Yasen ate his breakfast and nodded at her with a touch less of his usual aloofness.

"Morning," he said and sipped his chai.

"Morning." Zarya picked up one of the cards from the table. It depicted Row, and his stern likeness stared back at Zarya as if he were on the verge of scolding her for every bit of mischief she'd gotten up to since he'd disappeared.

"Where is he, Aarav?" she asked, feeling an uncharacteristic wave of melancholy for her pseudo-father. Despite herself, Zarya was worried and perhaps even missed Row's steady presence. He was always so sure of himself. Always knew how to handle anything. It was one thing she admired about him.

"I wish I knew," Aarav said, the cards snapping as he shuffled them. "He'll be back. I doubt he's easy to kill."

Zarya pushed out a puff of air. "I suppose."

"Let me show you the basics." Aarav grabbed the card out of her hand and inserted it into the deck.

"No, please," Zarya said, throwing her head back and covering her eyes with her arm. "Spare me from the competitive games of men and boys. I'll die happy knowing I never learned the rules or ever bet a round."

Yasen snickered. "She's just scared she won't understand it," he said with a challenge in his tone.

Zarya waved a dismissive hand. "Oh, please, if the two of you can figure it out, I'm sure a smarter-than-average donkey could grasp the rules. Besides, I want to visit the library."

Yasen's smile turned into a groan as he slumped down in his chair in mock agony, and she slapped him playfully on the arm.

"Stop it! I'm not making you go with me. You have your silly cards, and I have my books."

Yasen sat back up and shoved a plate topped with crispy fried dosa in front of her. "Fine. But eat something first. You're still recovering."

She tamped down on her smile, assuming that if she drew any attention to the way he was worrying about her, he would either deny it or shut down. But she was warmed by it all the same.

"Fine," she said, pulling the plate in front of her and digging in.

After breakfast, Zarya asked for directions to the library and learned there was more than one. She hoped she'd have time to explore them all, but she asked for the biggest one to start with. She'd had little opportunity to explore her magic in private and was hoping the Ravanas' library would have something that might be useful.

To date, she hadn't been able to get her hands on any reliable books on magic. When she'd asked around, she was told the only ones in Dharati were housed in the palace and were only accessible to those who had permission from the queen. Zarya thought about what Vikram had said about yakshis wanting to keep their magic pure and wondered if this withholding of knowledge was a nefarious tactic on their part.

Nevertheless, she had wanted to avoid arousing attention or suspicion by requesting access to them. How would she explain to the magnificent Rani Vasvi why a simple human girl from the swamps needed to read about magic?

She stood in the doorway for a moment, taking in the vast library. A giant staircase spiraled up the center of the room, allowing access to the rows and rows of shelves that stretched overhead. Giant globes sat on the floor, and Zarya passed them, taking in the sights of continents far away that she only hoped she might visit someday. The world was so large and hers had been so small for so many years.

She roamed the stacks, exploring shelves at random, picking up books and flipping through the pages. She wondered if there was someone she could ask for help, but as always, she was wary of revealing too much to strangers.

As if reading her thoughts, a voice pierced the quiet. "Can I help you find something?"

She spun around to find Vikram leaning against a shelf with his arms folded and one ankle crossed over the other. He looked especially handsome today in a dark kurta and fitted pants. Usually so buttoned-down in his soldier's uniform, she'd never seen him dressed so casually.

"Just looking for something new to read," she said. "How did you know I was here?"

"Yasen mentioned you'd gone in search of books, and I figured you'd head for the biggest library first. Before you leave, you should visit the one off the conservatory. It's smaller but even more beautiful."

She nodded. "Thanks for the tip. I'll keep it in mind."

Vikram unfolded himself and approached her, stopping when there was only a foot between them. "I could show you if you like."

"Vik—" She stopped herself, not sure what she wanted to say. She'd been thinking about the events of yesterday over and over. Of what she'd learned and what his future would be. Also, of how Amrita had ambushed her before she'd fallen into bed last night.

Did she want to continue a relationship with someone who could never truly be hers?

"I know I broke your trust," Vikram said. "But I want to try to earn it back."

"To what end? You can't be with me openly, and I have no interest in sneaking around with you. Amrita. She—"

She wasn't sure how to voice what the princess had told her last night.

"Amrita told me what she said to you."

"Oh. How do you feel about that?"

"I would... be open to it... if you were. The imposition of celibacy is an archaic rule that many believe should be done away with centuries ago. It was intended as a failsafe to protect the purity of the yakshis and nothing more. Not everyone would look down on me if I were to break it, and I can live with the judgment of those who would. They have no idea what they're talking about." His expression sharpened. "And I wasn't lying when I said how I feel about you."

Zarya hesitated. She cared for him, too, and despite everything, she believed he had a good heart. There was no denying she was attracted to him, but she wasn't sure if this was what she wanted. She'd barely had the chance to live. How could she even know what she wanted yet?

"Okay," she replied. "I need time to think about it. It's not that I don't also care for you, but it's a lot to consider."

A spark of joy lit up his eyes, and she resisted the urge to tell him not to get his hopes up. She didn't want to hurt him, and she also didn't know how to let someone down easily.

"Thank you. That's all I ask," he said. "I can be patient."

She nodded and smiled then. "Sure. Of course. Thanks for not pushing me."

He levered himself off the shelf where he'd been leaning. "Now, can I help you find anything? I know this place quite well. Unlike my friend Yasen, I happen to like reading."

She laughed and shook her head. "If it's okay with you, I'd rather just explore on my own. A library like this is something I've only dreamed of. I might be here for hours."

"Of course," he said, placing a hand over his heart and then tipping his chin. "Enjoy yourself. Feel free to send word if you decide you need a guide."

"I will."

He left her alone, and she let out a breath, confused about him and this strange situation she now found herself in. Putting it out of her head, she continued her quest for a magic book, scanning the shelves and picking up anything that looked promising.

As she rounded another stack, she felt a barely perceptible tug. It pulled at her like a carp caught on a fishhook, the sensation similar to what she always felt in the dream forest. Zarya wondered again about Rabin and when her dreams might take her back to him. Where was he now?

She wasn't sure if her reluctance to continue anything with Vikram might be due, in part, to her mysterious entanglement with Rabin. She could never tell anyone about how *he* made her feel. He was a phantom conjured from her imagination. He felt real, but was he? How could she ever tell anyone she was smitten with a ghost?

There were days when the entire incident seemed like a fantasy, no more solid than mist. But the pain had been real.

The release of her magic had been, too. And the flame she'd invoked. When Rabin had touched her, that had felt more real than anything.

The fishhook tugged her through the rows. She ran her hands along the books, allowing herself to be swept along on the crest of this benevolent wave.

There.

It grew stronger when she passed that row of shelves.

Zarya stopped and backed up. The sensation intensified as she stepped into the row, brushing her hands along both sides. Just below eye level, a small book grabbed her attention. It had a green leather cover with faded gilt lettering. She ran her fingers over the words. *Aazheri ka Jadoo.* It was written by Professor Amit Dhawan.

Professor Dhawan? That seemed like too great a coincidence not to mean something important.

As she flipped through the first few pages, the spark that now lived inside her flared, a warm glow flushing through her limbs. Her entire body hummed with energy, like a fuse waiting to detonate.

It took her a moment to realize her magic was reacting to the book in her hands, and she was sure this was exactly what she needed to help finally learn the answer to some questions she'd been asking every day of her life.

THIRTY-ONE

Zarya tucked the book into her bag next to the one with her mother's picture in it—she always kept it close by.

As she made her way back to her room, she passed guests heading to the great hall for dinner. She'd been in the library longer than she'd realized. They swept by on a stream of chatter, decked out in finery, cocktails already in hand.

She changed into her own pale pink sari, covered in sparkling silver beads, but she was distracted by the book of magic.

It seemed almost sentient, the way it kept pulling her in.

She decided to skip the party. There were plenty of people —enough, she hoped, that no one would miss her. She slung her book bag back over her shoulder and snuck out of her room, passing more guests who paid her no attention.

As she wove through the crowd, she spotted Aarav in conversation at the foot of the main staircase with Vikram and Yasen, and ducked away quickly.

Down the hallway, she found another set of stairs to take her to the main level and then went in search of a back way into the gardens.

After imploring a servant for help, Zarya located a secluded exit and burst into the fresh air, finding the sky awash in gorgeous shades of pink and orange as the sun began to set.

Peri whispered behind their hands as she swept through the winding paths. Zarya pressed a finger to her lips, beseeching them to keep her secret as she skipped the party. Several of them covered their mouths and turned away with impish looks, thrilled to be included in the game.

She made her way through the garden and to the stretch of forest that lay beyond, intending to find a spot that would provide adequate cover. As she approached the tree line, she stopped and turned back to the manor, studying the way the windows glowed in the falling light, the sounds of music and chatter drifting on the air.

Confident no one had seen her, Zarya ducked into the trees. Though all the forests of Daragaab were beautiful, this one seemed to have an especially wondrous quality to it. She wasn't familiar with the variety of the trees, but they bore slender silvery trunks and branches that hung with berries encased in fibrous cages of intricate lace as delicate as spiderwebs. Zarya wondered if this was evidence of Gopal Ravana's power or if this was yakshi magic at work.

Stepping lightly through the moss, she came to a clearing, the ground covered in thick green grass and dotted with bursts of pink and yellow flowers.

The noise and light of the house had faded behind her, and Zarya hoped she was deep enough into the trees to evade notice. Though she realized she did still have an audience, catching sight of a few bold peri hiding beneath the flower petals.

"You will keep my secret, won't you?" she asked, smiling as she flipped open the first book, the page with her mother's picture falling open from memory now.

How she wished she'd had the chance to know this woman.

Even in the drawing, Aishayadiva Madan had a spark and a light in her eyes. A sense of determination, like she was destined for something. Zarya traced the lines of her mother's face, wishing she knew where she was and what had happened to her. Was she really dead like Row had claimed?

With a longing sigh, Zarya closed the book and picked up *Aazheri ka Jadoo*, flipping it open to the title page, once again surprised at the serendipity of finding a book written by Professor Dhawan.

Next, she turned to the introduction page, reading the words:

All magic comprises the five elements. Air, water, fire, earth, and spirit. The manipulation of magic occurs through the combinations, permutations, varying strength levels, and natural affinities of the magic wielder.

While Aazheri can manipulate all five elements of magic, the same cannot be said of those whose gifts are tied to a single element.

Singular elemental magic is largely wielded by the non-Aazheri races—yakshi, rakshasa, vidyadhara, agni, merdeva, Niramaya healers, peri, etc. Their magic is limited to the boundaries of their kind and is performed through acts of the physical body or mind, such as the raising of hands, the flicking of fingers, or even the clucking of the tongue. Devakin power can be passed through singular elemental magic users, resulting in magic that is typically diluted from one's ancestors.

The far more interesting and complex magic belongs to the Aazheri. Through the combined use of elemental anchors, Aazheri have the ability to wield spells. Most Aazheri possess a fire anchor at a minimum, but the more powerful the Aazheri, the more anchors they will be able to access. Low-level Aazheri may have two or three anchors, while the strongest have five and a connection to each of the elements.

Anchors appear in different forms and are unique to every Aazheri, though often similarities can be drawn in those of the same family lines. Some may construe anchors as points or shapes or something entirely different. Some access them through their head or heart or hands, but again, this quality remains unique to each Aazheri.

She stopped reading and considered Professor Dhawan's words. At least now she really understood what the anchors meant. Rabin had told her to seek out her fire anchor the night he'd shown her how to light the flame in her hand.

Something fluttered in her chest, and Zarya closed her eyes, sure her anchor must reside in her heart where she'd noticed that initial spark. With her thoughts concentrated on fire, she held out her palm, and there—she felt it.

Fire, it whispered to her.

But did she have more anchors? With her eyes closed, she focused on the flickering light inside her, noticing how the fire anchor grew brighter the more she concentrated on its presence.

On instinct, Zarya imagined a breeze for air. For earth, the smell of fresh soil and blooming flowers. A trickle of water and the sensation of standing under a gentle rainfall.

She wasn't sure what might represent spirit, but then she thought of Koura, and that had to be aligned with Niramaya. Healing and life.

She focused on each of the elements as her fire died and retreated into blackness.

With her face scrunched in concentration, she was trying to retrieve the fire anchor when a blinding light exploded inside her chest. She felt it split apart like a comet detonating, light flaring behind her eyelids.

After a moment, it subsided, and in its place hovered a glittering five-pointed star. It spun so fast its edges blurred to form a circle, and then it stopped, pausing for a moment, before it spun in the opposite direction.

Zarya gasped.

Fire. Water. Air. Earth. Spirit. Five. She had all five of them.

Hot tears stung her eyes, and in that moment, she finally became something more than the sum of her lonely existence. More than a girl who'd been imprisoned by the sea. More than she ever dreamed possible. From this day on, she was a part of something. Something big and wide and important. She wouldn't allow anyone to ever make her feel small again.

She looked down to see that her little peri friends had grown bolder while she read, inching closer, lolling about in the grass at her feet.

Two performed a pantomime of falling in love, their gestures wild and their expressions gleeful as they collapsed dramatically into one another's arms. Zarya rewarded them with applause, and they bowed to her like actors on a stage before she resumed reading.

Aazheri magic is performed both from drawing on single elements and combining them to bring about additional nuances and consequences. For example, a protective spell against fire can be created by drawing on the wind, fire, and spirit anchors in varying degrees and proportions. Unfortunately, there is no formula for any spell—each Aazheri must learn to wield each in tandem with their own unique strengths and abilities. This book provides only a framework on how to bring about a particular outcome.

New magic wielders may find their power limited and often erratic, particularly when they are experiencing strong emotions. It requires practice and patience to see magical gifts grow and to discover the necessary combinations to produce the desired outcome. And for some, the limitations of nature will impede that progress. For some, the very nature of their gift can only take them so far. While there are a few whose power has seemed almost bottomless, most will find a limit to it as they fully mature.

Nature only gives us what we can handle, and there is many an Aazheri who has wasted their life trying to fight what the gods intended. It would be wise for the practicing Aazheri to understand that from the beginning.

Zarya contemplated the five points of her anchors, teasing out the distinct elements. Each produced a different spark as she cycled through them. Fire, hot and searing. Wind, cool and light. Water, icy and dense. Earth, thick and grounding. Spirit, shiny and illuminated. Each anchor with its own personality, its own signature, its own essence. It was intoxicating.

She flipped through the book, looking for mention of the sixth anchor she'd heard Suvanna talk about, finding only a brief mention near the end.

Of course, one cannot have a comprehensive discussion on Aazheri magic without recalling the now inaccessible sixth anchor that once belonged to only a handful of powerful Aazheri—the most notorious, of course, being the Ashvins. They combined this sixth strain with the basic elements to perform magical acts that had rarely been seen before and haven't been accomplished since. While it was a measure borne of necessity to snuff out these brothers' abilities, it will also forever be a loss to our kind. Without it, we are but a fractured part of the whole.

This was the darkness that Suvanna had been so afraid of. The "tainted magic" she had talked about.

Something about the words "a fractured part of the whole" sent a chill skittering to the back of her neck. Zarya had always been an anomaly, as far as she could tell. Row seemingly had no idea what her star magic was or where it came from. What if *she* were tainted?

Slowly, she closed her eyes and tried to call it, dreading the outcome.

The darkness.

Of course, nothing happened. She let out the nervous breath trapped in her chest, shaking her head with a wry laugh at herself. What a silly thing to even contemplate. She was going to start jumping at her own shadow next.

With a hand thrust out, she focused on a bubbling stream at the edge of the clearing, sliding her consciousness along her water anchor. Slowly, a droplet peeled up from the surface, where it hovered for all of two seconds before falling with about as much force as a single raindrop.

She sighed as she lowered her hand.

It was something, at least. Kind of.

Focusing on a breath of air, she succeeded in making a few blades of grass rustle. Well, perhaps it was one blade, she thought glumly as she peered into the greenery. Peri now sat with their legs crossed, chins in their hands, watching her and clapping enthusiastically with each new discovery. They were the perfect audience. Excited enough to keep up her confidence without making her self-conscious during her fumbling attempts.

Zarya tried a healing spell, attempting to smooth over a thin cut on her arm with a draw on her spirit anchor. After she was done, she twisted her arm, trying to catch slivers of moonlight, but it didn't appear she'd made much progress.

She read on, finding a spell Dhawan had penned for creating a burst of fire.

Fire and air.

Using the book's instructions, she drew on her fire anchor, feeding in ribbons of air bit by bit until it suddenly caught, igniting into a spray of sparks that jumped a foot above her head, exploding like the fireworks she'd set off with Row and Aarav on the beach for Diwali.

The pop echoed through the peaceful stillness before the sparks drifted harmlessly to the earth.

"Woah," came a voice from behind her, and Zarya whipped around. Momentarily blinded in the darkness, she blinked.

"What did you just do?" Yasen asked, stepping out from the shadows. "How? When did this happen? Why are you *hiding* out here?"

"I'm not hiding," she snapped.

"It looks like you're hiding." He crossed his arms over his chest and arched an eyebrow.

"I wasn't ready for everyone to know yet," she said.

Yasen dropped his arms, his skeptical expression softening. "Okay, but I don't understand. How long have you known about this?"

Zarya recounted a few details about that agonizing night in the forest, careful to omit the full truth of both her old star magic and Rabin's role in freeing her from Row's binding.

"But this is good news, isn't it? Why are you concealing it?"

"It is. I just don't understand who it's good for. I think the Chiranjivi want something from me, Yasen." She gestured in the direction of Dharati with her chin. "Kindle, Suvanna—I've heard them talking about me, and I need to understand what they want before I reveal the truth. Row always said this had to be kept hidden, but I never knew why."

Concern flickered across his face. "Okay, but don't try this on your own. It could be dangerous. I've heard of new Aazheri who've blown up entire buildings when they've come into their power."

"I'll be careful, I promise." She bit her bottom lip and then confessed, "I can barely light a match."

Yasen smirked and sat down in the grass. "So, show me," he said, eyes sparking with mischief.

She dropped down next to him and retrieved the magic book, flipping through it as he lay on his side, his long body stretched out, resting on an elbow.

"I was about to try this one. The bubble of memory. For the forgetful, trying to figure out what they forgot, a combination of spirit, air, and fire."

"Sure," Yasen said. "I don't really know what you're talking about, but it sounds good."

She rolled her eyes and crossed her legs with her back pressed against Yasen's outstretched thighs.

The peri watched intently while one crawled up onto Yasen's head and luxuriated in his silver locks. Making a sound of annoyance, Yasen plucked the peri off and dropped her on the ground. She jumped up, hands on hips, and kicked the dirt in front of her.

"Don't climb on me. I don't know where you've been."

The peri blanched with indignation and stomped over to sit next to one of her friends, throwing dirty looks at Yasen with her spindly arms crossed.

Zarya laughed before concentrating on the three different anchors as they pulsed and shifted, seemingly eager to do her bidding.

A flare of spirit. A spark of fire. A ribbon of air.

It was instinctual, like an equation laid out before her.

A small white bubble of light was now hovering over Zarya's hand. It expanded and spun slowly before it turned transparent like mist escaping a glass bottle. A moment later, it revealed a hillside covered in green grass beneath a clear blue sky, the sun high overhead. Laughter came from a distance as two young girls with long, dark hair ran into the picture. They both wore ornately decorated salwar kameez, one a vibrant purple and the other a ruby red, covered in black beads and lace.

Behind them walked a couple arm in arm, watching the girls and laughing with love in their eyes. Their parents, no doubt. The man was dressed in a tailored jacket, and the woman in a bright emerald sari draped in folds. Her dark hair was swept to the side and pinned with a large flower and a piece of black netting.

Zarya twisted her hand, trying to get a different look at the scene. The people seemed familiar somehow, like the tune of a song she couldn't remember the lyrics to. The girls were throwing themselves down the hill, rolling to the bottom, then hauling themselves back up to the top again and again. They'd kicked off their black shoes, each with tiny heels and bows that matched their suits.

One of the girls, who looked like the older sister—she might have been about eight or nine—came into clearer focus as she ran to the edge of the bubble. Zarya let out a breath of surprise as she recognized her necklace—a tear-shaped turquoise pendant about the size of a thumbnail suspended from a gold chain.

The same necklace she had worn every day of her life.

The scene froze just before the bubble burst, mist rising into the air, sparkling in the moonlight.

"What was that?" Yasen asked, sitting up.

"I think… that was my mother. She was wearing the same necklace." She grasped her pendant. "I've always had this. Row said it belonged to her."

"And the other people?"

"I don't know. A sister, her parents? I've never seen any of them. Where did that come from?"

"I have no idea. It certainly wasn't my memory."

"Memory? It wasn't my memory, either."

"Well, it must have been," he said, tapping the book that he'd pulled towards himself. "It says here the spell recalls lost memories."

"But that isn't my memory. I don't remember that."

"Maybe Row told you about it when you were young, and it lingered there in the back of your mind." He grabbed her braid and tugged it gently. "Besides, it says it's for lost memories. Looks like you just found one."

"I suppose," she said. She tried to picture it again, but the image kept slipping away.

"What about you?" she asked.

"Me?"

"What kind of magic do you have? Do all rakshasas have it?"

"Nope." He rolled onto his back and tucked his arms beneath his head. "I have no magic other than the usual enhanced hearing and sight and near immortality. And incredible good looks, of course."

"Well, I guess that's not so bad."

"True, I could be a lowly human with their near blindness and fleeting lifespans."

Zarya gave him a playful punch in the stomach.

"Oof, what was that for? You're not human," he said.

Zarya paused. He was right. She wasn't human anymore. Or never had been. Not really.

"Still, that's not nice."

He chuckled.

"Some rakshasas have magic. Usually those of higher nobility who've mated with yakshis. Most don't. The Ravanas all have it, of course. Gopal has a lot. Vikram, not as much. His brother was very strong. Some say he was nearly as powerful as a full-blooded yakshi."

"What about your family? Who were your parents?"

"I'm Diya's nephew. Her sister was my mother. Diya brought me here to live with the Ravanas after my mother died in a fire that almost killed me, too. No one knows who my father was."

"I'm so sorry, Yasen."

He gave her a tight smile.

"Who do you think they are?" Zarya asked, returning to the vision she'd just conjured. "What happened to her sister and her parents? My aunt? *My grandparents?*"

"I have no idea," he said, staring up at the darkened sky. "But they must have lived in Gi'ana."

"Really? How can you tell?"

"From the way they're dressed. That's the style there."

Zarya mouthed the word. *Gi'ana.*

The western realm ruled by King Adarsh, at least until he passed the crown to his daughter. She uncrossed her legs and lay down in the grass next to Yasen. The peri arranged themselves around them, mimicking Yasen's position with their hands behind their heads as they all watched the stars above.

"Have you ever wondered who your father was?" she asked him.

At first, he didn't answer, and she wondered if she should apologize for touching a sore spot. But then he said, "Every day of my life."

"You need the Bayangoma, too."

"The what?"

"It's a story Row used to tell me about birds who know secrets. I always wished they could help me find out who my parents were. Maybe they could do the same for you."

Yasen was quiet for another moment.

"Yeah. That would be nice."

THIRTY-TWO

When Zarya and Yasen returned to the manor, dinner was still in full swing. Mouth-watering aromas and strains of music filled the corridors, and it was clear the festivities would carry on well into the night.

"Do you want to go in?" Yasen asked. "We're both dressed for it."

She shook her head. "I'm kind of tired. I think I'd rather get some sleep."

"Okay. I'll make your excuses. I should head back in for a while."

"Thank you."

After bidding Yasen goodnight, she returned to her room. Using her magic had been a drain on her already wearied system, and suddenly she was exhausted. She noticed someone had come to dim the lights and turn down the covers. The bed looked so inviting that she walked over and lay down, intending to close her eyes for just a moment before she changed.

She stared at the ceiling, thinking about what she'd seen in the time bubble.

Gi'ana. Was that where her family lived? Were they still

there? Her mother and father must have been Aazheri, too. Professor Dhawan's book said Aazheri were born of two magical parents. After floating adrift for so long, Zarya was experiencing a distinct sense of coming together. Scattered pieces finding themselves amongst the layers.

It all meant something.

Her captivity. The mystery of her family. The secret of her magic. These were not spontaneous events. They were connected and woven like intricate silk rugs, the pattern yet to reveal itself.

It felt only like a few moments later that she opened her eyes and found herself lying on the grass inside the dream forest.

A rush stole through her, goosebumps peppering her skin.

Finally.

Every night before falling asleep, she'd hoped for it. Her earlier exhaustion melted away in the face of breathless antici- pation. She pushed herself up, dusting off bits of grass that clung to her sari and peered into the darkness of the trees, searching for any sign of movement.

For any sign of *him.*

When she saw nothing, she picked up the hem of her skirt and headed for the tree line. The grass was soft and cool and tickled her bare feet.

As she drew closer, she caught a flash in the darkness. The crescents of dark eyes reflecting in the moonlight. The sight ground her to a stop halfway across the clearing, where she waited, letting the fabric of her skirt settle over her feet.

The air in her lungs suspended at the rustle of leaves, signaling his movements through the trees. What was it about him and this place? Why did she keep returning here? Was this a message? Or a sign?

She ignored a string of intrusive thoughts that suggested *this* man might be what Row had been so afraid of all this time. But that couldn't be right.

Firstly, she didn't want to admit it because she wanted to keep returning. Secondly, it wasn't possible that a place that instilled such a sense of peace could be bad. Besides, it wasn't like she had a choice in the matter.

Rabin finally emerged and paused as their gazes caught. He approached slowly, then stopped in front of her, searching every inch of her face as if trying to memorize every line and detail he saw.

This place and this rakshasa were also part of the pattern. More threads, more pieces joining to form the whole. This wasn't a place to fear. This, too, was her destiny.

"You look... beautiful," he said, his voice jagged. He wore a pale grey kurta with the top few buttons opened to reveal the hard lines of his chest and something dark tattooed on his skin. Sleeves rolled up to his elbows revealed more dark marks covering his forearms. His dark, gold-flecked eyes were lush waves in a bottomless sea. Without her shoes on, he was even taller tonight. Bigger. Grander. Filling her entire view like a mountain that refused to be ignored.

"I was supposed to go to a party," she replied, gesturing to her elaborate sari. The words came out in a whisper. She could never catch her breath around him.

The corner of his mouth curved in the barest movement. "Supposed to?"

"There have been a lot of parties this week." When he raised his eyebrows in question, she added, "I'm visiting a friend in the countryside."

"Were you dancing, Zarya?"

She smiled and grabbed the edges of her skirt, swirling it back and forth. "I did."

He tilted his head and then stepped closer so they were

almost touching. Zarya's heart thrummed so hard it felt like it had slipped off course.

Rabin held her gaze for what felt like an eternity before he reached out and gently brushed his thumb across her cheek. She exhaled as her eyes fluttered closed at the contact, and she barely resisted the overwhelming urge to lean in and press her nose to the curve of his throat.

"I didn't get a chance to properly thank you for helping me," she said, still trying to find her breath, lost somewhere down at her feet. "You saved me."

Rabin wrapped his fingers around the side of her neck, his thumb sweeping along her jaw. Zarya placed her hand on his as a hungry flame flickered in her belly.

"Dance with me," he said, the words a restrained whisper, twisted with an authority that made it sound like an order.

She shook her head. "I'm not very good at it."

"We'll see about that," he said, wrapping an arm around her waist and pulling her close. Their bodies flush, the hard planes of his chest and stomach aligned with her softer curves, reducing her knees to jelly and turning that needy place below her navel molten with heat.

She rested one hand on his shoulder while the other joined with his, their fingers interlacing, his broad hand reducing hers to delicacy.

She stared up at him as he moved them both, turning her over the soft grass like they were floating over clouds. She was acutely aware of every place he touched her, the blood in her limbs rushing to find him.

"Have you been practicing? Your magic?" Rabin asked as they swayed as one.

She nodded. "A little. That's what I was doing when I skipped the party tonight."

His face registered some kind of amusement. Not a smile;

he was too intense for that, but a touch of approval danced across his gaze.

"Your anchors? Did you find them?"

She gave another nod as his thumb swept over her lower back, that simple gesture scattering her thoughts into a constellation of shooting stars.

"There are five," she said, and he seemed to go still for a heartbeat. Another emotion flickered on his face. Was it fear? Had she imagined it? There was nothing to fear here. Nothing to fear from *her*. His hand and his touch—this all felt like home.

He moved closer, the air between them humming with a hidden promise. Zarya's ribs and chest struggled to expand as her breath hitched. He searched her face, and she understood then that she was caught in something bigger than herself. Something bigger than she understood.

His eyes dropped to her mouth, and she licked her top lip, wondering if he was going to kiss her. This felt different than it had with Vikram. That had been fun and exciting, but this, this was the difference between being crushed under a pebble versus a boulder.

Gods, how she wanted to kiss him.

"Where are you, Zarya? Tell me that," he said, interrupting her reverie.

"Daragaab," she whispered, not sure if she should be revealing that, but he'd charmed the words from her throat. "Near Dharati."

She caught the barest spark of surprise in his eyes, accompanied by a conflicted flutter of emotion in her stomach. He drew her hand to his mouth and flipped it over before he pressed his lips to her palm. Every nerve and sense honed into that spot, and she did her best not to dissolve into a puddle at his feet.

"I'm on my way," he said, and it was her turn to be surprised. "Don't move."

Then he let go of her and walked away.

"What?" Zarya whispered. "What do you mean?"

He glanced over his shoulder with a look that suggested he was far from done with her.

"Wait!" she called.

But she woke up and the dream was over.

She lay on her bed with her skin flushed and her breath heavy, heat stirring in her stomach and the space between her thighs. Her hand slid over her skin as she pictured him. His beautiful face and the curves and edges of his body. Rounded shoulders and thick arms. Broad chest and carved jaw. She wanted to trace her fingers over every line and groove until she'd committed them to memory.

Her hand slid lower, fingertips dipping beneath her waistband and then her underwear, not at all surprised to find herself wet. She lifted her knees and then let them fall open as she pressed a finger inside her body.

Her eyes fluttered closed as she imagined the forest and the way he might touch her. His hands, so big and rough, but with the skill of a musician expertly tuning an instrument. She imagined his mouth on hers. On her breasts. On her stomach. His head buried between her legs as he made her back arch and her hands clench in the grass.

Zarya was no stranger to these sorts of fantasies. In the cottage with only her romance books to keep her company, she'd had plenty of time to explore herself whenever Row and Aarav would leave her alone, often for days at a time. She'd never had trouble using her imagination, and with Rabin filling her thoughts, she'd never had such vivid material to work with before.

He was quite possibly the most delicious man she'd ever seen.

A small gasp escaped her lips as her fingertip slid over her clit, sending a wave of electric shivers up her spine. She wondered what it would be like if Rabin did this? Would it be fast and hard or soft and gentle? Maybe some of both.

She'd wanted to stay in that forest forever. With him. Exploring these feelings and emotions twisting in her chest.

But he'd said he was coming.

He'd told her not to move.

Gently, she continued touching herself, winding herself closer to the edge. Her neck arched as she inhaled shallow breaths, her knees shaking and her heart skipping.

She'd been trying to convince herself he wasn't real. That he was only a dream. That he couldn't hurt her. Not really. But what if he came?

What if the things Row had always feared were real? Had she unwittingly stumbled into the path of danger? What if everything she'd been doing was wrong, and here she was lying on her bed, having erotic thoughts about a man with nefarious intentions?

Zarya circled her clit harder, waves of warmth cresting into her impending release, her hand gripping the bedsheet. Her hips shifted as she moaned, and then she flew apart as soft ribbons of heat dispersed through her blood.

When she was done, she lay like a starfish on the bed, staring up at the ceiling.

"Fuck," she whispered into the empty room.

THIRTY-THREE

"Always aim a swift kick at a man's most prized possession," Zarya said as she instructed Amrita the next day, practice swords gripped in their hands. Amrita giggled, her cheeks turning pink at the suggestion as Zarya offered a wicked grin. "Don't forget to keep your left side up and never, *ever* let them see you sweat."

Zarya whirled and knocked the sword from Amrita's shaking grasp. The amber-eyed yakshi clapped her hands in jubilation.

"Zarya," she said, breathless, "where did you learn all this? You are so brave!"

Zarya picked up a glass of water from a nearby table. She sat down on the low wall surrounding the courtyard where she was practicing with Amrita. She was due to return to the city tomorrow, and they were sneaking in the lesson she had promised.

"The man who raised me," Zarya said, before pressing her lips together. The title was a close enough approximation of the complicated role Row played in her life.

The man who imprisoned me for twenty years seemed a little dramatic, even to her.

"He thought everyone should know how to defend themselves against an enemy, and I was no exception."

Amrita sat next to her, wiping a sheen of sweat from her forehead. "Vikram told me about that wicked man. What was it like being confined for all those years?"

"Lonely. Confusing and frustrating, but mostly just lonely."

Amrita nodded in understanding. "I get lonely, too. It's nice when Vik and Yasen come to visit me in the palace, but I don't have any other friends. There are always a lot of people around, but no one talks to me unless they want something."

"Why do they keep you so... hidden from everyone? And why did you leave after the fire? You haven't seen your mother since then?"

"Gopal thinks I'm safer here. After all the terrible things going on lately, he doesn't want anything to happen to me, and the compound is heavily guarded against the blight." Amrita's smile was tight. "Royal heirs tend to be closely guarded in general. I don't have a lot of freedom, which is why I don't leave the palace much, even when I'm in Dharati."

When Zarya had first seen Amrita, she had assumed her existence must be so filled with freedom and purpose. That as a princess, she'd be allowed to do anything she wanted, but Amrita also lived in a cage of someone else's making, just like Zarya had for so long.

"She's not entirely devoid of personality," Amrita said. "My mother. Vik and everyone else just see a wall of bark and a woman who can't speak, but I can talk to her. She's warm and funny and kind. People don't see that. They only see what she isn't."

"She is beloved by her people. They kept vigil for hours after the fire. They must see some of those qualities in her."

"Yes, perhaps."

Zarya picked up on a wave of anxiety in Amrita. "I'm sure they'll feel the same about you."

"Oh, I'm not worried about that. I mean, yes, I want to be a good queen, but my mother taught me her ways. I am sure I can be what the people of Daragaab need, just as she has been. Perhaps I can be more."

"More?"

Amrita sighed. "Mother avoids confrontation. Daragaab's borders are secure, not by her will, but rather that of a strong army and a commander who expanded her territory so wide in the last hundred and fifty years that no one dares touch us. And if it were up to her, we'd never fight for anything ever again."

Zarya gave the princess a shrewd look, realizing Amrita was not as naïve as she pretended to be.

"But the days of our security are nearing their end. There is unrest in the north—the vanshaj are fighting back against their treatment. And who can blame them? Punished for a millennium for something done by two fabled kings? Who even knows if they were real anymore? And the blight is a threat to all of us. It wasn't my mother who summoned the Chiranjivi to help. It was Tarin who finally convinced her we needed them. She'd rather ignore problems and hope they go away."

Zarya laid a gentle hand on Amrita's arm.

"The people of Daragaab are very fortunate to have you as their future queen."

Amrita dropped her head, letting out a deep breath.

"So, what is bothering you, then?"

"I'm nervous about the joining," she said, looking up, her cheeks turning pink.

"The joining?"

She lowered her voice, leaning close to Zarya. "The seeding, specifically."

"I'm not sure I understand."

"During the ceremony, mine and Vikram's spirits will be joined to create a new heir. There's a pool of water we both enter where the spell is performed. Amrita's voice dropped to a whisper. "And we do it... in the nude."

Her eyes bulged, and Zarya barked out a laugh. "The fate of the world doesn't trouble you, but getting naked in front of the man who will speak for you for the rest of your life does?"

Amrita chewed her lip. "Well, when you put it like that."

"Wait," Zarya said. "An heir? Like getting you pregnant?"

Amrita shook her head. "In the technical sense, yes, but it's done through magic, not... the way you're thinking. The seed of new life will be laid inside me, and then one day, I'll be able to release it when we deem the time is right."

"Oh. I see," Zarya said, though she wasn't sure if she really understood. She made a mental note to do some reading on the subject later.

"I haven't ever... you know, done *that*." Amrita waved her hands, and Zarya leaned in.

"What? Had sex?"

Amrita's cheeks turned pink. "Yes. Don't say that out loud!"

"But why not?"

"Because I was never encouraged to talk about such things," Amrita said, her shoulders rounding in.

"Well, I wasn't, either, but I'm rarely a fan of doing what I'm told," Zarya said, and Amrita sat up and grinned. "And, my friend, it seems a crime that you must go into the beyond without having been ravished a little."

Zarya raised her eyebrows, and Amrita covered her face.

"I don't know. Would I enjoy it? I hear the men talk about it, and they must enjoy it very much."

Zarya huffed out a snort. "In my very limited experience, it wasn't all the stories make it out to be. But I'm strongly beginning to suspect that mine was broken."

Amrita's mouth opened into an *o*, and they dissolved into fits of laughter.

"Come on," Amrita said, wiping tears from her eyes. "We should go in. Lunch will be ready."

As they stood, Zarya caught sight of the rigid form of Gopal Ravana. He was beelining for them at a clipped pace, his arms swinging at his sides. Zarya's lip curled as the nawab stopped a few paces away.

It was disarming how much he resembled Vikram, slightly broader and a few years older, despite several hundred years separating them. His emerald-green eyes glittered with a malice she could never picture on Vikram.

"Amrita," Gopal said without looking at her, his gaze locked on Zarya. "Go inside."

Amrita squeezed Zarya's hand and scurried off without a word.

Zarya schooled her features into irreverent boredom as she faced Vikram's father. "Can I help you?"

"I see you. I see him looking at you."

Zarya rolled her eyes. Apparently, this family's favorite pastime was watching Vikram watch her.

"I don't know what you're talking about," she said, picking an imaginary piece of dust off her sleeve.

"Do you think I'm a fool?" He took a step closer, eyes blazing. He towered over her, but she refused to back up.

"I don't know what you are."

"My son will soon be Steward of Daragaab. I will not let some filthy *human* bring shame on my family's legacy."

She snorted. "Steward. Yes, because that's clearly what he wants."

Gopal's expression darkened. "Watch yourself, little girl. I will not tolerate words against my family. I do not want my son anywhere near you. You will stay away from him."

He stepped closer, his humid breath warming her face. She resisted the urge to flinch away, understanding he was the kind of man who'd feed off her fear and then happily lick his fingers clean.

"I'm just a little girl," she said, spitting the words out. "What could I possibly do? Not that it's any of your business, but there is nothing going on between me and your son. So please, get out of my way."

Gopal's eyes gleamed with a feral light. It was a blessing things were over with Vikram because Zarya couldn't ever imagine being anywhere near this man on a regular basis. Poor Amrita.

"I hope Vikram sees you, too," she added, deciding he was already pissed and nothing else she said would make much difference. "I hope you get what you deserve because you don't deserve a son like him. And the people of Daragaab certainly don't deserve a ruler like you." She took a step back. "I'm late for lunch."

Gopal stood rooted to the spot as Zarya skirted around him. She retreated to the safety of the house, trying to keep herself from breaking into a run to put as much distance as possible between her and this foul rakshasa.

THIRTY-FOUR

After they returned to Dharati, Zarya couldn't seem to sit still. There was something stirring in her blood, like an itch buried under her skin that she couldn't scratch. It felt like a breath held, waiting on the edge of something, but she didn't understand what.

The city itself felt like it was under siege. While they'd been at the Ravana estate, there'd been another breach of the wall. The vetala had struck again, this time knocking down one of the garrison doors and spilling into the city before the Khada could put them down. More people had died, and the queen's condition hadn't improved. It was obvious her magic was failing, and there was no telling what would happen if she didn't make it. How long could the city fight off the demons without her magic to protect them?

Yasen had picked up on Zarya's restlessness and suggested they go for a drink. They now sat in a bar in the heart of the city, and she suspected he'd needed the distraction as well.

"And then what happened?" Zarya asked, taking a draft of her ale. She clutched her stomach with laughter as Yasen recounted the time he and Vikram had broken into Gopal

Ravana's study to steal a rare bottle of absinthe from his liquor cabinet. The Ravana guards had convinced the two young rakshasas that absinthe imparted powerful properties of virility on whoever drank it, so Yasen and Vikram thought they'd test the theory before a night of partying.

"After drinking about a quarter of the bottle, I went blind." Yasen gagged, his face turning green at the memory. "And the only thing it gave us was a three-day hangover. I puked so many times it felt like my heart had come out of my throat."

He shook his head and laughed. "Gods, what a couple of idiots we were."

A warmth bloomed in Zarya's chest. Yasen's unrestrained laughter was like a secret song—it was such a rare and beautiful thing.

"We were both in agony," he continued, still chuckling. "We were lying on Vikram's bed, and we couldn't move at all. The room was spinning, and Gopal came in absolutely furious. I must have been hallucinating because I swear he turned into a fire-breathing dragon. It scared me so much that I fell off the bed and cracked my elbow on a post.

"I'm not sure if he was angrier that we had gotten so drunk or that we'd wasted his precious bottle. Probably the latter, if I know him. He kicked us both out of the house and made us sleep in the garden for a week. It rained the entire fucking time. I think he was somewhat satisfied that we'd learned a lesson when we dragged our sorry wet asses back inside."

"Not to drink absinthe?" Zarya asked, raising a brow.

"Right, or just to hide it better."

She snickered. "A good lesson indeed."

They fell into a companionable silence while Yasen stared at his glass. Then he took a drink and thunked it down on the bar. "Our punishment was light that time. Or mine was, anyway."

Zarya's gut twisted at the acid in Yasen's voice. "What do you mean?"

"It never went over well when Vik tried to assert his independence over his father. One of the worst incidents was when one of Vik's cousins fell in love with a vanshaj." Yasen rolled his shoulders and shifted uncomfortably in his seat.

"When they were caught together, Gopal was sent for. It was considered a scandal. He ordered the woman beaten to death. She was dragged into the back courtyard, and Vik tried to stop it and get his father to see reason. It wasn't her fault, and it would have accomplished nothing, but Gopal was in a rage. He wouldn't be swayed. When that didn't work, Vikram threatened to leave and abandon his role as steward, just like his brother had. I'd never seen him raise his voice to his father like that. I'd certainly never seen him stand up to him before.

"But that was the wrong thing to say because the nawab fucking lost it. He was so angry he was frothing at the mouth. So, he ordered me beaten next."

A gasp escaped Zarya's lips. Yasen stared into his glass again, and she waited for him to collect himself. When he spoke again, his voice was rough.

"They beat me within an inch of my life. I was recovering for weeks; they broke nearly every bone in my body. Vik didn't leave my side the entire time. The woman died, and Vik's cousin was sent away, never to be seen again.

"But the message was loud and clear. From that day on, Vikram toed his father's line. Of course, once in a while, he's slipped up in the eyes of the nawab, and I'm the one who always suffers for it."

Zarya placed a hand on his arm. "I'm sorry. That is monstrous. Why do you stay here, Yasen?"

He shrugged, but the movement was stiff.

"Vik is the only true family I have. And I can't leave him

alone with Gopal. He's too soft-hearted. His father would eat him alive."

"That's why he's going through with the joining."

"Yes. He'd rather die than let me face his father's wrath ever again."

"No wonder you were so angry about the two of us."

He shook his head. "No, I wasn't concerned for myself. I want him to be happy, and he was happy with you. I was angry he was leading you down a path you couldn't follow."

"That is so unfair. How can you be so resigned to this?"

"I've learned to accept my role in this life. I don't know what else I'd do, anyway." His smile was bitter.

Zarya puffed out her cheeks and let out a long sigh. "I do feel for Vikram. Can you imagine? Never being able to feel anyone's touch? Never being intimate again?"

"Oh, I know," Yasen said. "We've discussed it plenty of times. Usually after several drinks. It's such an archaic practice, but the nobility is so entrenched in their ways. Meanwhile, most of them are busy fucking their mistresses behind closed doors while their wives tend to their households with fake smiles plastered to their faces. It's hypocrisy at its finest."

"Well, one good thing came out of it," she said after a minute, giving Yasen a sidelong glance.

"What's that?"

"Thanks to Vikram's omission of truth, you stopped scowling at me and are almost tolerable now."

He snorted. "Thanks, you're kind of tolerable yourself." Yasen grinned at her, and Zarya's throat constricted. "Why are you looking at me like that?"

"It's so embarrassing," she said, "but I was so alone. I had no one, and now everything has changed. I have Amrita and you, and even Vikram. And it's like finding a life raft in a storm. Sometimes I thought the reason Row kept me hidden was because no one wanted me around."

Yasen furrowed his forehead. "Oh, Zee."

"It's okay," she said, shaking her head. "I don't believe that anymore. I know better now."

"Good, because that isn't true." He paused. "I listened to you and Aarav arguing on the beach a few weeks ago."

"I know. Thank you for watching out for me."

"You were growing on me like a fungus." He winked and took a drink. "What happened between you two, anyway? It can't be just jealousy."

She let out another long sigh and shook her head. "Maybe our relationship isn't his fault entirely."

He tipped his head in question.

"I don't really understand how it all started. For as long as I can remember, he always disliked me. Even when I was a child, he was borderline cruel. Aside from leaving me behind every chance he got, he'd sometimes lock me out of the house at night when Row was away and do petty things like knock my food over or trip me when I passed. Insidious things that in themselves weren't much, but over the years, a void grew between us.

"He's a bit older than me, and I've always assumed he hated playing babysitter so often. When Row was around, he ignored me completely, but Row was away often. And I wasn't exactly the most compliant kid." She looked down at her hands, needles of guilt prickling under her skin.

"You were a child, Zarya. That wasn't your fault," Yasen said, sensing her contrition.

She gave Yasen a small smile. "When I was fourteen, something happened that cemented our relationship forever. Row had been gone for a couple of weeks, and he had a strict rule about Aarav bringing visitors to the cottage. It was expressly forbidden, and it was because of me. Because *I* always had to stay hidden. I suppose that's another reason Aarav disliked me —like I had any choice in the matter.

"One night, Aarav went to the nearby village to go drinking.

It was just after sunset when he returned with a group of friends, including a woman I could tell he was absolutely smitten with."

Yasen grimaced, and she laughed.

"I saw them coming and went to hide in my room. Aarav must have told them I was there because a little while later, one of his friends found me. He was obviously stone drunk, and he stumbled into my room and grabbed me. Pushed me against the wall, put his hands on me, and licked my neck. It was awful. I was paralyzed, and I couldn't move. I couldn't scream, and I'm not sure anyone would have stopped him, anyway.

"To this day, I hate how I just froze. Row had me training with a sword since the day I could walk, but at that moment, I forgot everything he taught me. I can still feel how rough he was. He was so feral and possessive, like I owed him something. It was the most terrifying thing I'd ever experienced..."

She shuddered. Yasen laid his hand over hers and squeezed it.

"Then Row showed up. Aarav shouted at everyone to hide, and they all scattered into the forest, including the man in my room. I was shaking so hard I couldn't breathe.

"But whatever his faults, I knew Row would protect me. I was vibrating with fear and anger, and I told him what Aarav had done and what that man had tried to do. Row was furious. He's always kind of scary, but this was something else."

Overwhelmed by the memories, Zarya stopped again and stared into her glass. She'd done her best to block out those moments over the years. Yasen rubbed her forearm gently. "You don't have to tell me."

"No, it's okay."

With a trembling breath, she continued.

"Row stalked into the forest and hunted each one of them down like animals—they didn't stand a chance—and he killed every one of them. I heard them screaming, pleading for their lives. But he didn't spare a single one. Then he lost his shit on Aarav and threw him out of the house for weeks.

"Obviously, Aarav was furious with me after that. I reminded him of what his friend had tried to do, but he didn't care. Aarav had lost the woman he loved, along with the only friends he had. Living out there sequestered in the forest must have been lonely for him, too, but I never felt sorry for him. The way I saw it, he was at least allowed to leave, while I always had to stay behind. But he's blamed me ever since."

She wasn't sure if she could face Yasen's disappointment in her, so she focused on her hands clasped around her glass. Zarya had told herself she deserved Aarav's condemnation, over and over. She had killed those people by running to Row. They would still be alive if she'd waited until they'd had enough time to get away.

Yasen took her chin and turned her head towards him. When she finally gathered the courage to look at him, she found only sorrow and understanding reflecting back.

"It wasn't your fault," he said, his voice just audible over the din of the crowded bar. "He was wrong to blame you, and you did nothing wrong. You were a kid and should never have been put through any of that. It was not your fault."

No one had ever uttered those words to her. No one had ever sat her down and looked at her and told her those deaths hadn't been her responsibility. Something tight and heavy fell away from her then, tangled ropes that unfurled and dropped to her feet in a pile of discarded baggage.

"Thank you," she whispered as Yasen stood, causing Zarya to flinch.

"What?" He scowled with his arms paused in midair. "I want to give you a hug."

"You do?"

"Yes, I do. You seem to really like them."

Zarya laughed, wiping her tears, and Yasen folded her into

his arms. He was warm and solid and comforting and felt like something close to the family she'd craved for so long. She wished she could bottle this feeling and keep it for the next time she was lonely.

"I haven't had very many of them in my life. Hugs, I mean," Zarya said as Yasen rested his chin on her head.

"I suppose I haven't, either. Maybe I see what the fuss is about."

After a minute, they pulled away, both somber.

"So much for our fun night of drinking," Zarya said.

"Well, Zee, the night is still young."

He held up his glass, and she grinned at him. "And when I get drunk enough, I'm going to go find that idiot Aarav and kick his bony ass."

Zarya burst out laughing, and they clinked their glasses just as Dharati's alarm bells began to ring.

THIRTY-FIVE

The bar fell silent.

"What is it?" Zarya asked in a soft voice before a series of sharp staccato blasts pierced the air.

"The queen," Yasen said, recognizing the signal as they jumped up and tripped into the streets, pushing their way through the already-thickening crowds.

A steady tide of bodies was spilling into the courtyard through the palace gates. Yasen and Zarya entered to find small clusters of Dharatis gathered together, some sitting on the ground with their legs crossed, while others used the walls for support, everyone watching the Jai Tree intently.

They caught sight of Kindle working in tandem with the palace guards to bring some semblance of order to the growing chaos.

"What's going on?" Yasen asked as they approached.

"Koura says Rani Vasvi's end is near. We're asking everyone to form a line if they'd like to pay their respects."

Over the next few hours, Zarya and Yasen did what they could to help. The courtyard hummed with chants and pleading, flickering with candles and lanterns into the night.

"Should we go in?" Zarya asked eventually. Vikram and Amrita had been inside all this time, and she wanted to see how they were holding up.

Yasen rubbed a hand over his face and nodded, a faraway look in his eyes.

She linked her hand with his, and at first, he studied their joined fingers. When he looked up, conflict furrowed his brows. Poor Yasen. Maybe he hadn't grown up chained to a shoreline, but he might have spent his life nearly as alone as she had.

She squeezed, trying to convey the message that she was here for him. He nodded and looked away quickly before they headed for the queen's throne room.

The doors had been repaired after the fire, offering some privacy during her convalescence. As they entered, the choking smell of charred wood filled Zarya's nose, while ashes swirled around their feet, clinging to their shoes.

Inside, the once verdant hall was torched beyond recognition. Gone was the springy coating of moss and in its place was nothing but scarred walls and ruined floors. Tears stung Zarya's eyes as she beheld the fading queen.

Rani Vasvi's peaceful face was just barely visible in the tangle of bark. Her eyes were closed, her features twisted in a rictus of pain. Her body heaved, the bark pressing in and out in shallow, uneven puffs.

Koura stood next to her with his large, dark hand on the wood, casting a warm light over the surface as he murmured soft words, offering whatever comfort he could.

Hand in hand, Vikram and Amrita were staring up at Rani Vasvi.

"Amrita." Zarya walked over and embraced her friend. "I'm so glad you're here."

"Koura sent word this morning that I should come to say goodbye."

"I'm so sorry," Zarya said.

Tears rolled down Amrita's smooth cheeks, her amber eyes red from crying. "I know it seems like we couldn't have been very close, but we were. Even like this, she was a good mother."

"It sounds like she was as wonderful a mother as she was a queen," Zarya said, taking the hand Vikram wasn't holding. Amrita smiled, gratitude in her eyes.

Yasen laid a hand on Vikram's shoulder, and Zarya watched as a thousand emotions crossed Vikram's face.

The queen's breaths were growing quieter, spacing further and further apart.

"Will you stay?" Amrita asked, looking at Zarya and Yasen. "Until the end?" She choked down a sob. "You both mean so much to us."

Zarya nodded, her throat too tight to speak.

They waited silently as the queen's face began to relax before she let out a long, shuddering breath that somehow spoke of the loss and triumphs, the pain and the joy, the smiles and the sorrow of a queen who had lived through so much.

Then she opened her eyes slowly, gazing out upon the four figures who watched her. A small smile curled in the warped wood just as Rani Vasvi closed her eyes once again and took her last breath, falling completely still as the life finally drained from her body.

Koura dropped his hand, his light winking out, casting the room into near darkness.

"She is gone," he said, his deep voice echoing through the hall.

"I'll tell them," Amrita whispered, turning to leave. Vikram, Yasen, and Zarya trailed after the princess, who was now a queen.

Amrita stepped into the courtyard and lifted her arms.

"Rani Vasvi has passed," she said, her voice strong and steady. "My mother would have been grateful for your presence here tonight. On her behalf, I thank you. She believed in kindness, and the loss of her light will be felt in Daragaab and across Rahajhan. Tonight, the sky has claimed another star."

Heads bowed, and murmurs dispersed through the crowd. Vikram placed a hand on the small of Amrita's back, and she turned to him, crying into his chest as he wrapped his arms around her. Zarya and Yasen stood shoulder to shoulder, watching them.

One by one, mourners approached, bowing and offering condolences. Vikram and Amrita, ever the gracious hosts, thanked them all as they filed past. The nawab and his wives approached. Gopal bowed deeply before Amrita as the women pressed their hands together in front of them and tilted their heads.

"My deepest condolences," the nawab said, his voice coated in honey, but Zarya didn't miss the cold calculation in his eyes. The queen's death no doubt played right into his plans to put Vikram in a seat of power.

Diya grabbed Vikram and Amrita, pulling them both into a wide, warm hug while she made soothing noises. The fiery-haired Vamika gazed about the courtyard, her expression suggesting she wished she were practically anywhere else but here.

Vikram's mother, Jasmine, gave her son a sharp nod, her dark blue eyes cold.

"Wonderful news," Jasmine said after she hugged Amrita, holding her at arm's length. "I have already spoken with the royal astrologer, and the most auspicious muhurta has been decided for your joining date. We'll have it here at the palace in five days."

"No, that is too long to wait," Vikram said, scanning the sky as if already anticipating the worst. "The queen's magic is gone. Amrita must take her place as soon as possible. I've already sent word to the Khada to recruit every single person who can hold a weapon to join the patrols. What lives out there is coming for us."

Jasmine pressed a hand to her chest. "We cannot just *throw* the ceremony together on such short notice. There is food to prepare and decorations to arrange. Invites to send to the other regions," she insisted. "Besides, there is protocol to adhere to. We must conduct the joining ceremony first. Then it will take another seven days to complete the transformation. It cannot be rushed."

"Fine," Vikram said, his jaw hard. "Then we have it tomorrow. Forget the food. Forget the decorations. Forget the invitations. The city cannot remain vulnerable like this for a moment longer than it must."

Jasmine pressed her mouth together, clearly not happy with this response.

"Mother," Vikram said, wrapping a hand around her shoulder. "We cannot delay. To do otherwise could mean Daragaab's ruin."

"Very well. It won't be easy, but I'll do my best."

She squared her shoulders like she was a soldier about to face a horde and not a woman being asked to plan a party on short notice.

"Thank you," Vikram said. He turned to Amrita. "Are you ready?"

The princess nodded, her posture straight and her expression determined.

"Of course I am."

"Good, then we'll need everyone's help, and we'll need to move fast. They're coming for us."

Vikram looked towards the city wall, along with everyone else who'd overheard their conversation.

An ominous shriek far in the distance pierced the night as Vikram's grim words repeated in Zarya's ears.

They're coming for us.

THIRTY-SIX

Despite the solemnity of the occasion, Vikram and Amrita's joining day dawned with a bright sun peeking over the horizon. Zarya slid out of bed and headed downstairs, where she made herself some chai and spiced scrambled eggs. A few moments later, Aarav came down with his arm slung around the shoulders of a pretty young woman who was giggling at something he'd just said.

"Good morning," Zarya said, raising an eyebrow.

Aarav grinned. "Zarya, meet Lekha."

Zarya smiled at the young woman, who bowed with a shy tip of her chin. "Nice to meet you, Zarya. I need to get going." She pecked Aarav on the cheek and scurried out.

Aarav watched her leave with a goofy expression on his face.

"Who was that?" Zarya asked.

"I met her in the infirmary after one of my shifts. She bandaged me up. She's going to be my date for the ceremony later." He poured himself a cup of chai and leaned against the counter, wallowing in his smugness.

"Well, aren't you just the most charming prince," Zarya replied, her mouth now full of eggs.

"I suppose Yasen is taking you?" Aarav canted his head in a gesture of pity, causing Zarya to frown.

"No, he's busy with Vikram. Sidekick duty and all that."

Did she need a date? And was it too late to find one? No, that was ridiculous. Maybe she'd meet someone later, she mused, the corners of her lips turning up at the thought.

Zarya went to answer a knock at the door, finding two women she'd never seen before, one armed with an enormous makeup kit, while the other held up a garment bag proudly. "The most esteemed future steward sent us to help you get ready, miss." They curtsied to Zarya. "We'll set up and call you in a moment."

They headed upstairs in a cloud of perfume while Zarya stared after them in surprise.

Aarav shook his head as he bit into a piece of roti. "That rakshasa is so completely in love with you."

Zarya gave him a sharp look. "I thought you said I had to stay away from them because rakshasas only had one thing on their minds."

He shrugged. "I have better things to worry about now."

She snorted a derisive huff. "It may surprise you to know men and women can be friends without it meaning more. He knows it's over between us." Zarya drew herself to her full height and looked down her nose at him.

"Whatever," he muttered.

Several hours later, Zarya had been thoroughly groomed and plucked and painted. They'd curled her hair in glossy ringlets, painted her nails in matte gold, and surrounded her hazel eyes with thick black lines of kohl.

Next came a lehenga that melted from gold to teal to bright pink to green, along with a matching pair of slippers and earrings dripping with stones.

"You are beautiful, my lady," said one of her helpers, her voice wistful, as Zarya swung her skirt back and forth in the mirror.

"Thank you. I am very grateful for your help."

After they packed up their belongings, Zarya followed them downstairs to find Yasen waiting on the sofa in the living room, one ankle crossed over the other knee.

She took in a sharp breath at the sight of him. His long silver hair had been brushed to a burnished gleam, with his braids neatly redone. An emerald sherwani, tailored to show off his muscled warrior's physique, hung almost to his knees, secured with a row of shiny gold buttons. The cuffs and collar were decorated with golden thread, while an elaborately embellished talwar adorned his hip.

"What are you doing here? You look amazing, by the way."

He smiled. "You look rather amazing yourself."

"A gift from our queen and her steward."

Yasen smirked and then bowed. "I came to escort you to the joining."

Zarya put her hands on her hips. "I don't need you to take me. I can handle myself."

"I know. But I wanted to escort my second-best friend on the most important occasion of my best friend's life."

She sputtered. "Did you just call me your *second*-best friend right to my face?"

Yasen grinned. "Listen, I figure you're lucky you made the list at all."

"Oh, you're such a charmer, aren't you? How are you still single?"

"It is a wonder."

She gave him a playful punch in the stomach, and he folded in half, clutching it dramatically.

He straightened up, his expression turning serious. "Are you okay?"

"Me? Because of Vikram? Yes, I'm totally fine. My plans tonight include meeting a tall, dark, and handsome stranger."

"Mmm, me too," Yasen said, a faraway look in his eyes.

With a mocking flutter of her eyelashes, Zarya took the elbow Yasen proffered. They crossed the street towards the palace, their gazes lingering on the high stone walls. The Khada had recruited as many as they could to help defend the city until Amrita could take her place in the Jai Tree.

With the sun currently high in the sky, the atmosphere felt less ominous, but a stillness hung over the city, everyone moving with care and speaking in hushed tones as if they were an army of crystal soldiers.

Zarya and Yasen went in search of the garden where the ceremony would take place but were stopped short by a harried woman blocking their path.

"Her Highness Rajkumari Amrita has requested your presence," the woman said curtly before spinning on her heel. "Please follow me."

Zarya exchanged a look with Yasen before doing as they were told.

"Not you!" The woman turned back, her eyes blazing as she shooed Yasen away. "You're to attend to the steward. *Now.*"

"I'll see you in the garden," Yasen said with a bow, clearly wanting to escape the woman's ire.

Zarya was then led to a wide set of double doors with a magnificent tree carved into the surface. The woman opened the door, ushering Zarya into an enormous bedroom decorated in green and gold. Amrita was sitting at a vanity, surrounded by attendants who were finishing her makeup. She stood up to greet Zarya.

The princess was a vision in a deep red lehenga, her ears, wrists, and throat covered in rivers of gold jewelry that sparkled with diamonds.

"You're breathtaking," Zarya said, emotion pulling her ribs tight.

"As are you," Amrita replied, sweeping towards Zarya with her hands clutched together. "Have you seen Vikram? How is he doing?"

"I haven't, but I'm sure he's okay."

"I don't believe that." Amrita sat on the edge of the enormous four-poster bed, and Zarya sank down next to her.

"It's an important day for you, too. Are you happy? Do you want to join with him? He's going to become your voice for everything. That's a lot of trust to place in someone."

Amrita sighed. "Of course. I trust him completely. It's him I worry about since his life will become a shadow of what it is. Besides, they need me to protect the city. I'm no use to anyone like this."

She spread out her hands.

"Amrita, that's not true."

The princess bit her lip and sighed. "It's okay. I know it is."

Zarya thought that was the saddest thing she'd ever heard.

"I have a favor to ask you. Will you stand with me during the ceremony? Yasen will be there at Vik's side since his brother isn't here, and it would be so nice to have someone, too. I'd be honored if it was you."

Zarya paused, wondering why Amrita didn't have someone who knew her better to do this, but Zarya understood what it was like to be confined by your own life.

"It would be my absolute pleasure."

The door opened and a servant in white robes entered. "We are ready to begin, Your Highness." He bowed so low his nose almost came to his knees. He straightened himself and gestured for them to follow. A pair of servants flanked their procession as they made their way through the resplendent palace, decorated with flowers and ribbons and swathes of colorful fabric. Despite what Vikram had said about keeping things simple, it appeared his mother had managed to put together a small and very opulent miracle in a very short time.

At the bottom of the stairs, Tarin waited, ready to escort Amrita. Zarya hugged her friend before she headed for the garden.

A royal-blue carpet lined the walkway that led to a shallow stone amphitheater, where guests lounged against an array of plush, colorful pillows. At the center stood a canopied pergola adorned with fresh flowers.

She grimaced at the way so much of this was set up to mimic a marriage between two people who loved one another when it seemed it was anything but. While she supposed it was intended to symbolize the joyousness of the occasion—just like a wedding—she couldn't help feeling there was something sinister about the entire thing.

Zarya entered behind the Ravana wives, who took their places near the front where their husband was already seated. As Zarya passed him, he pinned her with a heated glare that felt like it might turn her skin to ash.

The Chiranjivi sat near the front as well. Apsara had traded her usual creamy leathers for a white-and-silver sari, her feathered wings spread behind her. Suvanna embodied her watery kingdom in a sea-green lehenga, while Koura wore a sherwani of pale yellow silk. Kindle was his usual elegant self in his black velvet coat with red trim. He nodded at Zarya with a warm smile as she passed.

She stepped under the pergola, conscious of the guests watching her from every side. Hundreds of lanterns, interspersed throughout the seating area, cast the whole scene with a soft glow. It was absolutely breathtaking, but it was getting harder to ignore the sounds coming from the other side of the wall as the sun was beginning to set. Why hadn't they done this earlier in the day? Not that it mattered. If the monsters were coming, it would make no difference what any of them were doing.

Next came Vikram, wearing a white sherwani and red turban, riding a white horse with a golden bridle as Yasen walked next to him, a hand on his sword hilt. Several other guards trailed behind them, while music played softly in the background. They joined Zarya under the pergola, all of them turning to await Amrita's entrance.

Clinging to Tarin, the princess emerged from the palace, sheltered under a piece of fabric suspended by four guards. They made slow progress, the elder astomi's steps stilted and shuffling.

Though he kept a careful smile on his face, Zarya caught the sadness reflected in Vikram's eyes. In a few days, Amrita would be crowned Queen of Daragaab and begin her transition. As he did his best to appear happy, Zarya felt a pang of regret for him and decided to forgive him for the lies he'd told. He was another person trapped in a cage of his father's making, and Zarya knew the lengths someone would go to when their freedom was threatened.

As Amrita reached the pergola, Vikram bowed before taking her hand and tucking it under his arm. They waited for Tarin to take his place in front of them.

As the current steward, he would be central to the process of transitioning out of his role and transferring his knowledge and the honor on Vikram. Today's events marked the first in a series of steps to bring about Amrita's physical change.

The ceremony consisted of long passages about time and nature and loyalty. More than once, Tarin's words were cut off by a distant shriek or scream. They couldn't hear the worst of the fighting from the palace, but it was obvious things were unsettled on the wall.

Vikram's distracted gaze kept wandering to some distant point beyond the garden as the ceremony dragged on. As he shifted from foot to foot, Zarya got the sense he wanted to snap at everyone to hurry things up, but it wouldn't hasten Amrita's transformation.

Zarya's thoughts wandered as she half listened to Tarin weave whatever magic was needed for this process, something nagging at the edges of her consciousness. It was that same restless feeling that had been bothering her ever since they'd returned from Vikram's family estate. The threat to the city was at the forefront of her mind, but there was something else underlying it.

She was chewing on her lower lip when Yasen caught her eye, inclining his head. *Are you okay?*

She nodded and drew her attention back to the ceremony, but she rolled her shoulders, feeling like her skin had become too tight.

Finally, it was time for Vikram and Amrita to perform the first exchange of their magic by linking hands and reciting a series of lines fed by Tarin. The guests watched in awe as ribbons of pale light dispersed from their linked fingers and wrapped around the princess and her future steward. It was both a symbol of their joining and the creation of an ancient binding that would see them become one.

As the ceremony finished, Tarin declared the first step was now completed. Vikram pecked Amrita's cheek as the audience clapped and cheered, maybe a little too loudly to drown out the sounds of the distant screeching. Holding hands, Vikram and Amrita returned down the aisle to congratulations and warm wishes.

Arm in arm, Yasen and Zarya followed behind them.

"That was... nice," Zarya said with a grimace before Yasen gave her a dry look.

"How bad do you think it is out there?"

He shook his head. "I don't know, but I predict this is going to be a very long week for all of us."

Guests were directed to another section of the sprawling gardens where the party continued. Vanshaj moved silently and efficiently among them, balancing trays of drinks and small bites along the edges, and in the center of the garden, musicians played, the soft strains of their music floating in the air. Couples gathered to dance around the large central fountain that had been left open for the purpose. All of it conspicuously backdropped by the sounds of their potential ruin.

Zarya was sure she wasn't imagining the way people were smiling just a little too much and laughing just a little too forcefully. This was supposed to be a happy occasion. One that signaled the next chapter in the queendom's history, and she couldn't blame them for wanting to lift the mood.

Vikram and Amrita moved to the center to take up a dance, their practiced steps spinning them in circles.

Zarya's heart broke as she thought about how neither of them would ever have the chance to fall in love with someone of their own choice. They'd never get to experience the small, insignificant moments that made up a life. Watching the sunset together. Waking up next to one another. Sharing a meal. Touching and holding one another.

Zarya sipped on her wine, looking up at the stars. She rubbed her chest as her ribs tightened. The sensation was similar to how she'd felt before the binding had left her incapacitated. She shook her head and pushed the thought away. She was still recovering, and the last week had been so full of activity. It was evidence of how far she'd come. Just a few short months ago she had been waiting for anything noteworthy to happen in her life, and now she could barely catch her breath.

She wouldn't have traded it for anything in the world.

Zarya watched Aarav dancing with Lekha. They were laughing about something, and a ripple fluttered in her heart.

Aarav deserved peace, too. Maybe he could fall in love again.

Those deaths hadn't been his fault any more than hers. Row was the one responsible, whatever mistakes either of them had made. As if he sensed her gaze, Aarav looked over, and she offered him a small smile. He nodded in acknowledgement before turning back to Lekha. If Zarya and Aarav could sort out their differences, then perhaps anything was possible.

Zarya moved to sit at the edge of the fountain, swaying to the music that was doing its best to drown out the rising cacophony outside. Everyone was trying to focus on the festivities, but she saw the way their eyes drifted past the palace. Maybe some of them had loved ones currently on the wall.

Apsara and Kindle were busy conferring in a corner, their heads bent together. Zarya knew they were discussing strategy for the ongoing protection of Dharati. Suvanna approached them just as a guard arrived with a message. She took it and showed it to the other two. While Vikram was busy with the ceremony, the Chiranjivi were busy fielding updates from the front lines and were ready to join the fighting if necessary.

Yasen sought Zarya out, sitting down next to her. She gave him an expectant look, and he growled low in his throat. "I told you, I don't dance."

"Please." She pressed her hands together. "Just this once? The demons might burst through the wall at any moment, and this will be our last night on this earth. Don't let me die this way."

"Gods, you are so dramatic," he said, and she grinned. "What do you need me for? There are plenty of eligible men here."

Zarya thrust her bottom lip in a faux pout. "I want to dance with *you*. One time. Please?"

With a sound of exasperation, he stood, holding his hand out. "Fine. One time."

Zarya jumped up and pulled him into the fray of swirling couples.

"Thank you," she said, her voice soft.

"For what?"

"For the dance."

He didn't say anything for a moment, and Zarya hoped he understood just how much he'd come to mean to her.

"Thank you, too. For being my friend and for understanding me. It's weird how you get me." Yasen spoke quietly.

"Does that qualify me for the role of first-best friend, you think?" she asked, looking up.

"Don't push it, Zee."

With a half-smile, he rested his cheek against her head as they swayed gently.

"A toast," Gopal shouted a few moments later, the music and dancing coming to a pause.

He raised a large golden goblet, a slimy smile on his face. He had many reasons to celebrate tonight. After years of scheming, the fruits of his labor had finally ripened.

"It's been—" A piercing shriek interrupted his words.

Gopal rolled his neck, looked skyward for a moment, cleared his throat, and pressed on.

"It's been centuries since the Ravanas have been so close to the throne, and the time has come at last for us to resume our rightful place. Alongside the Vasvi family, of course," he added, throwing an ingratiating smile to Amrita. Zarya scoffed, crossing her arms over her chest when another sound interrupted the nawab.

But it wasn't the shriek of a demon this time.

It was a deep, rumbling voice that floated out over the garden, signaling a shift that pulled Zarya's attention to a newcomer, who now stood at the edge of the crowd, his stance sure and loose, a hand resting on the hilt of his sword.

"Well, isn't this beautiful? I'm thrilled you've finally got your wish, Father."

Silence gripped the scene as the man strode forward.

Zarya stopped breathing as her heart tripped over itself.

It was Rabin.

His eyes flashed with darkness, intent on the nawab. His black armor was of a different style than the palace soldiers—a tunic and tight pants of light leather, black boots, all cut in an unusual and angular fashion, his black hair tied with a strip of leather. He was huge. Bigger than he'd seemed in her dreams.

Color drained from Vikram's face, and Gopal Ravana sputtered, the goblet slipping out of his hand and clattering onto the table.

Rabin strode to a stop in front of Vikram and Amrita, his steps as heavy as thunder.

Palace guards lining the perimeter of the space stared as their whispers floated across the garden. "Commander Ravana." Many raised fists and pressed them to their hearts. Some kneeled with their heads bowed.

Rabin watched them, his expression radiating unquestioned authority and registering no surprise that they were falling at his feet.

"Rabin," Vikram whispered, stepping forward. Emotions warred on his face—confusion, anger, wonder.

Taking Amrita's hand, Rabin pressed his lips to the back of it. "Your Majesty, congratulations, and welcome to this wretched family." Turning to Vikram, he clamped a heavy hand on his shoulder. "Sorry, little brother. I seem to have missed the ceremony. I guess my invitation got lost."

"What are you—" Gopal said, his face red and his words failing him. "What are you doing here, Rabindranath?"

"Aren't you glad to see me, Father?" He stepped forward, tilting his head at the nawab. "It's been so long. I thought you'd be thrilled to have me here for such an important family occasion."

"You shouldn't be here," Gopal hissed, his eyes narrowing.

Zarya, who had been too stunned to move or even breathe, suddenly snapped.

"This is your *brother*?" she practically shouted, the words bursting out.

"Zee, what are you doing?" Yasen pulled her back. "Zarya, what's wrong?"

Rabin turned at the sound of Zarya's voice, and now he was staring at her, those endless eyes burning as the drums of warning resonated in her head. Her fingers went numb, her breath failing as he stalked towards her.

She tried to say something, but the words died in her throat.

He was real.

She hadn't been sure until this moment.

He was blood and flesh and muscle and bone, and he was Vikram's *brother*. The one who had run away. Whose joining this was supposed to be. The one who had made her feel something she didn't have a name for.

He came upon her like a rolling tide, backing her up against a stone pillar. He caught her wrist in one of his large hands and pressed it against her chest. She clutched his arm, trying to pull him away, but he was iron and steel and marble.

Then he leaned in, his jaw hard, and his mouth pressed into a line. He was raging, his gold-flecked eyes a simmering, roiling vortex. Zarya was paralyzed, unable to do anything but stand there gaping at him.

"*You*," he snarled, the sound like fury and fire and lightning, his voice so low only Zarya could have heard. "How *the fuck* have you been entering my mind?"

THIRTY-SEVEN

What? Zarya's brow crumpled with confusion as she struggled against both Rabin's grip and his fury.

"Let go of me," she snarled, pressing her free hand to his rock-solid chest, trying to shove him out of her space. What was *his* problem? She hadn't been entering his mind. If anything, she could blame *him* for entering hers. The way she couldn't get him out of her head couldn't be natural.

She *knew* she'd been deluding herself and that forest had to be the product of some kind of wicked power. But she understood almost nothing about her own magic, and his conviction had planted nagging seeds of doubt.

"I didn't do anything," she hissed, bewildered by this abrupt shift in his demeanor. The last time she'd seen him, he'd nearly kissed her. Or so she had wanted to believe.

Once again, she attempted to wrench herself from his grasp, and then fell still. The air around her twisted. Suddenly, she couldn't breathe as her ribs contracted, and something jagged spiraled straight to her toes like she'd swallowed an iron burr. It was a presence borne of what haunted Daragaab's darkest corners every night. One molded into sharpened talons that were gleefully tearing this place apart.

Another piercing shriek carried on the night as every head swung towards the sound, this one undoubtedly closer than any had been before. Zarya's blood turned cold, clogging her veins.

"They've broken through the walls," she whispered, understanding with alarming certainty that something very, very bad was about to find them.

Rabin swung around to look at her as his grip softened. "What?"

"They're coming." She said it louder now. "In the sky."

He stepped back without dropping her wrist, scanning the area above.

Overhead, black shapes were filling their view, swooping and diving straight for the startled guests. It all happened in slow motion as realization sunk in. There was a pause, inertia holding everyone in place, the unholy sounds echoing against the night before awareness clicked like a lock breaking open.

Suvanna had called it the darkness and Koura had refused to name it.

But whatever it was, it had just arrived to claim them all.

Kindle jumped up on the ledge of the center fountain and shouted, "Everyone take cover!"

That's when panic erupted.

"The kala-hamsa," Zarya said, recognizing the scarlet-plumed birds. "The eggs. They must've hatched."

"We must protect the princess," Kindle said, spinning around, searching for Amrita. If anything happened to her, they would all surely be lost.

On the far side of the garden, Vikram was already throwing orders at his soldiers to secure the area and protect the guests. Zarya noticed their hesitation as they looked to Rabin for a heartbeat before they moved to obey Vikram's commands.

Vikram seemed to have noticed it, too, his expression

turning acidic before he selected four guards to escort Amrita to safety and another six to shield his mother, as well as Diya and Vamika. The women compressed themselves into a huddle, picking up their long skirts before they ran for their lives.

Like the eggs they'd hatched from, the kala-hamsa varied in size—some like eagles and others like doves. They used their sharp beaks and talons to shred clothing, grab hair, and gouge into skin as guests screamed in their attempt to scatter for cover.

A whoosh and a thump vibrated through the garden as an elephant-sized kala-hamsa landed in the center of the chaos, its eyes glowing red and its plumage ruffling with bright green, blue, and yellow feathers.

Then it stretched out its neck and let out a shriek so loud and penetrating that Zarya winced at the pressure on her eardrums. She sucked in an alarmed breath as it swung its enormous head and looked directly at her and Rabin.

Rabin yanked Zarya behind him while drawing his sword, swinging at its head in one fluid movement. His blade bit into flesh, slicing deep, spraying a shower of black blood as it screamed again, so loud the foundations shook. A shudder rolled over its feathers before it launched itself back into the air, shrieking and cawing as it circled overhead.

This was one of the few times Zarya had gone anywhere without a weapon since she'd arrived in Dharati, and she uttered a curse that she'd been caught unprepared. She scanned her surroundings, finding a fallen guard screaming for help while a kala-hamsa pecked at his face.

She lunged for his abandoned sword, scooping it up and cleaving her blade through the bird's neck. It exploded in a shower of dark ichor, the two halves of its body landing with a splat.

Breathing heavily, she looked around, the sour taste of dread coating the inside of her mouth. The garden turned into a nightmare, the stench of blood and fear filling the air.

"You should take cover in the palace," Rabin said, coming up behind her and grabbing her arm, his grip firm. "Go with the princess. Run."

His voice was different from the dream forest. Less muted, but just as authoritative. She glared at him, more than a little irritated by his less-than-warm greeting. Not authoritative. *Bossy*. Who did he think he was?

"Leave me alone. I will do no such thing."

She tore her arm from his grasp and backed away as he moved to fill her space.

"It isn't safe out here," he growled, his jaw hardening into steel.

"I'm perfectly capable of taking care of myself."

Zarya then noticed a kala-hamsa streaking towards Rabin. To prove her point, she shoved his massive bulk out of the way and slashed the bird from the air. It dropped like a stone, landing at his feet.

Zarya grinned as a flicker of confusion crossed his perfectly crafted face. She didn't wait to hear what he might say next. Instead, she took off, hurling herself into the mess.

More and more birds descended into the garden, and Zarya swung left and right, trying to cut them down. Talons raked the soft flesh of her cheek, and she grunted at the bright spot of pain before she felt the warm trickle of blood.

"Zee!" She spun around to find Yasen jogging towards her, his gaze honing in on her injury.

"I'm okay," she said, wiping the blood away.

"Stay close to me," he said, and they fell into sync, moving side by side as Yasen brought down beasts with military efficiency. Zarya's technique wasn't quite as tidy but still effective enough as she took out her share of the shrieking birds.

She caught a glimpse of Rabin, his entire presence like a magnet pulling her in. He moved like a sandstorm, nothing coming close as he hewed down entire groups of demons at once, their bodies exploding in showers of blood that glittered like ink against the night.

Across the garden, Apsara fought with a bloody sword in one hand, calling down spears of ice with the other, impaling birds and pinning them to the earth. Next to her, Suvanna held two curved blades as she spun and danced like an apparition, graceful as waves rolling on the shore.

Zarya spotted a giant naga slithering down the wide center path. She ran towards it, lifting her sword as the serpent curled, lifting its head to eye level. Before she could react, it lunged, its sharp front teeth slicing against the skin of her stomach. Zarya cried out, using the momentum of her swing to cleave her sword against the naga's neck.

Her blade melted into soft flesh, slicing clean through. After the head landed at her feet, she kicked it away, her foot tangling in her long skirt that was now filthy beyond redemption.

Zarya clutched her bleeding stomach, bending in half as she tried to catch her breath. The wound was aching, blood draining out and soaking into her clothing.

How she wished she were wearing her usual kurta and leggings right now. Since the beautiful garment was already ruined, she used her bloodied sword to slice away the bottom half, leaving her legs free.

When she was done, she scanned the garden, finding Vikram fighting off a dakini, bloodied flesh hanging from its maw. Covered in dark iridescent scales, it stood the height of two men on thick legs with clawed feet, its long fingers tipped with more sharp claws.

Needing a moment to recover, she watched Kindle spool ribbons of fire from his fingers as demons cowered from the heat. She found Koura, his expression thunderous as he slashed down their foes. Gone was the gentle healer, in his place was a fearsome warrior who fought with the same intense passion he reserved for the care of his charges.

Aarav roared as he descended on a pack of vetalas, their jaws dripping with blood and gore. After he finished them off, he spun on the next group, facing them without an ounce of fear.

"Do your worst, you maggots!" he yelled, and Zarya realized this was what he'd been born to do. Joining the Khada had unleashed something he'd been missing, with its brutality and its cruelty but also with its noble purpose. Something that spoke to him in a primitive way.

A rumble beneath her feet sent her spinning around, searching for the source. She found Rabin bent on one knee with a fist planted on the stone path. A jagged line formed before splitting open, demons speared by points of earth that shot up like a mountain range from the ground. They toppled along the sides of the peaks, disappearing into the rift, dozens falling to their deaths before he sealed it shut, silencing their echoing screams.

Shouts of alarm rang out beyond the palace walls. The demons were also terrorizing the city, but there wouldn't be enough soldiers to help them all. No one had ever imagined an assault of this magnitude.

A nearby chorus of screams drew Zarya's attention to a group of trembling courtiers who hadn't yet found shelter in the palace. They stood cowering beneath a dakini, its body covered in thick, black scales and corded with sinewy muscle.

"No!" she cried out when she spied Amrita amongst the group, clinging to the Ravana wives. Where were her guards? Her question was answered a moment later as she registered the heap of bodies lying at the demon's feet, the soldiers mutilated almost beyond recognition.

Zarya covered her mouth to quell the bile climbing up her throat. She had to do something.

Running towards them, she shouted, "Over here!" hoping to distract it away from the princess.

"Help them!" she screamed as the dakini finally noticed her presence.

She came to a halt as it stared at her, paralyzed by the satisfied look in its eyes. The corners of its horrible mouth tipped up before it lifted its head to the sky and let out a series of short, shrill whistles. A signal or a call?

Deciding that couldn't mean anything good, Zarya forced herself to move, raising her sword and swinging for its neck. Yasen appeared and charged from the other side. The demon ducked as she swung, her blade hissing through empty air.

Several more guards joined in, surrounding the demon, while more attempted to reach the princess to escort her to safety.

The dakini swung out a massive arm, its claws slashing through Yasen's thigh, carving four deep bloody grooves, forcing him to stumble back. Zarya screamed, but Yasen shook it off, recovering quickly before he took another swing at the dakini.

She went in for the kill while it was distracted, arcing her blade into the spot between its shoulder and throat, the edge biting into its stiff tendons before it threw its head back and roared.

It was a minor victory because she was immediately hurled off her feet and thrown through the air. She landed on the pavement with a smack that knocked the breath out of her, her elbows and palms tearing at the impact.

The elephant-sized kala-hamsa stood over her, its enormous feet caging her in. It bent down and shrieked in her face as she scrambled on her hands and feet, her chest still too tight to draw a proper breath.

Using a long talon, the beast snagged the remains of her skirt, dragging her closer. Somehow, she still had a hold of her sword, and she slashed at the bird while attempting to anchor herself to the pavement, her nails ripping as it towed her in.

The bird then raised a huge clawed foot, and she watched

as it slowly descended, thumping on top of her. Her remaining breath whooshed from her lungs like she'd been flipped inside out. She scrabbled and kicked, trying to free herself from its grip, panicking as her ribcage verged on the brink of collapse.

A gust of wind tousled her hair as the bird began to flap its massive wings.

"No," Zarya wheezed as she fought harder, realizing the thing was about to take off with her as its unwilling captive.

"Zee!" Yasen cried as he grabbed at her feet. Zarya felt the brush of his hand against her ankle, but he wasn't fast enough. She slipped away as she was lifted higher, the noise from the fight receding as the ground moved away.

The bird's talons squeezed her so tight she was growing desperate for breath, her heart thrashing like a moth trapped in a thimble.

As they ascended into the sky, the bird lurched, thrown off course. Zarya caught a glimpse of Apsara below, her hands pointed at them. The bird swooped, dropping several feet as Zarya's stomach launched into her throat before righting itself.

An arrow of fire blew past her vision as Kindle released his magic, but the kala-hamsa evaded the shot with more ease than something that large had a right to. It aimed its head at the ground and opened its mouth as a stream of bright green flame shot out, striking Kindle in the chest, sending him flying.

Zarya was having difficulty organizing her thoughts, both from the adrenaline burning through her veins and the increasing lack of air. Beads of panicked sweat slicked her skin. Her sword still clutched in a death grip, she swung it up, attempting to hack away at the bird's foot or ankle or anything that would make this fucker let her go.

The world beneath her grew smaller.

Apsara appeared in the air like a divine goddess coming to deliver her from this nightmare. Her magnificent wings flapped madly as she hurled bolts of ice at the demon. But a flock of smaller kala-hamsa appeared, diving for Apsara and attacking. They wrestled her in the air as she tried to fend them off while Zarya lifted higher.

They were well above the city now, the world below rendered into miniature. Zarya gagged, a sour wash of fear climbing up her throat.

As she tried to gather her fraying nerves, another horror materialized before her eyes.

An iridescent black dragon swooped alongside her, only slightly smaller than the bird, with black leathery wings, a shimmering black hide, and a wide jaw filled with needle-sharp teeth. A fact she learned when it opened its mouth and bellowed with a howl that seemed to vibrate the very molecules of air she was still trying desperately to suck into her lungs.

The dragon dove, its speed like a flash of lightning. She closed her eyes, waiting for the inevitable snap as she was swallowed in those tremendous jaws. She wasn't sure which ending was worse. Being shredded to ribbons or facing whatever this forsaken bird wanted with her. Maybe it had a nest of babies, and Zarya was their freshly caught worm.

The kala-hamsa lurched, and they fell several feet, the bird's talons digging viciously into her skin. She screamed, though the sound was a feeble whimper because she still couldn't get enough air.

The dragon circled away before it doubled back, snapping at the kala-hamsa. She wasn't sure if it was her addled brain, but it seemed to be attacking the *demon* rather than her. Maybe it was just trying to kill it so it could keep Zarya all to itself.

Still clinging to her sword, Zarya again tried to penetrate the tough skin of the bird's foot. The movement was awkward from her position, and she couldn't find the right leverage, but she kept trying until her grip slipped. The sword bounced off its armored foot, and the blade flew from her hand, spinning away and plunging to the earth. She watched it fall, a sob sticking to the roof of her mouth.

The bird had recovered, and they were rising again. Zarya caught a fleeting glimpse of the dragon surrounded by a flock of kala-hamsa. It bucked, its long tail and neck swinging before it let out a roar so anguished and broken that she felt it echo into the marrow of her bones.

Zarya tried to think. Tried to come up with some way to save herself. She was going to die. Of that, she was certain.

She stopped writhing and forced herself to calm down, taking the deepest breath the bird's tight grip would allow.

And then she felt it. A vibration. A call. Or rather, she felt *them*.

The stars.

Up here in the sky, where she was so much closer, the same feeling that flooded her veins every time she drew on her magic filled her now. She wasn't sure how she knew, only that some part of her had always felt like they belonged to her. That they were hers to command, as they had always been.

It had only been light and an illusion of power, but now, her magic had been freed. Now it was something more.

The kala-hamsa turned south, taking them over the city. And then she understood something else. This beast hadn't chosen her randomly tonight. It had taken her for a purpose, and she was sure that if it reached its intended destination, something might break forever.

She closed her eyes and the five points of her anchor flared to life, spinning and waiting, quivering with anticipation. She had no real idea of what she was doing. She didn't understand this magic or how it worked. But she had to try *something*. And she had to do it fast.

Working on some ancient instinct etched under her skin, she imagined the kala-hamsa burning. She imagined the strength of the stars. She asked them to come to her aid.

Her anchors glowed, their essence calling from somewhere deep, deep inside.

Now she knew their presence had always been with her—she just hadn't recognized it for what it was. This gift she'd been given had always been an invisible force that guided her, bringing her to this moment. Shaping her into the person she was now and the one she would eventually become.

Like the toss of dice in a game she didn't know the rules to, Zarya drew on each of her anchors, slow and steady, each with the same intensity, gathering them together into a fist. A little bit of everything, because right now, she needed it all.

The ribbons gathered, forming a whole, wrapping themselves into a glittering sphere.

And then it shattered.

Light, or rather an absence of light, black but sparkling with a million glowing points, burst from her hands in silky, endless ribbons of brilliant darkness.

It seared through the demon, crackling as it filtered through sinew and tissue and bone. It flowed out of the bird's eyes and mouth. The kala-hamsa shrieked, a mournful cry that signaled its last breaths before it exploded into a spectacular supernova, dissolving into a mess of feathers and flesh.

And then Zarya was falling.

THIRTY-EIGHT

The wind whistled in her ears, and her hair whipped around her face. Her stomach slid into her throat as she fell, her limbs circling into nothing. She squeezed her eyes shut, knowing she was about to die.

It seemed to take forever. She was weightless, her lungs finally open, her body numb and dead to every sensation. Distantly she wondered if she'd feel it when she hit the street or whatever building she was about to collide with. Or would she die immediately?

Suddenly, she lurched, her limbs snapping, as a black shadow surrounded her, throwing her off course. The sharp pain of teeth closed around her waist, and she had only a moment to register she was now trapped inside the jaws of the black dragon.

It landed amid the sounds of mortar and stone crumbling and shattering.

Her neck jolted from the impact, but the massive dragon's body cushioned the worst of her fall. Released from its teeth, she tumbled end over end before she came to a jarring stop. Dust filled her lungs and eyes, dragging out hacking coughs as tears streamed down her cheeks. The world above her spun as she lay staring at the sky with her chest heaving.

She was alive. Somehow, she was on the ground, and she was alive.

Eventually, she made out the hazy edges of the surrounding buildings. She was somewhere in the city, wreathed by rubble and debris, the air fogged with dust.

The dragon had saved her? But why? Or had it been trying to capture her for itself?

She tried to move and groaned. Her body ached, and her wounds burned, pain searing every inch of her skin. She was broken. She couldn't move. Pain threatened to pull her under. Her eyelids fluttered shut before they snapped open, only to slam closed again.

Maybe this *was* how she'd die. After everything—this tiny taste of life and freedom—this was how it ended. Gods, how she wished she could have done so much more. Seen everything. Been everywhere. But she would have to content herself with knowing that at least she'd had these last few months.

She'd finally been properly kissed. She'd found Yasen and Amrita, her first true friends. She'd started to bridge the divide with Aarav, even if they still stood miles apart.

Rabin. She would never understand what to make of any of that. She knew she had felt something, and he was real, not a ghost, but clearly, whatever had happened in the forest had only been an illusion. She thought of the way he'd stared at her with nothing but the blackest of hate. The way he'd spoken to her like he thought she had been the one deceiving him.

What an asshole. It was better this way. Now she could die and not have to suffer a lifetime knowing the man who had so thoroughly enchanted her was actually a grade-A dick.

And Row. She wondered if she would remember him even when she was gone. The lies and the secrets and everything he had kept from her. The worst part was never knowing what he'd been hiding.

She flexed her hand against the ground where it rested, her fingers catching on tiny pieces of stone littering the floor. She flipped up her palm and stared at it, thinking of the strange black light that had come from her fingers. What had that been? Was *this* what Row had been hiding? Was this why he'd wanted her to keep her magic a secret? What did any of it mean?

She groaned as she shifted, her body aching in protest, needing another minute before she tried to move. Her eyes fluttered closed again, and she let out a deep sigh, holding herself as still as possible, hoping it might hurt less. It didn't really work.

The city was unnaturally quiet. It reminded her of the eerie stillness of the swamp where she'd spent so much of her life. It almost felt familiar. Like a warm blanket.

Would anyone find her here? Would they come looking for her? How long would it take?

Her head throbbed, so she tried to stop thinking. Tried to just rest and wait for death to come. Every time she closed her eyes, she saw it—that river of blackness sprinkled with stars. Like she truly held the sky in her hands.

The star anchor in her heart flickered to life, spinning as it sent warmth into her limbs.

At that moment, no one was there to see Zarya. She was surrounded by a haze of dust, lost amongst the rubble, and even if someone were coming, it might be hours before they found her.

If anyone had been there to see her, they might have seen the way her mouth opened in a small gasp.

Because her five-pointed anchor had changed.

That warm and welcoming presence continued to spin in her heart, but now... it had six points. She stared in her mind's eye, hardly daring to comprehend what she was seeing.

The star glowed and spun faster like it was showing off. Telling her to look at what it had accomplished.

Fire. Air. Water. Earth. Spirit.

Darkness.

Zarya's breath twisted in her lungs as she choked on the tears running down her cheeks.

Darkness.

She tested it, feeling its texture and shape.

It was weighty and solid with presence. If the air was light and the water was cool, then the darkness was a forbidden smoky swirl, curling around the pillars of an abandoned civilization.

She continued crying, still coughing on the dust burrowing in her lungs, not understanding what to do with this knowledge.

The darkness.

She recalled the ominous words in Dhawan's book. The lost piece of the Aazheri. The brothers who'd lost control and needed to be tamed.

It had nearly been the end of everything.

And now it lived in her.

After a lifetime of loneliness, Zarya had suddenly never felt so alone in her life.

Her vision swirled, the ground underneath her spinning, before everything went black.

THIRTY-NINE

When Zarya awoke, the sky was just beginning to lighten, the haze of dust finally settling. She waited, surprised to see she was still alive. She shifted slightly, and every muscle and tendon in her body wrenched in agony. The wounds on her back and her stomach and her legs and every last inch of her burning skin were hot and tight.

Fuck.

Now she wished she had died.

She lay on the ground for another few minutes, summoning the energy to stand. Somehow, she'd survived the night, and Zarya wasn't a quitter.

Sucking in a deep breath, she maneuvered her arms under her and heaved herself up, pushing back to settle on her heels. The movement shot pain through her back, where the worst of her injuries seemed to be concentrated. She took several more deep breaths, trying to put last night's events into order. And that's when she remembered.

She searched inside herself, looking for her anchor star, hoping that she'd just been mistaken. That, in her nearly dead state, she'd imagined it.

Her star flared to life, springing open like a flower welcoming the sun.

Six petals. Six anchors.

There it sat, slightly dimmer than the others. Less like the sparkle of stars and more like the glow of twilight over an inky pond. She shook her head, wishing she understood this. Wishing she had someone she could talk to. But it was all clear now.

This.

This was what Row had been hiding.

The darkness.

She recalled the way Suvanna had talked about it. About the vanshaj and their eternally tainted magic. Of the way Dhawan's voice had wavered when he spoke of a time when darkness covered the world.

She, Zarya, was the evil they all feared.

It was then she knew she had to get out of here. She had to go back into hiding. There was still time to fix this. She hoped.

But, gods, she couldn't move.

She scanned the area where she sat, finally able to see her surroundings without a screen of dust clogging her vision. It seemed she had landed on the flat roof of a building, one of the walls completely shattered.

But she wasn't alone.

Rabin lay on the other side of the small courtyard on his back with his eyes closed and his dark hair spread around his head in a tangle.

What was he doing here?

She blinked heavily, her eyelids weighed down. It didn't matter why he was here. She had to get away from him and this place. Summoning all of her strength, she heaved herself onto her hands and knees, her body screaming in protest.

She pushed herself up to stand, wincing at the pain that shot through her legs and arms and back. She stretched, hoping to find a pocket of relief. She hesitated, and then sighed, before she made her way over to Rabin. She should at least see if he was alive before she abandoned him.

Slowly, she approached and then fell to her knees. He was still. She couldn't tell if he was breathing, so she leaned down, placing her ear against his heart, hearing a gentle beat. Why did that bring her such an overwhelming sense of relief? She moved, hovering close to his face, feeling for a gentle tickle of his breath.

He was alive. She stared at him, recalling the moments they'd shared, wondering which parts had been real and which had been only an illusion. When she closed her eyes, she remembered the way he'd looked at her with fire and fury and a coldness that suggested he had been so close to killing her.

She looked around, wondering how to get out of here. There was a gap in the rubble she might be able to climb through. But she couldn't leave him like this. Could she? When she looked back, she let out a yelp of fright. His eyes were open, and he was staring up at her.

Like a phoenix rising from the ashes, he sat up and shook his head.

"Are you all right?" he asked, but she was already standing up, backing away.

Whatever had happened between them, she had to let it go. A plan was already forming as she hobbled away, gritting her teeth with every step.

It had always been her intention to leave the city. Go somewhere Row would never find her. Now she needed a place *no one* would ever find her. She had to hide. Lock herself away again. Row had always claimed it had been for her own protection.

But now she understood he had never been protecting her.

He had been protecting everyone else *from* her. From the darkness. From whatever evil lived within her.

"Where are you going?" Rabin called, but she ignored him. She reached the wall, using her hands to brace herself before she heaved herself over the rough stones. Her feet were bare, her shoes having fallen off somewhere in the night, and she winced at the stabs of pain against her soles.

"Zarya!" came Rabin's deep voice.

A rock slipped out from under her, and she screamed as the entire mountain of rubble slid. She pitched forward, rolling down with the stones until she came to a stop under a shower of pebbles.

"Fuck," she moaned. Gods, everything hurt so much.

There was a clatter above her, and a shadow blocked out the sun. She opened her eyes to find Rabin scooping her into his arms.

Oh no. She did *not* want his help.

"Put me down," she protested, shoving his chest and wriggling her legs.

"I'm not letting you out of my sight. You have things to answer for."

"What things? What are you talking about?!"

She managed to wrestle herself from his grip, tripping out of his arms and nearly stumbling to the ground. He reached out to help her, but she wrenched her arm away.

"What is your *problem?*"

"How did you do it?" he asked. "Did my father put you up to it? Are you his spy?"

It took several seconds for Zarya's brain to catch up. What was he going on about?

"You mean the forest?"

"Of course, I mean the forest," he said, dragging into her a tight alleyway. With her back pressed against the wall, he towered over her, his hands planted on either side of her head. She was trapped here, the sounds from beyond the alley dimmed to a hush.

"Your father?" she asked with a derisive laugh. "You've got to be kidding me."

"Then how, *witch*?"

She blinked at the insult.

"If I don't tell you, are you going to slam me into the wall and try to tear off my arm again?"

"You're exaggerating." His tone was low and dangerous, but she saw something flicker in his expression. Regret? Shame?

With a snort, she pushed away from the wall and attempted to scoot under his arm.

"Tell me," he said, stepping closer, closing off her escape route.

Zarya bit the inside of her cheek as her traitorous body reacted to him. Even with him looming over her like an angry bear, her heart flipped in her chest.

"I can't," she hissed. "You know that! I barely had any magic when I first met you. You're the one who released it! *You* helped me!"

"Keep your voice down," he growled, peering out towards the street as if anyone would be listening to them right now. He pulled her deeper into the recesses of the alley, where the air was cooler.

"Stop it!" she protested. She wasn't sure if she should be scared, but she was more annoyed than anything. When they stopped again, they were even closer, the space so narrow he was forced to line his body against hers.

Without realizing it, she had gripped his waist when he'd pushed her back. Hard planes flexed against her hands, and despite everything, she wanted to touch him everywhere. The warmth of his skin through the thin fabric made her breath catch.

Something hot and ardent flared in his eyes, and her stomach tightened. She squeezed her own eyes shut, willing images of beheaded naga into her brain to shut out the pounding in her head, the thrumming in her veins, the ache below her navel. It was no use.

"What are you hiding?" Zarya asked, turning the inquisition back on him. "What don't you want anyone to hear?"

"No one needs to know what you've been up to."

"I haven't been up to anything," she said in exasperation. "You've been in my head as much as I've been in yours. I didn't even know who you were until you showed up."

Even as she denied it, Zarya knew she understood so little about her power. Some of it had leaked out before Rabin had released the binding. What if she *had* created the forest?

"Why did you help me with my magic just to come here and snarl at me?"

"I'm not snarling at you." His lip curled, and she gave him a pointed look before he smoothed his face. "You were in pain, and I wanted to help you. No one should be denied their magic." The last sentence was spat out as if he was furious about it.

"I haven't been coming into your dreams. I thought you were coming into mine. You're the one who came here to find me."

"I didn't come to find you. I came to see my family, and you were here. Rather conveniently."

Zarya scoffed, still clutching the fabric at his waist. "Liar. You left. No one has heard from you in years. Why did you show up now? Where were you, anyway?"

Rabin shifted, the former army commander clearly not used to being questioned. "Because I wanted to see what kind of danger you posed." His wide shoulders were tense. "Who you were."

She shrugged. "If you find out, please do enlighten me."

He narrowed his eyes.

Despite the blood rushing through her veins at Rabin's presence, at his face, at his body, at his closeness, she was also done with this infuriating line of questioning.

"The dragon. It was you, wasn't it? Why did you save me from falling?"

His jaw tightened. "I'm a soldier. It's my duty to protect the helpless."

"You seem to have a lot of excuses, and I am *not* helpless. How dare you?" Zarya was aware she sounded shrill but didn't care.

"No. You're not." He arched a dark eyebrow. "I won't make that mistake again."

Zarya lifted her chin.

"Who taught you to use a sword?"

"Why? Are you going to be a pain in their ass, too?"

"Answer me," he growled. "Stop deflecting every question."

"The man who raised me."

They stared at one another.

"Why are you here, really? Where did you come from? And very conveniently, right after Vik and Amrita were joined? Wasn't that supposed to be your fate?"

He didn't answer her question, something warring in his gaze.

"You're here because you felt it, too." Her quiet voice filled the air with static as Rabin went entirely still.

"I don't know what you're talking about."

"Don't lie to me. We have a connection. Something brought us together in that forest. Some kind of magic beyond both of us. It was..." She trailed off, unable to find a name for what she'd felt with him in the woods. For what raced through her now.

"You're imagining things." His voice was low with strained fury.

"Why are you fighting it?" She cocked her head to the side, wishing she could peel him open and root inside his thoughts. "Tell me what you're hiding."

"All those years with your magic bound addled your brain. You and I aren't anything."

Zarya whispered, "You feel it. I know you do."

But now she was beginning to doubt herself. Had it been all in her head? Had her lonely spirit created a fantasy that didn't exist? Surely, this *thing* couldn't have just been her? Even now, there was an energy between them that was impossible to ignore.

"Tell me," Zarya said, their faces inches apart. "Tell me you felt nothing in the forest and that you feel nothing right now."

Rabin inhaled a ragged breath as he placed a finger under her chin, the rough stone pressing into her back. When he tilted his head, her heart clutched, and her stomach plunged into her feet. As their eyes met, she saw it. Desire. Heat. Longing.

They both stopped breathing, and awareness exploded in every cell of her body. Rabin was going to kiss her, and Zarya had never wanted anything so much in her entire life.

"I. Feel. Nothing," he said in a dead voice, his eyes shuttering to coldness.

A sheet of ice split her in two, her limbs shaking as Rabin dropped his hand and stepped away. His boots rang like funeral bells as he strode down the quiet alley and disappeared from view.

Suddenly dizzy, Zarya slid to the ground and braced her arms on her knees. She took a deep breath, trying to calm her stuttering heart and willing herself not to cry. She had things to do. She had to flee. That was her goal.

She forced herself up and hobbled into the street, taking in the extent of the destruction for the first time.

The city was in ruins. There were dead people and demons everywhere she looked, buildings on fire, and the ground torn up in every direction. Dozens of soldiers and medics were swarming like bees spreading help to everyone who needed it.

"Zee!" Zarya looked over to find Yasen jogging towards her, and she almost collapsed in relief. "Oh, thank the gods."

He wrapped his arms around her, her legs buckling, right before he scooped her up. He started walking, and soon they came in sight of the palace. He passed through the gates and into the courtyard where a makeshift hospital had already been erected.

Yasen settled her onto a cot and crouched down. She noted the bandage already wrapped around his leg where the dakini had clawed him last night. Had that really only been hours ago?

"Rest here. I'm going to get you some help."

Zarya dozed in and out of waking, her eyes fluttering open when she felt a pair of warm hands on her stomach. Koura stood over her, his glowing yellow light knitting the worst of her injuries back together.

When he was done, she lay on the cot, feeling the vestiges of pain seep away. Now her mind was clearing again, and she remembered what she had to do.

Curling into a ball, she wrapped her arms around her legs and then pressed her forehead to her knees while she sobbed.

The darkness.

Fucking Row. She had never been angrier in her life. How could he not have told her this? How could he have let her live blind to what she was? She would never forgive him for this. Not that it mattered anymore. Once she got out of here, she would disappear and never talk to anyone again. Loneliness was her destiny. It was a good thing she'd had a lot of practice.

Breathing heavily, she searched inside her heart. The secret star responded, called by her thoughts. The sixth anchor was still there, reminding her why she couldn't remain in Dharati. Of why she had to do what she'd always done.

She didn't want to leave this life she'd created. She thought of Yasen and their friendship, but she would have to let him go. He deserved better than her. He deserved everything. She wondered if Amrita had survived the attack and how Vikram was doing. She prayed that none of the Chiranjivi had died, no matter her complicated feelings for them.

"Zarya." Yasen was standing over her. "You're not going to believe this, but Row is back."

Once again, it took her several long moments to weave through the tangle of her muddled thoughts. She pushed herself up slowly.

"Where? Where is he?"

"I can take you to see him. Do you think you can walk?"

Suddenly, she wasn't tired anymore. Row was back. She staggered to her feet, relieved to see she wasn't quite as weak as she had been before Koura had healed her.

"I can walk," she said with a determined set to her jaw. "Take me to him."

Yasen led Zarya through the palace into a large room scattered with sofas and tables. A bank of windows overlooked the sea, under which Row sat on a plush chair, holding a glass of whisky. A tightness around his eyes suggested he hadn't been sleeping much.

"Row," she said, her voice hard as his gaze flicked up.

Zarya strode into the room with her hands balled into fists. She vaguely registered there were others also in the room, but she only had eyes for her former captor. The man who had raised her. The man who had left her and was now sitting here completely unharmed, having a fucking drink.

Relief loosened his shoulders at the sight of her.

"Zarya," he said softly, before he placed the glass next to him and stood, arms hanging stiffly at his sides as if he might embrace her, and that's when Zarya finally snapped.

She stomped up to him, cocked her arm, and punched him square in the face.

FORTY

"Don't *Zarya* me!" She launched herself at Row while Aarav and Yasen held her back. "Where have you been? You left me! You locked me up, and then you left me!"

"Zee! Calm down," Yasen said as she stopped fighting his hold.

Zarya glared at Aarav, who let go of her arm, his hands raised.

Row's nose had given an audible crunch when it had connected with her fist, and blood dripped down his face. A servant handed Row a cloth that he pressed against it.

Slumped in his seat, he regarded her warily.

"What was that for?" His voice thick, he pulled the cloth away, examining the stain. Zarya turned to Yasen, who still held on to her. He slowly let go. *I'm right here*, his expression read.

She whipped back to Row. "What was *that* for? You've been gone for months. I thought something terrible happened to you!"

"I didn't realize you cared that much, Zarya."

"I don't," she said, unable to control her voice. "I was

worried about *me*! You disappeared! I might have died trapped in that cottage. You are *supposed* to protect me. You told me enough times that's your job."

The red haze of her rage clearing, Zarya took a deep breath. All the Chiranjivi were present, as well as Vikram and Dhawan. Koura was now helping Row with his nose. She nearly groaned at noticing Rabin leaning against the wall, an amused tilt to his perfect mouth.

Great. Not only was she desperate and pathetic, but now she looked like a raving lunatic. Zarya wished the sea would swallow her whole. She glared at him, hoping he would take the hint and leave.

"I had to go," Row said as Koura pulled away. "Quietly. Quickly."

Worn and defeated, Row was not the solid pillar of confidence Zarya was accustomed to. Something had crushed his spirit. With trepidation, he peered at Zarya, as though what he needed to say took great effort. "I heard a rumor about your mother, Asha."

The blood drained from every limb in her body. "My mother?"

Row sighed, rubbing the back of his neck. "Will you please sit down?" She hesitated. "Please, Zarya?"

Arms crossed, she dropped herself into the velvet seat across from him.

"It's been almost twenty years since I've heard the barest whisper of Asha," he said. "I've tried to discover her where-abouts, but I've come up against nothing but dead ends. I'd almost given up hope.

"But then a few months ago, I was in a tavern in the vanshaj quarter, and I overheard a story about the queen's secret return to Gi'ana."

Zarya's head began to pound as she connected the points of what he was saying.

"The queen of Gi'ana is... was... my mother?" she asked, choking on the last word.

"Yes, Zarya. If you'll give me a chance, I'm going to try to explain everything."

She couldn't seem to make herself speak, so she simply nodded as he continued.

"I began asking around. While most dismissed the rumors, some believed in Asha's return. It was the most promising bit of news I'd received in decades.

"Worried the trail would disappear, I set out immediately. There wasn't time to return to you. I couldn't risk losing her again. I released the magic tethering you and assumed you'd figure it out eventually. Testing your cage was one of your favorite pastimes."

He gave her a careful smile, but Zarya exhaled an angry breath.

"Why didn't you send a message?" she asked. As she digested his words, she focused on the minutiae first, not ready to thoroughly examine the rest.

"I couldn't risk it being intercepted. For your safety or Asha's."

Yasen interjected from where he'd sat next to Zarya. "You spent all those years keeping her hidden from everyone, and then you heard the merest hint about some long-lost queen, and you let her go? Just like that?"

"I wasn't going to be able to keep Zarya there much longer," Row said, his head bent. "You were already so restless, and you're an adult now. I couldn't keep you locked up there forever. I've always known that. It seemed like the time had come."

Zarya's throat was so tight it felt like she'd swallowed a bucket of rusty nails.

"You were in love with her. Asha. My mother," she said. "I

overheard them talking about it." She gestured to Apsara and Kindle.

"You shouldn't have been able to hear that," Kindle said, straightening. "My house is warded."

"Well, I did," she replied, before she closed her eyes, another question bubbling up her throat. She was so afraid of the answer, but asking was as inevitable as the sun in the sky and the tides of the moon. "Row? Are you my father?"

The expression then on Row's face was unbearable. As if she'd reached into his chest and shredded his heart into scarlet ribbons. His eyes shone with something she'd never seen before and wondered if she'd ever see again.

"Oh, Zarya. I'm sorry, but I am not your father."

Focusing on her hands, she willed the tears burning her eyes not to fall. Again, there was the spiraling loss of something she'd never realized she wanted, despite her complicated feelings for the man in front of her.

"Then who is?" she whispered, the sound small and feeble.

"I'm getting to that part. It's a long story." Row reached over to lay a hand on her knee.

"When you were born, Asha kept it a secret. She had other children already, four of them. The only people present at your birth were the midwife, two servants, and me. She'd hidden the pregnancy and, during the last few months, retreated to one of the royal country houses to disappear for a while.

"I didn't understand why at first, but assumed the king, her husband, was not your father. Why else would she be hiding? But she wouldn't tell me. You were born, and Asha asked me to eliminate everyone present, which I did, much to my shame. I was blinded by my love for her."

Zarya grimaced at Row's admission.

"They said she didn't return your feelings?" she asked, again gesturing to Apsara and Kindle, who both looked chagrined that they'd been caught gossiping like market wives.

"A rumor we spread together so as not to arouse suspicion." A serene expression grew on his face as he paused, lost in his memories. "She loved me as much as I loved her, but we had broken off our relationship years earlier. Asha was the married queen of Gi'ana, and I was a mere servant from another kingdom. We could never be together."

Despite everything, Zarya's heart broke for Row. No one should be denied their love for one another.

"Asha placed you in my care and asked me to keep you secret. To protect you because your father couldn't ever know of your existence. Your life would be forfeit. She was so terrified that I didn't question it. I would have done anything for her. So I went as far away as possible, and that's how we ended up on the southern shore of Daragaab.

"After we left Gi'ana, I didn't know what became of your mother. Rumors surfaced shortly after that she had vanished. Some said she died, but I never accepted it, sure I would sense it if she were gone.

"But I did what she asked. I kept you a secret. I protected you."

Feeling every eye in the room on her, Zarya was silent. When she spoke, her voice was raw. "But why couldn't you tell me any of this? It would have changed everything if I'd known."

Row rested his head in his palms in a gesture of shame. Then he sat up and stared Zarya directly in the eye.

"I was scared. I didn't know who I was protecting you from, so I kept everything from you."

"Including my magic," she accused. "You didn't want me to know I'm Aazheri. You let me think that bit of magic was all I was capable of."

Row shook his head. "No. That wasn't me. It was your mother. She bound you as soon as you were born. I tried everything to break it. I traveled all over Rahajhan to find someone with the ability to lift the curse."

Zarya blew out a long, slow breath.

"All those times you were gone, you were trying to help me?" Zarya tilted her head at Row, seeing him in a different light for the first time. "Why?"

"Because I didn't want you to be vulnerable. Your mother was wrong to keep you from your magic. If someone dangerous really was after you, you needed every tool at your disposal. It's why I pushed you so hard to learn how to defend yourself. It was the only thing I was able to give you to ensure you were strong.

"How did you break it, Zarya?" Row asked, leaning forward. "How did you finally access your magic?"

Like fingers trailing up her spine, Zarya felt Rabin's eyes on her. When she remembered what a fool she'd made of herself earlier, demanding he admit feelings he didn't have, her cheeks flushed. She was careful not to look at him as she gave Row the abbreviated version of events she'd shared with everyone else.

Row seemed perplexed, but before he could pull apart her lies, she plowed ahead, asking, "You said you were getting to the part about who my father is?"

Row sucked in a deep breath and nodded. "It took me many years to puzzle it out, but there is only one man ruthless enough."

"To do what?"

"Your mother was no ordinary queen. When she was crowned rani of Gi'ana, an oracle foretold she would be the one to bear a child who possessed nightfire—a gift that hadn't been seen in Rahajhan in a thousand years.

"Every child Asha birthed was welcomed with much fanfare, but alas, they were all ordinary Aazheri. Powerful Aazheri, but none could wield nightfire. Of course, most dismissed it as a fanciful notion, and after four children, it seemed they were right."

Row took a deep breath. "I don't know how they met or how she became pregnant with his child, but the Raja of Andhera believed the prophecy. Obsessed about it. Until the very end, it seems."

Blood pounded in Zarya's ears as the pieces of this story fell together.

"Nightfire?" she whispered. "Is that what I did?" She held up her hands, remembering the sparkling black light that had shot from her fingers.

"We all saw it," Kindle said, coming to stand next to Row. "Last night, when you released it, you confirmed something I'd wondered about you from the moment I saw you. You looked so much like her, there was no mistaking who your mother was, and I wondered if the prophecy had finally come true."

"Me?" Zarya asked, her mind reeling. "I have some crazy ancient magic?"

Of course, now they all knew. Knew she could use magic, and that she had been lying to them.

"I'm sorry I didn't tell you. I wanted to figure things out first," she said to them all.

Kindle shook his head slowly. "It doesn't matter now. What matters is you saved us all."

She sat up straighter. "What do you mean?"

"Your nightfire dissolved every demon between here and the forest. One moment they were there, and the next, they were just... gone."

Zarya released a shaky breath.

"It only affected the demons?" she asked, wondering about that strange six-pointed star and her new ability. They had to be connected somehow.

Kindle nodded.

"Zarya," Row said, pulling her attention to him as he picked up their conversation. "Given that you have nightfire, I'm more sure of it than ever. The gift could only have been the product of the two most powerful Aazheri ever to live. I believe your father is Raja Abishek of Andhera."

More silence as they all stared at her, open mouthed.

"What does that mean?"

"She's a princess," Vikram said, a touch of awe in his voice. "Of two realms."

Row scoffed. "Hardly. You've got four older siblings, including two sisters, and all from a pure alliance. You are, at best, illegitimate, and they'd sooner lock you up than recognize you as part of the royal family."

Even Row didn't miss the hurt on Zarya's face.

"I'm not telling you this to upset you, but I know what you're thinking. You have always craved this. Your half-brothers and sisters may be willing to meet you, but they wouldn't welcome another possible claimant to the throne. A female Aazheri who can wield nightfire—you are only a threat to them. The king is getting on in years, and your eldest half-sister Dishani has waited years for her crown."

"I still don't understand the need to hide her," Yasen said.

Row looked up at Yasen and then back at Zarya. "You may have no place in Gi'ana, but there is no doubt that if Raja Abishek had known of your existence, he would have hunted you down. This is what Asha feared. Abishek would find a way to wield you to his own ends."

"What ends?" she asked.

"Magic can be taken, Zarya. It is old and mostly forgotten magic, but Raja Abishek has always had a fascination with the darkness. Has always wanted to release it and use it. What you can do, Zarya, it's not just a way to channel the stars; some say it's a way to *control* the darkness."

Control the darkness. She shook her head, confused by this onslaught of conflicting information.

"You think he wants to take it from me," she said. All her life, she'd wanted a family, and now Row was telling her the man who might be her father wanted to hurt her.

"It must be what your mother feared."

"I knew it." Suvanna stalked forward. "Didn't I say it? It is *his* king who is doing this. The blight *is* the darkness."

"Abishek hasn't been my king in decades, Suvanna." He sounded dejected, defeated. "But you may be right."

Suvanna crossed her arms in smug satisfaction.

"Row?" Zarya asked as all eyes turned to her again. "What of my mother? Did you find her?"

Row's face twisted into a mask of intense pain and longing. He shook his head. "It seems it was another false rumor. I found no trace of her. I fear that what I've dreaded for twenty years is true. Though I have never stopped believing for one day, I don't think I have the strength to hold on to hope anymore. I fear she is truly gone."

With Row's hope, Zarya's died, too.

"You didn't need to keep any of this from me," she said, not restraining the accusation in her tone. "I would have listened to you. Done what you asked to stay safe."

Row searched for his next words. "I'm sorry, Zarya. I was wrong. I should never have kept you in that house, and I should have told you the truth. All of it. I was afraid. I convinced myself the danger was so great that I caved into the fear, letting it control me."

Zarya said nothing, scrubbing a tear that slipped down her cheek.

"I wanted to give you the answers you sought all those years. Now that you have them, I'm sorry none of it is what you hoped for."

"And now what?" Yasen asked. "Isn't Zarya in danger now?"

"Perhaps," said Row, "but there is no reason to think Raja Abishek has any idea Zarya exists. "

"But people saw my magic."

"Most would have no idea what they saw. The only other solution is to go into hiding."

Hiding. A few minutes ago, that was exactly what she had intended to do. But now, she wasn't sure if that was the answer.

"Could I help with the blight?" she asked, holding up her hands.

"I think you could," Kindle said. "When I tested you for magic, it was my hope this was what I'd find."

"Then I'm not going anywhere," Zarya said. Row opened his mouth, but she cut him off. "No. I've said from the beginning I wanted to help, and if I can make a real difference, then I'm staying."

Row dipped his head. "I can understand that, but you'll need to be careful."

"So, what do we do, then?" Yasen asked.

"We need to find out what Abishek knows," Row said. "If he knows Zarya exists."

"And if he does?" Zarya asked.

Row clasped his hands, his forehead furrowing. "Then we have to ensure you never fall into his hands."

"Absolutely," Yasen said, putting his arm around Zarya, pressing a kiss to her temple. She gave him a tentative smile.

None of this was what she had wanted. Her dreams had always been simple. A life outside the cottage. A family. Friends. Love. To learn that her family by blood only wanted to use her or dispose of her was forcing her to come to terms with realities she'd never imagined.

She'd been too naive to navigate this world on her own.

But she wasn't on her own anymore.

She looked around the room. At the faces that had become so familiar to her over the last few months.

Apsara came to stand behind Zarya and placed a hand on her shoulder. "If he does come for you, we will all protect you."

Zarya looked at her, something warm and honeyed erupting in her chest. Her vision blurred with tears.

A family. Of a sort.

And maybe the only one she'd ever truly have.

A LETTER FROM NISHA

Dear Reader,

I want to say a huge thank you for choosing to read *Heart of Night and Fire*. If you enjoyed it and want to keep up to date with all my latest releases, just sign up at the following link. Your email address will never be shared, and you can unsubscribe at any time.

www.secondskybooks.com/nisha-j-tuli

This book was written at the height of the pandemic in the summer of 2020 and will always have a special place in my heart. It was the moment when, after years of dreaming and thinking about it, I finally knew it was time to set out on the journey to become an author. To be here a few years later, sharing this story with you, still feels surreal.

If you loved *Heart of Night and Fire*, please consider leaving a review on your favorite platform. And if you'd like to get in touch, I love hearing from readers! You can join my Facebook reader group, send me an email on my website, or message me on Instagram.

Love,

Nisha

KEEP IN TOUCH WITH NISHA

www.nishajtuli.com

facebook.com/NishaJT

twitter.com/NishaJT

instagram.com/nishajtwrites

tiktok.com/@nishajtwrites

Printed in the USA
CPSIA information can be obtained
at www.ICGtesting.com
LVHW090747100923
757690LV00007B/48